the *Sunday Times* bestselling author of over twenty nov⌐
published in more than thirty countries and her books have sold
to Hollywood.

For all the latest news from Carole, visit her website, follow Carole
on Twitter or join the thousands of readers who have become
Carole's friend on Facebook.

www.carolematthews.com
@carolematthews
Facebook.com/carole.matthews

Praise for Carole

'All the warmth and wit we expect from Carole . . . Perfect'
Bella

'Matthews is one of the few writers who can rival Marian
Keyes' gift for telling heart-warming tales with buckets of charm
and laughs'
Daily Record

'Witty, funny and incredibly touching, this is perfect for lifting
the spirits'
Heat

'Simply brilliant'
Closer

'A feel-good tale, fun and thoroughly escapist'

Novels by Carole Matthews

Let's Meet on Platform 8
A Whiff of Scandal
More to Life than This
For Better, For Worse
A Minor Indiscretion
A Compromising Position
The Sweetest Taboo
With or Without You
You Drive Me Crazy
Welcome to the Real World
The Chocolate Lovers' Club
The Chocolate Lovers' Diet
It's a Kind of Magic
All You Need is Love
The Difference a Day Makes
That Loving Feeling
It's Now or Never
The Only Way is Up
Wrapped Up in You
Summer Daydreams
With Love at Christmas
A Cottage by the Sea

MORE TO LIFE
THAN THIS

CAROLE MATTHEWS

SPHERE

First published in Great Britain in 1999 by Headline Publishing Group
First published in paperback in 2000 by Headline Publishing Group
This paperback edition published in 2013 by Sphere
Reprinted 2014 (twice)

A CIP catalogue record for this book
is available from the British Library.

ISBN 978-0-7515-5139-6

Typeset in Sabon by Palimpsest Book Production Limited,
Falkirk, Stirlingshire
Printed and bound in Great Britain by
Clays Ltd, St Ives plc

Papers used by Sphere are from well-managed forests
and other responsible sources.

To saints, saviours and general keepers
of the sanity ...

Dave 'The Rave' Sivers, comedy writer extraordinaire and part
of the S&M Fun Factory ...

John Gough, for being a very special person ...

Gareth Gwenlan and the Montreux Gorillas ...
(They came back with me ...??!!)

Stephen 'Wadders' Waddington, a major techno mate ...

Eileen Quilter-Williams, who was there
from the very start ...

Sue Galtrey, for much-valued friendship ...

Kevin Stokes, who has restored my faith
in human nature ...

And, as always, to Sheila and Pauline, for duties
above and beyond the call of friendship.

In the search to find ourselves,
do we ever stop to count the cost of what we've lost?

Chapter One

'We're far too young to be doing this, Jeffrey.' Kate looked round the crumbling village hall and put her equally crumbly fruit cake down beside her tepid cup of tea.

'What?' Her husband looked up from the bright yellow book of National Open Gardens.

'This.' Kate gestured at the peeling paintwork. She lowered her voice. 'Everyone else in here is potential Zimmer-frame material.'

Her husband peered over his glasses at her. 'It's not that bad. You do exaggerate.'

'Can you see anyone here who isn't likely to be in the Post Office next Tuesday, drawing their pension – apart from us?'

Jeffrey surveyed the room. He took off his glasses and had a closer look. His mouth twisted uncertainly. 'We've just caught them at a bad time.'

'I think we're the ones who are at a bad time.'

At this, he put down the book with a sigh and folded his arms. 'What's that supposed to mean?'

'We've turned into trainee pensioners.' She tugged her dark hair back from her forehead with a frustrated jerk, showing the spark of her vivid blue eyes in their full glory. 'We can't walk a hundred yards without feeling faint and

1

needing to be resuscitated by Battenberg, angel layer cake and tea with too much milk.' Kate picked up her cup and put it down again disconsolately.

Her husband looked puzzled. 'But I thought you were thirsty?'

'I am thirsty – but that's not the point. We are in the prime of our lives,' she said emphatically. 'We should still be passionate about things.'

'I'm still *very* passionate!'

She flopped back in her orange plastic chair, causing it to wobble on its rickety legs. 'About what?'

'I liked that bubble pond and splashy fountain thing in the last garden – Whatsit Cottage,' he ventured, scanning the book to find it, without success. 'Didn't you think it was nice?'

'And that's being *passionate*?' Kate picked up a fragment of her cake and tossed it in her mouth. 'We've not yet climbed the hill to forty and we're behaving as if we're ready for our first SAGA holiday.'

A hurt look flashed across Jeffrey's face. 'Don't you enjoy nosing round other people's gardens?'

'Yes, I do. But perhaps I'd enjoy doing something else more.'

'Like what?'

'Like rollerblading or windsurfing or rock climbing.'

Her husband frowned at the dregs of cold tea in his pale green utilitarian china cup complete with designer chip. 'You've no sense of balance for rollerblading. You hate getting wet and you don't like heights.'

2

'Well, something else then!'

'The children enjoyed our outing today,' he reasoned.

'Doesn't that worry you?'

'No, I think it's rather nice.' He smiled benevolently in their direction.

Kate followed his glance to the Women's Institute home-made produce stall, where a cornucopia of handwritten labels and cellophane-wrapped sponge cakes graced a wonky trestle table. 'They're looking at home-made jam,' she said disbelievingly. 'They're ten and twelve years old and they're looking at home-made jam – *happily*.'

'Well, what's wrong with that?' Jeffrey asked.

'Look at them. They don't argue. Ever. They play nicely together. They sit and watch *Neighbours* without fighting over the channel changer. And I can't get a twitch of interest out of them for the lust of *Heartbreak High*.'

The father of Joseph and Kerry Lewis cracked his knuckles, a tried and tested indicator of supreme exasperation.

'I mean,' she continued drearily. 'When did we last have to go up to their schools and be lambasted about their disruptive behaviour?'

'Never!'

'My point, exactly.'

'What do you expect?' Jeffrey's brow creased in consternation. 'We've brought them up nicely. Would you rather they were behind the bike sheds dropping Es or shooting up heroin?'

'They should be old enough for a bit of illicit smoking,

at least. I've searched both of their bedrooms and there's nothing. *Nothing*.' Kate flicked back her mop of raven hair. 'Sonia said Andrew's got three copies of *Playboy* and a packet of multi-coloured condoms, ribbed for extra sensitivity, hidden under his bed already.'

'He's eleven years old!' Jeffrey looked disgusted. 'Isn't she the one with the problem, not us?'

Kate ignored him. 'They shouldn't be like this, Jeffrey,' she went on, her eyes troubled. 'They're quite happy to be dragged round looking at gardens with their parents on a Sunday afternoon when they should be locked away in their bedrooms, playing computer games and trying to find pornography on the Internet. They actually *like* fresh air.'

'It isn't a crime.'

'It isn't normal either.'

'What were you like at their age?'

'Little Miss Goody-Two-Shoes,' she said miserably. 'I couldn't move an inch for fear of incurring my parents' disapproval. I was nurtured to death in a meticulously kept semi-detached emotion-free box.'

Jeffrey smiled sadly. 'I was the same,' he said. 'It was called good parenting then – in the days before social workers were invented. They did their best.'

'That's not what I want for *our* children,' she sighed. 'I want them to be free to make their own mistakes, I want them to run before they can walk and do what *they* want to do, not what they think they're expected to do!'

'They're young. They're still finding their feet. Give them time.'

4

She pointed surreptitiously at them. 'But jam, Jeffrey, *jam*. We have two middle-aged children and it's all our fault.'

'I know you worry about this but let's not have a fight today.' He reached out and took her hand. This wasn't the first time that Kate had made these kind of noises, and Jeffrey didn't want to cause a scene. 'They're all right,' he said gently, 'really they are. Perhaps they'll be late developers.'

'I must have potty trained them too young,' Kate said. 'It causes them to be repressed as adolescents. I read it in *Parent and Child* magazine. They're too perfect and it's all because I was fed up with lugging truckloads of Pampers from the supermarket.'

'Don't be ridiculous, you're a wonderful mother! You should be proud of them.'

'I know.' Her voice wavered.

Jeffrey stood up, causing his chair to screech across the wooden floor. The roomful of pensioners looked up from their iced cherry fancies and glared at him. He smiled apologetically. 'Let's make a move,' he told his wife. 'We seem to have exhausted the delights that Great Brickworth gardens have to offer.'

Kate picked up her cardigan from the back of the chair and slipped her hand in his as they walked to the door. 'I've spoiled the afternoon now, haven't I?'

He squeezed her hand. 'Of course you haven't.'

The children fell in step behind them. 'Can we have some jam, Mummy?'

'We've got a cupboard full of it at home.'

'Yes, but this has big lumps of strawberry in it,' Kerry insisted. 'Not like that horrible processed stuff from Sainsbury's which is full of artificial colour and preservatives and probably gives you ME.'

'Why don't you make jam any more?' Joe asked.

'I've been busy.' *Doing what?* 'I'll make some this week,' Kate promised.

'Great!' They raced ahead into the sunshine.

It was one of those sweltering Mediterranean-type days with an impossibly blue sky – one of those days when you can believe global warming is really happening and isn't just something made up by bored scientists to keep themselves in a job. And yet as they began to walk back to the car, the welcome heat that was searing into the skin of her arms singularly failed to bring any warmth to Kate's soul.

'You're quiet,' Jeffrey said.

'Sorry.'

'You know,' he fiddled with her fingers, 'I think this is more about you feeling restless than anything to do with the children. They're perfectly content.'

'I know.' She squeezed his fingers back. 'I wish I could feel so delirious at being fobbed off with the vague promise of home-made jam.'

'Maybe you should stop thinking about making jam and do something more interesting. Get out more.' He stared at the lane ahead of them. 'I know you've not been finding things easy recently.'

She stopped and looked at her husband. Her other half. Jeffrey was so sure, so confident, so at home with himself. If he was her other half, why didn't he make her feel whole any more? Where had their oneness gone? The children didn't need her, either. Not like they used to. They loved her, as Jeffrey did, but they didn't *need* her. So long as there was a meal on the table, clean socks in the drawer and someone to drive them around in the car, they were perfectly self-sufficient individuals. She had been a wife and mother for longer than she cared to remember – even longer than Richard Whiteley had hosted *Countdown*. They'd had the best years of her life and now she no longer knew who she was. Her brain had been sucked dry by domestic duties until she felt like one of those sad women on TV ads who get their meagre kicks out of sniffing the fresh lemon tang of their new-improved fabric conditioner. Suddenly, the fulfilment she had experienced from being the hub of her family had flown out of the window, along with the ability to drink more than two glasses of wine without getting pissed and endure more than two consecutive late nights. The feelings of doubt and insecurity that had been bobbing below the surface of her consciousness broke water. 'Do you think I'm boring, Jeffrey?'

'Of course I don't.'

'I do.' She snapped a stem from the lavender bush that cascaded over the weathered stone wall next to them and twisted it in her fingers, inhaling its soothing scent. 'I've nothing interesting to say these days. My whole life revolves round the home. I feel like a hamster on one of those little

7

treadmill things. I scurry around wearing my legs out for no good purpose. My week is spent shopping and cleaning and cooking and making sure that the kids are washed and ironed and ready to go to school. I do nothing for myself.'

'You go to the gym with Sonia.'

Kate gave a sad little laugh. 'It's not exactly the meaning of life, is it?'

Jeffrey turned to her and the look of bewilderment on his face churned her insides. 'I had no idea you were *so* unhappy,' he said quietly.

'I'm not,' she said. 'Truly, I'm not. It's just that . . .' Suddenly her throat had closed and there was a nasty hot stinging behind her eyes. 'It's just that . . .' She gulped the tears away. 'There must be more to life than this.'

'What more do you want?'

I want to feel alive again. She trailed her hand along the rough stone, enjoying the pain on her soft skin. Anything rather than the numbness there was inside. 'I used to wake up in the morning wondering what new challenges the day ahead would hold. I couldn't wait to get out of bed! Now I just wonder how much of the ironing I'll be able to get through before the kids come home and need feeding. I don't measure my pessimism by whether a wine glass is half-full or empty – the ironing basket is my gauge.'

She turned to Jeffrey, but the expression on his face said that he was lost when it came to sorting out her problems. *She* was the sorter-outer in their household. The lawnmower

8

breaks – Kate fixes it. The washing machine floods – Kate mops up after it. The goldfish dies – Kate digs the hole, buries the fish and provides the tissues for the weeping children. Kate also arranges replacement goldfish, having trawled half the pet shops in the surrounding area for its identical twin.

'What do you want to do?' he asked, with the air of a man who isn't sure whether he really wants to know the answer.

'Perhaps I should get a job,' Kate said. 'I don't even know what I could do. Shorthand, telex machines and manual typewriters were all the rage when I was last in an office. I'd have to update my skills. How would I cope?'

'You could do something completely different.'

'Like what? I don't even get the time to think about what I might be able to do.'

She was a nineties woman. Wasn't having it all the key to the meaning of life? What did *all* mean, exactly? She'd got the big house, the nice car, the executive professional husband, the 2.4 children and the cupboard full of Fruit 'n' Fibre. What was she supposed to want now? A taxing job and the joy of juggling home plus career and doing neither well? Voluntary work? Would two days a week in an Oxfam shop reeking of old clothes make her feel like a valuable part of the human race again?

'Maybe you need to get away by yourself for a few days,' Jeffrey suggested. 'I don't know, maybe to a health farm or something. Have some quality thinking time.'

'Go away?' Kate was shocked. 'Without the children?'

9

'It's not unheard of.'

'Without you?'

'It might help.' Jeffrey didn't look convinced that it would.

It might help or I might decide I never want to come back again. Where would I go? What would I do? Who would remember to feed the cat?

'It's a thought,' she said uncertainly. 'Would you mind?'

'Of course not.' They'd reached the car – a top of the range Mercedes supplied by Hills & Hopeland Chartered Accountants. Jeffrey blipped the remote-control central locking and the kids leapt inside. He turned and scuffed his thumb across her chin. 'Not if it makes you happy again.'

The tears threatened to splash out of her eyes, a bit like the bubble pond that Jeffrey had so admired and she had thought so pathetic. She got into the car, swallowing down the emotion that had lodged in her throat. Jeffrey slid in next to her. How could she feel so far away from this man who was physically so close to her, a man she had known for over half of her life. He patted her knee gently. 'The kids and I could manage without you.'

'Could you?' It came out more bitterly than she intended.

'For a few days,' he said with a smile that was as sweet and as uncomplicated as Gary Lineker's.

That smile had been the reason she married him.

Jeffrey swung the car into the narrow country lanes and the car purred effortlessly along. Kate looked at her husband as he concentrated on the road. He was a good man. Kind, thoughtful, a bit intense. He had what her mother called 'intellectual good looks', which essentially meant he wore horn-rimmed glasses. His brown eyes were gentle, but you could never quite tell what was going on behind them. His face was smooth and youthful, with a high intelligent forehead that could be attributed to the steady retreat of his fair hair. 'Staid' was his middle name. Jeffrey was the sort of man who could work the video recorder – all of it. Even the special functions that no one ever used and were written half in Chinese and half Latvian. He knew how the self-timing oven worked, how to record a new message on the ansaphone and had read the manual supplied with every piece of electrical equipment in the house. From cover to cover. He liked having thirty-two equally spaced drapes in the lounge curtains and was even known to count them on occasions. Over the years she too had become accustomed to a certain amount of regularity in curtain folds.

In the back of the car the children were smiling like a pair of Rubens cherubs. They started to sing 'Ten Green Bottles'. The countryside whizzed by. The canary yellow fields of rapeseed, a sprinkling of scarlet poppies in the hedgerows, birds flitting from telephone wire to telephone wire.

'And if one green bottle should accidentally fall . . .'

That's just what she felt like. As if she was teetering on top of a wall like an unsteady bottle, waiting to see how long and how far the fall would be, and how much the process of being smashed would hurt. She looked at her handsome husband and her beautiful children and a cold shiver ran down her spine as she wondered if anyone else ever felt as if they were living in an Enid Blyton story.

Chapter Two

'You look really fed up,' Kate observed as she towelled her hair dry, grateful that the changing rooms were, for once, warm and not too smelly. It might be one of the most exclusive health clubs in the area, but even the lady members were still prone to bouts of cheesy-feetedness.

'I am,' her friend Sonia agreed.

'What is it? Sex or Weight Watchers?'

'Weight Watchers. I've put on half a stone.'

'Half a stone?' Kate looked at her friend in dismay.

'Since last week.' Sonia collapsed on the bench, stuffed her sweaty T-shirt in her holdall and pulled on her knickers.

'How did that happen?'

'I was permanently hungry.'

'I thought you could eat unlimited vegetables.'

Sonia glanced sheepishly at her friend. 'How was I supposed to know that Cadbury's Caramel wasn't a vegetable?'

'Sonia!' Kate laughed.

'I hate you,' her friend said vehemently, shoe-horning herself into her jeans. 'You just don't understand what it's like. You're the only woman in the world who has trouble keeping weight on.'

'I look after myself.'

'So do I,' Sonia protested.

'The difference is I look after myself with a healthy diet and exercise.' Kate looked at her sagely. 'You look after yourself with Mars bars and Bacardi and Coke.'

She came and sat down next to her friend, struggling to pull her leggings over her damp skin. 'I really don't know why you worry,' she said comfortingly. 'You look great, Son.'

'I've put heaps of weight on over the years.'

'Not that much, surely?'

'I used to weigh seven pounds, three ounces.'

Kate laughed. 'Well, I think you look good as you are.'

Her friend hung her head and examined her pink Nike trainers intently. 'I feel I have about as much sexual allure as a Fray Bentos steak and kidney pie.'

'Are things no better between you and Kev?'

'He still views sex as a non-participant sport, if that's what you mean.'

'Oh, Sonia.'

'Do you know,' she said lightly, 'a vigorous sex session burns off a hundred and sixteen calories. That's equivalent to one whole HobNob. I try to use it as part of Kevin's calorie-uncontrolled diet. It adds a whole new dimension to "Do you fancy a quick cup of tea and a HobNob, darling?"' She looked sadly at Kate. 'He just never takes me up on it.'

'Jeffrey and I are no different,' Kate admitted. 'We'd rather watch *Inspector Morse* than make love these days.'

14

'That's really sad,' Sonia commiserated. 'I can't stand John Thaw.'

'Sex isn't everything in a relationship.' Kate didn't sound convinced, even to her own ears. Their bed seemed to be getting wider and wider as the gulf between them grew. Jeffrey treated her like his favourite sister, not like the red-hot love machine that she felt burning inside her. 'It's important to have companionship, shared interests and mutual respect.'

'If you believe that, you'll believe anything,' Sonia snorted. 'I'd rather have a good bonk any day of the week. Or every day of the week,' she added after a moment's thought.

Kate rested her elbows on her knees and put her head in her hands. Her legs felt leaden, even after the hour of 'Lean-Burn, High-Octane' stepping and they matched the heavy feeling that permeated the rest of her body. Why didn't she enjoy anything any more? She always seemed to feel vaguely detached, as if none of this was really happening to her – and everything felt like such an effort. When had her get up and go got up and gone?

'I'm thirty-five years old,' she complained, 'and already I feel I'm on the slippery slope of middle age.'

'You're exactly middle-aged, if you believe the Bible. All we get is three score years and ten – if we're lucky.'

'Thanks, Sonia, that makes me feel a lot better.'

Sonia slipped a shapeless jumper over her head. 'Look,' she said kindly, 'you shouldn't think of yourself as thirty-five. Think of yourself as two seventeen-and-a-half-year-olds rolled into one. That's much more fun.'

Kate shook her head sadly. 'There must be more to life than this. Jeffrey's working harder and harder just to stand still. The days seem to melt into one another in an endless stream of drudge.' She twisted towards her friend, just as Sonia was surreptitiously removing a squashed Toffee Crisp from the pocket of her jeans. She stopped guiltily, caught in the act.

'I'm depressed now,' she informed Kate. 'And my sugar levels are dangerously low after all that exercise.'

Kate didn't even hear her. 'Do you know how pathetic my life is? I've even started to worry that my floating candles will sink.'

'Sad,' her friend agreed.

'I have developed an addiction to watching small scented candles in assorted pastel shades glide serenely across ornate bowls of tap water. I feel suicidal when I see them starting to tilt halfway through dinner, plunging Delia's Beef in Designer Beer into darkness.'

Her friend regarded her with pity.

'And they always do sink,' Kate continued. 'I feel my negative vibes influence them. It's karma.'

'It isn't, it's the *Titanic* principle. One heavy object, one expanse of water, one impending disaster.' Sonia proffered a bite of the Toffee Crisp. Kate declined. 'You're lucky that you have so little to trouble you.'

'I know, I should be grateful, shouldn't I? I should be happy.'

Sonia met her eyes. 'But you're not.'

'No. It's not that I don't love Jeffrey,' Kate said hastily.

'Hm. That particular sentence usually precedes goodbye and a dramatic slamming of the door.'

Kate sniffled miserably.

'So what are you going to do about it?' Sonia prompted.

Kate tilted her chin decisively. 'I have decided to confront my velvet-lined rut of a life, take it by the throat and give it a thorough shaking!'

'I constantly feel like doing that to Kev,' Sonia conceded. 'And, pray tell, how is this "thorough shaking" going to proceed?'

Kate hesitated. 'You'll laugh.'

'I won't.' Sonia held up her Girl Guide salute. 'May God strike me dead!'

'Promise?' Kate took a deep breath. 'I've booked myself on a week's T'ai Chi course at Northwood Priory.'

Sonia looked at her po-faced. 'T'ai Chi? Isn't that what ancient Chinese pensioners do in the parks?' Sonia pressed her lips together and tried to look suitably serious.

Kate said defensively, 'Yes. It's a Chinese system of exercises that promote physical and mental well-being. It happens to be very trendy at the moment.'

'And Alvin Stardust's all the rage too.'

'It's *not* funny,' Kate said irritably. 'I'm leaving Jeffrey, the kids and the Dyson bagless vacuum cleaner behind and I'm doing something for me!' She pointed at her chest. 'I'm going to have a week away from them all to think about what *I* want from life.'

17

'We could go up to London together,' Sonia suggested. 'We could see the Chippendales, get drunk on Bacardi and Coke at ten quid a throw in some trendy bar and then bop till we drop at one of those sweaty nightclubs filled with Arab tourists.'

'You make it sound so appealing, Sonia.'

Kate picked up her bag and slung it on her shoulder. Sonia followed, struggling to keep up as Kate crashed through the swing doors; passing a litter bin, she greedily licked her Toffee Crisp wrapper before throwing it away.

'When did you last let your hair down?' she shouted. 'That's all you need.'

'I don't want to let my hair down. I want to find myself.'

They had reached their cars. Usually, the light nights filled Kate full of energy that had her digging the garden borders until bedtime, but this year even the long hot summer days and balmy nights had failed to lift her spirits. Could you get postnatal depression ten years after the children were born?

'Take me with you.' Sonia's voice broke into her thoughts.

'No.'

'Go on, go on, go on!'

'No way.'

'It'll be great crack!'

Kate leaned on the roof of her BMW. 'I don't want "great crack". I want some quiet time to think about things.'

'I'd like some quiet time too,' Sonia insisted. 'Let me come – please.'

18

'No.'

'I can do quiet.'

'You can't. And anyway, I want to be alone.'

'You sound like bloody Zsa Zsa Gabor.'

'It was Greta Garbo. And you still can't come.'

'When are you going?'

'I'm not telling you.'

'You'll miss me.'

Kate smiled. 'I know I will.' She opened her car door. 'Don't be cross with me, Sonia. I need to do this by myself.'

'Well, personally,' her friend said sulkily as she flounced across the car park, 'I don't see how waving your arms around for a week just outside High Wycombe is going to change anything!'

Chapter Three

'Jeffrey, I'm going away for seven nights.'

Her husband glanced up from his copy of *Accountancy Weekly* and smiled encouragingly. 'I know.'

Kate lay on her back, Jilly Cooper abandoned on the bedside table. She had tried to arrange her hair seductively across the pillow, but her efforts had gone unnoticed. And there was a limit to how far shoulder-length hair would drape anyway. Their next-door neighbour swung into his drive, the beam of his headlights swooping across the bedroom ceiling. It reminded Kate of when she was a child and how she used to lie awake watching for the headlights of her father's car to make their kaleidoscope patterns across the knobbly surface of the woodchip wallpaper in her bedroom – for only then could she sleep soundly, secure in the knowledge that he was home safely. Tonight the memory failed to comfort her.

'Seven *whole* nights,' she repeated.

'I know,' he murmured, turning a page. 'You'll enjoy it.'

She propped herself up on an elbow. 'I've never been away before. Apart from two nights in a maternity ward.'

'I know,' he said and patted her leg.

'And then you set fire to the cat while you were making toast.'

20

Jeffrey took off his glasses and rubbed his eyes. 'He was only mildly singed though, rather than burnt to a crisp. Unlike the toast.' He pointed with his glasses. 'You were wearing that nightie when I came in to tell you.'

'Was I?' *Was I?* The thought horrified Kate. What was she doing still wearing a nightie that was ten years old? A maternity nightie, to boot! Jeffrey must be mistaken. 'It was probably a similar one.'

'No,' he insisted. 'It was definitely that one. I remember the pink rosebuds.'

Kate looked down at the faded grey-pink rosebuds that adorned the threadbare material. This was her favourite comfy nightie. Her mind did a reluctant flashback. *Grief, he could be right!*

'Have you put plenty of food in the freezer for the kids?' her husband asked.

'Is that all this means to you?'

'No,' he said patiently. 'I just wanted to make sure we were all organised.'

'*We* are very organised, thank you,' she said crisply.

'I'm not complaining,' he reassured her. 'Just checking.'

'Well, I've been considerably more organised than filling the freezer with food.' She sat up and hugged her knees to her chest. 'I've arranged an au pair.'

Jeffrey looked flabbergasted. 'I don't want an au pair!'

'Of course you do,' Kate insisted. 'Every man wants an au pair. It comes with midlife crisis, and the urge to buy a racy little sports car instead of a Vauxhall Astra. What's more, you'll be the talk of the office.'

21

'I don't want to be the talk of the office.' He rubbed his hands over his face slowly and deliberately. 'Besides,' he said tightly, 'I can manage perfectly well.'

'You can't.'

'I can.'

'The cat incident merely serves as a benchmark of your domestic capacity.'

'You should have discussed this with me first.' He looked at her with his I-am-very-serious face on and she noticed, for the first time, the fine lines starting to etch into the smooth skin on either side of his mouth. Soon they would be as bad as hers. 'I'm not sure that I want a stranger roaming round our home while you're away.'

'I couldn't discuss it with you because I had to make a quick decision. She's not going to roam, she's going to work. And she's not a stranger. She's Jessica's nanny. The family are going on holiday to Disney World and were leaving her behind for two weeks to water the plants and the pets and so forth. Jessica said she'd be happy to come over here on a daily basis and look after you lot as well.'

'*She* might be happy, Kate, but I'm not.' Jeffrey scowled until a little bump formed between his eyebrows. 'Not happy at all.'

'Jessica said she's wonderful. So organised.'

'How would Jessica know?' Jeffrey pointed out. 'She couldn't organise a piss-up in a brewery.'

'She could!'

'What about the barn dance fiasco? That was Jessica's

little baby. When we arrived, complete with checked shirts and jeans, the place was still two foot deep in cow pats!'

'Now you're just being Victor Meldrew for the sake of it,' Kate said dismissively, remembering that it had taken them so long to shovel the manure out that no one had any strength left for do-se-do-ing. 'Take my word for it, this girl's wonderful. She's a six-foot hunk of Australian beauty with tits like Emma Noble.'

'Really.' That failed to raise even the same level of interest as *Accountancy Weekly*.

'Yes. *Really*.'

'So that's it. I'm going to be sharing my home, my *one* place of refuge, with an air-headed Aussie for a week?'

'I wouldn't have put it quite like that,' Kate bristled. 'But that's about the sum of it.'

'Fine.'

Kate snuggled up to her husband. 'I thought I was being helpful,' she said. 'I didn't want you under any more pressure than you already are.'

'We're talking about looking after two kids for the week – my kids! And by your own admission, two extraordinarily well-behaved ones.'

'They take a lot of looking after, Jeffrey,' Kate warned him. 'They need constant chauffeuring. Kerry has a busier social diary than Tamara Beckwith. Just getting the pair of them to where they need to be on time takes a blend of mathematical precision and divine benevolence. Having Natalie here will take the pressure off.'

'Natalie?'

Kate nodded. 'Natalie Lambert.'

'I suppose she's about sixteen and straight out of Ramsay Street.'

'She's twenty-eight, very capable and she is, indeed, from Melbourne. And she's coming tomorrow morning to have a look round, so that I can show her where everything is before I disappear.' *For seven whole days!* A shiver of panic rippled through Kate as her gaze caught the ready-packed case standing by the wardrobe. 'Then you'll have the rest of the day by yourselves for you to get fed up playing the bountiful father, and she'll come and take over on Monday. By which time you'll be glad to get back to work and will be eternally grateful that I found her.'

'Fine.' He closed his magazine decisively and put it on the bedside cabinet.

'You've finished *The Joy of Accountancy*, then?' She couldn't keep the hurt out of her voice.

'I never get time to read it at the office.' Jeffrey slid down in the bed. 'Are you ready to go to sleep?'

Kate wriggled down too, burrowing against his side, feeling the warmth of his skin through the dreaded nightie. His face was pale and drained and she felt a surge of affection for this quiet, sensitive man. She traced a finger slowly over his chest. 'I'm cold.'

'Do you want to put on a pair of my socks?'

'No, I don't want to put on a pair of your socks!'

'You know what your feet are like once they get cold – they'll be blue all night.'

She moulded herself against him seductively. 'I'd prefer a cuddle.'

'I thought you were tired.'

'Well, I am a bit.'

'So am I.' He reached out and switched off the light. 'It's been a very long week.' Plumping his pillow, he turned towards her. 'By the way, your hair's all over the place.'

She stared at him open-mouthed, the effect lost in the darkness.

'Night, night,' he said sweetly, and pecked her lightly on the cheek.

Kate felt the tears well up. *I'm tired but I'm not too tired! I'm going away for a whole week, Jeffrey. Doesn't it warrant a more romantic goodbye than this?*

Her husband turned his back to her, snuggling down into the duvet, and within moments had started to snore gently with the snuffly wet sighs of a contented hedgehog. It was Saturday night – normally the only night she could guarantee that they would make love. Kate looked down at her aged rosebud nightie and wondered if that might offer a clue as to why her husband didn't feel the slightest bit inclined to ravish her any more.

Chapter Four

It was Sunday morning in sunny suburbia. The packed suitcase had now moved down to the hall, and was waiting expectantly by the front door. The children were sitting at the kitchen table doing their homework and singing along chirpily to the pop songs on Radio 1. Was there no one in this house who was remotely bothered about her abandoning them, leaving them to fend for themselves for a week? Everyone was so sodding cheerful! Even the cat, Erstwhile, who was normally welded to the top of the central heating boiler, had vanished on one of his few forays into Bedfordshire's wild beyond. They couldn't wait to see her gone, obviously.

'You can get through life without endless swotting, you know,' Kate said loudly to the back of her children's heads. 'Why don't you watch an old episode of *Neighbours* on video?'

'This isn't just ordinary homework,' her daughter informed her condescendingly. 'It's a very important project, Mum. And you do want me to work hard, pass all my exams and follow in the footsteps of Cherie Blair and become a QC, don't you?'

'Wouldn't you rather be a ballerina?'

Kerry frowned. 'How much do they make a year?'

'Probably not as much as a QC and you're burnt out by the time you're twenty-eight.'

Kerry sucked the end of her pen. 'Perhaps I could be a ballerina until my knees go and then be a QC.' She returned to her scribbling.

Kate made herself the tenth cup of chamomile tea she'd had this morning in the vain hope that one of them must soon hit the spot and start to relax her. Jeffrey came in from the garden, tugging his muddy boots off by the door. He had a smear of mud on his cheek and she resisted the urge to reach up and wipe it away. She was still smarting after his cold shoulder last night; what's more, this morning he had been up and out of bed with the lark without so much as a farewell fondle.

'Hi.' He kissed her cheek. 'I've watered the hanging baskets.'

Riveting. 'Thanks.'

'One less thing for you to worry about.'

'Yes.' And the alarming thing was, she *had* been worrying about the hanging baskets. This would have to stop.

'What are you two doing?' he asked the kids.

Kerry looked up. 'A project on popular pesticides in African agriculture.'

'That's nice.' He raised an eyebrow at Kate.

'Dinosaurs,' Joe obliged.

'Coffee?' Kate suggested.

'I think I need some,' Jeffrey said.

'They don't have lessons in school these days,' Kate observed while spooning some Nescafé into a mug. 'They have optimum learning experiences and projects.'

Jeffrey took the mug of boiling coffee from her. 'Things just aren't the same as when I was a boy.'

'No,' Kate agreed wistfully. 'There's electricity for a start.'

'Very funny.' Leaning against the kitchen cabinets he crossed his long legs and sipped his coffee.

They'd recently had the kitchen refitted. Another part of this restlessness that had taken up residence in Kate's body was the urge to redecorate. She had been terrified for one brief moment that this sudden homebuilding instinct was an early warning sign that she was pregnant – before she remembered that Jeffrey had braved the vasectomy clinic and the ensuing infected testicle with much complaining and recourse to antibiotics. It was distressed. The kitchen. Distressed is fashionable, so the builder had said. Which meant they had a brand new kitchen with designer scuffed and chipped paintwork. The only thing that seemed to be truly distressed was her husband – firstly, by the price and secondly, because he couldn't see anything wrong with the pristine stripped pine kitchen that it had replaced.

'So, when's this au pair coming?' Jeffrey enquired with stage-managed reluctance.

Kate glanced at her watch. 'She should be here even as we speak.'

On cue the doorbell rang.

'See how reliable she is?' Kate breezed out to answer the door. 'She'll be the answer to our prayers.'

Jeffrey rolled his eyes heavenwards in silent disagreement.

'Gidday,' the apparition in front of him said in a broad Australian twang. He fully expected her to add 'cobber'.

'This is Natalie,' Kate said from somewhere far away in the distance.

This girl was what Kevin would call 'totally babetastic'. Kate was right when she said that Natalie was six foot tall – she'd just failed to mention that most of it would be legs. Legs that appeared to end only beneath three inches of highly insubstantial material. Even Joe looked up from his dinosaur project, transfixed.

'Natalie Lambert.' The vision spoke again and reached out for the hand that wasn't clutching his mug so hard that his knuckles had turned white.

'Hi,' he croaked as nonchalantly as he could manage.

She squeezed his hand, crushing his fingers to the point where he would never be able to play the piano again. But then he had never been able to play it anyway.

'Everyone calls me Nat.'

'Hi, Nat,' he croaked again, sounding in serious need of Strepsils. 'Jeffrey,' was all his voice could cope with by way of introduction.

'You've got a smut,' she said and spat on her thumb and rubbed it heartily across his cheek, fixing him with lazy slate-grey eyes that said DANGER – TROUBLE AHEAD.

He saw a brief frown wriggle across Kate's forehead.

29

Natalie – Nat – winked at him. 'That's better, Jeffers.'

Jeffers?

'I'll show Natalie round.' Kate spoke out of the haze again.

'F-f-fine,' he swallowed.

Natalie smiled at him and something that he didn't realise was extinguished lit up inside his heart. She had more lips than Julia Roberts and wraparound teeth that gleamed pearly white from a golden tanned face. Slinging her backpack over her shoulder, she followed Kate from the kitchen with the elegant saunter of a racehorse that knows it's about to win the race.

'We won't be long,' Kate informed him loudly. 'I need to be going soon.'

'Right. Right,' he said. 'Right.'

Natalie turned on the kilowatts again. She had masses of impossibly bleach-blonde hair – honey-coloured, threaded with tresses of pure white. It cascaded in wisps over her face, enhancing her beauty considerably, and she looked as if she hadn't combed it since she got out of bed. Jeffrey gulped at the thought. When he managed to tear his eyes away from her face, he noticed that she was wearing a short denim jacket and a striped skimpy top that looked stretched to breaking point. Kate had been right about the Emma Noble chest.

Jeffrey took off his glasses and massaged his forehead. The palms of his hands had gone clammy and his heart was thundering like an express train. There was a damp line of perspiration on his top lip, and the kitchen felt a lot hotter than it had a few moments ago. No one had ever made this sort of impact on him before, not even Kate, who was, in a completely different way, a very beautiful woman.

His wife was as dark as Natalie was light. Her hair was always slightly unruly, despite her best efforts, but most days she gave up the fight with the hair dryer in favour of breakfast. He didn't think she had any tell-tale grey strands, but it was a while since he had looked that closely. Her best feature was her eyes – striking, vivid, a make-believe blue from the strong end of the artist's palette. Strangers noticed them across crowded rooms. They say that the eyes are the windows of the soul, and every emotion Kate experienced flashed through them, sparking them into life without her needing to speak. She would have made a useless poker player and he knew that he had been ignoring the unhappiness in them for too long. Kate had the subtly rounded slimness of a woman who had borne two children. *His* children. But the waif-like form belied her solidity and substance while, for all Nat's physical impact, there was a slightly surreal air to her that made you feel she was likely to float tantalisingly beyond your grasp the minute you reached out for her.

Behind Kate's efficient façade was a vulnerability that drew people to her like iron filings to a magnet. Jeffrey had always felt an overwhelming desire to cherish and nurture her, to do right by her. Since the day he first met her as a callow youth, he knew for certain that he loved her and would one day marry her. Had this diminished over the years until they had become a weak and pallid imitation of the real thing, like vending machine coffee? He thought not. So what were these feelings for Natalie, with her come-and-get-me confidence? Lust? Desire? Passion? Feelings that were certainly unacceptable in a married, middle-aged man!

This girl had pulled his eyes out, polished them off with her shirt-sleeve and pinged them back into his sockets, so that now everything seemed brighter, more sharply in focus. How long had he been walking round myopically like Mr Magoo? His mind ran over the video play-back of her walking into the kitchen. It had already lodged itself in his brain for ever. With a slightly shaking hand, Jeffrey picked up the cold dregs of his coffee and swallowed them down in one.

Natalie Lambert was, quite unequivocally, the most terrifying person he had ever met in his life.

Kate was fussing as she came downstairs. She knew it, but couldn't help it. It was one of the more alarming signs that she was slowly turning into her mother. Casting a sideways glance at Natalie, she chewed on her fingernail. There was no doubt that she seemed terribly capable, it was just that she looked the sort of girl who would be more comfortable sprawled across a bed in one of Andrew's copies of *Playboy* rather than wielding a steam iron through a pile of school blouses. If only she'd looked slightly more like Hyacinth Bucket. Kate wondered if she was really happy to leave

Nat in charge of her domain for a week. Could Jeffrey, as he so vociferously pointed out, have really coped by himself? Probably not. The thought, at least, gave her some comfort. *Some* comfort. Some *small* comfort.

Kate turned again to Natalie. 'So, are you happy with the arrangements?'

'Happy as a sandboy.'

She certainly looked as if she was; she had been grinning widely since she'd walked into the kitchen. Had Natalie grinned quite so much when she'd seen her at Jessica's house? Had she really seemed quite so tall and quite so beautiful when viewed in another setting? Too late now; she had made the arrangements and it was no time to be getting cold feet about the prospect of another woman rooting through her laundry basket. Perhaps she was being overly protective. Jeffrey had behaved very strangely when he met her, but then he was never very comfortable around women. He wasn't a man's man either; he was a potential loner and only relaxed with someone when he had known them for years. He had been dead-set against the idea too, which probably didn't help.

Kate glanced at her watch. 'I must be off. Registration is at twelve o'clock and it will take an hour or so to get there.' She started down the stairs. 'Now, I told you that Kerry has her keyboard lesson on Monday night at seven o'clock, while Joe's at swimming club. Then Tuesday is Guides night and Joe is at football practice . . .'

'Don't worry,' Natalie assured her with a widening of her smile. 'You've written it all down for me.' She waved the piece of paper bearing the weekly chart of activities to prove that she still had it. 'We'll be right.'

'Now, everyone has their own copy, including Jeffrey, so don't let him tell you that he hasn't. And there's one stuck to the fridge too as a central reference point.'

Jeffrey came out of the kitchen as they reached the bottom step. 'You're sounding like your mother,' he said. 'And you're going to be late unless you get your skates on.'

'I just want to make sure everything goes smoothly.' *Stop it! You're in panic mode! She'll be thinking you're old and confused. Fortunately, she doesn't know your mother. This is supposed to be the day you're going to stop thinking for everyone else and think of yourself! Remember?*

'Ah, I'm sure we'll all get along fine, Mrs Lewis.' Natalie smiled at her husband. 'Won't we, Jeffers?'

Kate felt strangely at a loss. 'If you could get here about eight o'clock tomorrow morning to give them some breakfast and see them off to school?' she asked Natalie.

Jeffrey stepped forward. 'Er, have you made any arrangements for the rest of the day, er, Nat?'

'No, Jeffers, I'm free as a bird.'

'Perhaps you'd like to join us for a spot of Sunday lunch at the pub. It'll give you an opportunity to get to know the children.'

Sunday lunch? In the pub? 'There's a leg of lamb in the freezer,' Kate interrupted. 'New Zealand lamb.'

'Oh, we don't want to bother with that, darling,' Jeffrey

laughed lightly. *She did. Every bloody Sunday. And didn't they all moan if she suggested otherwise!* 'The kids will love eating out for a change.'

'It won't take long to defrost in the microwave,' Kate insisted.

'A pub lunch sounds great,' Natalie beamed, looking straight through her.

'I thought we'd go to the Bridgeman's Arms and then maybe have a walk through Ashridge Forest while the weather's fine,' her husband said nonchalantly, as if it was something they did every Sunday.

'That sounds cool. I haven't been there yet.'

Kate scowled. This wasn't the vision of them sitting missing her that she'd anticipated. 'I should be off,' she said brusquely.

'Let me put your case in the car.' Jeffrey picked it up and strode outside.

Why the rush?

She went into the kitchen. 'Are you going to come out and wave me goodbye?' she asked her children a little wistfully.

They both stood up from the table. 'I'm glad Natalie's going to look after us while you're away,' Kerry said happily. 'She's pretty.'

'Yes.' Kate felt her heart sinking further towards her newly purchased soft-soled shoes.

'Andrew thinks she's a babe. When we were all playing at Aunty Jessica's house, he said he'd seen Natalie walking round the house in her knickers and her bra.'

'Oh, did he?' Kate's heart, which was now somewhere round her ankles, missed a beat.

'He's probably lying,' her daughter said loftily. 'You know what boys are like.'

Kate glanced at Joe. He looked immensely cheered by the prospect of seeing Natalie in her knickers. She wondered what Jeffrey would think of it.

They all trooped out across the gravel to the waiting BMW. Jeffrey held the door open and she kissed the children goodbye. It felt as if she was leaving them for ever. She wanted to throw herself at their feet and tell them that she'd changed her mind, she was quite happy to remain in a rut and Natalie could naff off back to Jessica's and look after nothing more vulnerable than a couple of cats and a goldfish. There was, however, some sliver of sense lodged in all this emotion that told her she would only regret it in the morning. A week wasn't a long time to give yourself after fifteen years of wifely and maternal devotion. *Was it?*

Kate turned to Jeffrey. She wanted him to take her in his arms and cling to her and beg her not to go. It was unlikely, given the audience of two inquisitive children and a bombshell au pair, that he would. And Jeffrey was not a demonstrative man. Even on her wedding day when she had arrived at the altar next to him, radiant and blushing, he had turned to her and said those immortal words, 'You look nice.' He was more a man of quiet passions. But even they seemed to have gone out of the window these days.

She wound her arms round his waist and felt his body stiffen. 'Will you miss me?'

'It goes without saying.'

'I'd rather you did say it.'

He lowered his voice. 'I'll miss you.'

'Lots?'

He checked the audience and lowered it even further. 'Lots.'

'Be good,' Kate said tearfully, as she kissed him briefly on the lips, before slipping into the car.

'And you.'

'Whatever you do, Jeffrey, please don't get *Ground Force* in while I'm away. I couldn't stand the thought of that blonde, breasty woman ripping up my herbaceous borders.' It was bad enough thinking of Natalie Lambert rummaging about in her freezer.

Her husband laughed. 'I won't, I promise.'

Jeffrey walked back and joined the children as she turned on the engine. Natalie stood behind them, resting her hands on their shoulders. It was a scene straight out of *Happy Families*.

Kate put the car into gear and started a reluctant crawl out of the drive. The children waved enthusiastically at her. Jeffrey raised his hand. It would have been better if he'd used it to blow a kiss.

'Have a nice week, Mrs Lewis,' Natalie shouted. 'Don't you worry about us!'

As Kate turned out of the drive, she realised she had never felt more worried in her life.

37

Chapter Five

Sonia opened the front door as soon as she heard the car in the drive. She bounded to the driver's door and peered in the window. 'You're late,' she said. 'You promised to be here by eleven.'

'I know,' Kate apologised. 'I had to show the au pair round and then I shot into Marks and Sparks on the way.'

'What for?'

'A nightie.'

'A nightie?'

'It's a long story.'

'Let's have a look.'

'Not now. We've got to be there by twelve to check in. I'll have to put my foot down as it is.'

Kevin and the boys had followed Sonia out of the house. 'By the way, Kevin's very jealous that you're leaving Jeffrey with an au pair,' she said.

'Yes,' her husband agreed. 'Particularly as Sonia's leaving me with Captain Birdseye.'

'You'll manage,' she said.

'We'll have to.' He gave Kate a can-you-believe-it? look. 'Anyway, Kate, how are you?'

'Fine, thanks, Kev.'

'That's not what I heard.'

Kate glowered at Sonia. 'What's she been saying?'

'That you were fed up with Jeffrey and life in general.'

'Well, I suppose that's it in a nutshell,' Kate said. 'I have no secrets with her.'

'Me neither,' agreed Kev, who was probably well aware that his prowess between the sheets was the regular subject of in-depth analysis. That might explain why he was so reluctant to embark on a performance – as Sonia might as well sell front row tickets. 'She reckons this T'ai Chi lark is all your idea.'

'I'm afraid it is.'

'Thought so. Didn't reckon that being taught to stand on one leg by ninety-year-old Chinamen was quite my dear wife's cup of tea.'

'I had planned to go on my own.' She cast a pointed look in Sonia's direction. 'This was supposed to be space for myself.'

Oblivious, Sonia hoisted two bulging suitcases into the boot.

'It was rather a *fait accompli* when she rang up and told me she'd booked herself on the course too.'

'Subtle as a flying brick. That's our Sonia,' her husband commiserated.

Sonia grabbed her boys by the hair and kissed them both roughly on the forehead. They resumed their game of trying to kick each other in the shins and Sonia flopped in the car beside her.

'Don't I get a kiss?' her husband asked.

'It doesn't normally bother you,' she replied.

'See what I have to put up with?' he laughed.

'There is one saving grace for this week, Kevin,' Kate said. 'At least I'm not having to share a room with her.'

'Be thankful for small mercies. She farts in bed.'

The boys raced to the car and tried to scale the sides of the BMW to climb in the windows.

'Get down,' Sonia shouted.

'Mummy,' Daniel whined, 'what's an orgasm?'

'I've no idea,' Sonia said sweetly. 'Ask your father.'

Kevin grimaced and banged the roof of the car. 'Have a good week. Don't get too excited and overdo it!'

'Bastard,' Sonia hissed out through her smile. She gave an excited little shrug to Kate. 'Come on then, James, don't spare the horses.'

Kevin stood rooted to the spot while the boys ran after the car waving.

Sonia waved back enthusiastically, while saying, 'Naff off, naff off, naff off,' under her breath.

Kate smiled. 'You are terrible.'

'I'm a free agent. For a *whole* week. A *free agent*!' Sonia bounced up and down. 'Woo! Woo!' she yelled. 'Let's give this yoga on legs some stick!'

'It would seem timely, at this juncture, to remind you that we are going there to have a quiet time of contemplation and renewal.'

'Bollocks to that!' Sonia jeered. 'I'm going to have some fun!'

Kate turned onto the dual carriageway and accelerated the BMW to eighty miles an hour. This was a great start to a stress-free week of winding down. Leaving her husband at the mercy of a gorgeous blonde and having to then cane it to get there on time, accompanied by Freddie Starr in female form. It didn't bode well for the rest of the week.

Sonia switched on the CD and let Kerry's M People blast out at full pelt, until it vibrated the door speakers. 'This is brilliant,' Sonia shrieked above the music. 'The open road, the wind in our hair! It's like a great adventure unfolding before us. I feel like Thelma and Louise!'

'Except we haven't shot anyone.'

'No, but I had an overwhelming desire to!'

Both of them laughed uproariously.

They drove along listening to the pounding music, until Kate decided it was time to save what was left of her hearing for old age.

'Sonia?'

'Oh no, this sounds serious,' she said. 'Do I need a cigarette?'

'No.' Kate shook her head. 'Anyway, you know I don't like you smoking in the car.'

'I won't light it.' She ferreted in her handbag. 'I'll just suck it, as the actress said to the bishop.' She put the unlit cigarette in her mouth. 'Go on then – I'm all ears.'

Kate fixed her eyes on the road ahead. 'Does Kevin look at other women?'

'If you put a blonde wig on a broom handle, Kevin would be after it.' She puffed on her unlit Benson & Hedges. 'Mind you, he wouldn't know what to do with it if he caught it.'

Kate laughed.

'Why are you asking? Does Jeffrey lust after other women? He hasn't ever struck me as the leering type.'

Kate shrugged. 'There are times when *Baywatch* has been on the television and he hasn't even looked up from the *Telegraph* crossword.' Then again, he never looked at her either. She had a good figure for her age and was lucky enough to be naturally slim, but she also worked at it. There was a lurking fear of developing a tummy as squishy as the Pilsbury Doughboy's, and drooping tits. Why couldn't Jeffrey see her as a desirable woman for a change, rather than as chief cook and bottle-washer?

'Kev's just as bad,' Sonia agreed. 'He's at that age where he thinks coming to bed smeared in Germolene or Deep Heat is an aphrodisiac.'

'Once upon a time I would have said that if a blonde and buxom wench walked into our kitchen in an itsy-bitsy bikini, she would have failed to raise a smile – let alone anything else.' Kate's brow creased with concern. *She* might not be the one raising Jeffrey's temperature, but she was convinced it had gone up a few degrees in the last couple of hours. 'Now I'm not so sure.'

'Don't tell me.' Sonia took a deep drag of the dummy cigarette. 'The lovely Natalie?'

'Oh, I'm just being silly,' Kate said with a shake of her head. 'This is the first time we've been apart for any length of time. Jeffrey's had the odd night away at conferences, but that's about it. He likes being at home.'

'But you're not sure whether you like him being at home with Miss Bondi Beach.'

'I thought it was a good idea, but now I feel as though she's intruding on my turf.' Kate glanced at her friend. 'Tell me I'm being silly.'

'You're not silly, you're completely mad,' Sonia said emphatically. 'I only caught a glimpse of her once, getting the milk bottles in from Jessica's front door. She had this strappy nightie thing on that barely covered her bum.'

Kate frowned.

Sonia continued unabashed. 'I wouldn't let her within a five-mile radius of Kevin. His testosterone level would shoot off the scale.'

'Thanks, Sonia,' Kate said. 'Your words have been a source of comfort and joy.'

'Speaking of nighties,' Sonia reached over for the Marks & Spencer carrier bag from the back seat and peered into it. 'Let's have a look at this then.'

'What do you think?' Kate asked, concentrating on the road.

Sonia curled her lip. 'It's a bit married woman, isn't it?'

'Is it?'

'Well, there's a sad lack of black lace and frilly little bits. Are you planning to be cold?'

'I thought it was nice.'

'Sorry – it's one very small step away from prissy pink rosebuds.' Sonia eyed it with disdain. 'Definitely married woman.'

Kate snatched it from her and threw it onto the back seat of the car. 'I *am* a bloody married woman!'

'Tell me about it.'

They continued in silence, until Sonia piped up again, with: 'I'm your best friend, right?'

I sometimes wonder. 'Right.'

'I can tell you anything, can't I?'

'Go on.'

'Well, I reckon you ought to go shopping with Kerry more often. Or me. Your fashion sense seems to have gone adrift somewhere along the line. You're a very attractive woman, my love, but you have a fixation for blue eyeliner and sad cardies that means you're never likely to grace the pages of *Vogue*. Yes, you've got trapped somewhere at *Women's Weekly* level. You need to think more SI rather than WI.'

Kate eyed her friend suspiciously. 'What's SI?'

'It's something I just made up,' Sonia admitted. 'Sexual impact. You know – *Pzazz*! I'd willingly die to be half as gorgeous as you, but you just don't use it to your advantage.'

Kate pondered. 'Do you think I should apply to go on *Style Challenge*?'

'*Challenge Anneka*, more like, for the scale of project we're taking on.'

Kate was feeling gloomy. 'Thanks.' It was true, she did seem to have developed an unhealthy attraction for all things Laura Ashley. She didn't seem to be happy unless her clothes had a sprig of blooming flowers on them

44

somewhere. 'I'm having a struggle with my self-esteem here, Sonia.'

'It's a passing phase,' her friend said glibly. 'Every woman goes through it. It's the time of life when Venus is in retrograde and the moon is in Uranus, or something. Don't worry, you just wait till you find yourself again, then you'll be rushing out to buy Lurex G-strings without giving a fig for what anyone else thinks.'

Kate somehow doubted it.

Sonia looked at her sympathetically. 'I hope you don't mind me saying this?'

'No, not at all,' Kate lied.

Why should she mind? She had no romance in her marriage, no clear sense of direction in her life, and her husband was currently wandering about the woods with an overwhelmingly wonderful, young Australian woman. Now her so-called best friend had just pointed out that she didn't even have the ability to pick the right blouse. Perhaps she should have looked for a course entitled *Goodbye Cruel World: How to Make Your Suicide Fun* rather than T'ai Chi. She'd been looking forward to a quiet week of contemplation. Venus in retrograde, Lurex G-strings? *Don't worry?* Now she had more to worry about than ever!

Chapter Six

The Bridgeman's Arms was packed and smoky.

'I'm going to die of passive smoking,' Kerry pointed out.

'We won't be in here long enough,' Jeffrey said, scanning over the heads of the crowd. 'Don't breathe in as often as you normally do and you'll be fine.'

'When I become a QC, I'll lead a case against cigarette manufacturers and get my own back,' his daughter informed him.

'Yes, darling.' Jeffrey began to push his way to the bar. 'What do you want to drink?'

'Mineral water, please. Still.'

'Joe?'

'Orange juice.'

'Natalie?'

'A glass of dry white wine, please, Jeffrey.' *Why had he expected her to say a pint of Fosters?*

Natalie took the children to find a table, while Jeffrey steadily elbowed his way through the crush and remembered why he and Kate no longer bothered to come out for Sunday lunch.

The children and Nat were looking at the menu when he returned with a bent tray laden with drinks. He had

46

been jostled so much that they were swimming in a puddle, and only Natalie's glass of wine had remained relatively intact. He was aware that his every move was being watched and he wondered what the other men must think, seeing him with this beautiful blonde who was clearly a good deal younger than he was. Did they think that he and Nat were a couple? It was amazing the number of heads she had turned, simply by walking into the place; he felt quite self-conscious being with her. She was obviously perfectly used to it, as she barely seemed to notice. He sat down next to her and put the drinks on the table.

'Kerry, mineral water – still,' he said. 'Joe, orange juice. Natalie, dry white wine.' He handed her the glass, and the tips of their fingers touched as she took it.

'Nice one, Jeffers,' she said with one of her radiant smiles.

He'd always been called Jeffrey. His parents called him Jeffrey. His schoolfriends called him Jeffrey. His colleagues called him Jeffrey. His wife called him Jeffrey. And his children, when they were being their watered-down version of rebellious, also called him Jeffrey. Now here was this long-legged, full-busted blonde calling him Jeffers. And he really rather liked it.

'Boy, it's hot in here.' Natalie shrugged out of her denim jacket, leaving the full-stretch skimpy striped top very much on display.

Jeffrey felt it had suddenly got a lot hotter. He needed a good slurp of his pint to steady his nerves. Was it his imagination, or did several men reach simultaneously for *their* pint glasses? Jeffrey tore his eyes away from her.

'Have you decided what you want to eat? They've got scampi and chips, Joe.'

'Too much saturated fat,' Kerry advised.

'I'd like a cheese salad,' Joe said.

'Natalie?'

'I'll have the beef curry.'

'Do you watch your intake of red meat, Natalie?' Kerry enquired politely.

'I watch everything I eat, Kerry.' She smiled again at Jeffrey. 'My eyes never leave the plate once.'

'I apologise for my daughter,' he said. 'She's on a one-woman crusade to save the planet.'

'Good on ya, Kez.' Natalie gave her a girl-to-girl nudge.

'And I'll have the vegetarian casserole, please,' Kerry said piously.

Jeffrey ordered the highly unhealthy scampi for himself, much to his daughter's disdain, but when the food arrived he found himself unable to eat. His stomach had locked to a tight ball of tension, a bit like it did when he had to make a presentation at work, and he merely picked at the soggy scampi and greasy chips. There was far too much adrenalin surging in his veins for him to have a snowball's chance in hell of ever digesting this little lot. Natalie clearly had no such inhibitions, and her beef curry was disappearing at an alarming rate.

She looked up and grinned, pointing her fork at his plate. 'Missing Kate?'

'Pardon?'

She pointed again. 'You're being picky with your food. I thought you might be missing Kate.'

It was ridiculous, but it was the first time his thoughts had turned to his wife. She would have arrived at Northwood Priory by now and he wondered if she would be all right. Normally, she was so capable and in control, the house ran along like clockwork, but she had seemed strangely agitated when she set off. Perhaps the thought of 'finding herself' was more scary than she had first thought.

He hoped that when she found herself, she also found that she still loved him too. Maybe their marriage had got into a rut. He saw it as comfortable and cosy, what family life should be about, but he could see that there were areas that couldn't be particularly fulfilling for Kate. She wasn't naturally a jam-making or cake-icing person, it was just something she had done out of habit over the years. Her mother always made jam, she was now a mother herself, ergo, she made jam. Ditto cake icing, potato stamping, Lego building, name-tag sewing and a thousand other things she did, essentially under sufferance, but always with a smile on her face.

It wasn't easy to see things from the other person's point of view, Jeffrey realised now, especially since he himself had always felt quite content. It was true that some days his work drove him quietly to the brink of insanity, and his blood plodded round his veins until he was sure he was on the road to a slow and certain death behind his desk at Hills & Hopeland. He was also certain that no one would notice until the end-of-the-month figures became overdue. On the whole, though, he had been happy with his lot. He stared across at Natalie, who appeared about to lick her plate. Until this . . . this . . . girl had come into his life and stirred up feelings that he thought were incapable of being stirred, let alone shaken.

'I thought you might be missing Kate,' Natalie prompted.

'Yes,' he responded automatically and hoped to God that he was.

It was a ridiculously hot summer by British standards. Day after day of unbroken sunshine followed each other with a regularity normally attributed to senna pods and All Bran. As a consequence there was a hosepipe ban and trite adverts kept popping up on television from the water companies concerned about water wastage, but seemingly unconcerned about pouring money down the drain.

They paid their fifty pence to a surly man in a flat cap and parked at the drive leading up to the Bridgewater Monument, a towering column of Aberdeen granite, topped, for some inexplicable reason, by a giant green fruit bowl. It was as tall and unattractive as it was pointless. A monument to the father of inland waterways. Canals to you or me. Quite. It dwarfed the minute National Trust shop next to it, where you could buy everything from a hedgehog-shaped pencil sharpener to a Scottish heather tea-towel, but nothing remotely of local interest. There was an ice-cream van flogging Magnums as if they were going out of fashion, and Jeffrey wondered how many of the sales ever saw the light of day on a tax return, acknowledging ruefully the fact that work was never very far from his mind.

They wandered towards the monument, Jeffrey marvelling at the British population's propensity to spend Sunday afternoons sitting on fold-up deckchairs behind their Ford Mondeos parked neatly next to a line of a hundred other cars, eating warm sandwiches and drinking cold tea from Thermos flasks. No wonder the first escapees from this green and pleasant land had perfected the art of barbecuing. Kerry and Joe ran on ahead.

'They're nice kids,' Natalie said as she sauntered along.

He was aware that their paths kept colliding as they walked side by side and he could feel Natalie's bare arm brushing against his skin. The difficulty was concentrating on walking in a straight line when there were so many other things that he was trying not to concentrate on. On the way here, Natalie had been sitting in the front passenger seat. Her legs had stretched interminably into the foot well of the car, making her feet disappear. It was the only bit of her he hadn't been able to see and had added a certain element of risk to negotiating the narrow roads through Ringshall. He wondered how she could be so uninhibited whilst wearing so little clothing. It had taken him all his courage to wear his shorts to lunch. Jeffrey was not a shorts man. It wasn't that he had bad legs, a bit on the pasty side perhaps, but he was more of a suit person.

'Very well-behaved,' she added when he failed to comment.

'Yes,' he said hurriedly. 'Although Kate worries that they're too docile. Most of our friends' kids have a rebellious streak a mile wide. These two are completely domesticated.'

'I don't think there's anything wrong with that.'

'Neither do I,' he agreed readily. 'She thinks it's unnatural that Kerry prefers to drink water to Coke and hates the taste of chocolate and that Joe's favourite food is salad. Is that unusual?'

'I'd say that's pretty unusual,' Natalie laughed.

'But not just cause to bring in a team of behavioural psychologists?'

'They're individuals.'

'Isn't that what they say about most psychopaths?' Jeffrey shivered. 'My word, I'm sounding like Kate now. I think they're perfectly well-adjusted, well-balanced, well-behaved children. She feels that Joe is an exact replica of her father, who is a sixty-five-year-old architect. Kate thinks our son isn't a child, he's a pensioner in school uniform. Joe spends his spare time innocently designing houses for the oppressed masses and my wife thinks he should be lying on his bed idling away his life trying to imagine what the Spice Girls would look like without their clothes on.'

'Do you?'

'What?'

'Try to imagine what the Spice Girls look like in the buff?'

52

'No!' Jeffrey felt himself blush to his hair roots. 'Of course I don't. But then I'm not ten years old any more.' Which served as a jolly good reminder. He had been very disconcerted to find, whilst prodding his scampi, that his mind was dwelling on what Natalie would look like without her clothes on. And it wasn't too hard. She left very little to the imagination.

'Perhaps he's taking after his father then?'

'Perhaps,' Jeffrey said cagily, sure she was making fun of him.

They walked along in silence, watching the children run in and out of the edges of the woods, the sun piercing the gaps between the trees. The scrubby driveway was dusty with dirt and the grass was parched and brown. Even the towering majestic oaks looked thirsty.

'How are you enjoying England?' Jeffrey asked politely, keen to get away from all discussions of nudity.

'Fine,' she said. 'Not that I've seen much yet. I've been into London a few times, but looking after Jessica's tribe keeps me pretty busy. I was going to have some fun this week, but well . . . I need the money. I want to do Europe.'

'All of it?'

'I don't plan to stay in one place very long,' she told him. 'I want to earn some cash, see some sights and then move on.'

'Where have you been so far?'

'This is it,' she laughed. Her chuckle was as hearty and uninhibited as the rest of her. 'Grand plan! First stop Bedfordshire!'

'I don't think Leighton Buzzard is necessarily repre-
sentative of the rest of Europe.'

'It's a nice little place,' she said, and gave him a sideways
glance. 'The natives are very friendly.'

Jeffrey tugged at his polo-shirt collar. That was another
thing. Kate always liked him to wear his T-shirts outside
his shorts, but he was happier when he was safely tucked
in.

They had arrived at the base of the monument.

'This is cool,' Natalie observed, shading her eyes to look
at the top.

'Well, it's big,' he conceded. Perhaps Australians were
like Americans in their preference for quantity rather than
quality.

'Can you go up it?'

'Well, you can,' he said uncertainly.

'Now?'

He looked at the white-haired old ticket lady shaded
by her National Trust umbrella; she had a hopeful glint
in her eye and was fingering her roll of pink tickets
expectantly.

'I've no head for heights,' Jeffrey confessed. 'It would
take a braver man than me to venture to the top of that
thing. It looks decidedly rickety.'

The children had joined them. 'Can we go up, Dad?'
they chorused, sounding suspiciously like two of the Famous
Five that Kate always accused them of being. 'Can we?'

He turned to Natalie for support. 'The steps are probably
really narrow and dangerous, like in a castle.'

'I'm Australian,' she pointed out. 'We don't have castles.'

'It'll be okay going up,' he warned. 'But just wait until you have to come down.'

'Where's your sense of adventure, Jeffers?'

He answered uncomfortably, 'I think it bypassed me. Like the Beatles and flares.'

'Come on.' She tugged his hand. 'Let your hair down. Feel the fear and do it anyway!'

'I take it from this gung-ho attitude that you're probably an exponent of bungee jumping?'

Natalie nodded, a fire in her eyes.

'Yes,' he said thoughtfully. *I might have guessed.*

'If you're good, I'll buy you an ice cream afterwards,' she promised.

He didn't know if he could cope with the sight of Natalie's tongue flicking lazily over a Magnum. 'I think I'd rather have a nice cup of tea,' he said, and Kate's voice popped out of his subconscious – *and perhaps some Battenberg or angel cake?*

'The view will be spectacular,' Natalie cajoled.

He knew when he was beaten. 'Go on then,' he said, magnanimous in defeat.

The white-haired old lady had already ripped the tickets off her roll and was proffering her Quality Street tin, in which Jeffrey deposited the requisite four pounds. 'You can go up as many times as you like,' she said cheerfully.

God, don't encourage them, Jeffrey thought. One near-death experience per day is quite sufficient for someone who is used to dealing with nothing more alarming than a bought ledger account.

The view from the top was spectacular. And it was a bloody long way down. Jeffrey curled his fingers over the top of the wholly insubstantial iron railing that bounded the viewing platform. He didn't know where this irrational fear of heights had come from – not inherited, he assumed; his father was, after all, a pilot in the RAF just after the war. Jeffrey liked his feet firmly on the ground, flying nothing more threatening than a desk. His breath was white hot in his chest and his knees were wobbling like jelly. Despite insisting to Kate that golf kept him perfectly fit, he wondered if it really did.

Natalie came and stood next to him. There was no discernible breeze, but fine wisps of hair trailed across her face and he longed to reach out and brush them away.

'You could bungee jump from here,' she said, looking down. 'Ah, it's gotta be about a hundred feet.'

'One hundred and eight,' he puffed. 'One hundred and eight feet and one hundred and seventy steps.'

She wrinkled her nose up at him. 'You counted them?'

'I read the information at the bottom,' he wheezed.

Natalie laughed. 'You're a funny guy.'

Yeah – hilarious.

When he had stopped shaking, he could appreciate that the view was indeed wonderful. It was a clear day and you could see out over Tring as far as Aylesbury in one direction and far past Leighton Buzzard in the other. Jeffrey turned to Natalie and pointed out into the distance.

'If you squint, you can see Hemel Hempstead from here.'

'That right?'

'It's where I work.'

'No kidding?' Natalie squinted obligingly. 'What do you do?'

Jeffrey grimaced. 'I'm an accountant.'

Natalie smiled. 'I had you down as an accountant sort of guy.'

'I take it that's not a compliment.'

'Not at all,' Natalie disagreed. 'You're a very thoughtful, sincere person. Not a lot of people have those qualities these days.' She shrugged. 'Maybe you just need to hang loose a little more.'

He wondered exactly which bit of him she wanted to 'hang loose'.

'Shall we head back down?' Natalie asked.

'I think the children have probably had enough,' Jeffrey agreed quickly.

'Are you ready to tackle those stairs?'

'Quite ready.'

As he was about to move, she put her hand over his. It was surprisingly cool, given the heat of the day, and he hoped she wouldn't notice how disgusting and sweaty his was. 'Was it worth the risk, Jeffers?'

'I think so,' he answered, heart hammering in his chest.

'It didn't hurt one bit, did it?' She gave him a winsome smile.

Jeffrey had to agree, that at that moment, he was feeling no pain at all.

Chapter Seven

The library at Northwood Priory was well stocked with leather-bound, serious-looking tomes – a distinct lack of Jilly Cooper and Jeffrey Archer adorning the polished shelves. There was a gentle hum of conversation buzzing on the air and the sun blistered its way through the stained-glass windows, making the trays of melting cream cakes look an unappetising shade of pale green.

Sonia curled up her nose at the curled-up cucumber sandwich, minus crust, that she held between her fingers like a dead fly. It was unlike her to be fussy with food. Kate helped herself to a piece of perspiring cheese and pineapple from a passing waitress. The canapés were wilting at an alarming rate in the heat and the ice-cold white wine was sliding down far too quickly.

Sonia sidled up to her. 'So this is where all the Greenham Common peace women got to.'

'Behave,' Kate instructed, trying not to stare at the group of cropped-haired women in embroidered waistcoats and gypsy skirts. Nose-piercing seemed to be popular with them – and they all looked so young. She suddenly felt even more middle-aged – a real old fuddy-duddy.

'One of the few benefits of getting old,' Sonia elucidated in between sips, whilst surveying the room, 'is that you don't have to worry about baring your midriff or going through the pain of having your belly button or your nose pierced.' She waved her glass expansively. 'Tell me,' she continued, 'exactly how do you eat your Weetabix with a tongue stud in?'

It was too disgusting to contemplate, Kate agreed. She just wished Sonia wasn't voicing her opinion quite so loudly. Particularly since every other woman in the room looked quite likely to have several parts of their anatomy pierced.

'There's somewhere in town where you can have it done while you wait,' she added loudly.

'Sssh,' Kate hissed. In vain.

'And I bet tattooing hurts like shit.' Sonia nodded, staring fixedly at an anorexic-looking woman with a snake banding her skinny upper arm. 'I've had electrolysis,' she said knowingly. 'The sting of a thousand bees.' She winced in remembrance. 'And while it might seem a very good idea to have GIRL POWER tattooed on your firm little derrière when you're eighteen, it's going to look a bit silly when you're sixty and half the letters have disappeared into folds of elephant skin. You could end up with GROPER on your bum,' she sniggered.

Kate tried to work out whether this was alphabetically or even politically correct, and gave up.

'Grief, it's hot in here,' she said, fanning herself with her serviette.

'Shall we go in the garden and check out the talent? There isn't any in here and I'm starting to sweat like that cheese.'

They wandered out through the French doors, onto an uneven terrace bearing little flowering mounds of saxifrage between the stones. The terrace was bordered by a sweeping manicured lawn, mowed into stripes with a meticulous touch that Kate could never quite understand. It was the sort of thing that Jeffrey could well turn to in years to come if she didn't nip it in the bud. There was a croquet lawn too, mallet and balls lying redundant against one of the hoops, begging someone to play. A towering Cedar of Lebanon spread its majestic branches earthwards to act as a natural signpost. One branch indicating the sheep-speckled meadows that sloped away from the Priory towards the dried-up river bed, and the other pointing back at the main house which had put on its party best and was glowing golden in the sun. It was built of a mellow sandstone, covered in the twisting, gnarled stems of a rampant wisteria, unfortunately no longer in flower, which reached up to the crenellated ramparts and gave it the air of a toy-town fort. The Benedictine monks had long since gone, and having been a hospital during the war and a mediocre public school, Northwood Priory was now enjoying a renaissance as an adult education centre.

'What's your room like?' Sonia said. They were housed in an attractive red-brick modern annexe, just behind the Priory. 'Mine's a bit pokey. Definitely lacking in the frills and flounces department. And there's no room to put anything anywhere.'

'That's because you've brought enough stuff to stay for the next forty-two years rather than a week.'

'I've never been able to travel light,' Sonia allowed. 'You never know what you might need.'

'I'm not sure your bikini will come in that handy.'

'I didn't know if they had a swimming pool or not,' she shrugged.

'If you'd read your blurb, you would have seen that *not* was the answer to that particular question.'

'I don't suppose I'll need the blow-up lilo then either.'

Kate chuckled. 'Possibly not.'

'You're not being very sociable, ladies,' a voice like a melted Milky Way said from behind her.

She turned and came face to face with its owner. A pair of the palest blue eyes she'd ever seen stared back at her. 'We're clinging together out of fear,' she said as lightly as she could manage.

'Surely not?'

Well, it was true in her case, but Sonia was clinging to her simply because she hadn't spotted anyone sufficiently fanciable to bother to pursue.

The newcomer held out his hand. 'Ben,' he said. 'Ben Mahler.'

Sonia thrust out her hand and clutched him in a death grip. He grinned good-humouredly, showing a slightly crooked front tooth which spoilt his heart-stopping smile and rendered it merely devastating. 'Sonia Buchanan,' her friend said, making her eyes go round and soulful like Ally McBeal's.

'Pleased to meet you, Sonia,' Ben said and turned to Kate.

She resisted the urge to wipe her palm on her dress and took his hand. His fingers were strong and sure. Warm. 'Kate Lewis,' she stammered.

'What course are you doing?' he asked politely.

'T'ai Chi,' she said.

'Both of you?'

'Yes.'

'What about you, Ben?' Sonia said girlishly, twisting her blonde hair round a finger.

He pursed his lips. 'Same.'

'I didn't have you down as a T'ai Chi-er.'

'I'm not sure that I am,' he admitted. 'I was booked on *The Beauties of Bordeaux* – the wines, not the women.' His eyes twinkled. 'But it was cancelled last week because the tutor died.'

'How awful!'

'Cirrhosis of the liver,' Ben explained. 'Hazard of the job, I suppose.' They all sipped their wine in a moment of reverent silence. 'I'd already booked the week off work, so I decided to come anyway and transferred to the next available course. I thought *Trying Out T'ai Chi* would suit me infinitely better than *Fun with Fur Fabric* or *Beaded Bags for Beginners*.'

They both laughed. Sonia more loudly.

Ben shrugged. 'It's just good to get away.'

Kate knew how he felt. It was a shame that she couldn't stop her mind wandering back to Jeffrey in the woods with Wonder Woman.

'Are you local to here?' Ben asked.

62

'Bedfordshire,' Sonia replied.

'Which part?'

She smiled in what Kate assumed was intended to be a seductive manner. 'All of me!'

He was polite enough to laugh. The sound was soft and gentle, like summer rain on canvas. It seemed somehow at odds with his appearance. Ben's face was classically handsome, with high cheekbones – the lot – but on first impression he looked rather aloof and arrogant. His hair was light brown, mousey if you were being unkind, cropped short in a fashionable style. Nice. There were flecks of silver-grey through it, picked out by the sun, which said that he was probably a few years older than he looked. Kate hazarded a guess at mid-thirties. Sonia clearly wouldn't have cared if he was mid-teens, she was totally besotted already.

'Where are you from?' Sonia asked.

'Surrey, originally – Richmond,' he answered. 'All of me, too.'

'What do you do?'

'I run an advertising agency in town,' he said. 'And now I live there too.'

By town, Kate assumed he meant London town and not High Wycombe town.

'And you?'

'I have my own health club,' Sonia said with a sweep of her arm. 'Nothing much,' she added, failing to acknowledge Kate's open-mouthed stare. 'Wall-to-wall mirrors, dance studio, sauna, jacuzzi, hi-tech gym. You know how it is?'

Ben looked impressed. 'What do you do, Kate?'

'I'm a housewife,' she said lamely.

He nodded with an attempt at an encouraging smile that may have been pity. 'That's nice.'

No, it isn't. It's a conversation-stopper. Perhaps I should have invented a glamorous alter ego like Sonia, whose only work since Andrew was born was a disastrous two weeks in Timpson's shoe shop before she was unceremoniously given the boot.

As expected, the small talk suddenly petered out and they both turned to Kate as if she was the one to rescue the embarrassed silence, having caused it. If they were looking for inspiration they'd come to the wrong place. It was years since she'd done this polite chit-chat thing and the strain was showing. It probably wasn't a good idea to ask Ben whether he'd finished his homework, which was the level of conversation she'd been having for the last five years. No wonder her mind felt like it had been put out to grass.

Kate shuffled from foot to foot and glanced at her watch. 'Oh, is that the time?' she said. 'I'd better go and get changed.' Her tummy had begun to churn nervously. 'The first class will be starting soon.'

'I haven't seen any little old Chinese men wandering around who look like they could be tutors,' Sonia observed.

'I'm sure they'll be here somewhere.' Kate scanned the sea of heads. 'Anyway, I'll see you shortly.'

Ben caught her eye. He seemed warmer than she had first thought. 'I'll look forward to it,' he said with a grin.

*   *   *

The T'ai Chi instructors weren't Chinese. Or little. Or even old. They were big and young and looked as though they had recently starred in a Bruce Lee-type movie. They wore baggy black trousers and white T-shirts stretched over rippling broad chests. Red sashes bound their nipped-in waists, and their whole demeanour said, Don't mess with me.

'I expected Fu Manchu lookalikes, not Arnie and Sly.' Sonia was exuberant.

'Me too.' Kate looked worried.

'I'm beginning to like T'ai Chi,' Sonia grinned. 'I could certainly do those two some damage.'

The instructors stood at the front of the class flexing their muscles in a very athletic manner, stretching in places that even Jane Fonda would fear to access. Apprehension crawled through Kate's body and she wished she had decided to 'find herself' while studying *The Excitement of Stumpwork Embroidery* instead. 'I think they're more likely to do us some damage.'

'Just think,' Sonia hissed under her breath, 'by the end of the week I could look like one of the Gladiators too!'

Kate was unconvinced. 'Which one? Deadly Lampshade?'

'Yes,' Sonia said tartly. 'And you can be Poison Dwarf.'

Ben was further along the row in the class. He looked good in his Nike sweatshirt and joggers. Kate examined her leotard, which showed up every wrinkle, crinkle, fold and flabby bit that existed. Every stretchmark was pounced on and signposted. Perhaps she should have bought something new from the shop at the health club – the one that Sonia didn't own – which had a big selection of brightly coloured wisps of material that purported to be exercise clothing. From tomorrow, her leggings and baggy T-shirt would reign, she decided.

Sonia was resplendent in a fake Armani ensemble bought out of a suitcase at Camden Market. She looked as if she couldn't make up her mind which one of the instructors she wanted to get her claws into first. Ben's more subtle charms had clearly receded into the distance faced with this onslaught of beefcake.

'Good afternoon, everyone,' the dark-haired instructor addressed the class. 'I'm Sam,' he gave a low bow. 'And this is Guy.'

The taller blond-haired one stepped forward and also bowed.

'We're here to introduce you to the Chinese art of T'ai Chi,' Sam continued. 'We hope we're going to have an enjoyable week of exercise. Before we start, if anyone has any particular problems, please let us know and we'll do all we can to help.'

My thirty-eight-year-old husband is deliriously middle-aged, my children are perfect to the point of nausea, I've got cellulitic thighs despite working out twice a week, my days have no purpose and my floating candles always sink. Other than that, life's a dream!

'The Chinese believe that everything in the universe is made of energy,' Sam explained. 'This energy has two basic essences – yin and yang.'

'*Ying Tong Tiddle I Po!*' Sonia added tunefully.

Kate kicked her in the leg.

Sam carried on regardless. 'When the body is out of order in any way, physically or emotionally, the yin and yang balance is upset.'

Kate decided her body was so out of order that her yin and yang probably needed to go on vacation in Florida.

'In practising T'ai Chi we're trying to re-establish that harmony, so that there's a better balance between the opposing aspects within ourselves – male and female, positive and negative, hard and soft, light and dark. Their characteristics complement one another, just as sunshine needs rain, and with a storm there is always a time of calm.'

'Just as bangers need mash and with Sooty there is always Sweep.'

'You're going to ruin this for me if you don't shut up!' Kate warned under her breath.

'The T'ai Chi form will help the body to become light and agile. It promotes health and vitality,' he promised. 'So if you've come here feeling stressed out and jaded, we'll soon have your energy levels topped up again.'

'I'm feeling considerably more lively already.' Sonia fluttered her eyelashes.

'The principles of T'ai Chi,' Sam continued undaunted, 'are very simple.' He sounded so encouraging and sincere it made Kate want to weep. 'Stay relaxed.'

Stay relaxed. Clenching your fists into tight little balls probably didn't qualify for staying relaxed. She let her hands fall to her side.

'Keep breathing,' Sam said with a laugh. 'I know it sounds silly, but you'd be surprised how people hold their breath when they're feeling tense.'

Breathing? Kate wasn't sure she had taken a breath since the larger than life Natalie Lambert had first sauntered through her front door. She gave a heavy lingering sigh.

'Work at your own level. Don't compete,' Sam told them all.

Don't compete. Kate looked nervously round at everyone else in the class. There were about twenty people there altogether and they all looked like serious competition. Even Sonia, who was totally weak-willed when it came to Fry's Turkish Delight, knew no fear when it came to keeping up with Mr Motivator. Kate shrank inside.

'Always keep your spine upright and the head suspended.'

Spine upright. Head suspended. Kate's head seemed locked to her shoulders in a way that was probably very seriously interfering with her yin and yang balance.

'Your waist should be free.' He circled his waist to demonstrate.

Her friend stared lasciviously at him. 'Just your waist, Sonia,' Kate hissed. 'Not the rest of your body too!'

'Watch the knees!' he warned, patting his kneecaps with his huge muscle-bound hands.

Your own knees or other people's? She sincerely hoped no one was going to be watching her knees, which she'd had a complex about since the age of thirteen when they had started to creak and crack alarmingly.

'And, finally,' he said, 'have fun!'

'I intend to have great fun,' Sonia whispered. She leaned closer. 'I bet you, if I wanted, I could have one of those two by the end of the week.'

Kate frowned her disbelief. 'Which one?'

'I don't care. Either will do.'

Kate tutted. 'I bet even at school you weren't known for being fussy.'

Sonia drew her eyebrows together. 'At least I wasn't called iron drawers.'

Kate had known that one day she would come to regret telling her that.

'Shall we begin by doing some gentle warming-up exercises?' Sam asked.

No, thanks, Sam, I think I'll go home now. Kate wished she had never started this. She wished she had been happy, at one with the world and content with her little lot as wife and mother. Why did she have to go stirring things up? A vision of the week stretched endlessly ahead of her. She wondered if Jeffrey was missing her or if Miss Bondi Beach already turned him into a surf junkie.

Across the room Ben looked suspiciously as though he wished he was opening a rather nice bottle of Château Grand Videau, instead of waving his arms around maniacally in an effort to loosen up. Kate caught his eye and he winked at her, taking her by surprise. How long was it since a man had winked at her? It wasn't a leery sort of wink, it was a we're-all-in-this-together wink, an I-am-on-your-wavelength wink.

There was a sudden upsurge in voltage to her sadly

depleted courage and she puffed out several sharp determined breaths like she'd seen American footballers do to psyche themselves up. *I can do this, I can do this,* she chanted to herself, *I can do this!* Ben grinned at her and she wondered, for a moment, whether she had said it out loud.

Feeling self-conscious, she turned her attention back to Sam and Guy, who were being terribly enthusiastic in their efforts to get the rest of them moving with some semblance of coordination. They swung their arms and circled their hips and Kate followed obligingly. They swooped towards the ceiling. Kate followed. They dipped to the ground. Kate followed. An awful cracking sound like the fire of gunshot ricocheted round the room, followed by a deathly silence. Even the lovely Sam and Guy stopped swinging. Kate felt every last drop of blood in her veins rush headlong towards her face and, to her abject humiliation, twenty pairs of eyes simultaneously swivelled to look in horror at her knees. She was right. It was going to be a *very* long week.

Chapter Eight

The familiar theme tune for the start of BBC golf programmes blasted out in the lounge.

Kevin accompanied it, tunelessly and with a wiggle of his hips. 'Da, Da, Da!' He kicked off his shoes and flopped down onto the sofa with a contented sigh.

Jeffrey passed him a beer and a long-stemmed glass. 'This is the life,' Kevin gloated. He looked approvingly at the can of Coors Light in his hand. 'Beer and golf on the telly. What more can a man want?'

Jeffrey sat down next to him. 'Quite a lot, actually,' he said. The room was looking spick and span, as always. Kate had polished every ornament they possessed to within an inch of its life before she left, and there was a waft of lavender room spray in the air, complementing the ubiquitous bowls of pot pourri that graced every surface in the house. She was a wonderful wife and homemaker, and wasn't content unless everywhere smelled of something floral. The place seemed empty without her; he hadn't realised before how much he missed her pleasant chatter that was constantly in the background, even when he was trying to watch something really interesting on television.

Kevin ripped the ring pull off his can and slurped the froth from the lid. 'Bliss!' He nestled the can in his lap and rubbed his hands together in anticipation. 'Now then, me beauties,' he said to the golfers quietly milling about on the television. 'Show Uncle Kevin exactly what you can do with a little white ball and forty-four inches of graphite!' He swung his feet onto the coffee table and wriggled down in the cushions. 'Watch and learn, Jeffrey,' he advised. 'Watch and learn.'

Jeffrey tipped his glass sideways and poured his beer carefully into it. 'Who's got the boys?'

Kevin waved his hand. 'They're staying with a friend round the corner. His mum's going to take them all to school in the morning. One night down, only five more to go!' He took another swig of his beer. 'The kids are sick to death already. Do you know, all Sonia's left is twenty-four boxes of fish fingers, a mountain of oven chips and two cartons of vanilla ice cream. Correction,' he waved his can, '*fat-free* vanilla ice cream. I ask you, how can you have ice cream without fat? That's like asking Pamela Anderson to look good in a polo neck!'

Jeffrey smiled. 'Kate's left a barrage of margarine cartons in the freezer containing a variety of wholesome meals all neatly labelled with the day of the week.'

'She is a fine woman, Jeffrey,' Kevin said solemnly. 'You should look after her.'

'I do look after her.' Even he thought he sounded defensive.

Kevin stared at him directly – or as directly as he could while keeping one eye on the progress of Ernie Els. 'Sonia said Kate's been a bit depressed lately.'

'Did she?'

'Tell me to mind my own business, my friend. But I know what these women are like.'

Jeffrey folded his arms across his chest and stared at the ceiling, even the paternal voice of Peter Alliss failing to soothe him. 'I'm not sure what's wrong,' he admitted. 'Recently she's become so restless. She's talking about rollerblading and rock climbing.'

Kevin pulled a sympathetic face that said, *At her age?*

'I feel she's looking for something I can't provide,' Jeffrey said wistfully. 'And I'm not sure that a week's T'ai Chi in Buckinghamshire will provide it either.'

'She'll be all right,' Kevin assured him. 'Do up the house a bit, buy her a few pretty frocks, tell her that her bum's not fat. They love that sort of thing.'

'We've already parted with a small fortune to make the kitchen look worse than it did before we started. Now she says she wants new bedroom fittings. The trouble is, I think that includes me too.'

'All middle-aged women start hankering after younger men, it's part of life. They get to a certain age, their tits start to connect with their knees and their hormones go completely to pot and suddenly the acne-ridden paperboy is looking very attractive. Trust your Uncle Kevin. You just have to let her ride it out.'

'So where does Tom Jones fit into this equation? He hardly counts as young and spotty, yet women of all ages still rip their knickers off whenever he gyrates his pelvis.'

'A one-off, matey. Universal appeal. Very few people have it.'

'Anyway, Kate's not like that,' Jeffrey said. 'She never looks at other men, however young. All she needs is a bit of excitement in her life. Something to make her day buzz. It must be very dull staying at home all the time.' But then it was very dull going to work all day. Wasn't life generally like this? Long periods of dullness, enlivened by the odd barn dance or a holiday in Majorca? It was how the vast majority of people lived without complaint.

'Are you happy, Kev?'

'Delirious.'

'No, seriously.'

'Good grief, Jeffrey, we're not nearly drunk enough to be having this type of conversation.' He shook his empty can and Jeffrey passed him another one.

'But are you?'

'There are one or two things that would improve my lot in life,' he confessed.

'Like what?'

'A twenty-five-year-old, sex-starved blonde would do for a start.' He gave a leering grin.

'Would that really make you happy?'

'It hasn't done Warren Beatty any harm. He's slept with Brigitte Bardot, Julie Christie, Joan Collins, Jane Fonda, Bianca Jagger and Madonna – to name but a few.'

'Yes, but is he *really* happy?'

'If he's not, it sounds a damn fine way to be miserable.'

Jeffrey cuddled a cushion to his chest. 'Kate says I'm not romantic any more.'

They paused to watch Nick Faldo tee off, a majestic

swish of his driver sending the ball hurtling into the wide blue yonder, and grimaced at each other in awe.

'I'm very romantic,' Jeffrey insisted. He took a drink of his beer and pointed his glass at the screen. 'That is a swing to die for.' He shook his head. 'Particularly when there isn't any golf on the television.'

'I know what you mean, Jeffrey.'

'I did feel old the other day, when I was watching Sue Lawley on the box and thought, Now *there's* a babe.'

'Sue Lawley?' Kevin looked appalled. 'Sad.'

Peter Alliss explained the principles of getting out of a bunker in fewer than twenty shots. Something that they had both failed to do on many occasions.

'While we're on the subject of babes,' Kevin said when there was a lull in the proceedings, 'how's the blonde with build working out?'

'Natalie? She's a very nice girl.'

'Yeah, right.' Kev spread his hands. 'I can't believe Kate has trusted you in a house alone with her for one whole week.'

'Why not?'

'You're a free agent – the possibilities are limitless!'

'So are you,' Jeffrey pointed out. 'And you're sitting round here watching golf with me on the telly.'

Kevin looked crestfallen. 'How very fucking depressing,' he muttered.

'I took her out to lunch today,' Jeffrey said as casually as possible, given the fact his heart had started racing at the mere mention of her name. He loved the feel of it on his tongue. Natalie Lambert. Natalie. Nat. 'To the Bridgeman's Arms.'

Kevin looked impressed.

'And then we went for a walk in Ashridge Forest.'

'*There may be trouble ahead . . .*' Kevin sang, using his beer can as a microphone.

'Not alone,' Jeffrey interrupted tersely. 'With the kids. There was nothing in it.'

'Yeah, and the band played "Believe It If You Like".'

'She's nice. Just a nice girl, that's all.'

'And she could do for your marriage what the M25 has done for hedgehogs.'

'Don't you think I know that?' Jeffrey snapped. 'I've never been unfaithful to Kate. She's a fabulous wife, a wonderful mother. She's all I've ever wanted.' *Until now?* a tiny insistent voice prompted inside him.

'You're being a bit touchy, old chum.' They both ooooed appreciatively as Ballesteros's ball landed six feet away from the hole and rolled sedately in with a satisfying plop.

'Sorry,' Jeffrey said. 'I'm just a bit edgy. I've got a lot on at work at the moment.'

His friend flicked an eyebrow at him. 'I thought it might be another type of figure that was keeping your mind whirling.'

Jeffrey passed Kevin another beer.

'Thanks,' he said, with a slurp and a stifled belch. 'Did you know, Jeffrey, that men are genetically programmed to fall in love with somebody who's half their age plus seven?'

'No, I didn't.'

'How old's the nubile Natalie?'

Jeffrey shrugged. 'I think Kate said she was twenty-eight, but she doesn't look it.'

'It's downright impossible to tell the ages of women between nineteen and twenty-nine. Those that are twenty-nine are still trying to make themselves look nineteen, and those that are nineteen are trying to make themselves look twenty-nine. What's a bloke supposed to do?' Kevin examined the contents of his beer can in his search for the answer. 'In reality, by my scientifically proven theory, Natalie is, in fact, too old for you. And that is a particularly sobering thought.'

Such a sobering thought that they both took a drink.

Jeffrey stared fixedly at the television screen. It was ridiculous! Here he was, a happily married, allegedly contented man, yet he couldn't get this slip of a girl out of his mind. Although he could hardly call her a slip of a girl – Nat looked as if she could drink most blokes under the table and was probably capable of a mean right hook if the occasion required it. His arms tingled with joy just thinking about her, and that was the least alarming of his bodily reactions.

He settled down next to Kevin on the sofa and tried to look suitably engrossed in the deliberations of Colin Montgomerie and his misbehaving putter. What was going wrong in their previously ordered and tidy little lives? He didn't seem to understand what Kate wanted any more, and now he couldn't even understand what he wanted for himself. Why, when he was watching his favourite sport in the world, was his mind continually turning to the pouting fullness of Natalie Lambert's lips? Before, the house could have burned down while Ian Woosnam was lining up a putt and he wouldn't have noticed. He would watch the putter take aim, strike the ball and follow the curved contours of the green, willing it in all the way. Now his attention was distracted by another type of curved contour and the ball was in the hole without him even realising it had been struck. He had no control over his viewing strategy. And no control, it would seem, over his emotions. Natalie Lambert was just a normal sort of woman – two eyes, two legs, too young. Why were his brain and his body so steadfastly refusing to believe it?

Chapter Nine

'I didn't think T'ai Chi would be so strenuous,' Sonia groaned. It was Monday morning, the first full day of the course, and Kate was already aching. They were standing with their legs splayed, hands on the grass in front of them, bottoms to the sky and had been like that for some considerable time. 'I must say our Sam seems very keen.'

'As mustard,' Kate agreed through clenched teeth.

'It's times like this when I'm glad I've got legs as sturdy as a kitchen table.'

'And relax,' Sam said to an accompanying chorus of relieved exhalations. 'Massage the lower back, like this.' He demonstrated, rubbing briskly. 'Now legs apart again, but this time bend the knees and sink into the posture.'

They all followed dutifully. 'This is Riding Horse stance,' he informed them cheerfully, clapping his hands on his thighs as Kate's legs started to wobble.

'Someone once told me horse riding was great for burning calories,' Sonia muttered in her ear. 'I went to the local stables and thrashed through the countryside for four solid hours.'

'Did it work?'

'Yes, the horse lost two stone.'

They both burst into a fit of uncontrolled giggles.

'Relax the breathing,' Sam said with an indulgent smile over his shoulder. 'Let go of the tension and sink further.'

'If I sink any more, I'll be like one of your blessed floating candles,' Sonia hissed. 'Sunk without trace.'

'Tuck your bottom under,' Sam instructed.

'I've got more bottom than him to tuck under.'

'Sonia, sssh! Concentrate!'

'You know the pencil test that you can do to see if your boobs are sagging? I can do that with my bum. There's enough overhang to keep an HB happily wedged there for days.'

'You're putting me off,' Kate giggled.

'Just look at his bum,' her friend continued undaunted. 'Did you ever see a butt that was so biteable?'

'I'm afraid it doesn't entice me at all,' Kate puffed, her efforts to hold the stance at maximum impact seriously hampered by Sonia's ramblings.

'Sink your Chi,' Sam encouraged. Kate wasn't quite sure where her Chi was, but she was pretty sure it shouldn't be focused on her instructor's rear end.

'Yes, that's the sort of bottom that just begs to have strawberry yoghurt licked off it,' Sonia said wickedly.

'And come up out of the stance.' Sam turned round to face them and Kate grinned to herself as she watched Sonia go pink in case he had heard.

It was true that she wasn't the slightest bit interested in sexy Sam's bottom, but her eyes had slid over in Ben's direction more than once in the last hour. He appeared to be managing the exercises with consummate ease, cucumber cool, while she felt like a hot, sweaty mess. It had taken the others all morning to get used to her knees cracking every five minutes.

'Like yin and yang,' Sam said when they had got their breath back, 'all the forces of nature are comprised of five elements – earth, wood, water, metal and fire. As we work through the week we'll be focusing on each of these elements in turn and what their essential essence means to us. By doing that, it will help you to get in touch with what's happening inside you.'

Sounds wonderful! I haven't a clue what's going on inside. Even the outside is a mystery sometimes.

'Today we're going to concentrate on the earth element, which is at the hub of all things. Its associations are nurturing, nourishing, being rooted, loving yourself.' His face softened. 'How can you love others, if you don't learn to love yourself first?'

Hot tears suddenly prickled behind Kate's eyes. *Do I love myself? Do I love Jeffrey?*

'We're going to practise this in a stance called Standing Firmly,' Sam said. 'Imagine that you're a tree, rooted deeply in the ground. Stand tall and straight, but with no tension in the body. Allow your Chi, your energy, to sink. Now visualise a silken thread coming from the top of your head to connect you with the heavens. This is the balance you're looking for.' His voice was hypnotic. 'Keep the breathing relaxed and focus on the earth, on caring and loving yourself.'

Kate's Chi was fluttering wildly inside her, battering

against her ribs like a bird against the bars of a cage. All sorts of unwanted, unbidden thoughts flashed through her mind. She had neglected herself over the years, not physically, but emotionally. She had given so much to caring for her family, there had been nothing left for her. Now she was a dry vacuum, like a sucked-in milk carton devoid of contents. *Sink, sink, sink!* she told her Chi. *No, no, not yet!* it said back.

'Let go of the effort,' Sam encouraged.

But the turmoil continued to whizz dangerously out of control in her brain, like a liquidiser left on full power without a lid.

'Ease out the body.' Sam's voice eventually drifted into her consciousness. 'Move gently from side to side.'

Her body was so heavy it felt like she was stuck in a hole. She looked round her as she swayed; no one else appeared to be having this inner battle. Was it only she who shared a body with the demon Doubt?

'You've worked very hard for your first day,' Sam said soothingly. 'This sort of stuff isn't easy to grasp straight away. It has to be worked at. The most important thing is to learn to love yourself.'

He seemed to be looking directly at her again.

'There's just one more thing I need to show you before we break for tea,' he continued. He put his right fist to his left palm and held it in front of his body. 'This is a martial arts sign which shows that you aren't concealing any weapons or have any ulterior motives. It says *I mean you no harm*. We use it as a sign of respect at the end

82

of each session.' With a certain amount of hamfistedness, the group eventually copied him. Sam bowed and the class responded accordingly. 'We'll meet back in front of the Priory in half an hour to do some relaxing work to finish.'

They wandered back to the house collecting bags, suntan cream and shoes on the way. It was wonderful working out of doors in the blistering sunshine, barefoot on the grass, and Kate wondered how long it had been since her toes had been in contact with the earth rather than shoved into battered old trainers or squashed into court shoes rushing at full tilt from one place to the next. They were clearly appreciating their new-found freedom and she in turn began to feel lighter and faintly invigorated as she moved across the lawn.

Sonia flopped into a deckchair. 'You get the tea today, Katie,' she begged. 'I'll do it tomorrow. Not too much milk – I'm slimming.'

'How many biscuits?'

'Three,' Sonia said. 'Or four, if they're chocolate.'

Kate joined the queue indoors for the teapot. Her eyes scanned the room, looking for Ben, but he wasn't there. She hadn't had a chance to speak to him today, primarily because they were late for breakfast. Foolishly, she had agreed to wait for Sonia to get ready, which took several changes of clothes and subsequent hair restyling. All that was left when they finally arrived in the breakfast room was cold sausage and greasy bacon, which Sonia demolished with relish and without a thought for the ensuing depression at the end of the week when her bathroom scales would go haywire.

She took two cups of tea and a pile of biscuits back to Sonia, who had managed to find some shade under one of the white linen parasols that now graced the terrace, fluttering gently like a line of clean washing in the breeze.

'Thanks.' Sonia gasped with pleasure as the tea hit the spot. 'I needed that,' she said, and tucked into the custard creams and chocolate digestives Kate had brought. She frowned at one before biting it in half. 'I can't for the life of me understand what five elephants have got to do with anything.'

'Five *elements*,' Kate corrected. 'You're not listening properly.'

'How am I supposed to listen with sex on legs standing right in front of me wiggling his butt?'

'You're supposed to tune into the *elephants*,' she teased. 'Then everything else ceases to exist.'

'Oh.' Sonia shrugged, her expression suggesting that the point had missed her by a mile. She selected another custard cream. 'Is line-dancing this difficult?'

Kate settled back in the bleached teak chair and lifted her hair from her neck, enjoying what little breeze there was cooling against her skin. Ben was sitting in the shade under a majestic towering pine; his tall frame looked tiny against its huge girth. He was talking animatedly into a mobile phone and she watched him, glad that her gaze was shaded by her sunglasses, wondering who he was ringing that could make him laugh so readily.

Sonia licked the crumbs from her lips. 'He seems nice,' she said. 'In a quiet sort of way.'

'Ben?'

'No, Saddam Hussein.'

'He's okay, I suppose.'

'You were staring at him very dreamily just now,' Sonia observed shrewdly.

'I was not,' Kate blushed. 'I was wondering whether Miss World had remembered to get the bolognese sauce out of the freezer for tonight's dinner.'

'If you say so.' Sonia drained her cup. 'Anyway, I thought you were here to get away from all that domestic crap.'

'I am. But it's not that easy to give up the habits of a lifetime.'

'And it's not that easy to forget about home when you've got Ken and Barbie's love child looking after your husband's every whim.' Sonia glanced knowingly at her.

'Jeffrey doesn't have whims,' Kate said calmly. 'He has schedules and timetables and boundaries. Boundaries that he *never* oversteps.'

'You're both so uptight these days, Kate. You need to let go a bit. Perhaps Jeffrey needs to find himself too.'

'I don't think Jeffrey's ever been lost,' she said wearily.

Her eyes strayed to the handsome man still chatting away under the tree. Snapping the phone shut, Ben stood up and strode towards their table, still without his shoes, cup and phone clutched in his hand. 'May I join you?' he asked.

Sonia stood up. 'Here, have my chair, Ben. I'm going

to get some more tea and biscuits. Anyone else?' She clattered her cup.

'I'm fine, thanks.' Ben slid into Sonia's chair and tossed his phone on the table with the casual air of a man easily able to afford the latest in technology.

'Do something to take her mind off her domestic crisis, if you possibly can,' Sonia advised, patting his shoulder. 'I've failed miserably.'

'I'll try,' Ben promised.

Sonia peered into his cup and sniffed. 'What on earth are you drinking anyway?'

Ben peered too. 'Blackberry and ginseng herbal tea.'

Sonia grimaced. 'Nice.'

As she walked past Kate's chair, she bent to whisper in her ear. 'Never trust a man who drinks herbal tea – he's bound to be crap in bed!'

She looked even more lovely when she blushed, Ben thought as he studied Kate over the rim of his cup. Not many women did blush these days. Not the women he mixed with, certainly. They were all hard and brash, keen to prove themselves better than men. Blushing would have been eschewed as a sign of feminine weakness. Perhaps it was. But it looked bloody attractive.

He'd noticed her the minute he'd arrived at the Priory, struggling with two huge suitcases, and he'd wanted to rush over like some latter-day knight in shining armour and rescue her. But he hadn't been able to find a parking space quickly enough, and by the time he was ready to do his good deed for the day, she'd gone.

Kate was a gorgeous creature, dramatically beautiful, but in an understated way, if that wasn't a contradiction in terms. Her eyes were wide, almost staring, and the most vibrant shade of cornflower blue. She was wearing make-up, but wasn't all glammed up to the eyeballs like the women he normally dated. Her hair was dark, raven, worn loose to her shoulders where it flicked up naturally and wasn't glued there with the aid of ten cans of hair spray. Her smile was warm and wide, her lips a deep dark natural red. She was tall, but slender, like a gazelle, slightly skittish in her movements. Her gentle manner made him want to crush her to his chest and hold her there until she was breathless with the power of his protection. He'd never experienced feelings like this before.

'I'd like to apologise for my friend,' Kate said, breaking into his reverie. 'She loves to embarrass me.'

He laughed. 'Her heart's in the right place, I'm sure.'

'Oh, her heart is,' Kate agreed. 'I'm just not sure about the rest of her vital organs.'

They both giggled.

'That's better,' Ben said. 'You look pretty when you smile.'

Kate turned pink again and studied her fingernails.

'So what's the domestic crisis?' he asked. 'If you want to share it, that is. Otherwise tell me to get lost.'

Kate folded her arms across her body and hugged her shoulders. 'It's nothing really,' she said, but he noticed the little dark flash in her eyes. 'I've left my home in the hands of a beautiful young woman with a body like Elle MacPherson.'

'Don't you trust your husband?'

'I trust my husband implicitly,' she replied. 'I'm just not sure about her.' Her mouth turned down at the corners.

'Your husband would be mad to look at another woman,' Ben told her sincerely.

'If there's one thing Jeffrey isn't, it's mad,' she said quietly. 'He's the most sane person on the planet.'

'You make that sound like a bad thing.'

Nursing her cup, she sighed heavily. 'Then I'm being very unfair to him,' she said. 'My husband is a lovely man. He's kind, he's gentle, he's neat.'

'Neat?'

'Neat.'

'I'm glad this isn't a job reference,' Ben observed. 'I'm not sure if I'd employ him.'

He noticed her close her eyes behind her sunglasses and lift her throat to the solitary waft of breeze. God, she was lovely.

'I'm not sure I would either,' she said softly.

'What does he do?'

'He's an accountant.'

Ben felt his smile widen.

'Chartered,' she added tartly.

'I'd have been more surprised if you'd said Turf.'

'Don't laugh,' she chided with a grin. 'Jeffrey loves his work. It suits him down to the ground. It's ordered, precise . . .'

'Neat,' Ben supplied.

'Neat.' Her eyes clouded over. There was a sadness deep inside her, and it came to him that he would like to find it, touch it and unfurl it like the tight bud of a delicate rose.

'I hope I haven't bored you,' she said.

'Not at all.' The truth was that Ben would have gladly talked to her all day; he just wanted to watch the movement of her mouth, the way her eyes flickered as she spoke, the flutter of her long, dark lashes, the expression in her graceful hands. He knew nothing about her, but every fibre of his being wanted to. Desperately.

Sam and Guy had resumed their positions on the lawn now and were swaying gracefully from side to side. The rest of the class were finishing their tea and starting to stroll back, keen to get on with learning the mysteries of the East.

'We'd better go,' Kate said, and stood up.

'I'll catch you up,' Ben said. He wanted to watch her walking away, enjoy her long loose-limbed stride.

Ben Mahler had everything that money could buy. A car that was the envy of the agency, membership of an exclusive health club, a penthouse flat overlooking Tower Bridge, a tiny tumbledown thatched cottage in the country. What he couldn't buy was something that could only be given freely – true love. He had dated some very beautiful women, enjoyed fleeting relationships that brought fleeting pleasure for a while. Why had this particular woman turned him inside out, upside down and left him gasping for breath? Out of all the women in the world, why her? She wasn't even available!

Ben watched Kate walk across the grass, kicking at it with her bare toes. His soul seemed to be crying out for her. He wanted her body. He wanted her love. He wanted her heart. She was married and she wasn't free to give it. The sooner he accepted that the better.

Ben put his right fist to his left hand and banged it firmly against the palm. A reminder. *I have no weapons. I am defenceless. I have no ulterior motive. I mean you no harm.*

90

Chapter Ten

Jeffrey stared out of the office window. His desk overlooked the staff car park, and it always annoyed him that the gravel was thin in patches and scraggy weeds pushed through the rock-hard ground underneath, making the whole area look tatty. Not very suitable for a thrusting dynamic firm of cut-throat accountants! He was tempted to bring his own hoe in and give it a tickle about, except that it was sure to render him a figure of ridicule.

He'd been with Hills & Hopeland for years, ten years to be exact, and had worked his way steadily up the ladder to a plateau. The comfort zone. Similar to the twilight zone, but with a better salary and a bigger company car. It was bad news when a man of his tender years was confined to coasting. The company was full of hungry young men – brought in when the senior partners were all pensioned off with cosy retirement packages. Except that these hungry young men were never hungry for *food*; they sat relentlessly crunching numbers, swallowing caffeine in various forms at a rate of knots, but never stopping to eat. Come one o'clock, Jeffrey yearned to go to the pub for steak and kidney pie and chips. His arteries screamed for a cholesterol fix. But there was always the fear lurking in the background, gnawing in his subconscious, that if he took his statutory hour for lunch, who would be at his desk when he returned? They didn't let the weeds grow round the personnel at Hills & Hopeland like they did the parking spaces.

His heart wasn't in the job today: end of year accounts for his least favourite client, a building company with a managing director who favoured the Bernard Manning school of charm, followed by some junior staff training and development work. He did this not because he was any good at passing on his knowledge acquired through years at the dirty end of accountancy, but because he was deemed to be the only person patient enough to deal with the exuberant ignorance of youth and focus them on the delights of the grindstone. He assumed it was some form of back-handed compliment.

His mind wasn't on the job either. It was still lingering on Natalie Lambert, who had arrived looking particularly sunny at the allotted time this morning and had proceeded to engage two rather startled and school-uniformed children in a Rice Krispie throwing fight. He had left the house to the cry of: 'See you later, Jeffers!' before any of the offending cereal had headed in his direction. The children were squealing with delight and possibly over-excitement by the time he had crunched across the drive and reached the car. Breakfast was normally a terribly sedate affair during which Kate dished out the packed lunches. He was to fend for himself today, hence the lusting for steak and kidney, as Kate had deemed Natalie incapable of preparing three rounds of sandwiches and a Wagon

Wheel. She would have fainted if she'd seen her hurling cereal across the table.

As it was he had worked through lunch without even a loo break, and was now on the point of starvation. He looked at his watch. Time to go. He'd just miss the traffic if he was lucky, which would give him some time to potter in the garden before they lost the light.

There was a strange smell drifting from the direction of the kitchen. Two strange smells if he was going to be absolutely accurate. One was definitely burning. Not call-the-fire-brigade burning, but burning nevertheless. The other was harder to identify. It was pungent, spicy, like sour curry and made his nostrils twitch in displeasure. Jeffrey paused with his key in the lock.

It was strange to come home and not be greeted by Kate's cheery voice shouting out from somewhere in the house. He offloaded his briefcase into the study and was gratified to hear giggling sounds coming from the kitchen.

'Keep still,' Natalie ordered as he pushed open the door.

Jeffrey stopped in his tracks. 'What the . . .'

Kerry was lying on her stomach in the middle of the kitchen table, giggling uproariously. Joe looked on in rapt silence, sitting amidst the cereal boxes that were still there from this morning. Jeffrey frowned. He could feel the furrows eating deep into his brow. A sea of luminous green sludge lay in a bowl next to her – the source of the foul stink – and Natalie was stabbing enthusiastically at the

93

bared cheek of his daughter's bottom with a small stick tipped with the same green goo.

'Don't wriggle!' Natalie barked. 'You'll make me blob!'

Kerry chuckled again. 'You're tickling me!'

Natalie looked up, hand poised on Kerry's buttock. 'Hi, Jeffers,' she said with a wall-to-wall smile.

Kerry rested her chin on her hands. 'Hello, Daddy.'

Jeffrey ran his fingers through his hair. It took a moment to be sure that his voice was going to be available for use when he opened his mouth. 'What the hell are you doing?' he stuttered.

'Ah, I'm tattooing Kerry's bum,' Natalie informed him, giving his daughter a hearty slap on the hide.

Kerry shrieked with laughter.

'Tattooing Kerry's bum?' Jeffrey repeated incredulously.

'It's not a *proper* tattoo, Daddy,' Kerry assured him brightly. 'It'll be gone in a couple of months.'

Jeffrey pulled out one of the kitchen chairs and sat down next to Joe. Then he inspected the bowl of green gloop. 'A couple of months. That makes me feel a lot better.' Kate would go *ballistic*. He pushed the bowl away. 'This stuff smells foul.'

'It's mehndi,' Natalie said. 'Henna.'

Jeffrey stared blankly at her.

'It's a brown dye,' she continued. 'It doesn't do any harm and it generally fades after a few weeks. I can show you mine if you like.'

She proceeded to roll up the sliver of Lycra that was her skirt.

'No!' Jeffrey held up his hand. 'There's no need for that. I'll take your word for it.' He needed a drink. A stiff one. 'What exactly are you tattooing on my daughter's bottom?' he asked politely.

'*I love Ronan Keating.*'

'And some sunflowers,' Kerry added.

Jeffrey nodded carefully. 'Ronan Keating?'

'Boyzone,' Natalie supplied. 'Lead singer.'

'Oh.'

'Daddy, you are such a saddo!'

'Quite probably,' he said. *Drink. Fast!*

'I want one too,' Joe piped up. 'I want MAN UNITED FOR EVER!'

'Don't be silly,' Kerry sneered. 'Boys don't tattoo their bottoms!'

'We could do your arm or your shoulder,' Natalie suggested pleasantly. 'Sean Bean's got *100% Blade* on his arm.'

Joe grinned with contentment. Jeffrey thought that he might pass out. There was a rush of blood to his head and a ringing in his ears. Sean Bean was a Hollywood film star and, as a direct result, could carry off such fripperies. He wasn't sure a ten-year-old schoolboy could. Kate would go *completely and utterly* ballistic!

Natalie resumed her task of daubing his daughter's rear end with dye with the supreme concentration usually only demonstrated by neurosurgeons. Now that he had got used to the unattractive whiff of the mehndi, the smell of burning was getting distinctly stronger.

'So why can I smell burning?' he asked.

'Ah, fun!' Natalie shouted, abandoning her stick in the bowl of goo and leaping towards the cooker. 'That's tonight's dinner!'

Jeffrey closed his eyes. *A whisky. Malt, perhaps. A double.*

Nat scraped around the bottom of the pan with a wooden spoon. 'That'll be right,' she said encouragingly. 'We'll hardly notice the black bits. Charcoal's good for you. Cleans out the digestion.'

Jeffrey stood up from the table. He wasn't sure he wanted his digestion cleaning out. Not by the bits that had flaked off the bottom of his saucepans anyway. He went over to inspect the damage. The empty margarine carton stood on the draining board, its label wet and smudged. WEDNESDAY – CHILLI CON CARNE. He checked the pan. It was chilli con carne all right, con black bits.

Jeffrey held up the carton. 'This is Monday,' he said.

'Good call, Jeffers,' Natalie grinned.

'But we're eating Wednesday's meal.'

'Are we?' Natalie peered into the pan.

Jeffrey scoured the various charts and rotas held by cutesy magnets to the front of the fridge. 'Monday is spaghetti bolognese,' he said.

'Is it?'

'You've got the wrong carton out.'

'Have I?' Natalie looked very unconcerned. 'Does it matter?' she ventured, stopping in mid-stir.

'No,' Jeffrey blustered. 'No. Not at all.' But it did matter.

A lot. Kate had gone to an enormous amount of trouble to cook the meals and label them all for the freezer, including an individual portion of a suitable vegetarian alternative for Kerry, and here was Natalie, heedlessly producing them out of order. God, he hoped Kate didn't ring tonight. How was he going to explain two tattooed children and burnt chilli con carne on Monday, when they weren't due to eat it until Wednesday. He turned to Natalie, feeling extremely flustered.

'You need to stay cool, Jeffers.' She gave him a long, lazy wink. 'It'll taste bonza whatever day of the week. You wait and see.'

In the event, he had to wait rather a long time to see. Kerry had to lie on the table with her mehndied bottom drying for forty-five minutes and Joe also had to have a small tattoo – by which time Wednesday's chilli had lost much of its heat. It seemed excessive to lay the dining-room table for burnt offerings and salad. Jeffrey had a drink, or several, while he waited. Natalie joined him, sipping white wine with a relaxed air of someone who is obviously used to obliterating dinners. She turned the radio up and danced round the kitchen, singing chirpily and making a performance out of cutting up an iceberg lettuce.

When the food eventually appeared on the table, it was dreadful. But the children ate it without complaint, chattering ceaselessly, still absorbed by their tribal marked bodies. Jeffrey ate his with equal compliance, chewing and swallowing every mouthful with stoic determination. It was the most disgusting meal he had ever eaten, but he didn't care. All he could do was wonder exactly what Natalie Lambert had tattooed across her firm round bottom.

Chapter Eleven

'Where's Sonia?' Ben asked as Kate approached him. The dining room at the Priory was already crowded and there had been a Charge of the Light Brigade-style rush for the best places. He patted the cushion next to him. 'I've saved two seats for you.'

'She's retired to bed with a stash of Mars bars and a headache. I think T'ai Chi's rather more strenuous than she envisaged.' Kate laughed. 'When I left her she seemed to be finding the effort of sitting upright rather taxing.'

'So she won't be joining us?'

Kate felt herself blush. *No, it's just the two of us.* 'It seems unlikely.' She slipped into the vacant seat opposite Ben aware that her pulse was hammering. 'Although she could make a miraculous recovery when she realises she's missing food.'

Ben chuckled. 'You two seem to be very close. Have you known each other long?'

'Years. We met in the maternity ward.' Why did she say that? It made her sound married and boring. *I am married and boring!* 'We've clung together ever since.'

Ben appraised her, slowly. 'You look nice,' he said.

'Oh, this is old,' she replied, self-consciously fingering her blouse. It was old. Why hadn't she taken more care with what she'd packed? Sonia had brought clothes for all occasions, all temperatures – every eventuality was catered for. Kate hadn't packed with more care, because she'd come here hoping to find herself, not someone else.

'Perhaps you'd care to join me in a glass of particularly good Fleurie?' Ben waved the bottle temptingly. 'As I was supposed to be on a wine-tasting course, it seems silly to deny oneself completely.'

'I'd love to.' She held out her glass. 'I feel we deserve it after all the exercise we've done today.'

Pouring the wine, Ben tasted it, savouring it in his mouth. He clinked his glass against hers. 'Here's to a good week, Mrs Lewis,' he said. 'May it be all that you hope for.'

Kate returned the clink. 'Here's to you, Mr Mahler.' She tasted the wine. 'A very fine choice,' she said.

'I like the good things in life,' he told her.

I bet you do.

There was a muted buzz of chatter in the dining room, giving it a relaxing atmosphere. The whole place still had the cloistered feel of a priory, with its flagstone floors, mellow stone walls and Gothic arches, and it felt as if the walls had absorbed the calm meditations of centuries of monks, and now quietly seeped them out as succour to their current highly stressed occupants.

'Your work must be very exciting,' Kate observed.

'Not really. I spent all day last Friday choosing models for a client's millennium calendar.' His eyes twinkled. 'It's a dirty job, but someone's got to do it.'

'Sounds like hell,' Kate agreed, straight-faced.

'And what do you spend your days doing, Mrs Lewis?'

'Very mundane housewifely things,' she shrugged. 'I spent a ridiculously large proportion of last Friday choosing biscuits in Tesco, for instance. Other than that it's the school run, school lunches, school homework. If you want a conversation about any aspect of school life, I'm your woman.'

'It doesn't sound as if you're very happy with your lot.' His mouth twisted in sympathy.

'I am,' she said, looking down at her skirt. 'Most of the time.' Taking a drink of her wine, she paused as she felt the warming flush of it travel to her cheeks. Kate forced a laugh. 'Why am I telling you this? I've forgotten what it is to have a proper grown-up conversation. You're probably not the slightest bit interested.'

'Of course I'm interested,' Ben said earnestly. His hand reached out and brushed hers. So briefly that it was gone by the time she noticed it. 'Go on.'

'I just feel,' she struggled past the tears which felt perpetually close to her eyes these days, 'that there's something missing.'

'I know what you mean.'

'How can you?' she cried. 'You look like the sort of man who has everything.'

'Do I?' The corners of Ben's eyes crinkled with amusement. 'I suppose I do. Materially.' Suddenly he was serious. 'But that doesn't mean I have everything I *want*.'

'Do any of us?' Kate asked. They stared at each other for a moment.

Ben sat back and folded his arms. 'So why T'ai Chi?' he said, breaking the silence.

She shrugged. 'I wanted to get away for the week. Have some time to think about things. "Find myself" if you want to be the hundredth person to take the piss.'

'I don't think it's funny at all,' he said. 'I think it's a very courageous thing to do. Not many of us are focused on where we're going in life. I admire you for it.'

'Thank you,' she said quietly. 'I feel no one understands what I'm going through. I'm not even sure that I do myself.'

'Try me.'

'It's difficult when you can't put a label on it. I'm not sick, I'm not suicidal. I haven't got a deadly virus. I just have an itching throughout my body and a twitchiness in my bones. My feet fidget all night long.' She twisted the stem of her wine glass in contemplation. 'I have a husband who adores me and two beautiful children who never put a foot out of place. So why doesn't it feel like enough? What else do I need to satisfy this . . . this longing that's inside me?'

'If you're lucky you may find some answers here,' Ben ventured. 'At least you've started your search. I think this is the right place too.' He gestured at the room. 'There's something very magical about the atmosphere. What was it Sam said today? "Be open to all possibilities."'

'Wasn't that shortly before he made us stay in Dragon stance for fifteen minutes?' Kate giggled. 'I was definitely open to the possibility of never being able to move my knees again after that!'

The waitress served them a starter of avocado, piled high with succulent prawns swimming in Marie Rose sauce. Dangerously high in fat and calories. Sonia would have loved it. Kate considered taking a doggy bag to her room except that would have meant leaving Ben and she was enjoying his company too much. More, probably, than was good for a married woman.

'How old are your children?' he asked between mouthfuls.

'Kerry's twelve, Joe's ten. It seems strange to be without them. I've never been away from home before.'

'Never?'

'Not without them.'

'I can't imagine it,' Ben said. 'I spend half of my life in hotels.'

And what about the other half? 'I needed a break,' she said. 'And now, after one night, I'm missing them.'

'Will they miss you too?'

'I doubt it,' she said. 'I nag them constantly. They'd never put cream on their athlete's foot if it wasn't for me.'

Ben laughed.

'Do you have a family?' Kate asked.

'No.' A shutter came down over his pale blue eyes and he took a long drink of the Fleurie. 'And what does your husband think about your quest for fulfilment?' Ben said eventually.

'Jeffrey?' Kate pushed her plate to one side. 'He's very supportive.'

'But not exactly in tune?'

'He can't see anything wrong with our life,' she admitted. 'Not that there is,' she added hurriedly. 'It's just that when you become wrapped up in your children and work and life in general, you lose some of the intimacy of being a couple.'

The avocado was replaced by roast lamb. Kate's mind wandered to the leg of New Zealand that would still be languishing in the freezer.

'Have you been together long?' Ben asked.

'It feels like for ever sometimes,' Kate murmured. 'Jeffrey was my first boyfriend. We were both still at school.'

Ben looked surprised and she wished she'd been able to say that they'd met at a candlelit champagne reception on a millionaire's yacht in the Bahamas, but she'd never even been on a sailing dinghy in Bournemouth. Ben looked as though he'd been on a lot of yachts in his time.

Kate shrugged. 'As you can tell, I'm not a woman of the world,' she said candidly.

He leaned forward, watching her closely but not in a lecherous way. 'That's part of the attraction,' he said.

Attraction! Kate felt a renewed red-wine flush gallop to her cheeks. Wasn't this where she was supposed to give a tinkling laugh, look coquettish and come back with some sparkling repartee? She was out of her depth with this. 'I think I'd better check on Sonia.' She stood up hastily.

Ben stood too. 'I'm sorry,' he said. 'I've embarrassed you.'

'No. No. Not at all.' Kate's skirt swished against her wine glass, knocking it over. A blood-red stain seeped across the white linen tablecloth. 'Now look what I've done!' She felt everyone was turning to watch her.

'Don't worry,' Ben soothed. 'I'll clear it up. Please, sit down again. Have some dessert. How about some coffee?'

'No. Look – I have to ring home. They're expecting me.'

'Don't rush away,' Ben pleaded.

'My goodness, is that the time? They'll be worried about me.' She turned and fled from the dining room, serviette still tucked in the waistband of her skirt.

Jeffrey wasn't at all worried about her. In fact, he sounded as though he couldn't wait to get her off the phone.

'Was the spaghetti bolognese good?' she asked.

'Fine.'

Clearly, he was still smarting about being lumbered with Natalie.

'Is she a good cook?'

'She has her own individual style.'

'Can I speak to the children?'

'They're in bed.'

'Already?' Kate frowned at her watch. It wasn't yet ten o'clock. They never went to bed before ten.

'They were tired.'

'Aren't they well?'

'No. Just tired.'

'Is everything all right?' Kate could tell he was being cagey. She just couldn't tell why.

'Yes. Fine.' It wasn't, you didn't have to be Einstein to work that one out!

'Is everything at work okay?'

'Same as usual. How's the T'ai Chi?' Jeffrey asked finally.

'It's okay,' she said. 'Harder than I thought.'

'Are there some nice people on the course?'

'Yes.' It was her turn to be cagey.

'I'm glad.' She heard Jeffrey sigh. 'I'd better go, we've still got to clear up after dinner.'

Clear up after dinner? Kate checked her watch again. Why hadn't Natalie cleared up straight after they'd finished eating? *She* always did. Kate held her breath. She wouldn't fuss. If there were dirty dinner plates on the table at this late hour, what did it matter to her? At least it meant they had all been fed.

'I'll speak to you tomorrow,' he said.

'Goodnight.'

'Goodnight.'

'I love you, Jeff . . .' The phone had already gone dead. '. . . rey.'

Kate replaced the receiver and the empty click echoed round her bedroom. The television was blaring away in the next room, but she felt cut off, isolated. What on earth was she doing here? She should be at home where she was needed and had a role to play. If she'd felt like a square peg in a round hole at home, this was even worse! She'd made a fool of herself with Ben, who was probably only indulging in a harmless bit of flirtation. It was probably something he did every day of the week, particularly with the line of work he was in. Sonia would be very proud of her.

We've got to clear up after dinner. Not *I've* got to clear up after dinner. Jeffrey had said that the children were in bed, so the other part of the *we* could only be Natalie. Kate stared hard at the rag-rolled wall of her small bedroom. It had been done in a rush and there were uneven patches that made it look just blotchy rather than a designer effect. So what was the awesome Australian au pair still doing in Acacia Close at this time of night? That really was devotion above and beyond the call of duty.

Chapter Twelve

They were standing in front of the Priory on Tuesday morning – another scorching summer's day – circling their hips, following the languid rhythm of the ever-cheerful Sam and Guy, a few wisps of clouds sauntering across an otherwise unbroken blue sky.

Kate felt shattered. She'd hardly slept a wink in her cramped, hard single bed, tossing and turning, trying to fathom out exactly what was wrong with her life. It would probably have been more comfortable if she'd laid out flat on her ironing board. Which took her mind back to Natalie. Tuesday was ironing day on the rota and Kate wondered how she would fare with a laundry basket full of school shirts and blouses and sensible white knickers. She hoped that Natalie would iron the tea towels properly and wouldn't simply fold them and stick them in the drawer.

Why was she feeling so jumpy? It wasn't that she didn't trust Jeffrey: he didn't have a deceitful bone in his body. One of the qualities she admired most in him was his loyalty. But he had sounded ever so strange last night.

Her back was stiff and creaking nearly as much as her knees, but she was starting to loosen up under the guidance of the instructors. Kate had always thought that she was quite fit, but T'ai Chi was reaching the places where step aerobics feared to go. Ben had smiled at her this morning before the class started, but hadn't come over to speak to her and Sonia. He probably thought she was a complete wally now anyway. Or a saddo, as Kerry would have said. Perhaps that's why she was feeling so wobbly. She'd been revelling in his attention far more than she ought to. After all these years with Jeffrey, how could she let her head be so easily turned by a bit of meaningless flirting?

'Did you sleep well?' she whispered to Sonia.

'No,' her friend hissed back. 'I spent all night dreaming that I had a big bum. It was so depressing.'

'Why?'

'Because when I woke up, it was true!'

On cue they stopped their synchronised hip wiggling. 'Now that you've been introduced to some of the basics, during the course of this week,' Guy said, 'we also want you to concentrate on the essence of the white crane. In China, this graceful bird signifies good fortune, harmony, calmness and beauty. It has strength, dignity and integrity. Concentrate on that when you are doing your T'ai Chi this week and see where it takes you,' he suggested.

'I'd like to concentrate on him and see where that takes me.' Sonia gave her a wink.

'Behave,' Kate laughed. 'This is meant to be serious.'

'Yeah, like horoscopes and crystal balls.'

'There is a movement in the T'ai Chi form called White Crane Spreads Its Wings and we're going to try to get the spirit of that by practising a white crane animal play,' Sam said. 'Just follow us.'

'To the ends of the earth,' Sonia breathed.

'Stand firmly, feet together. Now bend one leg and lift the foot to knee height,' Sam instructed. 'Hold it there. This is Crane stance. Now raise the arms, palms upward, open to the sky, a wide sweeping movement. Majestic. Imagine the powerful beating of the wings of a beautiful white crane. Turn the palms and lower your arms; at the same time bend the standing leg and lower the raised one.'

Kate wobbled alarmingly.

Sam smiled encouragingly. 'Now we'll repeat that on the other side. Slowly. Rhythmically.'

Kate felt more like a scruffy old crow. Standing on one leg was never as easy as it looked. It was all a question of balance – something that was difficult to achieve without effort. She frowned herself into position.

'Relax the face!'

Was he looking directly at her?

'One more time,' Sam urged, looking for all his worth exactly like a magnificent crane in flight. Bastard, Kate thought. 'Half close the eyes and gaze into the distance, across the fields. Pretend that you're flying effortlessly through the air, carried by gentle thermals. Light, unfettered.'

She tried a few more tentative flaps. Heavy and dismally fettered.

'Keep it going,' Sam urged. 'Are you flying yet?' He flapped his arms gracefully. 'You may not feel it instantly – sometimes it requires a leap of faith to believe that you can do it.'

Kate glanced round. Everyone else looked as if they were flying through the air. She was grounded. Rooted steadfastly to the floor. Stuck.

'And let your arms come gently to rest by your sides,' Sam instructed. 'Stand quietly for a moment. See how that feels inside. What are the emotions?'

Disappointment. Disappointment that I can't move forward. Disappointment that I can't even do something as simple as pretending to be a bloody bird for ten minutes!

'Let's finish there,' Sam said. 'Turn the body gently from side to side. Ease out.' He beamed encouragingly. 'Go and have a nice cup of tea. Sit quietly for a few minutes.'

Sit quietly – with Sonia? Some hope!

'I think it's your turn to get the tea today, Katie,' Sonia said, flinging herself on her back on the grass.

'I did it yesterday,' Kate reminded her.

'You do it today, then and I'll do it for the next two,' she said, shading her eyes against the sun.

Kate sighed. 'Biscuits?'

'Is the Pope Catholic?'

Kate queued up with Sam and Guy who chatted animatedly and seemed indefatigable in their enthusiasm for life. It was a long time since she had felt like that, optimistic and ready to cope with all that life threw at her. Perhaps life's handfuls got bigger the older you got. Her eyes drifted towards the garden. Ben had taken up residence under his tree again, phone clamped to his ear. He didn't look as if *he'd* had any trouble soaring high in the sky. The words 'high-flyer' were stamped all over him.

'You look as if you need that cup of tea, my little friend,' Sonia observed. 'You seem decidedly peaky this morning.'

'I didn't sleep very well,' Kate told her. 'Apart from the fact that my bed is about as comfortable as a plank studded with two-inch nails, I had a very strange telephone conversation with Jeffrey last night.'

'*All* my telephone conversations with Kev are strange,' Sonia puffed. 'They're complaining about the lack of variety in their diet. Fish is good for the brain, I told them. It'll improve your IQ. And heaven knows, Kevin's could do with some improving!' Her eyes followed Sam and Guy who emerged from the Priory bearing their hard-earned cups of tea. 'Don't they make you want to bite the back of your hand every time you see them?'

'No,' Kate said.

'I wonder if they'd consider a threesome?' Sonia mused.

Kate stared at her, outraged. 'I can't believe you're talking like this! You're a happily married woman with two lovely children.'

'I think you need to rephrase that.' Sonia looked at her sanguinely. 'A married woman with two children. I'm not sure that the children have been lovely since they came out of nappies, and happy is something I was a long time ago. Shortly before I met Kevin.'

Kate put her teacup down on the grass. 'Well, I hate to disillusion you, but Guy is *blissfully* happy, is devoted to his wife and has two *wonderful* children – his words, not mine – and a mortgage the size of Manchester. He has an

112

ageing Labrador called Marmalade and a mad mother to look after and is, probably, kind to all other small furry animals and sundry life forms. It's quite likely that he doesn't even stamp on spiders.'

Sonia huffed offendedly. 'He sounds like a real fun guy!'

'Sam is also deliriously in love and is about to propose to the rather gorgeous blonde Scottish girl with glasses over there.' Kate helpfully pointed her out.

Sonia peered disappointedly at the object of Sam's desire. 'He needs his eyes testing,' she grunted.

'This means, essentially, that neither of our two instructors is available,' Kate concluded.

Her friend wagged a finger knowingly. 'Show me a man who's not up for an illicit fling and I'll show you a chocolate cake with no calories.'

Kate toyed with her cup. 'Are things really so bad between you and Kevin that you'd consider an affair?'

'Yes.'

'Seriously?'

Sonia sat up and hugged her knees. 'Yes, seriously.' Her voice sounded small and sad. 'I feel that I've become Invisible Woman. I've tried everything, but he never looks at me any more.'

'Isn't there any romance left?'

'Romance?' Sonia scratched her chin. 'Hang on, I'm sure I used to know what that word meant.'

They both fell on the grass and chortled. Kate noticed that Ben had finished his phone call and was watching them from beneath the shade of his tree.

Sonia's voice pulled her back. 'Don't you think that Kevin and Jeffrey will be ogling the barmaids at the golf club while we're away?'

'The only things that Jeffrey looks at lustfully these days are golf clubs in the pro shop.' *At least I hope they're the only things.*

'I sometimes wish I played golf,' Sonia said dreamily. 'At least I could guarantee getting my hands on a stiff shaft once a week.'

They sniggered childishly again.

Kate looked up at the sky. 'Why did we fall in love with men who are dispassionate about us?' she asked, plucking absently at the cool grass.

'When did we become dispassionate about ourselves?'

Kate rolled over onto her tummy and sucked a strand of grass. 'Do you ever fake your orgasms?' she asked.

'Constantly,' Sonia admitted.

'Does it fool Kevin?'

'No,' she said thoughtfully, 'but it sometimes fools me.'

They both shrieked uproariously.

'Why?' Sonia asked.

'Oh, nothing.' Kate brushed the question away. *I do. I have to these days.* The spark had gone out of her marriage and she wondered if it was possible to ever get it back. Jeffrey had never taken her to dizzy heights of passion. Their love-making had always been quiet and comfortable, years of having the children to consider, she supposed. It had never been adventurous either. They'd never made love outdoors, unless you could count a few exploratory fumblings on the park swings as teenagers. For years she'd subjugated an urge to roll in the breaking surf or frolic naked in a secluded field. Jeffrey was not a natural frolicker. Now he seemed to think they'd had good sex if it started at eleven o'clock and he could still be asleep by quarter past. The whole thing seemed like such an effort.

She looked over at Ben who was lying propped against the tree, arms folded, eyes closed, dozing. Why did her heart start vibrating like a pneumatic drill whenever he was less than ten feet away from her? Would making love with Ben seem like a routine chore – just something else to be fitted in around destringing green beans and putting down slug pellets? Could *she* ever consider an affair?

Kate grinned to herself. It was as ridiculous as it was out of the question. Ben Mahler was probably surrounded by beautiful, switched-on career women every day of the week. What could he possibly see in her – a mousey little housewife, whose last proper job had been as a shorthand typist in a building society thirteen years ago? She thought of Jeffrey, the considered, intense, serious person she had married. He was a good man. A good, steady man. She should be happy. What would it take for the fireworks to sparkle between them again? Kate knew what Sonia would have said. They both needed a rocket up their backsides!

Chapter Thirteen

Jeffrey felt terrible about lying to Kate. He couldn't ever remember doing it before. The children hadn't been in bed when she called last night. They were in the lounge playing Twister with Natalie. Kerry was so excited about having *Ronan Keating* on her left buttock that she would have blurted it out to Kate instantly, and there was no way he wanted her to know about the tattoos so early in the week, otherwise she would have jumped in the BMW and high-tailed it back home quicker than you could say Boyzone.

It was getting to the end of another dreary day in Hills & Hopeland. The mind was willing, but the flesh was extremely weak, and the out-tray had failed miserably in its quest to keep pace with the in-tray. He knew exactly how many extra weeds there were in the car park, though, and had been enjoying a pleasant daydream involving running through foam-tipped waves hand-in-hand with a lithe blonde beauty who, for the sake of marital harmony, should remain nameless.

The shrill ringing of the telephone made him jump at the same time as a wave was about to knock him over in his reverie.

'Jeffrey Lewis,' he said, trying desperately to sound businesslike.

'Daddy?' Kerry's voice was tremulous.

'Hello, darling.' Why was she ringing him at work? He'd be home in half an hour – it was five o'clock. As the alarm bells started to clang his daughter broke into a racking sob.

'What is it, darling?' He could feel perspiration breaking out on his forehead. 'Tell me.'

'I can't!'

'Why? What's happened? Has Flopsy died?'

'I don't think so.' There was more sobbing down the phone.

'Then what is it?'

'It hurts, Daddy!' she wailed pathetically.

'What hurts, poppet? Tell me, please.'

'It hurts! I need you.'

'What have you done? Have you fallen?'

'I can't tell you.' Her voice was interspersed by heaving breaths. 'You'll be cross.'

'I won't be cross,' Jeffrey promised. 'And where's Natalie? Why isn't she with you?'

'She's not here.' The crying was becoming hysterical.

'Don't move,' he barked. 'I'm on my way home.'

He punched his next-door neighbour's telephone number into the mobile phone as he grabbed his jacket and headed for the door. 'Domestic crisis,' he shouted to the senior partner as he banged the door and raced down the steps to the car park. It was engaged. Damn Mrs Barrett, she was always on the bloody phone! Where the hell was fucking Natalie when he needed her?

* * *

117

The Merc was approaching warp speed when he careered into the drive of number 20, Acacia Close, spraying gravel into the vibrant red salvias in the borders. He yanked the front door open and raced in. The kitchen was empty. He flung open the lounge door. Joe was sitting in the corner, arranging a platoon of plastic soldiers in front of a battalion of *Star Wars* characters. Blood-curdling battle noises were coming from his mouth; in true male fashion he seemed oblivious to the female distress being aired on the sofa, where Kerry lay curled up in a ball hugging a cushion to her middle. Her sobbing had dried to a feeble snivel, but her face was stricken and pale. Natalie was wiping her forehead with a facecloth.

'What's the matter?' He could hardly squeeze the words out.

The snivel increased and turned rapidly into a sob again.

'Don't cry, darling,' he said helplessly. He turned to Natalie who looked the picture of calm. She simply mouthed something at him and he had no idea what it meant.

'She said it hurts,' he gasped. 'Is she sick?'

'It does hurt!' Kerry took up wailing again.

'You said you were going to be brave, Kez,' Natalie admonished. 'It was going to be our little secret.' She squeezed Kerry's hand. 'I think you're going to have to confess.'

'Confess?' Jeffrey wanted to slump into the nearest armchair, but feared if he did, he'd never get up again.

Kerry cried harder.

Natalie met his perplexed gaze directly. 'She's had her navel pierced.'

'Her what?'

'Her belly button,' Natalie expanded. 'She's had it pierced.'

Jeffrey slumped into the nearest armchair. Speechless.

'She said she'd always wanted it done.'

Jeffrey hoped this was a follow-on dream from the Bondi Beach one and soon he would wake up and still be safe and sound behind his desk at Hills & Hopeland. 'She's twelve years old!' he said faintly. '*Always* is a very short time.'

'She didn't think it would hurt so much,' Natalie explained calmly. 'But the pain doesn't last long.'

'I take it you know this from personal experience?'

Natalie nodded. *My God, a tattooed bum and a pierced belly button!* Jeffrey closed his eyes against the vision.

'By tomorrow, she won't know it's there.'

'But I will,' Jeffrey shouted. He pointed at Kerry. 'And very soon your mother will!'

'You promised you wouldn't be cross,' Kerry howled.

'I'm not cross, Kerry,' he said. '*I'm furious!*'

She howled even louder. How on earth was he going to explain this to Kate? This made eating chilli con carne on Monday instead of Wednesday pale into insignificance.

He turned on Natalie. 'And where were you when she needed you?'

'I was at the chemist, buying surgical spirit to bathe it. You didn't have any.'

119

'That's because we're not accustomed to having our bodies pierced on a regular basis,' he shouted.

'It's very handy to have in,' Natalie assured him.

'Get out,' Jeffrey said through clenched teeth. 'You're fired!'

Her head snapped up and there was a pained look in her eyes. 'Fired?' she said. '*Fired?*'

'Fired,' he repeated flatly.

'Don't you think you're being hasty?'

'No, I don't.' Jeffrey held up his hand.

'Is that it?'

'We can dress it up as a discussion if you want, but the conclusion will be the same.' Jeffrey set his jaw. 'Leave now, Natalie. I never want to see your face in this house again.'

Kerry bawled with renewed vigour, and Joe, Darth Vader abandoned, was looking as if he'd like to join in.

'Wouldn't you like time to consider this?' Natalie pleaded. 'We'll laugh about it in the morning.'

'I doubt it very much,' Jeffrey said crisply. 'Now kindly take your hands off my daughter. You've done quite enough for one day.'

Natalie stood up and walked to the door.

'Don't go!' Kerry cried.

Natalie met his eyes and shook her head sadly. As he heard the door close quietly behind her, he realised his hands were shaking violently.

Jeffrey had left the kids with Mrs Barrett for the evening. Kerry still hadn't forgiven him; neither had Joe. Now he sat gloomily on a high stool in Kevin's kitchen. There appeared to be tomato ketchup smeared copiously over every flat surface including the floor. 'I've sacked Natalie,' he said miserably.

'The Body?'

'Yes. She's gone.'

'Never!' Kevin looked at him in disbelief. 'You get the chance to spend the week alone with those legs and, instead of *getting* her in the sack, you *give* her the sack!' Kevin scraped burnt fish fingers into the bin. 'What happened?'

Jeffrey rubbed his eyes. 'It's too tawdry to go into.'

'Does it involve the intimate and mutual exchange of bodily fluids?'

Jeffrey glared at him. 'No, it does not!'

'Oh.' Kevin looked hideously disappointed.

'She took Kerry to get her belly button pierced,' Jeffrey said tightly.

'Her belly button?'

'Yes.'

Kevin rubbed his chin. 'And that's it?'

'Isn't that enough?' his friend snapped.

'Not really, mate,' Kevin replied.

Jeffrey felt his heart sink and three more wrinkles etch themselves into his face. 'Well, it is in my book.'

'It must be a pretty bloody tame book then. Who wrote it – Barbara Cartland?'

Before Jeffrey could protest, a car pulled up in the drive. Kevin looked out of the window. 'Aye, aye,' he said, rubbing his hands together. 'Mrs Shaw's here. We can go now.'

121

Jeffrey followed him into the hall, where Kevin let in an elderly, slightly nervous-looking woman.

'They're in there.' He pointed at the lounge and she followed him in. 'It's very good of you to come at such short notice, Mrs Shaw,' Kevin grovelled. 'As I explained, we're off to visit a sick friend.'

The boys were stationed on either side of the lounge – one with a sub-machine gun, one with a bow and arrow. Both had walkie talkies. They looked up and smiled angelically at the babysitter.

'Now, you two,' Kevin warned. 'Remember, hamsters are sensitive creatures. I don't want to come home and find Little Ham cowering in his cage again. Do you hear?'

Two butter-wouldn't-melt-in-my-mouth faces beamed at him. 'Yes, Dad.' Their attention returned to the no man's land of the Ikea hearth rug.

Kevin turned to Mrs Shaw, whose hair already seemed to be whiter than when she had arrived. 'Just keep them away from matches, superglue and any sharp or particularly blunt objects and we shouldn't have a repeat of last time.' He nodded to her reassuringly.

Reluctantly, she took her coat off. 'Don't be late,' she said faintly.

'We won't.' Kevin winked as they closed the door.

'Sick friend?' Jeffrey asked.

'You'll see.'

The golf club was unusually quiet, even for a weekday night. A few stalwarts were scattered through the Tartan lounge, putting their lives to rights over a pint of Theakston's Old Peculier.

'Evening, Frank,' Kevin said to the barman. 'How's the cold?'

'Gedding bedder, thanks,' he sniffed.

Kevin turned to Jeffrey and shrugged. 'Now call me a liar.'

'You're a liar,' Jeffrey obliged.

'Two pints of Theakston's, Frank,' Kevin said.

They took their drinks and sat down at a window table, watching the keen golfers practise their putting on the manicured green outside.

'I've got a joke for you,' Kevin said, smacking his lips as he put his pint down. 'An elderly billionaire is talking to his stunning young wife. "If I lost all my money," he asks her, "you'd still love me, wouldn't you?"'

Jeffrey raised his eyebrows.

'"Of course I would," she cried, "and I'd miss you too!"'

He laughed politely.

Kevin scratched his head. 'Not funny?'

'Just not in the mood,' Jeffrey said apologetically.

'Regretting dispensing with the services of Miss Australia?'

Jeffrey nodded, when what he really wanted to do was close his eyes and weep. He would never see Natalie again.

'I'm beginning to think I've acted like an intolerant prat,' he admitted.

'True to form then,' Kev said.

'Thanks.'

'You didn't really give her the flick because of the heinous crime of belly-button piercing?'

'I did.'

'She must think you're a right wanker.'

'Kerry could get septicaemia or hepatitis!'

'Or she could get a bucketload of street cred in the playground tomorrow,' he pointed out. 'Girl power and all that. You've accelerated your child's blossoming into womanhood. You should be happy.'

'Kate will go ballistic,' Jeffrey cringed.

'Women are always going ballistic about something.' Kevin shrugged dismissively. 'It could be a lot worse,' he said sagely. 'You don't know how lucky you are with your kids. I think mine have signed a pact with the devil in return for our souls. They'll probably pierce their own belly buttons given half the chance – with one of my screwdrivers. Then there'd be hell to pay! I spend a disproportionate amount of my life at the A and E department at Milton Keynes General. I'm on nodding terms with all the staff. I'm hoping to get an invite to the Christmas party.' He smirked lasciviously. 'All those nurses in stockings!'

Jeffrey tutted.

'And here's you,' Kevin continued, 'one little teeny tiny crisis and you're acting as if the whole world's falling apart. You're getting very middle aged in your outlook, old buddy.'

'You sound like Kate,' Jeffrey said, surprised. 'I'm sure

she thinks I'm an old stick-in-the-mud. How can I prove to her that I can move it and groove it with the rest?'

'Don't use words like "groove it" for a start,' Kevin advised. He hugged his Theakston's to his chest. 'Can I ask you a question?'

Jeffrey looked suspicious.

'Would you rather play a round of golf or play around with Melinda Messenger?'

'Well,' Jeffrey contemplated, 'the golf would certainly last longer.'

'Danger. Middle-aged married man thinking.' Kevin held up a finger. 'There should be no hesitation in answering that question if all of your love cylinders were still firing.'

'I'm not sure where my *love cylinders* are.'

'I rest my case.' Kevin preened himself.

Jeffrey watched enviously as a man in checked trousers on the putting green holed ball after ball without faltering. 'Do you know,' he said, 'that in one lifetime we spend an average of six months on the loo and only two weeks French kissing?'

'No!'

'I read it in Kate's copy of *Cosmopolitan.*'

'That bloody magazine should be banned. Sonia reads it too. She thinks it's the ruddy Bible. According to *Cosmo,*' he sneered, 'all men over thirty-five are crap in bed.' He looked mortally wounded. 'I'm fabulous,' he said. 'Not quite as athletic as I once was, but still fabulous.'

Jeffrey wasn't sure that he had ever been fabulous. But he wanted to be. Disconcertingly, he'd thought a lot about it since Natalie arrived. She'd made blood flow in places that were previously as stagnant as their garden pond. Jeffrey put down his pint. Solace wasn't to be found in the form of alcoholic consumption, he decided. 'I've had enough, Kev. I'm going to push off home. I'll only bring you down too if I stay around in this mood. You'd be better off sharing Lemsip stories with Frank.'

'Nonsense.' Kev picked up Jeffrey's glass and headed towards the bar. 'A few little pints of best bitter will do you the world of good.'

'Just one then,' Jeffrey agreed reluctantly.

'This is Theakston's finest therapy for a broken heart,' Kevin assured him.

'I haven't got a broken heart.'

His friend leaned on the bar and stared directly at him. 'Are you sure about that?'

Jeffrey avoided Kevin's eyes and turned to the window as a means of deflecting his knowing look. The man with the hot putter had gone and the sun was low in the sky, the still softness of dusk filtering in through the trees. He hadn't answered Kevin and the question hung in the air like the cigarette smoke all around them. *Did* he have a broken heart? The truth was, he wasn't at all sure.

Chapter Fourteen

Ben was sitting surrounded on all sides by the redundant Greenham Common women. They were all wearing loud tapestry waistcoats and one girl had a single cotton braid twined through her long crimped hair. She was giggling loudly at everything he said. Too loudly.

Kate and Sonia were late getting to the dining room because Sonia couldn't decide between the red velour Dash sweatshirt or the Marks & Spencer cotton stripes, and all the good places had gone – i.e., the ones next to Ben. Instead, they were sharing a table with four elderly women from Farnborough, who were, apparently, having great *Fun with Fur Fabric*. Kate took a deep breath and tried to sink her Chi to her *Tan-Tien*, now that Sam had told her exactly where it was. Looking away from Miss Giggly Tits momentarily, Ben caught her staring at him. He smiled and she hurriedly returned her gaze to her lasagne, feigning rapt attention and noting that her Chi had gone completely to pot and was whizzing round her body totally unfocused.

'I'm knackered,' Sonia complained. She rubbed her neck. 'Here was I, thinking I'd be spending the week swimming, saunaing and sunbathing, and all we've done is bloody *exercise*.' She said it like a dirty word.

'This is an exercise course.'

'Don't I know it!' Sonia hugged herself carefully, as if she thought she might break.

'Anyway, I thought you liked exercise. You go to the gym twice a week.'

'That's not because I like it. It's because my body requires large amounts of Toblerone and I have to go to the gym in order to accommodate that need.'

'I see.'

'I should never have let you persuade me to come,' Sonia said resignedly. 'I thought at least I'd have lost a few pounds by now, exercising morning, noon and night.' She pinched at her waist. 'Not a sausage. I wanted to go home slim and svelte and sexy and make Kevin mad with desire, but a steel band could still play "Yellow Bird" on the dimples in my thighs.' Sonia prodded her. 'Kate!'

'What?'

'You're not listening to me, are you? You keep looking dreamily at the beautiful Ben.'

'I do not!' She lowered her voice in case the four elderly ladies suddenly found their conversation more riveting than fur fabric.

'And he keeps mooning at you.'

'He does no such thing!'

'He does.' Sonia inclined her head. 'He's doing it again.' She smirked. 'Look at him.'

'I will not!'

'I think he fancies you.' Sonia twiddled her eyebrows in the style of Groucho Marx.

'And I think you're mad!'

'Go on, give him a look.' She made encouraging nudging movements with her elbows.

Kate scowled. 'What sort of look?'

'You know.' Sonia rolled her eyes seductively. 'A vampish, come-to-bed-and-ravish-me look.'

Kate sighed. 'I could never do that sort of look even when I was young.' She prodded the remnants of her lasagne. 'That's probably why I married the first man I ever dated.'

Sonia tutted.

'And besides,' Kate continued in a whisper, 'I don't want him to come to bed and ravish me. He's nice. He's pleasant company. End of story.'

'You are so boring,' Sonia moaned, letting her fork clatter to her empty plate.

'And I happen to be in love with my husband,' Kate insisted.

Sonia sensibly let the subject drop. She looked round at the dessert table, her eyes passing quickly over the fresh fruit salad and settling on anything that involved double cream. 'I'm off to the calorie gallery,' she said decisively. 'The chocolate centre in my brain needs serious restoking, and only Death by Chocolate will do.' She stood up. 'I could practise my wood element though, by having some white chocolate log too.'

'I don't think that's quite what Sam meant when he said you should incorporate T'ai Chi into your daily life.'

'I'm doing my best,' Sonia huffed. 'Do you want some?'

'No, thanks.' Kate shook her head. 'Shall I go and get us some coffee?'

'You go through,' Sonia said. 'I could be some time.' A naughty twinkle flashed in her eye as she took up her spoon and headed purposefully towards the waiting desserts.

'Black, no sugar,' Ben's voice said next to her ear as she poured herself some coffee.

Kate's free hand flew to her chest. You could always tell when a man was coming because they jingled. Their pockets were full of loose things that chinked together in a little tune. Old or young, scruffy or smart. Corporate executives were the worst offenders. And headmasters. They all jingled. Except Ben. He was conspicuous by his lack of warning jingle. 'You made me jump,' she laughed nervously. 'I was miles away.'

'Back home?' he asked.

'No,' she admitted.

'Want to tell me where?'

She poured him the requested coffee and handed it to him. 'I was wondering why everyone else looks so contented as soaring white cranes and why I feel I've as much coordination as Daffy Duck.'

'Ah.' Ben raised a finger. 'Appearances can be deceptive.' He sat on one of the wicker sofas and stretched his long legs out before him. 'We're all probably struggling just as much.'

'I was hoping you'd say that,' she beamed, 'even though I don't believe it.'

130

'It'll come,' he assured her. 'It's not always easy to cut your ties and get airborne.'

She sat opposite him. 'Do you have ties?'

Ben stirred his coffee thoughtfully. 'Only the ones I make myself,' he said.

Kate gazed out into the garden. The sun was low and golden, still holding the warmth of the day. Four men from the *Confused About Computers* course were whacking the croquet balls with gusto and looked equally confused about the rules of the game. Strains of classical music filtered through the speakers, filling the evening air with the gentle sound of strings.

'My children love classical music,' she said, turning back to Ben. 'Vivaldi, Mozart, even boring old Bach. They get it from Jeffrey. I, on the other hand, coerce them into listening to Radio 1. I think children of their age should only listen to classical music when they go to the dentist.'

'You worry about them, don't you?'

'Constantly,' she admitted, and drained her coffee. 'I'd better go and find Sonia,' she said, 'and rescue her from the dessert trolley.'

'You worry about everyone.'

'I know.' She gave an apologetic laugh. 'I took it up when I stopped biting my nails.'

'I'm going for a walk,' Ben said. 'Take what's left of the evening air.'

'Have a nice time,' she said.

He cocked his head on one side, appealing. 'It was an invitation.'

131

'I know.' Kate stood up. *I'm scared of being with you, can't you tell?* 'I'll see you in the morning.'

'Goodnight,' he said with a sad smile.

Scrawled in untidy red letters, the white Nobo board in the reception hall read DEAD! GONE TO BED. SONIA.

Uh oh. Death by Chocolate – *now* what? It was a good job she'd come here for rest and recuperation, not excitement. Perhaps an early night would do her good too.

Ben came and stood behind her. 'You've been deserted,' he observed.

She folded her arms in resignation. 'It's that dessert trolley I told you about.'

Ben looked puzzled.

'I suspect a severe overdose of Death by Chocolate.'

He laughed. 'Come on, you've no excuses now,' he urged. 'You can join me on my walk.'

'But I haven't got a cardigan with me,' Kate replied.

He laughed. 'I don't think you'll freeze to death. It's the middle of summer, after all.'

And he set off, pushing through the modern revolving door that looked incongruous in its mellow medieval setting. Kate fell into step behind him, quickening her pace to catch up with his long stride. They strolled across the lawn, over the lengthening shadows and into the canopy of trees, an indigenous mix of oak, copper beech and sycamores, that bordered the grounds. A narrow bark path led the way to a set of overgrown steps and they threaded their way down through the nettles and thistles, Ben holding back unruly branches that threatened to spring out and bar their way.

They emerged onto a narrow lane lined with chocolate-box cottages that looked as if they had been untouched for centuries – except for the television aerials and the phone lines and the fact that, on close inspection, the neat white picket fencing that united their fussy, flowery gardens was made of uPVC. Kate sighed inwardly. That was what her life was like. As pointless as uPVC picket fencing. What earthly purpose did it serve? It didn't keep anything in, it didn't keep anything out and even its decorative properties were questionable. This might have been the middle of summer, but a cool breeze sprang up, rustling the leaves on the trees and she shivered slightly.

'Cold?' Ben asked, concerned.

'A little,' she said. In fact her bare arms were a mass of goose pimples.

'Let's walk in the last of the setting sun,' he suggested. 'It's chillier in the shade.'

They crossed the street, admiring the overflowing hanging baskets that adorned every porch, their blooms only slightly faded from the relentless sun of the last few days. As they walked, she could feel the air crackle between them, like an electric force field. His arm hung casually next to hers, six inches away at least, yet it felt as if he was pressed close against her. She was aware of his every movement as if they were joined together. *Do you feel it too, Ben?*

Ben glanced sideways at her and his eyes said yes. He

133

stroked her arm lightly and her flesh stood to attention at his touch. 'You've got goose pimples,' he said.

Kate rubbed her arms vigorously. 'Not enough fat to keep me warm,' she joked.

'I wish I could be chivalrous and whip off my jacket and place it gently round your shoulders like they do in films. But I don't have one, so I'm afraid you'll just have to shiver.' His expression was woeful. 'Unless . . .'

'What?' she asked cautiously.

'I was going to say that I could put my arm round you and you could huddle against me for warmth.' The devastating smile twitched at his lips. 'But even the thought of it has turned your face pale.'

'You're laughing at me,' Kate said.

'No,' he said softly. 'No, I'm not.'

She glanced at her watch. 'I'd better get back. I should phone Jeffrey.'

'Ah,' he said. 'Lucky Jeffrey.'

'Now you *are* laughing at me,' she chided, stronger now that she'd mentioned her husband's name.

'Yes,' he said, eyes twinkling in the fading light. 'I am.'

They walked in silence, not entirely comfortable, until Ben stopped to pluck a white rose from an old-fashioned rambler that tumbled over the wall of the end cottage. 'A beautiful rose for a beautiful woman,' he said, presenting it to her.

'Thank you.' It was a long time since she had been given roses. Not since Joe was born. She twirled it in her fingers and inhaled its sweet scent. 'It smells wonderful.'

He studied her seriously. 'Do you know that every rose has twenty-five petals?'

'No.' She didn't, but it was the sort of thing that Jeffrey would know.

The rose was just beginning to open, only the outer petals accepting the sun. At the centre the bud was still tightly closed, waiting for the right time to unfurl and show its beauty.

'I'll count them when it opens,' she said. 'And see if you're lying.'

'I never lie,' he said earnestly.

They turned back towards the Priory, walking down the High Street as the quicker option. The pavement was made of intricate patterns of block paving and studded with Victorian-style bollards that were neither use nor ornament, so narrow in parts that they had to walk single file. Ben guided her in front of him, his hand hot in the small of her back. Comforting and discomfiting at the same time. It was one of those streets that are full of prissy little shops selling dried rosebud topiaries in gilded terracotta pots, antique cribs and hand-made writing paper. Wonderful for passing tourists, but selling nothing remotely useful to the resident populace, who, no doubt, had to trek off to the nearest Tesco's to purchase even a tin of cat food or a bar of soap. Kate eyed the contents with as much interest as she could summon for designer teddy bears and wooden cats, trying to keep up a pace that was less than relaxing.

The light was fading fast, the night air chill and damp.

It made the lights from the Priory look warm and welcoming as they approached.

'Safe and sound,' Ben announced.

'Yes,' she said, wondering whether she would ever feel safe and sound again.

'A quick nightcap in the bar?'

'No, I'd better . . .'

'Phone Jeffrey,' he finished.

'Phone Jeffrey.' She fiddled with her fingers.

'Are you enjoying the course, Kate?' he asked.

'Yes.' *I just thought that finding myself would be easier than this. I've got feelings running riot round my body that shouldn't be allowed out without a safety warning and a hard hat. And now I think I feel more confused than ever.* 'Are you?'

'Yes,' he said. 'More than I expected.' He twitched his eyebrow. 'But then I expected to be learning about *The Beauties of Bordeaux*, not the beauties of Buckinghamshire.'

'Oh.' There wasn't a lot else she could say.

'Will you be at the session before breakfast tomorrow?'

'I don't know.' She scuffed her feet against the tarmac drive. 'I'm not at my sparkling best in the morning.'

'Feeling the cold dew between your toes is very enlivening. It's one of the best feelings in the world.'

What are the others, Ben Mahler? She smiled softly at him. 'I'll take your word for it.'

'Goodnight, Kate,' he said.

'Goodnight.'

He leaned forward and kissed her gently on the lips. It

136

was soft, tender, warm and it made the world tilt very slightly on its axis. Turning away from her, he strode towards the Priory, raising his hand in a wave without looking back. She followed his movement until he was out of sight, clutching the thorny stem of the white rose. As he disappeared from view, she put her fingers to her mouth and felt where his burning lips had been.

Chapter Fifteen

Solace *was* to be found in the form of alcoholic consumption, Jeffrey decided. They had abandoned Kevin's car at the golf club after they lost count of how many pints of Theakston's Old Peculier they had downed, and had shared a taxi home. It was very, very late and Kevin had been safely deposited at his house to relieve the possibly now demented Mrs Shaw and the beleaguered hamster. Jeffrey was feeling rather peculiar himself as the taxi headed towards Acacia Close. What was there for him at home? he thought self-pityingly. Two sleeping children. An empty bed. An absent wife and instead of the gorgeous Natalie, the grizzled features of Mrs Barrett, who was babysitting for him. He sank into a deep and remorseful depression. And it was all his fault.

What did it matter that Kerry's belly button was now mutilated beyond belief? Was it important in the scheme of things? Was it life-threatening? Possibly, when Kate found out. The thought sobered him briefly. He should apologise to Natalie for overreacting, and he should do it now. He sat bolt upright.

When he managed to locate it, Jeffrey tapped the driver's shoulder. 'Wait, wait,' he said. 'I don't want to go home. I want to go to Jessica's house. Now!'

The taxi driver pulled over to the side of the road and turned in his seat. 'Jessica's house?'

'Yes, yes!' *Why didn't I think of it before!*

'Can you be a little bit more specific?' the driver said, using all his Cockney charm. 'Do we have an address for Jessica?'

Jeffrey looked puzzled. 'An address?'

'It tends to help. Where does she live, mate?'

'Near me,' he said helpfully.

The driver sighed patiently. 'What about a name? Is she known as anything else other than Jessica?'

'She's my wife's friend. She organises the barn dances like piss-ups in breweries.'

'Does she now.' The driver picked up his radio and spoke to the control. 'Margaret,' he said to the woman on the other end, 'do you know a woman called Jessica that organises barn dances and lives near Acacia Close? She's a friend of . . .' He looked at Jeffrey for inspiration.

'My wife,' Jeffrey supplied.

'Who is?' the driver asked with the studied patience of a man who is used to dealing with inebriated passengers.

Jeffrey tried to look alert. 'Who is what?'

'*What* is your wife's name?'

'Kate Lewis, of course.' *Was the man an idiot?*

'Kate Lewis.' The driver rubbed his face. 'Of course.' He repeated the name into the radio. 'She's a friend of Kate Lewis.'

The line crackled and buzzed and it reverberated in Jeffrey's head.

'Jessica Hall,' the answer came amidst the static. 'She lives in Palfrey Avenue. Number twelve.'

'Cheers, Margaret,' he said. 'I owe you one.'

'No problem.'

The driver turned to Jeffrey. 'We're off to Jessica's house, mate,' he said. 'Are you sure you don't want to do a quick kerbside quiche while we're stopped?'

'No,' Jeffrey assured him. It wasn't his stomach that was sick, it was his heart. His stomach was like cast iron.

Number 12 was in complete darkness as they bumped into the drive. The driver hunched over his steering wheel. 'It don't look as though this Jessica's in,' he observed.

'She's in Florida,' Jeffrey said helpfully.

'Hang on – I thought you said ...'

'Someone else is in,' Jeffrey assured him. 'I know she is.'

'Are you sure?'

'Yes. Absolutely positive,' Jeffrey said expansively as he handed some notes to the driver. 'Thank you, thank you.'

The cabbie counted out his fare and gave Jeffrey his change. 'I've taken a two-quid tip, mate,' he said.

'Take more,' Jeffrey urged him. 'You deserve it.'

'I deserve a bloody medal!' The driver looked at him anxiously. 'Wouldn't you like me to wait for you?' he asked. 'You're not all that steady on your pins, old son.'

'I'm fine. Really.' Jeffrey tried to pat him jovially on the back and missed. 'I'm fine.'

'Well, I hope whoever's in has got plenty of strong black coffee,' he said. 'Go easy.' And the taxi drove out of the drive, its headlights swinging away, leaving Jeffrey alone in the pitch black of the night.

He unsteadily perused the darkened house. There were probably more signs of life on Mars. He tiptoed up to the door. It wouldn't do to ring the bell – it might startle her. Crouching down, he pushed open the letterbox. 'Natalie,' he whispered, trying not to wake the neighbours. 'It's me, Jeffrey. I've come to apologise.'

He waited. For an answer. For a light to be switched on. Nothing.

'Natalie!' he said more loudly. 'It's me, Jeffrey. Let me in.' He paused with his ear to the letterbox. 'I need to talk to you,' he added when there was still no response.

'Please!' He stood up and waited, beginning to feel the cold air pinching through his shirt and wondered vaguely what had happened to his jacket.

He rapped viciously at the letterbox and rang the bell for good measure. It echoed eerily through the hall. Cupping his hands round his mouth he shouted: 'NATALIE!'

A light went on in the house next door but Jessica's house remained steadfastly in darkness. Where could Natalie be? Perhaps her bedroom was round the back of the house.

Jeffrey tiptoed along the side of the house, using the wall to feel his way in the darkness and stopping to shush a noisy hedgehog that was snuffling haphazardly ahead of him. It was all going quite well until he fell over the dustbin. He stubbed his toe, kicking it over – the metal lid clattered noisily to the ground, scattering its contents in his wake and making a ginger tom who'd been having a nice nap on the top shriek with terror. Jeffrey joined in, sprawling full length on top of a rotting chicken carcass and assorted debris. He dragged himself to his feet, hiccuping, and began hopping down the path nursing his toe and trying to escape the tangle of Chinese takeaway cartons that had become attached to his trouser bottoms like sweet and sour limpets.

He emerged into a vast expanse of inky garden, dismayed to see that there was no hint of a light to welcome him. Jeffrey wiped his hands on his shirt, smearing chicken grease and mayonnaise down the front, before picking up a handful of gravel from the edge of the path, weighing it in his hand, drunkenly surveying the range of windows, looking for one that might suitably belong to a resident au pair. End one, frosted, bathroom. Middle one, small – study? Hadn't he and Kate been to a party here years ago? Another fiasco like the barn dance involving a poorly plotted murder mystery, if he remembered rightly. Jessica had been dressed to kill and her food was much the same. Did he go upstairs to the loo? He probably hadn't dared, lest he discovered he was the corpse. Other end, double window – spare bedroom? He'd give that one a go.

Jeffrey took aim. The window was showered in a flurry of small stones. 'Natalie,' he coo-eed. 'It's Jeff-ers!'

His heart sank when, after a few moments, her beautiful face still hadn't appeared at his chosen window. They never had this trouble in films, did they? One little pebble aimed at a window and the heroine never failed to appear with a cherubic beam and overflowing negligée.

Scooping up a bigger handful, he aimed less carefully, in an overhand throwing style not much practised since his premature departure from the cricket club, shortly after the premature birth of his son. The stones ricocheted against the window and, narrowly missing Jeffrey's head, fell in a noisy hail onto the patio at his feet.

'Natalie,' he hissed in the loudest stage whisper possible. 'Wake up!' The dead in several nearby cemeteries were waking, but still Natalie did not appear. Wrong window, Jeffrey concluded. He moved along the house and repeated the process. Small gravel, large gravel and even a bigger handful of gravel, but to no avail. Did this woman sleep for Australia?

He searched round the garden until he'd found a nice large rock. It was jagged and mossy, and supported a crop of sedum 'Autumn Joy'. It was the sort of rock that in a state of sobriety would scream at you DO NOT THROW AT WINDOWS! Jeffrey heaved it to shoulder height, did a couple of Geoff Capes-style warm-ups and launched it full tilt at the window he first thought of.

The sound of shattering glass set up a posse of barking dogs and the few remaining dead that had slept through the rest of the entertainment no doubt sat up and said, 'What was that dreadful noise?'

Jeffrey was perplexed. *Where was she?* He stood gaping, until he realised that the shrill noise wasn't coming from a ringing in his ears, but from the burglar alarm which, unlike Natalie, had awoken from its beauty sleep and was performing its specified task in life perfectly. Lights were starting to go on all over Palfrey Avenue – all except in number 12. It was time for a sharp exit. *Where could she be at this hour of the night?*

'Natalie,' he cried desperately, above the noise of the burglar alarm. 'I need you!'

Nothing. *Nada*. Naff all. Jeffrey's shoulders sagged. He set off for home at an unsteady jog, swerving out of the gravel drive after checking there were no keen Neighbourhood Watch vigilantes waiting to apprehend him. What had he been thinking of, coming round here in the dead of night, trying to win the affection of a woman ten years his junior? He couldn't believe he was doing this. Staid, sensible Jeffrey Lewis trudging the streets half-cut, half-dressed, half out of his mind with desire. What would Kate think?

The night was bitterly cold now and a breeze had struck up, wafting the smell of chicken grease and decaying food from the front of his filthy shirt to sting his nostrils, making his stomach heave majestically. Contrary to the taxi driver's warning, he didn't need a kerbside quiche. Instead, hanging onto a particularly obliging conifer with hands covered in grit, staid and sensible Jeffrey Lewis produced a perfect pavement pizza.

Chapter Sixteen

It was Wednesday morning at Northwood Priory.

'This morning,' Sam said cheerfully, 'Guy and I are going to demonstrate the T'ai Chi sword set.'

They hadn't even started and their smiles were in unison. Their matching red T-shirts picked out the long red tassels that fluttered in the breeze and hung from the long straight swords both men carried tucked to their sides, the highly polished metal glinting in the sun.

Guy took over. 'The sword represents the water element,' he explained. 'Light, quick, flowing. Working with the water sword helps us to gain an insight into the ever-changing flow of our lives. And remember, every person has an element to which they are particularly drawn – be it water, wood, fire, earth or metal.'

Kate wasn't a water element person, that was for sure. Wherever she was going, it wasn't with the planned flow of her life; on the contrary, she seemed to be paddling against it as fast as her legs would carry her, but still getting nowhere. She wasn't so much a sparkling, bubbling spring as pond sludge. This morning she felt weighted and leaden inside; she didn't make the early session before breakfast. It wasn't that she hadn't been awake. She had – for most of the night, a great deal of which had been spent staring at the flawless white rose which shone out pearlescent in the darkness from its new home in her toothbrush mug on the dressing table. The reason for languishing in bed was that she didn't want to appear too keen to be with Ben, although she had an overwhelming urge to rush out in her tracksuit and stand on wet grass with him in her bare feet. He probably had lovely long, straight toes, she thought, remembering the brief glimpses of his bare feet she'd already enjoyed.

Also she had phoned home before going to bed and the babysitter, Mrs Barrett from next door, had told her that Jeffrey was out and she didn't know when he would be back. *Out with whom? Out where with whom?* That had kept her mind buzzing until at least two o'clock. Jeffrey didn't go out on week nights. It was against his religion. He liked his eight hours' sleep and was always up bright and breezy so that he could be in work before anyone else. What was the saying about the mouse playing while the cat was away? Not Jeffrey, surely?

'My word,' Sonia said with longing, rousing Kate from her thoughts. 'Sam and Guy are a sight to gladden the heart of a bored housewife on a Wednesday morning.'

'I was reading their brochure in bed last night. It says that they're so highly trained in the mystic arts that they can actually see the energy flow, the Chi part of T'ai Chi, passing between people.'

'Really?' Sonia's interest perked up. 'Do you think I could train mine to go all pink and throbbing and shout "Take me, take me"?'

146

'I think it's probably doing that already,' Kate replied drily.

'Probably,' Sonia agreed good humouredly.

Kate wondered, with a brief tremor of alarm, what colour her own Chi was and who it was heading towards. As Sam and Guy began to swish their swords powerfully, she stole a glance at Ben. He seemed distracted this morning and had already spent a long time with his phone clamped firmly to his ear after breakfast. His welcoming smile had been distinctly half-hearted.

'Heavens above!' Sonia collapsed on the bench. 'Those two are just so gorgeous. Look at their muscly ankles.'

Kate said patiently, 'For the twentieth time, Son, we're supposed to be admiring their style and mastery of the ancient arts rather than ogling parts of their firm young anatomies. Anyway, you can't fall in love with your instructor. It's such a cliché.'

'Clichés are only clichés because they occur so often.' Which was quite philosophical considering the majority of Sonia's conversations revolved round Jaffa Cakes.

'So which one is the object of your very fickle affections today?'

'I think the jury's still out on that one,' Sonia said after a moment's consideration. 'But neither of them would need to douse himself in Hi-Karate aftershave before I'd want to chase him.' She cupped her chin in her hands. 'Just look at the angle of dangle on that.'

'I take it we're talking about the tassel on his sword?'

She let out a long shuddering sigh. 'Whatever.'

147

'I don't believe you.' Kate shook her head.

When Sam and Guy came to the end of their routine, Sonia turned to Kate. 'Hey, where did you disappear to last night?' she asked. 'I got up to get a drink of water and the light wasn't on in your room.'

Kate could feel herself flushing. 'I went for a walk.'

'On your own?'

'No,' she said hesitantly, 'with Ben.'

'With Ben?' Sonia raised her eyebrows.

'It was perfectly innocent,' Kate insisted. 'He felt sorry for me because you'd abandoned me.'

'Did he try it on?'

'Of course he didn't.' Her fingers went guiltily to her lips.

Narrowing her eyes, her friend scrutinised her closely. 'Are you sure?'

'Of course I'm sure!' She felt her skin change from scarlet to puce.

Sonia shook her head, bemused. 'I don't know what's wrong with men these days,' she said.

Kate didn't know what was wrong with herself these days! She had desperately wanted Ben to kiss her and had desperately wanted him to stop when he did. It felt too right, too good, too inevitable. Her mind was whirling like the waltzer in a fairground and her stomach was doing pretty much the same. She wondered what her Chi would think of that.

'Now then,' Sam said, clapping his hands to get their attention, 'it's your turn to work with the swords. Be very careful with them. These are training swords, so they aren't sharp. Work together and you won't hurt yourself.'

Which was a shame, Kate thought, because at this moment she'd like nothing better than to throw herself on one.

Ben was watching Kate from under the shade of the tree. Occasionally, he forced himself to look up, peering through the vivid green branches to the cornflower-blue sky so that he could pretend he wasn't. There was a gentle breeze, breaking up the humidity of the past few days and he was glad of the relief. His palms had been sweating far too much since Sunday for his liking. He hoped he looked relaxed; he felt anything but. His stomach was groaning and gurgling and it wasn't just the fact that he had opted to miss lunch. He hadn't wanted to sit near Kate – no, that was wrong. He had *desperately* wanted to sit near Kate. He wanted to sit next to her feeling the electricity from her body tingling over him, the scent of her skin delighting him. He wanted to watch her nose wrinkle when she laughed, her fingers toying with her fork . . .

Ben sighed to himself. This was wrong. She was someone else's wife – Jeffrey's. That's why he was sitting alone under a tree, starving to death and wondering how to stop himself from falling over the precipice of unrequited love. If it wasn't too late already. If he had any sense he would leave the course, go home and go back to work – walk away while he still had his sanity, if not his heart, intact. The lure of the T'ai Chi wasn't so great that it should keep

149

him here. Why couldn't he have fallen for one of the million or so mini-skirted women who minced past his offices every day in teetering high heels, their wiggling bottoms saying: 'I'm available! Come and get me!' Why a wife and the mother of two children, for pity's sake?

If he couldn't bring himself to leave, he'd have to try other tactics to distract himself. He punched a number into his phone and jammed it to his ear.

'Mahler Bell Associates.'

'It's Ben,' he said without preamble. 'Can you put me through to Fiona, please.'

'Sure.' The holding music started. A tinny version of 'I Got You, Babe'. Grief, he would have to get that changed, it was terrible.

'Fiona here,' a chirpy voice said after a moment's wait. 'Hi, Ben. What can I do for you?'

'Fi, is the Bradley package sewn up?'

'Just about,' she answered.

'How just about?'

'It needs a few bits and pieces finishing off.'

'Like what?'

'Photos marking up. A bit of basic donkey work.'

'Could you do it this afternoon?'

'Yeees,' she said hesitantly. 'You know they don't need it until the end of the month. There's no sweat. I thought you were supposed to be on holiday.'

'I am.'

'So where's the fire?'

In my heart! 'I'm just feeling edgy about it.'

'Why? They've been clients for years. They'll love it. They've loved everything else we've done.'

'Can you do me a huge favour?'

'How huge?' she said suspiciously.

'Can you bring it out here for me to have a look at tonight?'

'*What?*' Ben could imagine her startled face and smiled to himself. 'You're in the middle of nowhere!'

'I'm just outside High Wycombe.'

'Exactly.'

'There is life beyond Sloane Square, Fi,' he said mildly.

'Yes, but it's very rudimentary! Does it have wine bars?'

'We could find out,' he offered.

'It's probably all *real* pubs, serving *real* ale and bunches of hops hanging round the bar,' she whined.

'Be a pal,' he pleaded.

'Don't tell me,' she said. 'You're desperate for my body and can't think of any other way of luring me into your evil clutches.'

'Something like that.'

'I don't know . . .'

'You never used to play so hard to get,' he teased.

'It's my new regime.' He could hear her drag deeply on her cigarette. 'I've resolved not to be a pushover any more . . . except on days with a D in them.'

Ben laughed. 'I knew you'd say yes.'

Fiona sighed resignedly. 'What time do you want me?'

'Seven-thirty?'

'And how the hell am I supposed to find this place without a tour guide?'

'I'll fax you a map.'

'Has technology reached such far-flung places?'

'Yes, and they stopped shoving children up chimneys too.'

Fiona grunted. 'Well, if I'm not there by eight, send out a search party. I'm probably being eaten by some restless natives.'

'You're a pal,' he said.

'And you're a pain!' The phone went dead.

Ben grinned to himself. Fiona could refuse him nothing.

Chapter Seventeen

The rasping sound in his head, Jeffrey realised, was the sound of butter being scraped over toast. Forcing himself from the bed, he picked his way through the trail of filthy clothes that lay scattered on the floor and went into the en suite bathroom. He gawped at the face which stared back at him from the mirror there with something approaching horror. His puffy eyes were barely discernible in his green blotchy face. The last time he had seen something so hideous was in Michael Jackson's 'Thriller' video, which he had banned the children from watching as he thought it was too scary. Now he was going to have to face them looking equally terrifying over breakfast. He couldn't remember ever having been in such a state before. After splashing cold water on his shell-shocked face, he ran his toothbrush round the birdcage of his mouth and belted his dressing gown tightly round him. Blindly, he followed the scraping sound to the kitchen.

It was Natalie who was buttering the toast. This stopped Jeffrey in his tracks. A rush of relief hit him harder than the splash of cold water just had, and he realised how much he had wanted to see her standing casually in his distressed kitchen once again. Kerry was sitting at the table spooning Crunchy Nut Cornflakes forlornly into her mouth. Her eyes were red and blotchy and her cheeks puffed and pale. They both looked sheepishly at him.

Natalie leaned against the work surface, clutching a J-cloth. 'I'm sorry,' she said, looking downcast.

He couldn't respond. His throat was as firmly stoppered as a port decanter.

'Would you like some muesli?' Natalie flicked the J-cloth at Kerry, indicating that she should pull out his chair. His daughter scrambled to oblige.

'Yes,' Jeffrey said, sounding somewhat strangulated, and allowed himself to be seated. A bowl of muesli and a cup of steaming hot fresh coffee were placed gingerly in front of him. It was the last thing he wanted, but he didn't dare say so.

'It doesn't hurt any more, Daddy,' Kerry said hesitantly.

Jeffrey sighed. 'Let's have a look.'

She untucked her school blouse from her skirt and proffered her non-existent tummy across the breakfast table. Her belly button was livid red and swollen around a tiny gold ring that jutted out. He couldn't believe he was even permitting this thought to traverse his mind, but he thought it looked sweet in an un-twelve-year-old sort of way.

Kerry fingered it tentatively, a look of pride on her emotionally wasted face. 'It stings a bit though.'

'Perhaps that will remind you what a very silly thing it was to do,' he said as sternly as he could manage, given the fact that he, too, had done a very silly thing. At least she had the foolishness of youth on her side.

154

'Yes, Daddy.' She tucked her blouse in carefully, only wincing once.

Jeffrey turned to Joe. 'Have you had any of your body pierced?'

Joe shook his head vigorously, a look of terror on his face. *Sensible boy. His father's son.* Or, at least, his father *used* to be sensible.

'Come on, you two,' Natalie ordered. 'You'll be late for school.'

'Daddy's late for work,' Joe said brightly.

'I don't think Daddy's very well,' Natalie said and their eyes met across the table.

Jeffrey hung his head and tried to ignore the sledgehammer that was pounding the inside of his skull. The children came and kissed him and he gave Kerry a special hug. 'Bye bye, darlings,' he said miserably. 'Have a good day.'

When the children's chatter had ceased and the front door closed, Natalie turned to him. 'Are you okay?'

'No,' he said, pushing his untouched muesli away.

She picked up two Alka Seltzer from the work surface and poured a glass of water. The plink-plink-fizz reverberated in his brain. Natalie sat down next to him and handed him the glass. 'I heard you come in at one o'clock this morning,' she said by way of explanation.

'Oh?'

'Mrs Barrett phoned me at about eleven o'clock. She was worried that you weren't home, so I came over and spent the night here.'

Jeffrey looked up sharply.

'In the spare room.'

Jeffrey closed his eyes and the insides of his lids whizzed psychedelic patterns in front of them.

'I stayed out of your way in case you were still mad at me.' She wrinkled her nose.

She was here all the time! All the time, she was here!

'Are you?' she asked when he didn't speak. How could he? Words were failing him.

'What?'

'Still mad?'

Mad? Insane, certifiable, out of his mind, demented, off his trolley, totally ga-ga? Yes.

'No,' he said, hanging his head further still. 'I'm not mad at you.'

'Shall I phone in work for you,' Natalie suggested, 'and tell them you're sick?'

'Yes, please,' Jeffrey said pathetically. He didn't think he was up to lying for himself.

Natalie pushed away from the table. She was wearing cut-off denim shorts and her smooth slender legs were tanned to a gorgeous shade of hazelnut brown. His heart and his stomach gave a synchronised lurch. She put the kitchen wall-phone to her ear and smiled at him sympathetically. Or it could have been pityingly.

'Gidday,' she said, brightly. 'I'm phoning for Jeffrey Lewis. He's not going to be in work today. He has a stomach disorder.'

A brain disorder more like.

156

'No, this isn't his wife,' he heard Natalie continue. 'His wife's away. This is the au pair. Okay. Bye.'

Well, that would ensure him several weeks' worth of ribald comments when he got back to work. Still, he had no one to blame but himself.

Natalie regarded him closely. 'You don't look so hot.'

Never in his life had he felt so intrinsically lukewarm.

'I have to go back to Jessica's house,' Natalie said. 'One of the neighbours called this morning. Someone tried to break into the house last night and smashed a window. They've arranged a glazier.'

A shard of reality splintered painfully in Jeffrey's brain and he felt the blood drain from his face.

Natalie frowned at him. 'Will you be okay? I'll come straight back.'

'It was me,' he said flatly.

'What?'

'It was me who smashed the window.'

'You?' Natalie started to laugh. It was a light tinkling sound – rather too reminiscent of the shattering of glass. '*You?*'

'Me.'

She put her hands to her mouth. 'I'm sorry, I shouldn't laugh.'

'Yes, you should,' Jeffrey said morosely. 'I deserve to be an object of derision.'

Natalie giggled again. 'What were you thinking of?'

He glanced up at her. 'I was thinking of apologising to you.'

157

'But I was here.'

'I'm fully aware of that fact now,' Jeffrey said tightly.

'Oh, Jeffers,' she said, progressing to an unrestrained guffaw.

He sat there, humiliation burning into his cheeks. The last time he had felt as shamefaced as this was when he was ten and was caught in the playground with his hand up Janet Eccleston's skirt.

'Of course, I'll pay for the damage,' Jeffrey said.

'I'll bring you the bill,' Natalie chuckled.

'Thank you. I'm not proud of myself, you know.'

'Going wild once in a while isn't something to be ashamed of, Jeffers. Maybe you should do it more often, then it wouldn't be such a shock to the system. That's my philosophy on life.'

'I'm not sure that it's mine,' he mumbled.

She came over and kissed Jeffrey on the forehead. 'You are very sweet,' she said.

Sweet?

'You go and get yourself spruced up while I'm away,' she instructed. 'You can't waste this wonderful day moping round the house with a hangover. I'll be back soon.'

When she did return – with a bill for £129.99 from The Smashing Glazing Company – Jeffrey had washed, scrubbed and brushed himself back into some feeling of normality. He was sitting at the kitchen table, ploughing his way through the strongest black coffee he could make in the largest mug he had been able to find, filled with remorse and muesli.

Natalie threw her backpack on the floor, turned a chair round and sat astride it, scrutinising him intensely. As his mother would have said, her legs went all the way up to the top. Jeffrey closed his eyes.

'You're looking very uptight again, Jeffers,' she noted.

He glanced up at her. 'Oh,' he said, pouring some more sludge down his throat in the hope that it would at some point get his caffeine receptors to respond.

'I rather liked you when you were a wild thing.'

Jeffrey's heart sank. She was teasing him again.

'Does Kate like the clothes you wear?'

'Kate?' He mulled it over briefly. 'She's never said. But then she buys most of them, so I suppose she must.'

'I hope you don't mind me being upfront, Jeffers,' she said earnestly.

Could you be anything else?

'. . . but I think you need to get a bit more chill in your dressing.'

'Chill?' He rolled the word round his mouth. 'Chill? You mean short-sleeved shirts?'

'I think we may have a long way to go.' She folded her arms across the top of the chair and leaned her chin on them. Her smile was guileless and, for a moment, she looked little older than his daughter. *What a terrifying thought!*

'I have to go into Milton Keynes to buy some new panties.'

Did I need to know that? Jeffrey was aware of how easily his brow perspired these days.

'Why don't you come with me and I'll give you a revamp.'

Jeffrey looked wary, which hid the fact that inside, his intestines were recoiling in horror. 'I'm not sure if my red corpuscles are up to revamping today.'

'It doesn't have to be anything major, just a little titivation,' she promised.

He wasn't sure if his red corpuscles were up to Natalie's titivation either. 'Perhaps another day.'

'There may not be another day, Jeffers. Trust me.'

'I've got a headache,' he complained.

'Then let's go and give your credit card some ache,' she suggested. 'The body can only cope with one type of pain at once. Believe me – your headache will completely vanish.'

Natalie tugged at his hand. 'Marks & Spencer is for wimps,' she said in a tone that dared him to argue.

But I like Marks & Spencer. It's a sensible shop for a sensible man.

'It's an accountants' shop,' she said. 'And what are we today?'

He looked at her blankly.

'Not an accountant at all,' she supplied. She frowned theatrically. 'I have seen the white Y-fronts in the washing basket, Jeffrey. They are not cool.'

'No,' he agreed. Kate had said so many times. It's just

that they were comfortable. They held him securely. He had never liked the feeling of flapping around in the breeze.

'White shirts are out too!'

'White shirts are out,' he echoed uncertainly.

Natalie dragged him across the concourse and away from the lure of good quality clothing at reasonable prices.

It appeared that citrus-coloured shirts were in. Lime green, orange and sunshine yellow. One or two of them had patterns. Jeffrey was still unsure. What might look good on Bondi Beach was sure to raise eyebrows at Hills & Hopeland. It was definitely a white shirt company. Hadn't he himself raised the odd follicle when one of the trainees had appeared in anything other than 'acceptable' colours – i.e., white? Natalie assured him that the bold colours flattered his skin and made him look less drained. It was a shame the same couldn't be said for his bank account.

He had escaped briefly for a caffeine recharge, while the aforementioned panties were chosen, and despite his complaints and his uncertainty that lime green really was 'his thing', he had enjoyed their day immensely. Natalie was fun to be with. She flitted round the shops like an impatient butterfly, flinging clothes around with casual disregard for the assistants' stony glares. She had posed in ridiculous hats and had made him do the same and had flung extortionately expensive scarves round her slender young neck. She had, dare he say it, made shopping a joy.

The last stop was the hairdresser's – the most exclusive in Milton Keynes, of course. A palace of natural wood, muted tones and soft jazz. Natalie led him in with the malicious glee of a *tricoteuse* – one of those old Frenchwomen who used to sit and knit as they watched someone go to Madame Guillotine. He liked his hair. It had been this style for years. He'd grown rather attached to it. Or rather, it had grown attached to him. Most of it.

He was to be at the mercy of Mark, the Ultimate Style Director – hairdressing's answer to God. And, not surprisingly, twice the price of any other mere crimper.

'Do your worst!' Natalie instructed, sitting down in the next seat and studying him intently.

Jeffrey tried hard not to look at the large amount of blond hair – his precious, thinning hair – that appeared to be amassing on the floor.

Mark did his worst. Once Jeffrey had got over the shock of feeling the wind blowing round his ears, he had to agree it wasn't half bad. He now sported one of those cropped affairs favoured by boy bands which gave him a certain rakish charm – even though he said it himself. Kerry would be delighted. He looked fearfully in the mirror and wondered what Kate would think. She'd probably give it a Paul Daniels. *How do you like it? Not a lot.*

Natalie was hyper – even more so than normal. Clearly pleased that the proposed revamp had gone according to plan, she clutched her small bag of new smalls while he was laden down with designer carriers, and sang all the way back to the car, which had a whole minute left to run on the parking ticket.

As he turned to manoeuvre the car out of the tight

space, she took his hand and he was lucky not to shoot back into the unsuspecting Metro behind them. She spread her fingers, interlacing them slowly with his and squeezed lightly. 'It's been a great day, Jeffers,' she said with a happy sigh.

'Yes,' he said, aware of his blood pumping against the warmth of her palm. Their eyes met and he felt his Adam's apple bob up and down.

'I'll remember it for a long time.'

'I will too,' he managed. 'Thanks.'

'I've bought you a little present for being such a poppet.'

A poppet? 'You shouldn't have.'

'Well, I did.' She produced a small bag.

'Shall I open it now?'

'I think so.'

He rummaged in the small carrier bag and pulled out a tissue-wrapped parcel. It contained two pairs of hipster-type briefs in soft clingy material with Calvin Klein's moniker emblazoned on the waistband. They were pale blue with navy over-stitching, and sported three little blue tortoiseshell buttons down the front. Jeffrey gulped.

'You should look good in them.' She smiled seductively.

He tugged at the neck of his shirt. *Is it hot in here, or is it me?*

'They'll make your bum look cute.'

'Thank you,' he said rather breathlessly, not entirely sure whether a cute bottom was up there on his list of 'must-haves'.

Natalie's eyebrows twitched in a faintly amused fashion. 'No sweat.'

But there was sweat. On his top lip, on his newly exposed brow and under his clammy arms. Returning the briefs to the safety of their carrier bag, he swung out of the car park on auto pilot. Why did she make him feel like this? There was a euphoria throbbing in his body that he didn't normally experience from excessive retail purchases. Was this the sort of thing people felt the urge to discuss on *Oprah*? It was an addictive feeling and he knew he wanted more.

He still had his headache though. Contrary to Natalie's prediction it hadn't completely vanished. The only thing that had completely vanished was an awful lot of money.

Chapter Eighteen

'That's it for today,' Sam said brightly. 'Let's bow out.'

Right fist, left palm. *I have no weapons. I mean you no harm.*

The problem with having no weapons, Ben decided, was that it left you defenceless in the face of a surprise attack. He looked longingly in the direction of his attacker who was inoffensively tucking her hair behind her ear.

They had spent the afternoon working with the sabre, a heavy, curving weapon representing the metal element. Blunt, hard, unyielding, cutting through. It wasn't his favourite weapon, it was too brutal. He much preferred the fluid flexibility of the water sword. Still, that was what he was going to have to be – blunt, hard, unyielding. For both of their sakes. If he continued to be soft and malleable, he would be lost.

Ben had been avoiding Kate all day and it was clearly bothering her. At times he had felt her eyes boring into his back and he had longed to turn round and smile at her. Now she was hovering on the edge of the group, fiddling with her tube of suntan cream and keeping one eye on him. Heaven knows, he wanted to be with her, but sometimes you have to be cruel to be kind. At the end of the day, this would be the painless route. It's just that being a heartless bastard didn't come easy.

He acknowledged her briefly as he walked past, quickening his pace.

'Hi,' she said, catching up with him. 'You've been quiet today.'

'Just preoccupied,' he said, which wasn't exactly a lie. He glanced unnecessarily at his watch. 'I've got to go.' *Chop her off at the knees with your sabre, Ben old boy.*

'Will we see you at dinner?'

'I'm going out tonight.' *Blunt.*

She stopped walking and stared at him. He avoided her penetrating eyes. 'Business,' he shrugged. *Hard.*

'Oh.'

He couldn't bear the hurt look on her face.

'Perhaps we'll see you in the bar for a drink afterwards.'

'I don't know.' His tone was too crisp, he knew that. 'I may be late.' *Unyielding.*

'Have a nice time,' she said, and he could tell that he had wounded her.

'You too.'

Fiona was late. But then she usually was. Ben was punctuality itself, and therefore by the time she did roll up to the door of Northwood Priory, he was just about ready to shred his fingernails. It was one of the many differences between them, not least their ages. She had been a tender twenty-six years old when he had first employed her two years ago. And she hadn't aged at all

166

since then, not emotionally, anyway. He knew she was consistently late because she was so disorganised and had an in-built disregard for Greenwich Mean Time, but he couldn't help but worry about her too. There was always the chance that she had got lost or had an accident. This was beyond the reach of the London Underground and, as such, uncharted territory for her.

It was a relief when her battered Peugeot smoked and clattered its way up the drive. Ben pushed himself away from the wall that he had been trying to lean casually against, when every fibre of his being wanted to rush into the dining room and consume soggy shepherd's pie with Kate.

Fiona flung her door open and he gave her a wry look.

'Sorry, Bens,' she said. 'Took a bit of a circuitous route. I can't cope with all these country lanes. All the bloody trees look the same.'

'Well, they're all green, I suppose.'

'Tell me about it,' she dragged on her cigarette. 'Can you get hay fever from trees? My nose has been running since I came off the motorway.'

'It's probably not used to breathing clean air.'

'True,' she said.

'Or is it some other substance that's irritating your nasal passages?'

'Don't turn into my maiden aunt so soon, Ben-Ben,' she scolded with a pouting lip.

'I worry about you.'

'A girl's got to have some fun.'

'Dabbling with illegal substances isn't fun, Fi. It's dangerous.'

'So is heading this far out of London,' she countered.

He smiled, defeated by lack of reason once again. 'Park up,' he instructed. 'We'll go in my car.'

'Don't be such a snob!' She patted the passenger seat. 'Get in – you won't catch anything. I've got to drive home anyway, so you might as well enjoy a drink. From the miserable expression on your face, you could do with one.'

Ben slid into Fi's car and screwed his nose up. 'We pay you a huge salary and you've just had a fat bonus cheque, can't you spend some of it on a decent set of wheels?' He poked his finger into a hole in the seat where foam padding peeped through. 'I don't know why you insist on driving this festering heap.'

Fiona patted the dashboard. 'Old Faithful,' she said with pride. 'It never lets me down. Not like some men I could mention.' She gave him a knowing look. 'I look after *it*. *It* looks after me.'

'But you don't look after it.'

'It's like my houseplants,' she assured him. 'It thrives on neglect.'

'And what about you? Do you thrive on neglect?'

'I'll try to do better, Aunty Ben,' she teased. 'Where are we going?'

She put the old car into gear and Ben pointed the way out of the Priory. 'There's a little pub down the road I thought we could try.'

'Isn't there a Chez Nico anywhere?'

168

'Now who's being a snob? Enjoy the local colour.'

'The local colour seems to be beige.'

Fiona was right, the pub was a bit beige. Designer old-fashioned with nicotine effect paintwork and, as she pointed out with her silk-wrapped nails, the predicted bunches of hops around the bar. Hard going for a girl who inhabited a world of Prada handbags and balsamic vinegar. The menu made a stoic attempt at modernity and Fi deigned to order a goat's cheese salad.

Sitting down, she slung her briefcase across her knees, looking out of place in her strappy Jimmy Choo kitten heels and shocking pink Versace suit. 'We might as well get this out of the way while we wait for the food,' she said, swishing the salt and pepper pots to one side. 'Da, da!' She opened a folder on the table with a flourish. 'The Bradley account!' Fiona produced a cigarette and lit it. 'Read it and weep,' she instructed.

Ben turned the folder round to face him and scanned it briefly. 'It's great,' he said.

She narrowed her eyes through her cigarette smoke. 'You've hardly glanced at it,' she said accusingly. 'Have a proper look!'

'I have,' Ben said defensively. 'And I've fully absorbed it.'

'Cursory is the word that springs to mind.' Fiona blew out a stream of smoke.

'It's great,' he repeated. 'You've done an excellent job.'

Fiona leaned forward suspiciously. 'Okay, what's wrong with it?'

'Nothing.' Ben sat back. 'I said it was great. Twice.'

'So why did you say it like that?'

'Like what?'

'*It's great.*' Fi did a Marvin the Paranoid Android voice. 'It sounds like the enthusiasm bypass was a total success.'

'It is great,' he reiterated. 'Wonderful. Marvellous. Fantastic. You're the best account manager in Mahler Bell.'

'Keep going,' Fiona said when he stopped.

Ben laughed.

'That's better,' she said. A look of concern wrinkled her brow. 'You seem so uptight. I thought this T'ai Chi lark was supposed to be relaxing.'

'It is,' he answered, sounding more tetchy than he wanted to. 'I've just got a few things on my mind.'

'Is that why you've dragged me halfway to the end of the universe, to pretend to be interested in the Bradley account? And why, stunning as it is, my brilliant peach of a presentation has failed to raise even the glimmer of a smile?'

Ben's smile glimmered. 'Sorry.'

'Problems?' she asked sympathetically.

Ben studied the table, picking absently at the whorls notched into the pine. 'You could say.'

'Ben "nothing-is-a-problem" Mahler has got problems?' Fiona looked incredulous. 'Well, it can't be your job,' she reasoned, 'the agency is going great guns. It can't be money either, because you could actually lend the Sultan of Brunei a few quid if he was ever strapped for cash.' She regarded him through the wispy smoke of her cigarette. 'So it must be an affair of the heart.'

'Yes, thank you for that brilliant deduction, Ms Poirot,' Ben said with a huff.

'What's the problem?' Fi looked puzzled. 'You're young, free and single.' She gave him a guarded smile. 'And not bad-looking.'

'Thanks.' He folded his arms.

'So?'

'She isn't.'

'Ah!'

The food arrived and Fiona prodded hers tentatively as if she had uncovered an unexploded bomb. 'Emotional baggage?' she queried.

Ben rubbed his hands over his eyes. 'A full matching set.' The teriyaki salmon that had been placed in front of him had suddenly lost its appeal. His stomach had gone into involuntary shutdown. No one had ever put him off his food before. 'One very sturdy suitcase of a husband and two lovely little holdalls.'

'Fuck!' Fiona breathed.

'Quite.'

'How far has it gone?'

'It hasn't gone anywhere.'

'So what's the problem?'

'I want it to.'

'Oh, Ben.'

'I know!' He held his hands up. 'You don't need to "Oh, Ben" me.'

'I thought I was supposed to be the emotional mess?'

'I'm just trying to keep you company,' he said sulkily.

'Do you want to talk about it?'

'There's nothing much to say.'

They both dollied their food round their plates, Fiona still regarding her goat's cheese suspiciously, until they had made such a mess it looked like they had eaten some.

Fiona edged her plate away. 'Do you want another drink?'

Ben shook his head.

'So, what now?' Fiona asked. 'We've pretended to look at the work I trailed all the way out here with for no good reason, we've done the food, neither of us want another drink – although I would recommend, from vast personal experience, that you get completely and utterly slaughtered.'

'It's not my way,' he said. 'You of all people should know that.' Ben pushed away from the table. 'I think we'd better leave.'

'We could go back to your place and have a sociable shag,' she said with forced lightness. 'I don't have to go home tonight.'

Ben looked at her sadly.

'Don't tell me,' she laughed bitterly. 'Thanks, but no thanks.'

'Oh, Fi.' He took her hand and squeezed it firmly.

'It was a stupid suggestion,' she said, pulling her hand away and grabbing her briefcase. 'I couldn't possibly stay out here, the atmosphere is too rarefied. I need to feel the drag of carbon monoxide in my lungs. Let's go and get Old Faithful revved up.'

* * *

172

Old Faithful was being mutinous. A string of expletives came from Fiona as the engine caught, chugged a bit and then faded to an abrupt nothing. 'Fucking car,' she shouted, banging her hand violently on the dashboard. 'You faithless bastard! What have I ever done to you?' She stamped her feet on the pedals and rammed the gearstick back and forth.

Then, sagging with resignation, she turned to Ben. 'I don't think it's going to start,' she said quietly. There were tears in her eyes and he wanted to hold her, but it didn't seem an appropriate time.

'Open the bonnet,' he instructed. 'Let me have a look at it.'

She turned on him. 'And what do you know about bloody cars?'

'Nothing,' he admitted helplessly.

Fiona sniffed. 'It's probably the thingamagig that's gone.' A tear rolled down her cheek. 'It's a very common fault. Do you think there's a garage open round here?'

'I think it's highly unlikely,' he told her.

Fiona looked like she was going to cry in earnest. 'Look,' he took her hand, 'why don't we go back into the pub and get the number of a taxi firm? You can take my car back to town for the rest of the week and I'll arrange to get Old Faithful fixed.' He tried to keep the irony out of his voice. 'Then you can come back on Saturday when the course ends and pick me up.'

'I might be busy,' Fiona sniffled.

He forced her to look at him. 'Doing what?'

'I don't know,' she said. 'I need time to think of something.'

'The course finishes mid-morning. We can spend the afternoon together,' he cajoled. 'I'll take you to Hampstead and you can pose.'

'You're a bastard, Ben Mahler.' Fiona wiped her nose. 'I hate you as much as I hate this car.'

'I know,' he said. 'Come on. Let's go and ring for a taxi.'

The taxi dropped them at the Priory. Ben paid the fare and they wandered over to his car in silence.

'Here.' He handed over his keys to Fi. 'You can play with my new toy until Saturday,' he said. 'Will that cheer you up?'

'It might do,' she said, but she sounded doubtful. 'What about Old Faithful?'

'Against my better judgement to send it to the knacker's yard, I'll arrange to have it towed in tomorrow and fixed.'

Fiona smiled reluctantly. 'You're quite sweet, really,' she said. 'For a bastard.'

'I'm not a bastard, just because I won't sleep with you.'

'I know.' Fiona sighed wearily.

'I'll phone you and let you know about the car. We can arrange a time for you to collect me then. Is that okay?'

'Fine,' she said.

'Drive carefully!'

'Do you want to check it for dents before I leave?'

'No. I trust you.'

'Yeah, and I trust you, Ben Mahler. About as far as I can throw you.' She got in the car.

'I mean it,' Ben said. 'Be careful.'

'I'll see you Saturday,' she called out, crunched the car into gear and roared off into the night.

Ben smiled to himself as he watched her leave. He was fond of Fi. Very. In some ways he loved her, but he wasn't in love with her. It would be easier if he was. She was a good friend to him, but then perhaps that was the worst thing you could say to a woman who wanted more from you.

The night was clear, the sky filled with stars and the air sharp against his cheeks after the fuggy warmth of the pub.

Ben glanced at his watch. It was late, but he might still catch the rest of the class in the bar. Should he go for a drink? Would Kate still be there? He checked her room, but it was in darkness. Perhaps she had already gone to bed. He should do the same. It was the safe and sensible thing to do. And he had never felt less safe or sensible in his life.

Chapter Nineteen

Sonia was smoking. Heavily. But not quite as heavily as she was drinking.

'Sonia,' Kate warned. 'Don't you think you've had enough?'

The bar at the Priory was called 'The Cloisters' but it was one area where the muted monastery theme had gone awry and had been replaced by a frenzy of orange chairs and the same shade of carpet. In one corner an out-of-tune piano sat unplayed, in another the four elderly ladies from *Fun with Fur Fabric* snoozed over empty glasses that had, some time earlier, contained Harvey's Bristol Cream sherry. It was how Kate had always imagined the waiting room to Hell would be.

'Don't nag me,' her friend objected. 'I've hardly had a fag all week and I haven't lost an ounce.'

'I don't think there are that many calories in cigarettes, Sonia.'

'There must be,' she retorted, 'because I hardly eat a thing. Very little else passes my lips, ho ho.' She took another swallow of wine and tucked into her third bag of salt and vinegar crisps. 'See, I only have to inhale near a chocolate eclair and that's two inches on my hips. I have a morbidly slow metabolism.'

Sonia leaned forward unsteadily. 'I'm going to let you into a little secret,' she said.

'Oh grief, I do wish you wouldn't,' Kate said.

Sonia lowered her voice until only those living in the surrounding three counties could hear her. 'I am going to use all my feminine wiles to lure sexy Sam into my bed tonight.' She gave Kate a gleeful confirming nod. 'Then I'm going to have my wicked way with him until dawn.'

'This is not a good idea, Sonia,' Kate advised. 'In fact, it's one of the worst ideas you've ever had.'

'I have my heart set on it.'

'It's not your heart I'm worried about. There are other parts of your anatomy that are in far more immediate danger. Please don't do this!'

'I want some romance in my life, Katie,' Sonia said firmly. 'In all the telephone conversations I've had with Kevin this week, not once has he said he loves me. Where has all the passion gone?' she asked, before she threw the rest of her wine down her throat.

'An affair is never the answer,' Kate cautioned.

'And what is?' Sonia snapped. 'I'm bloody sure that a week's T'ai Chi in monastic splendour isn't.' She rounded on her friend. 'Have you found the answer to your problems yet?'

'No,' Kate admitted quietly. In fact, she was now more confused than she had been when she arrived. She had missed Ben desperately tonight. Every time the bar door opened – and it wasn't that often – she had turned round to see whether it was him. One night without his presence and she was ragged with nerves. What was she going to be like at the end of the week, when the course was over and there was no chance of her ever seeing him walk through a door again? Even the thought of it was unbearable. And she still couldn't find the sodding wherewithal to soar like a crane! Everyone else was flying majestically over the lush carpet of rolling hills and fields, and she was still firmly attached by feet of clay to the croquet lawn.

'I've tried everything I can think of to get Kevin interested,' Sonia said morosely, 'with the exception of prancing round the bedroom naked with a rose stuck up my bum, and nothing does the trick. Now I just want to have some fun and damn the consequences.' She slammed her empty wine glass down on the table, jolting awake the *Fun with Fur Fabric* quartet. 'I need a proper drink!'

A proper drink, it would seem, was half a bottle of sambuca purchased from the barman, who had been obliged to polish an inch of dust from the label just to locate it. Sambuca, it appeared, was not a strong favourite at Northwood Priory. Sonia brought it back to the table and poured them each a measure of the lethal clear liquid. Then she flicked her cigarette lighter over the glasses and with an exuberant rush of pale blue flame, the sambuca set itself on fire.

'Sonia!' Kate leapt back.

'I'm practising my fire element, which has been sadly neglected this week.'

Kate laughed and they blew the flames out together. Kate puckered her lips as she tasted the aniseed flavour strong and warming in the back of her throat; Sonia swallowed hers in one. She set her glass down with a faint watering of her eyes. 'Another?' she croaked.

'Hang on – I've hardly started this one.'

'You always were a slow drinker.'

Sonia was downing her fourth glass by the time Kate had finished her first. There would be tears in the morning, as sure as hangovers are hangovers.

'You are being too boring for words, Kate Lewis,' Sonia said drunkenly. 'When have you ever done anything daring?'

When indeed?

'Watch this,' Sonia invited. She took a mouthful of sambuca, gargled it noisily and then spat it out in a steady stream while holding her cigarette lighter under it. Tongues of flame shot across the table, licking fiercely at the droplets that had splashed on its surface.

'Shit!' Kate said, unsure whether to be shocked or admiring. As party tricks go it was quite a show-stopper.

Sonia giggled uproariously. The *Fun with Fur Fabric* Four, now fully awake, decided that *Fun with Flame-throwers* was too much for them and, clutching their handbags to their chests, they left hurriedly. Thank God the barman's back had been turned, thought Kate.

'Sonia,' she hissed. 'We've come here for spiritual enlightenment, in case you've forgotten. I don't think a sambuca-spitting contest is quite what we need.'

'Don't you believe it,' Sonia slurred. 'I've had more spiritual enlightenment through the bottom of a flaming glass,' Sonia stabbed a drunken finger, 'than you've had hot dinners.'

'Or hot alcohol.'

'Loosen up, Katie.' Sonia's eyes were beginning to point in different directions.

Sam chose that moment to enter the bar, grinning all over his cherubic face. Kate prayed he would sit somewhere else, but Sonia saw him and lurched at the poor man, pulling him down to the seat next to her.

'Some sambuca, Sam?' Sonia lisped.

'Well . . .'

'Kate, get Sammy some sambuca!' She screeched with laughter. 'Some *sam*buca for *Sammy*!'

Kate raised her eyebrows at him. Clearly, it was a six-glass joke.

'Just to be sociable,' he said hesitantly.

Kate poured him a sociable amount.

'Thanks,' he said, politely raising his glass in a toast, at which point Sonia flashed her cigarette lighter under his nose and set fire to the sambuca, narrowly missing setting fire to Sam.

Kate closed her eyes.

Laughing uproariously, Sonia kept her lighter going and lit another of Benson & Hedges' finest.

'Wanna ciggy?' she asked Sam, with it bobbing up and down attractively between her lips.

'No, thank you.' He frowned disapprovingly. 'I'm afraid I think it's a filthy habit.'

'It is.' Sonia smiled seductively and nudged him in the ribs. 'And I've got lots more too.' She blew a smoke ring and leaned heavily against Sam's arm, pinning it to his side. For a fearless martial arts expert, he looked pretty terrified.

'So whaddaya reckon to all of this T'ai Chi malarky, Sammy?' Sonia asked dreamily.

'Well,' he stammered, 'it's about harmonising your body's internal energy with the forces of the universe.'

She slowly wagged her finger at his nose. 'Yes, but does it work?'

'It takes years of constant practice to attain mastery.'

'You see,' she said in a very wobbly way, 'it all sounds just a bit touchy-feely to me. Whereas my friend Kate, here – my very, very, very good friend Katie . . .'

'Sonia!' Kate warned.

'She thinks it's going to solve all her marital problems.'

'Sonia!'

'I, on the other hand, swear by step aerobics.' She smiled drunkenly at him. 'You can't beat a bit of up, down, up, down, up, down and some buttock clenching. What do you think, Sam?'

'Er . . .'

Sam's dark hair framed his face in lazy waves that threatened to turn Shirley Temple-ish when they grew too long; it curled over his collar, eschewing the current fashion for Bruce Willis baldness. Sonia selected a strand and wound it lazily around her finger.

She nuzzled closer to him. 'I find you terribly attractive,'

181

she confessed girlishly. Her hand stroked his arm through his shirt. 'You're very well built, aren't you?' she said with admiration as she squeezed his muscle tentatively. 'Firm.' She fixed her eyes on his. 'Hard men are good to find.'

Sam coughed uncomfortably.

'Sonia, I think it's time I took you back to your room,' Kate suggested.

'When did you turn into my mother?' Sonia glared at her. 'Next you'll be reminding me to wash behind my ears.'

'I just don't want you saying anything you'll regret,' Kate said.

'It's better to say something you regret, than not to say anything at all,' Sonia said boldly.

'Actually, it isn't, Sonia. It's better to keep your mouth firmly shut, particularly following an excess of sambuca.' She tried to look her friend earnestly in the eyes, but Sonia's pupils had started a slow and steady rotation.

'Do you find me attractive?' Sonia continued unheeding and almost unconscious.

'Well, I'm engaged to be married,' Sam said hesitantly. 'Although we all possess an inner beauty . . .'

Sonia's head snapped up. 'Is that the same as "Get lost, you fat, ugly dwarf"?'

He glanced at his watch. 'My goodness, is that the time?' he said brightly as he stood up.

'Don't go!' Sonia pleaded, clinging to his thigh.

'I'm taking the early morning session.' Sam shook his

leg in an attempt to dislodge her. 'I think I'd better be making tracks.'

'Probably wise,' Kate agreed.

Sonia let go, allowing Sam to beat a hasty retreat.

'Fattist bastard!' she shouted after him. 'I'm not overweight! I'm just undertall!'

'Sonia, you're showing yourself up. It's time we went to bed.'

Her friend shook her fist at the door. 'So what if I've got more chins than the Chinese phone book?' She began to laugh wildly.

'Look,' Kate waved the empty bottle at her, 'there's nothing left to drink, and the bar –' *thankfully!* '– is closed for the night. Come on. Let's go to bed.'

'Alone?'

'It's for the best,' Kate said kindly.

Sonia looked extremely miserable. 'He's probably gay,' she said.

'He's about to get married.'

'It's a well-known fact that ninety-five per cent of gay men are married.'

'I think you're getting mixed up with it's a well-known fact that Domestos kills ninety-five per cent of all known germs.'

Sonia's head sank towards her chest. 'I knew it was something like that.'

'Come on.' Kate helped Sonia up, heaving the dead weight of her friend's arm over her slender shoulders.

'Why does no one fancy me, Katie?' Sonia asked

tearfully. 'Not even my own husband. I can smoulder along with the rest of them, can't I?'

'It's actually the carpet that's smouldering,' Kate said with alarm as she bent to retrieve a glowing cigarette butt from the floor. Stubbing it out in the ashtray, she added it to the pile of dog ends with a wrinkle of her nose.

Sonia began to cry. 'He's never going to love me now,' she sniffed. 'I've made a complete fool of myself!'

'No, you haven't. You would never have been compatible. Sam said he was a wood element.'

'You mean he's a complete blockhead?'

'Probably.'

Sonia brightened considerably. 'What element do you think I am?' she asked as they lurched towards her bedroom.

'Quite possibly putty,' Kate said.

'I'm going to change,' Sonia swore. 'I'm only going to love Kevin from now on. I know he wouldn't win a Fabio lookalike competition, and he may be a boring old fart sometimes, but I could do a lot worse. He is the mother of my children, after all, a good provider and he makes a mean chicken curry when the occasion warrants it.' She burped at the thought of it.

'I think it's a wise decision.'

If it was so damn wise, why couldn't *she* feel the same about Jeffrey? Why did she lie awake at night tormented by feelings of darkest longing for Ben Mahler? All that Sonia had needed was the oblivion of sambuca to find the answer. Why couldn't life be as simple for Kate Lewis?

Chapter Twenty

There was a limit to how many fish fingers one could reasonably consume in a lifetime, Kevin decided, and he was fast approaching it. And, by the expression on the boys' faces, so were they.

'Can't we go to McDonald's?' Andrew pleaded.

'No,' Kevin replied, juggling the fish fingers onto a plate while trying not to burn his own fingers. 'You'll be late for school.' It was Thursday morning and his cupboard, much like Old Mother Hubbard's, was bare.

'But I don't want fish fingers for breakfast,' Daniel joined in the rebellion. 'We had them for tea last night and they were horrible then. You don't even cook them right like Mummy does. She doesn't do them with black bits round the edges.'

'Look,' Kevin ran his hand through his hair. 'The cereal's run out, there's no bread and I can't find anything else vaguely edible, unless you count dried pasta. So fish fingers it is.'

'What are we having with them?'

'Beans.'

They both grimaced. 'Can't we just have the beans without the fish fingers?'

Kevin thought for a moment. 'No,' he said decisively.

'I've cooked them now. If you want to eat off the à la carte menu, you have to order beforehand.'

'Can't we go to the supermarket?' Andrew ventured. 'It's very easy. You just fill a trolley up with things you like and then pay the lady at the end. Mummy does it all the time.'

'I do know what supermarket shopping entails,' Kevin snapped. 'I have been once or twice.' But he had to admit to himself he couldn't quite recall the last time he had graced Safeway's with his manly presence.

Daniel's lip started to quiver. 'I want Mummy to come home now,' he said, sounding sniffly. 'I don't like her being away doing Typhoo any more.'

'T'ai Chi,' Andrew corrected.

'I don't care what it is! I miss her!'

Kevin agreed with Daniel's sentiments wholeheartedly. He too was missing Sonia desperately. The dishwasher was full and so was the sink. These were the last clean plates and there were no mugs left, except the prissy ones with geraniums on that her mother had bought them and they were always the last resort. The laundry basket in the bathroom was stuffed fit to burst and was reeking of little boys' socks. He had even lain awake in bed last night missing the feel of her ice-cold feet tickling against the back of his legs in an effort to get warm.

'How many more getting-ups is it before she comes home?'

'Only two,' Kevin said brusquely. 'She'll be home on Saturday.'

'But that's ages away,' Daniel whined. 'I want her to come home now!'

'Well, she can't,' his father said. He eyed the fish fingers and a spark lit up in his brain. A slow sneaky smile spread across his lips. 'Unless . . .'

They were in McDonald's fortifying themselves for the master plan with Big Macs, chips and solidified banana milkshakes. It was 8.30 a.m.

'Now,' Kevin said. They all leaned their elbows on the table and the boys listened attentively. 'Which one of you is going to stay at home and which one of you is going to school? Shall we toss for it?'

'Why can't we both stay at home? That way she's more likely to rush back,' Andrew reasoned. 'If she gets a move on, she could be back in time to cook our lunch.'

Kevin considered this carefully. It was very true. And if they were both at home it was less likely that sibling rivalry would come into play and also less likely that one of them would spill the beans. And if the beans were spilled, blood would also be.

'Remember,' he warned, with a severe pointing of his finger, 'we are all dead men if your mother so much as gets the slightest whiff of a rat. Are you with me?'

'Yes, Dad.' They both nodded their heads.

'I mean it,' he said sternly.

The nodding reached epidemic proportions.

'Just do it,' Daniel said solemnly.

'Okay,' Kevin said. 'Step one of Operation Mummy Come Home. Countdown.'

'Five, four, three, two, one,' they all said together. 'Go!'

Kevin pulled his mobile phone out of his pocket.

'I'm not very well,' Sonia wailed.

'I'm not very surprised,' Kate said.

Her friend was kneeling on her bathroom floor with her head in the toilet bowl, making alarming noises and revisiting her sambuca experience from the inside out.

She pulled her hair back from her face and eyed Kate groggily. 'I can't believe it took just one little drink to get me so plastered!'

'Yes, but I think it was the ninth or tenth of those little drinks that tipped you over the edge.'

'Are there many calories in sambuca?' Sonia asked queasily.

'I wouldn't worry, most of the ones you consumed are heading out of Buckingham's main sewer and towards the North Sea by now.'

'I'll never drink again,' she said, panting heavily.

'Oh, I expect you will.' Kate sat on the edge of the bath and ran the dampened facecloth over her friend's forehead.

'Never,' Sonia heaved. 'Never again will that poisonous stuff pass my lips.' She looked at Kate with red-rimmed eyes. 'How ever am I going to face Sam? He'll think I'm such an idiot! Why didn't you stop me? You're supposed to be my friend.'

Sonia sagged to the floor and Kate lifted her gently up again.

'I'm not enjoying this T'ai Chi business,' Sonia told

188

her. 'I knew all along it wasn't my thing. I'm much better with something that involves loud disco music and mirrors. I don't think I'm cut out for meditation. I *hate* being a bloody white crane.' Sonia started to cry. 'And I miss my lovely boys,' she wept. 'And I miss my lovely Kevin!'

Kate was wishing she could make her friend feel better when the bedroom telephone started to ring. 'I'll get that,' she said, gratefully slipping out of the bathroom.

After a moment, she popped her head back round the door. Sonia was now lying slumped against the bath. 'It's Kevin,' she said. 'Are you in a fit state to speak to him?'

Sonia grabbed the receiver. 'Sweetie,' she cooed. 'How are you? How are the boys?' Her face was suddenly ashen. She turned to Kate. 'My babies are ill,' she whispered.

Kate sat down next to her friend. 'What's wrong with them?' she asked.

'What's wrong with them?' Sonia asked Kevin. She turned back to Kate. 'They're spotty!'

'*Spotty?*' Kate said. 'They've had chickenpox and measles, haven't they?'

'Both.'

Kate scratched her chin. 'It could be an allergy.'

'Kate thinks it might be an allergy.' Sonia held her hand over the receiver. 'He thinks it's worse than an allergy.'

There was a stifled muttering from the other end of the phone.

'*Much* worse,' Sonia stressed.

'Has he called out the doctor?'

'Have you called out the doctor?' she demanded. 'He says they're asking for me.' Sonia's eyes filled with tears. 'They need me!'

'Then I think we'd better get your bag packed.'

'I'm coming home!' she cried down the phone. 'Tell them Mummy's coming.' Sonia replaced the receiver and sniffed into a piece of toilet roll. 'He's going to leave them with Mrs Shaw while he comes to get me.'

'I could have taken you,' Kate insisted.

'No, no, it's fine. But I feel really bad leaving you,' Sonia said, flinging clothes into her case so fast that her hands were blurred. 'I know how much you wanted me to come.'

'I'll be okay. It's only another two days.' *Only another two days with Ben.*

Sonia stopped the unending river of clothes midstream. 'A lot can happen in two days.'

'Look,' Kate reasoned, 'I've been on this planet for thirty-five years and not a lot has happened. I think I'll be safe on my own.' *Will I?*

Her friend continued her packing, her hangover getting better by the minute. 'Go and have some breakfast. Kev will be here by the time you've finished.'

'I couldn't leave you,' Kate said. 'I'll wait here.'

'Aren't you starving?'

'No. I'm fine.'

'Couldn't you just eat a nice juicy fat sausage?'

'No.'

190

'You might see Ben.'

Kate leaned back on the bed and regarded her friend. 'Does this mean, by any chance, that you want a nice juicy fat sausage?'

Sonia looked up. 'Well, now you come to mention it, I am a bit peckish.'

Regurgitated sambuca obviously didn't spoil the appetite. But then with Sonia, not a lot did.

'Why don't I go and get us both a sausage sandwich and bring it back here?' she offered.

Sonia grinned. 'What a jolly splendid idea!'

Kate was leaving the dining room with a tray piled high with toast, sausages and a pot of tea, when Ben appeared round the corner. His hair was still wet from the shower and his skin had that just-shaved glow. He was so unbearably handsome he made her legs go all quivery. His smile was warm and friendly again and she was relieved that the coolness that had sprung up yesterday seemed to have disappeared just as quickly. She wanted to touch his damp skin, his smooth cheek, and run her fingers along the firm contour of his jaw.

'Breakfast in bed?' he said chirpily.

'Room service for Sonia.' Kate nodded at the sausages. 'Apparently they're the best cure for a sambuca hangover.'

'Sambuca?'

'Yes.' She gave him a look that said, You wouldn't believe it if I told you. 'Last night she took it upon herself to try to make The Cloisters a little less cloistered.'

'Did she succeed?'

'Admirably.'

Ben chuckled. 'I can believe it. I was going to come into the bar last night. When I got back.'

'I wish you had.' She looked up at him and his eyes answered hers.

'I wasn't late,' he said.

'Oh.'

'I thought it was better if I went straight to bed. Alone,' he added.

'Oh.' Kate shifted the weight of the tray to her hip.

'Shall I carry that for you?'

'No, thanks. I can manage.' Kate laughed. 'If you had come back into the bar last night, you could have helped me to carry Sonia!' She shuffled uncomfortably. 'She'll be wondering where I am.'

'I take it she won't be at the first session this morning.'

'She's leaving,' Kate said. 'Her husband has just phoned to say the boys aren't very well.'

Ben's face creased with concern. 'I'm sorry to hear that.'

'I'm not entirely sure Sonia was,' Kate answered. 'I doubt it's anything serious. You see, our Sam was an unwitting part of the sambuca experience and I don't think she knew quite how she was going to face him this morning. It only sounds like the kids have got a bit of a rash, but Sonia took it as a perfect excuse to hightail it out of here.'

'Now she'll never know the meaning of life.'

'I actually think she does,' Kate said. *Or, at least, she's a darn sight closer to it than I am. And she's lucky to have found out so soon.* Kate shuffled on the stone floor. 'Did your business go well?'

'My what?'

'Your business meeting. Last night.'

'Oh, that!' Ben looked guilty. 'Yes, fine.'

'I'd better be going,' Kate said. 'There's nothing worse than cold tea.'

'Cold toast?' Ben suggested.

She grinned. 'We'll have both in a minute, if I don't get a move on.'

It was Ben's turn to scuff the floor. 'Are you going to be on your own tonight then?' he asked and she thought she saw him blush faintly.

'Well,' she hesitated. 'Yes.'

'Perhaps we can escape,' he said in a slightly shaky voice. 'Leave the fur fabric-ers behind and be by ourselves for a while.'

'Mmm,' she said and hoped that he'd heard it because it barely came out.

'I'll see you later then.'

'Okay.'

Ben winked at her and went into the dining room.

Her hands were trembling so much that the teacups were rattling in their saucers. What did 'a while' mean? An hour? Two hours? The whole night? Kate set off back to the bedroom with the tray. Sonia might have the constitution of an ox, but the way Kate's insides were lurching, there was no way that these sausages

193

were ever going to pass her lips. She looked at the mountainous tray of congealing food. Oh well, all the more for Sonia to take to Weight Watchers the minute she got home.

Chapter Twenty-One

They watched Kevin's car pull up outside the bedroom annexe and Sonia wiped a smear of sausage grease from her mouth.

'He's here,' she said excitedly as she clunked her suitcase closed.

'Are you sure you've got everything? The lilo and the bikini?'

Sonia nodded confidently.

'The evening dress and the hiking boots?'

'I think so.' Frowning, her friend checked round her room. 'Are you going to be all right on your own?'

'I'll be fine.'

Sonia grinned. 'I'm sure Ben will look after you.'

Kate felt herself flush. 'Don't keep Kevin waiting.'

There was a knock at the door and one very harassed-looking husband stood on the other side of it.

'Are they okay?' Sonia said, her voice high with worry.

Kevin's face had anxiety written all over it. 'They're fine,' he said breathlessly. 'They need you. We all need you.'

Sonia fell into his arms and he held her tightly, squeezing her as if he never wanted to let her go. Over his wife's shoulder Kevin's face broke into a cheeky grin and he winked wickedly at Kate.

'*Rotter!*' Kate mouthed.

'*Desperate!*' Kevin mouthed back. He tenderly wiped a tear from Sonia's cheek. 'Let's get you home,' he said.

Sonia and Kate trailed after him as he carried her cases to the car and loaded them into the boot. It was another glorious morning and the fountain tinkled merrily into the large pond in front of the bedrooms, encouraged by the gentle breeze. Kate kicked aimlessly at the gravel that spilled over the edge of the path.

'Have you seen Jeffrey this week?' she asked casually.

'We went to the golf club for a drink on Tuesday.'

So that's where he was. 'Did he seem okay?'

Kevin flushed guiltily. 'You know Jeffrey.'

Kate's brow creased to a frown. *I thought I did.* 'Is he missing me?'

'Like the desert misses the rain.'

She smirked reluctantly. 'Charmer!'

Kevin fluttered his eyelashes. Sonia was wringing her hands together and fidgeting from foot to foot.

'I hope the boys are better soon,' Kate said. Personally, she thought they'd be recovered beyond recognition, given an hour or two.

Sonia squeezed her shoulder. 'Don't worry,' she advised. 'You'll crack that white crane thing. It's easy. Just relax.'

Relax. It's easy. Since the minute she'd clapped eyes on Ben Mahler, every fibre of Kate's body had been on red alert. Relaxation, like cellulite-free thighs, was a thing of the past.

'Well, I've got plenty more chances to practise today,'

she said. 'Speaking of which,' Kate glanced at her watch, 'I'd better get a wiggle on. Class is about to start.'

'Which of the five elephants are you trying to harness today?'

Kate searched her brain. 'Wood.'

'I won't miss much then, I'm already as thick as two short planks!'

'Apparently, it's to do with blossoming and growing.'

Sonia looked at her earnestly. 'I hope it helps then.'

Kate huffed in an unconvinced way that was meant to convey that it didn't matter whether it helped or not. But it did.

'Take care,' Sonia said, kissing her cheek. 'I'll see you on Saturday, perhaps. Ring me the minute you get home!'

'I will,' she promised. 'See you.'

Sonia lowered her voice. 'Say goodbye to Sam for me.'

Kate gave her a warning look. 'I will.'

She nudged her friend theatrically. 'Don't do anything I wouldn't do!'

Kate sighed. 'I don't think my imagination stretches that far.'

'No, but someone else's might!' she said.

Sonia slid in the car next to Kevin, waving excitedly as she fastened her seat belt and Kate shut the door behind her. She clearly couldn't wait to get home, even on the pretext of ailing offspring. *If only I could feel the same!* Instead, Kate was dreading the moment when the course ended and she had to return to her home in the land of twee and her neatly ironed tea towels. She watched her friend drive away from the Priory, waving until the car turned out of sight. There was a lump in her throat, but she felt a mixture of relief, elation – and terror. For the first time in years she was completely alone and answerable to no one. No husband, no children, no best friend. She was free to do whatever she wanted. Kate let her hand fall to her side. If only she knew exactly what that was.

'T'ai Chi is all about mind intent,' Sam said.

Kate's mind was intent on anything but T'ai Chi. And, for once, she couldn't pretend it was because of Sonia's constant babble. Her thoughts were wandering all over the place, following the birds, listening to the rustle of the leaves on the trees. There was something wonderful about this time of year, the full flourish of beauty that nature had promised in spring before the colourful fading of autumn and the stark death of winter. They were on the croquet lawn and she was holding a stick – a broom handle to be precise – which she was pointing at the woods, far in the distance, beyond the grazing sheep, beyond the dual carriageway, beyond the point where sharpness of vision gave way to indistinct sunkissed haze. She felt very silly and it was making her arms ache.

'We want to focus the wood energy from inside us to the wood energy of the trees on the ridge. Use your mind intent to visualise your Chi flowing along the stick, reaching out to the trees and beyond to connect with the universe.'

The universe. It was a larger concept than she was ready

to confront on a Thursday morning. The course was getting harder, she was tired from all the exercise, emotional from all the soul-searching and hyper from the cha-cha-cha her heart insisted on doing for most of the day and a goodly part of the night. And she was missing home and not missing home both at once.

'The wood element represents growth, being flexible, bending with the gentle movement of the wind.'

Was she flexible? She wasn't averse to drinking full-fat milk rather than skimmed if she was forced to. She regularly tried a different washing-up liquid in response to commercial pressure – lemon and lime, spring blossom, traditional soapy-smelling dark green stuff – they had all graced her windowsill at some point. And now she and Jeffrey were thinking of putting a wooden floor in the dining room. How flexible was that? But when it came to matters of the universe . . .

'If we're frightened of growth, we can become brittle and inflexible in both our hearts and our minds. Wooden.'

Was that what happened to people over seventy? Did they all need to get out and wave their walking sticks at the trees? *Is that where I'm heading?*

'By extending your focus out of yourself, you allow a deep internal stretch.'

Sam's soporific voice was making her eyes roll. All this standing around and doing nothing but concentrating was exhausting. Her mind was always busy, but it wasn't used to lingering on one thing for anything more than a nano-second.

'Free your thinking,' he commanded. 'Don't be stuck. Let yourself move forward.'

Kate dragged her concentration back to the broom handle. Now her shoulders were tensing up and she was gripping it for grim death. She took a deep breath and relaxed her grip and let her shoulders ease away from her ears.

'Feel as if the wood is coming to life in your hands. Imagine feelings of hope, new beginnings, starting afresh. From little acorns, mighty oaks grow.'

This freeing of your thinking was all very well for people who didn't have to worry about French exchange trips and school play rehearsals and making sure that netball/ football kits were taken in on the ordained day and that music lessons were practised for.

'Are you feeling alive, awake, like a tender young bud waiting to burst open in spring?'

No, Sam, I'm not.

And then it happened. Nothing much. It was barely discernible. There was a ripple along the stick. A shiver. As gentle as a butterfly brushing against her hand. Kate's Chi started to panic. *Breathe, breathe, breathe.* She waited, feeling the anticipation wriggle in her belly. It happened again. There was a movement. Hardly there at all, but it was there nevertheless. And it terrified her so much that she dropped the stick.

Chapter Twenty-Two

The Superman curtains were closed in the boys' bedroom, blocking out the brilliant morning sun and plunging the room into an atmosphere of subdued gloom.

Sonia tiptoed into the room. 'Hello, darlings,' she whispered. 'You'll be all right now, Mummy's here to look after you.'

Pitiful groanings came from the twin beds. She sat down on Daniel's bed and stroked his forehead. It was beaded with perspiration and his hair was matted to his head, soaking wet with sweat. His cheeks were flushed and feverishly hot and there were livid maroon spots covering his entire face. He was wearing sunglasses.

'How are you feeling?' she said sympathetically.

'Poorly,' he croaked. 'Very poorly.'

His matching Superman duvet was tucked tightly round his chin and Bart Simpson's head peeped out from beneath to nestle comfortingly against his neck. Sonia prised the duvet away from him and fished for his hand under the covers. It was burning hot. She felt his forehead again.

'You're burning up,' she said. 'I think you're running a temperature. Mummy's going to get the thermometer from the bathroom.'

As she moved on the bed there was a sloshing sound.

Sonia's brow furrowed and she reached under the duvet, knocking Bart out of the way, rummaging around until she located the hot water bottle. She waved it in front of Daniel's sunglasses. 'A hot water bottle?'

'I felt cold,' he squeaked.

She moved again and there was another rubbery slosh. '*Two* hot water bottles?'

'Very cold.'

She went over to check on Andrew, who was lying prostrate, arm above his head, murmuring incoherently. He too was feverish and burning. He too had two hot water bottles lodged against him in the bed.

'I think we'll have these curtains open,' Sonia said, swishing Superman across the window and letting the sun stream in, catching a flurry of scattering dust motes in its path. The boys groaned and writhed like vampires caught out at dawn. She smiled secretly to herself.

Daniel clutched his duvet in panic as she pulled it down. 'I want to have a closer look at these spots,' she said firmly. His pyjamas were buttoned all the way up to his neck. Sonia started to undo the buttons.

'No!' He stopped her hand.

'I want to see if they're on the rest of your body.'

'I don't think they are,' he said fearfully.

In fact, they stopped very abruptly in a neat little line at the neck of his pyjama top.

'This is dreadful.' Sonia shook her head and stared closely at the livid marks on his cheeks.

Daniel's face clouded with panic.

She rubbed at one of the spots with her thumb. Lip liner. Elizabeth Arden. Paradise Plum. Her mouth set in a grim line. 'I don't think I've ever seen such a bad case.'

Daniel tried to clutch at his sunglasses as she swiftly removed them. His eyes were circled with deep pink making them look red raw and swollen, as if he hadn't slept for a fortnight. She recognised the signs instantly. Boots Number Seven. Coral Pink blusher. Applied too thickly. The whites stared back at her in terror.

Kevin came into the room behind her and slipped his arms round her waist. 'How are they?'

Sonia cuddled into him. 'They are very, *very* sick children,' she said solemnly.

'No, we're not,' Daniel blurted.

Kevin shot him a warning look.

Sonia smiled indulgently at him. 'Mummy's brave little soldier.'

Kevin nuzzled her neck. 'We've missed you.'

'And I've missed you.'

He kissed her ear lobe. 'I'm glad you're home.'

'So am I,' she said. 'And just in the nick of time.'

'What do you reckon to these two?'

'I think they need a lot of tender loving care,' she said sweetly.

Both boys smiled weakly back at her.

'They must rest in bed and do nothing until those terrible, terrible spots have gone completely.'

Andrew grinned, whipped off his sunglasses and reached for his Game Boy.

'That means being absolutely still with no stimulation of any kind until it's time to go back to school on Monday.'

Andrew put his Game Boy down sullenly. 'But it's only Thursday,' he protested.

'Then it will give you a lot of time to think,' Sonia answered.

Daniel sat up, his face blanched with alarm. 'What about *The Simpsons*?'

'And no television until your eyes have fully recovered – you don't want them square as well as red, do you?'

They both stared at their father, troubled eyes pleading beneath the circles of Coral Pink blusher.

Kevin grimaced sympathetically. 'I think we'd better leave you to rest,' he said. 'I'll pop in and see if you're feeling any better a little bit later.'

Sonia saw him wink and give them a thumbs-up sign out of the corner of her eye. She hid the grin that twitched at her cheeks. She'd get them back for this, she thought. She wasn't sure how and she wasn't sure when, but it would be expensive.

Sonia and Kevin backed out of the room and closed the door.

Kevin pulled her to him. 'I'll check on them later,' he said. 'I expect they'll get better a lot quicker now that you're back.'

Sonia lifted an eyebrow. 'I shouldn't be at all surprised.'

'They're good kids, you know.'

'They take after their father.'

He wound his arms tightly around her. 'Are you glad you came home?'

'Yes,' she smiled. She was. She was sorry to have left Kate to fend for herself, especially when she seemed to be struggling so much to get to grips with this T'ai Chi palaver. Sonia couldn't see the attraction herself, it was all too quiet and sedate. Too much time to think and not enough action. On any front. Still, it had worked out well for her in the end, at least. There was nothing like a bit of abstinence to make the heart grow fonder.

'And how are you feeling?' His hand travelled down her back.

'Fine.' Sonia yawned.

'I bet all that strenuous exercise has left you feeling very sleepy.'

'Mmm,' she agreed, snuggling against him.

His hand stroked the nape of her neck. 'Do you think you could do with some bed rest?'

'It's nearly lunchtime,' she objected feebly.

His mouth grazed along the line of her throat. 'What better way to work up an appetite?'

She giggled as, with a heartfelt groan, he lifted her into his arms, carried her to the bedroom and kicked the door shut.

Chapter Twenty-Three

There was an air of unrestrained desire between them now that Sonia had departed. Ben's eyes lingered on Kate that bit longer, the looks held a touch more meaning, the loosening hip rotations had taken on a new dimension, and every time she bent over she was aware that her bottom was being closely watched. It was a long time since any of her body had been ogled and it was an empowering feeling. The rest of the class had receded to background scenery, hazy blurs against which she and Ben stood out in terrifyingly sharp relief.

Guy was taking the class today with Sam hovering in the background. The poor chap had seemed immensely relieved when she told him that Sonia wouldn't be continuing with the course, and who could blame him? It probably wasn't every day that a woman hurled herself at him. Kate didn't think T'ai Chi groupies were a recognised phenomenon.

'Gather round,' Guy said, marshalling them into a circle.

She stood close to Ben, both of them with their arms hanging loose by their sides; even the nearness of him was electrifying and she could feel all the tiny hairs on the back of her neck tingling with excitement.

'Sam and I are going to demonstrate Pushing Hands. This is a Chi sensitivity exercise and the purpose of it is to develop an awareness of what is happening in someone else's body by tuning in to the subtle flow of their energy. We need to learn to move in stillness and be still in movement, if we are going to attune ourselves to the life force of another person's vibrations.'

Vibrations? So that's what she was feeling.

'In martial arts terms, this is how we would neutralise and deflect an unwanted approach in a relaxed and careful way, so that we don't hurt ourselves.' He and Sam stood facing each other to demonstrate, a few feet apart, the outside edge of their right hands resting gently together, just above the wrist. 'Circle your bodies slowly,' Guy instructed, 'keeping your hands in contact at all times. Move from the waist. Use the energy from the belly, the *Tan-Tien*, not the force of your arms. As one advances, the other yields.' They moved slowly, rhythmically, in unison, their arms drawing invisible spheres in the air. 'Feel what your partner is doing.'

It was mesmeric to watch them, and momentarily distracted her attentions from Ben. When they stopped, they bowed to each other. 'Now,' Guy said. 'Find yourself someone to work with and take it from there.'

It was obvious that she and Ben would turn to each other.

'May I have the pleasure of this dance?' he said, breaking the tension.

'You may,' she replied glibly, listening to the loud thump that had already set up inside her. Would Ben be able to hear it? Probably from where he was standing.

They took up the posture as Guy had shown them and Kate felt her heart falter for an instant as their hands touched. It was the lightest of contact, but for the effect it was having on her. Her breath leapt from her belly to high in her chest and doubled its speed. *Relax, relax, relax! Breathe, breathe, breathe! Remember your antenatal classes!* Ben's breath appeared to be hideously normal; it was going in and out in all the right places and he didn't seem to be going puce in the face as she felt she was.

'Okay?' he said.

She nodded in response and they started to move together, gently, tentatively. Their eyes locked onto each other's and she saw Ben swallow deeply as their bodies turned and swayed in slow, deliberate motion. Turning their hips to mirror each other's image, they moved in a sensuous pattern like the faint ripple of movement in deep, deep water. She cleaved to him in her advance and yielded against the pressure of his body as he circled towards her, their hands and their eyes never breaking contact. Her breath sank to her belly and she could feel it rising and falling, settling, deepening, following the even symmetry of Ben's calm, steady breath. As he exhaled, she drew him into her, feeling the ebb and flow of his essence flood inside her. Her body was bathed inside with a golden light, suffused with a feeling of such peace and tranquillity that it made her want to weep with joy.

Guy clapped his hands. *No, don't bring me back! Not yet!* she pleaded silently. They stopped circling, but the motion carried on spiralling down within her. She let her hand fall to her side, but she knew that they were still connected by an unbroken cord of energy.

'Let's leave it there,' Guy said. 'Time and tea stop for no man! Discuss the feelings you experienced with your partner during the break.'

Kate sank to the grass, singing inside, buzzing and alive as if she'd been scrubbed down with a Brillo pad. Never before had she experienced anything like this. How could they have communicated so much without speaking? How could their inner thoughts, movements, the cadence of their breath reach such unity?

Conversely, how could she and Jeffrey talk so much and say so little? Since she had arrived here, their telephone conversations had been remote and mundane. Somewhere between the altar and number 20, Acacia Close, Jeffrey had turned into Monosyllabic Man and she had become One Line Woman, their exchanges mainly involving barked instructions regarding domestic minutiae. When had they last talked about anything that mattered? They hadn't wanted deep and meaningful conversations when they were teenagers, they'd wanted to snog in dark spaces, like the understairs cupboard at her mother's house. Then when the children had come along, there hadn't been time. And now there was the time, there wasn't the inclination.

When she had phoned home last night, Jeffrey had sounded terrible, as if he was suffering from the after-effects of a cold, and the children had been distracted by clearly riveting homework projects on the origins of teddy bears (Kerry) and dormant volcanoes (Joe). A mere five days away from home and already she felt as if she no longer existed for them. So long as there was a meal on the table and a car to ferry them around, anyone could fill her place.

Ben lay on his stomach next to her. The vibrations between them were still palpable.

'Do you want to talk about how you feel?' he asked.

She shook her head. 'I'm not sure that I can find the right words to say it.'

'Me neither,' he said.

'Perhaps later.'

He nodded his consent. 'I've arranged a picnic hamper for us tonight,' he said. 'I thought we could find somewhere quiet across the fields.' His eyes searched hers for approval. They were softer, bluer, more vulnerable than she'd seen them before.

'That sounds lovely.' *That sounds dangerous!*

Ben glanced over to where the tea was being served. 'I could do with a nice cup of tea.'

It was just what Jeffrey would have said. 'I think we both need one.'

He grinned. 'What do you think the chances are of us getting a biscuit now that Sonia's left us to our own devices?'

'Infinitely better, I should say,' Kate laughed.

'Shall we try it?'

He took her hand and pulled her to her feet and, for a moment, the bubble cocooned them once again. What were the chances of getting something infinitely more satisfying than mere digestive biscuits, Kate mused, now that they were indeed left to their own devices?

Chapter Twenty-Four

Jeffrey sat nursing his head in his hands. He still felt like an alcoholic in the throes of recovery, and had swallowed Resolve all of Thursday, standing the packet on his desk at Hills & Hopeland as a tangible reminder of his foolishness and his resolve to pull himself together. There had been a few behind-the-hand sniggers pertaining to Natalie's phone call, but the others were all wise enough to see that he needed handling with kid gloves.

Like Joe's project, Jeffrey felt he was a dormant volcano, with something simmering deep below the surface, just waiting to break through. He was clearly giving off *handle with care* vibes as no one had commented on his radical new hairdo and the word 'peaky' had been bandied about by several of the secretaries – enough for him to leave work early and retreat to the safety of Acacia Close. He swung the car onto the Leighton Buzzard road, glad to be ahead of the crawl of homeward-bound traffic, but unsure whether his home was still the haven it had once been. Wasn't it now a place where danger lurked?

The danger came in the very welcoming form of Natalie – who relieved him of his briefcase and handed him an ice-cold beer as soon as he walked through the door.

'You're early,' she said.

'I couldn't take any more,' Jeffrey sighed. His suit felt as crumpled and jaded as he did and his non-iron shirt looked distinctly as though it had never seen an iron. But how his crestfallen spirit had lifted when he had seen her standing there with her legs going all the way up to her Australian armpits.

'Take a shower,' Natalie instructed. 'I can start dinner now that you're here.'

'What's on the menu today?' he asked, enjoying the refreshing shock in his parched mouth.

'I have to confess,' she said, looking suitably penitent, 'to veering from Kate's brilliantly prepared regime. Thursday was supposed to be pork casserole and new potatoes, or we could have had the spaghetti bolognese that we should have had on Monday when we had the chilli.' Natalie wrinkled her nose. 'I thought it was too hot for any of them.'

'Right,' Jeffrey said, still sweltering unpleasantly inside his suit.

'I'm preparing some traditional Australian fare instead,' she said with a grin.

He raised an eyebrow. Didn't they eat kangaroo, termites and disgusting-looking grubs?

'Barbie!' Natalie gave one of her raucous laughs. 'Sometimes you have to revert to native stereotyping.'

Jeffrey smiled with relief. 'It sounds great.' At least he would be responsible for burning the food tonight.

'Don't be long,' she warned. 'The coals are just about ready.'

212

'You've *lit* the barbecue already?'

She looked perplexed. 'Yes.'

'Oh, fine. Fine,' Jeffrey said, trying not to sound completely in awe and truly thankful that he'd been saved the usual embarrassment involving firelighters, lighter fuel, several boxes of Swan Vestas and rubbing two Boy Scouts together in an attempt to tap into his long-abandoned caveman instincts and produce flame.

Jeffrey stood in the shower and let the soothing water wash over his body and cleanse the grime from his skin. His soapy hands massaged his belly and he was pleased to assess it as still firm. It hadn't sagged despite years of sitting behind a desk – so golf must be good for something, if not for the soul. Other parts of him were equally firm, he thought as his fingers travelled further down, which wasn't so good – not when your wife was in the next county looking for the meaning of life. Perhaps the meaning of life was here, after all, growing hard in his hand. Everything these days seemed to revolve round a man, a woman and you know what – films, books, television, newspapers, politics – they were all littered with images and stories of sex. It was surprising in a way that he hadn't been tempted earlier. *Tempted to do what?* Seduce a girl young enough, if not to be his daughter, then at least his younger sister? What was happening to him? Where had the straight, sensible, work-focused, family-loving husband and father of two gone? Where had he gone and when was he likely to come back?

Jeffrey turned off the shower and immediately punished himself with a rub down that was more brisk than it needed to be. He threw on his shorts and a clean T-shirt from the pile of ironing that Natalie had left neatly stacked on the bed and looked at himself in the mirror. Grief, he could feel himself ageing by the minute! He picked up his aftershave, Givenchy Gentleman, and splashed himself liberally with it. His side of the bathroom cupboard was bursting with matching soap, skin balm, shower gel and antiperspirant – none of which he had cared to use before. But now he went downstairs with a light step, glad to know that he smelled of 'a delicious blend of exotic, mood-enhancing spices'.

Natalie was standing over the cooker, an apron tied round her slim waist, stirring a pan intently. She looked up and smiled, and his spirits soared even higher.

'Try this, Jeffers,' she coaxed, wafting the wooden spoon laden with sauce at him. 'It'll blow your socks off.'

He wasn't wearing socks. Kate had long since dinned it into him that socks and sandals didn't mix.

'This is Mrs Lambert's patented barbecue sauce,' she informed him. 'Guaranteed to make your barbie go with a zing.'

Jeffrey approached cautiously. It looked like the sort of sauce that could melt work surfaces. Natalie held the spoon aloft. He offered his mouth up to accept the spoonful of sauce, resting his hand on the tiny span of her waist. Their eyes met and he held her hand as he steadied the spoon and closed his mouth carefully over it. Natalie swallowed hard, as did he. His fingers curled round her wrist and stroked the tender skin on the inside with his thumb, completely oblivious to the scalding piece of onion that was gleefully sintering itself to the roof of his mouth.

'Isn't that the best thing you've ever tasted?'

Jeffrey nodded, mute in his emotion.

Natalie moved towards him and he could hear her breathing; he could feel it fast and hard in her breast beneath the plastic apron.

'You smell nice . . .' she said huskily.

Although he wondered how she could tell above the cloud of garlic that was emanating from Mrs Lambert's barbecue sauce. Perhaps the Givenchy Gentleman was more potent than he thought.

'. . . like an old English country house.'

Most of them smelt musty and damp to Jeffrey, as if there was a rancid relative left rotting in a cupboard somewhere, but Natalie was Australian and probably had little, if any, experience of old country houses and, therefore, harboured romantic notions about them. At least, he hoped that was the explanation.

She reached up and stroked her fingers tenderly across his lips and he caught them with a hesitant kiss.

'Sauce,' she said.

'Daddy!' Kerry ran into the kitchen. She stopped in her tracks and stared at them. They jumped guiltily apart and Kerry regarded them each in turn, narrowing her eyes imperceptibly. 'The barbecue's ready,' she said crisply and turned and ran out again.

215

Natalie stirred the sauce furiously.

'I'm sorry,' Jeffrey said.

She shook her head, but didn't look at him. 'Don't be.'

'I can assure you, I don't normally do that sort of thing.'

'I know.'

'I'll take the salad out, shall I?'

'Yes,' she said tightly.

He didn't know what else to say, so he picked up the salad. When he turned back she was staring out of the window, spoon still clattering round the pan.

Contrary to expectations, the sausages weren't burnt and neither was the lettuce limp. Natalie, it appeared, was a mean cook when it came to deliberately trying to burn something rather than trying not to. Kerry, amazingly, had eschewed her all-meat-is-murder stance and was tucking into one of Natalie's home-made beefburgers. It was a good job it hadn't been down to him to go out and club the odd mammoth to death to provide food, Jeffrey thought, for he was totally knackered and would probably struggle to pull the wings off a few innocent flies. The fine art of barbecuing had always eluded him and he tried to avoid being pressed into service more than once or twice per summer. Wasps were always a good excuse. His chicken was always incinerated to the point of charcoal on the outside, yet still raw and bleeding inside. A bit like he felt now. He sat in the garden lounger, plate balanced on his lap, and tried to admire his flourishing geraniums rather than flourishing parts of Natalie's anatomy. What was the opposite of Viagra? Whatever it was, he needed to take some and quick, before his errant libido went completely off the rails. He bit the end decisively off his perfectly grilled sausage.

To prove he was a new man, Jeffrey offered to tidy up while Natalie served dessert – also unburnt – in the form of pavlova. Kerry helped him to clear up the debris. He was scraping chicken skin and sweetcorn husks into the swing bin when she cleared her throat.

'You and Mummy aren't going to divorce, are you?' she asked, studying the colourful array of magnets that adorned the fridge freezer in commemoration of every family holiday they'd had over the last five years.

'No.'

'Not ever?'

Jeffrey folded his arms and regarded her paternally. 'No.'

'Children of divorced parents don't grow as tall,' she informed him. 'The continued wrangles over custody and maintenance stunt the growth of the developing vertebrae and I want to be a supermodel.'

'I thought you were going to be a QC?'

'I want to be the first QC who can also earn twenty thousand a day for getting up in the morning.'

'I see.'

Kerry kicked at the kitchen table. 'Are you?'

'I love your mother.'

'That's not the same. Clarissa Roddick's parents say they still love each other, but they just can't live together any more.' Kerry eyed him directly. 'That's why Clarissa has to spend every weekend in a pokey flat being nice to her daddy's silly new girlfriend.'

'That must be difficult for her.'

'She's always sick.'

'Clarissa?'

'No, the girlfriend. Clarissa says she spends half the night groaning.'

'Oh.' Jeffrey covered the smile that played at his mouth with his hand. Kerry looked sullenly at him. 'I don't want to spend my weekends in a pokey flat,' she said. 'I like it here. I've got my own CD player.'

'Is that all?'

'And I shouldn't have to live with uncertainty at my age.' He noticed she was fingering her belly-button ring distractedly.

'The only thing in life that's certain is uncertainty, Kerry,' he said kindly. 'But, don't worry, your mother and I are very happy together.'

Are we? He pulled his daughter to him and cuddled her, kissing the top of her head. If so, why was his wife currently away trying to find what was missing in her life, and why was his penis suddenly behaving like a jack-in-the-box at the mere sight of a leggy blonde?

At least his daughter looked appeased. 'I don't want any pavlova,' she said, wrinkling her nose. 'All that cream!'

Jeffrey was looking forward to it immensely.

'Too many dairy products are bad for your arteries. Can I have an apple instead?'

'Have whatever you want, darling,' he said. *This is*

probably the only time in your life when things that are bad for you hold no hint of temptation.

Food finished, the children decided to go inside to watch TV and Natalie brought another bottle of wine out of the fridge. She poured Jeffrey and herself a glass and sat in the swing chair, rocking backwards and forwards, studying the horizon. The sun was still high in the sky, the longest day recently past, and the garden looked soft and mellow in the golden light. The clear yellow flowers of the evening primrose had opened and their heady scent was hanging in the air.

'That was wonderful.' Jeffrey massaged his straining stomach appreciatively.

'We're born with an inbuilt ability to barbecue,' she said. 'Can't do much else though.'

'You seem to get by all right,' he said.

Natalie patted the cushion next to her. 'Come and sit here.'

'Is that wise?'

She shrugged.

Reluctantly, he left the safety of his lounger and crossed to where she sat. He flopped into the flowery comfort of the swing, catching its genteel rhythm and trying to keep a sociable distance between his and Natalie's legs. Neither of them spoke, only the squeaking of the springs that he had been meaning to oil for months, filling the silence.

Jeffrey gulped his wine. 'I'm sorry I overreacted the other night,' he said.

219

'It was my fault,' Natalie replied, curling one leg under her. 'I should have asked your permission to mutilate your daughter.'

'I wouldn't have given it, you know.'

Natalie stared at him frankly. 'That's why I didn't ask.'

They giggled at each other.

She ran her finger round the top of her wine glass. 'You're a very nice man, Jeffrey.'

He snorted derisively. 'Very nice, very boring, very married.'

'You're a potential himbo, Jeffers,' she said. 'But you just need to let go a little. You take life too seriously.'

He rested his head against the back of the swing. 'I can't help it,' he said. 'Even at school I was the only one who'd be worrying about equilateral triangles while all the other boys were reading the *Beano*. I've always been like this.'

'But sometimes you feel trapped?'

I didn't used to. Not before this week!

'You love your wife, you love your family . . .'

'I hate my job.'

'. . . But, occasionally, you want some time on your own, to be yourself, to forget your responsibilities, to let your hair down.'

'Yes.' *No, it was never like that!*

Natalie rested her hand on his thigh. 'I understand how you feel.'

His eyes were glued to the slender suntanned hand that was burning its imprint into his shorts. *Do you? How? I don't understand myself.*

220

He'd never expected marriage to be all moonlight and roses. It was a bit like the descriptions in a holiday brochure. In the pictures, everything looks idyllic, but it's only when you're there that you realise that the hotel isn't quite as glossy as it seemed and they omitted to mention it's the rainy season which means it's going to bucket down for the best part of the fortnight. And every time you do manage to go on the beach, you get sand in your picnic lunch. He'd never minded the sand in his sandwiches, that was an intrinsic part of what it was all about. It was the good bits that you took away with you, that carried you through the rest of the year. That was marriage. Lots of gritty sandwiches with a bit of snatched sunbathing in between.

Natalie sat up in the swing. 'Let's do something mad tomorrow.' Her eyes were twinkling with excitement. 'Have some fun. It's my last day. We should do something special to mark surviving the week.'

'Like what?' He wasn't sure what constituted Natalie's idea of fun.

'I don't know.' She twirled her wine glass absently. 'I'll have to give it some thought.'

It sounded terrifying. 'I've got to go to work.'

'Ah, phone in sick again, Jeffers. They'll never suspect you're bunking off. I bet you're a model employee.'

It was true, he hadn't had a day off sick in years. Even when he had a cold he just dosed himself up with Day Nurse and struggled on. The idea wriggled deeper into his brain and, like the pavlova, it was very tempting. 'What about the children?'

Kerry and Joe came out and sat on the grass. 'What *about* the children?' Kerry asked warily.

'I'm trying to persuade your father to do something wild tomorrow!'

'We've got school.'

'Couldn't you give it the flick for the day? It's nearly end of term anyway. I bet you're hardly doing any work – right?' Natalie was well into her stride.

'We could go to Alton Towers,' Joe piped up.

'I've always wanted to go there.' Kerry added. She was clearly having a night off from being an eco-warrior, and forgetting for once that one of her passions in life was to save the countryside, not contribute to its erosion by supporting what she called tacky commercial enterprises.

It was possibly the last place in the world that Jeffrey wanted to go. A damp day out in Dorking would be infinitely preferable.

'Yes, yes, yes!' Joe said, starting to dance round the garden.

No, no, no! thought every fibre of Jeffrey's being.

Natalie was looking blank.

'It's a theme park,' he explained. 'White-knuckle rides. Everything designed to induce vomiting in those of a nervous disposition. Like Disney but without Mickey Mouse.'

The width of Natalie's grin could have broken records. 'Sounds great!'

'Can we go, Daddy?' Kerry urged.

'I don't think so.' Jeffrey was hesitant. 'It's not really

my cup of tea.' A nice cup of tea was more his cup of tea. And Kate wouldn't approve. 'You're supposed to be at school. What would Mummy say?'

'She's away,' Kerry pointed out. 'She doesn't need to know what we get up to.'

Quite.

'Please! Please!' Joe begged.

'Well, maybe,' Jeffrey said reluctantly. 'But that's my last word on the subject.'

Joe was boinging round the begonias like Zebedee on speed. 'LET'S! DO! IT!' he cried, punching the air.

Jeffrey shrank back into the garden swing, which was starting to give him motion sickness. Let's not, he thought.

Chapter Twenty-Five

This was madness, Ben decided, as he peeped inside the heavily laden picnic hamper complete with bottle of champagne, punnet of strawberries and the traditional red and white gingham cloth. Sheer unadulterated madness. He fussed with the glasses and cutlery that the Priory had also supplied, and then glanced at his watch. Kate would be waiting for him. It wasn't too late to back out. They could eat their picnic on the lawn in front of the Priory, with the Greenham Common women and the Fur Fabric Four as chaperones, rather than in the very romantic – and secluded – spot on the edge of the woods that he had recklessly chosen for them earlier in the day.

He tidied the cloth back over the hamper and headed out to where he had arranged to meet Kate. She stood with her back to him, wearing a floral sundress and flat strappy sandals. Her fingers tugged anxiously at her hair and he recognised, with some relief, that she probably felt the same as he did – as nervous as hell and with as much confidence as an emotionally retarded seventeen-year-old.

'Hi,' she said shyly.

'I've brought the picnic,' he said inanely, wondering what else she would think he was carrying in a wicker hamper. 'I thought we'd go up through the woods.' *Please look outraged and say you'd rather stay within screaming distance of the Priory.*

She crinkled her eyes against the sun as she smiled. 'That sounds nice.'

It's not nice! I'm trying to pretend to myself that I'm not hoping to seduce you. Don't encourage me!

They walked out across the croquet lawn, both aware of the slight lull in conversation as they passed the other course members who were enjoying a pre-prandial sherry under the fluttering butterfly umbrellas on the terrace. Several pairs of eyes swivelled to follow their progress.

'It's a lovely evening,' Kate said.

'Yes.' *Scintillating conversation, Ben!*

They pushed up through the cool shade of the woods, Kate walking slightly ahead of him where the path was too narrow to fit side by side. Golden shafts of sunlight dappled through the dark green leaves, shifting and swaying, so that they had to concentrate on their footing to avoid tripping over tree roots that snaked half-hidden over the surface of the sun-baked mud. It made talking impossible, which was just as well because they seemed to be finding it pretty impossible anyway.

'Through here,' Ben indicated when they reached the clearing he had earmarked. They ducked through the gap in a hawthorn hedge and emerged into a gently sloping area of lush green grass which banded a field of tall yellow corn. The fields stretched out as far as the eye could see, punctuated by the odd lone-standing farmhouse and abandoned tractor. The corn wasn't ripe yet for harvesting, but a few more weeks and it would be razed to the ground, as unattractive as day-old designer stubble. But, for now, it swayed magnificently in the hint of a breeze.

'What a beautiful setting,' Kate said, pulling the hair back from her forehead and tilting her face to the evening sun. 'It's hard to believe that we're only down the road from the nearest Tesco's.'

Ben laughed as he set the hamper on the ground.

'I'm sorry,' she apologised. 'Domestic duties are never far from my mind.'

'Do you assess everything by its proximity to supermarkets?'

'Not everything,' she said.

A woodpecker swooped across the field and landed in a nearby tree and began drilling maniacally into the bark in an attempt to find its dinner. At least they didn't have to knock themselves half senseless before they tucked into their picnic, Ben thought. Although for some reason, he seemed to be behaving like he was half senseless anyway.

Ben squatted on his haunches. 'I've spent too much time in London lately.' He shaded his eyes and stared into the distance. 'I've got out of touch with the countryside. I think you lose something of yourself when you're surrounded by nothing but buildings all the time. I've got a cottage in the Mendip Hills that I haven't been to in ages. It's thatched and full of spiders wearing hobnail boots. I like to go there and walk.'

'Alone?'

He looked back at her. 'Sometimes.'

'I don't know when it happened,' she said wistfully, 'but my interest in nature seems to have diminished to fussing around with bedding plants and a few hanging baskets. What I don't know about Miracle Grow isn't worth knowing. Perhaps that's what's sapping my soul.'

'I hate to see you unhappy,' Ben said.

'I'm not unhappy.' She sank down and plucked at the lush grass. 'Not really. I'm confused. What was it Sam said about T'ai Chi helping you to see things in perspective? If you could still the mind, it would be like looking into a pond without the distortion of any ripples on the surface. The image would no longer be fuzzy.' Kate looked unconvinced. 'I came here to have time to think about what I want from life, but instead of being clearer, the water seems to be a darn sight more muddy and the ripples are growing into extremely choppy waves.'

'Perhaps you're just going through a bad patch?'

She grinned at him and joked, 'It always makes me think of a field of cabbages when someone says that.'

He shrugged. 'Everyone has them.'

She gazed into the distance. 'I think it's more than that.'

Ben moved next to her, plucking a tall stalk of corn on the way. He chewed the end thoughtfully, twirling it slowly between his teeth.

'I thought I had everything I wanted,' she told him softly. 'Two lovely children to fulfil my maternal longings, a good, kind husband. We have a pleasant home. No money worries. No dandelions in the lawn.' She looked at Ben. 'And then suddenly one day, it isn't enough.'

Ben continued to stare out over the cornfield.

'Why can't I be content to stay at home and breed babies, the way mothers used to? Why can't I make my life revolve around producing home-made pastry and turning shirt cuffs to make them last that little bit longer? I'm thinking of joining the ranks of other women who go out to work and slave their bollocks off to afford the latest Volvo. For what purpose? I already drive a BMW, for heaven's sake!'

'How are they managing without you?' he asked practically.

'Fine, I expect.' She gave him a careworn smile. 'I've arranged an au pair to look after them. Not that they need it. Jeffrey is a terribly capable man, when he has the time. He's read the owner's handbooks for both of our cars. What's more, he knows where he's filed them if he ever has to refer to them again. How can I live up to that? I struggle to remember where the petrol goes, let alone how to open the bonnet. I haven't a clue what half of the buttons do. His standards are so exacting.'

'Does he miss you?'

'I honestly don't know,' Kate answered. 'He hasn't said so. Our conversations have been very stilted and I haven't even phoned him tonight. There's no intimacy in our relationship any more. All the passion has gone out of it.' She lowered her voice and looked away. 'We make love every Saturday night with the light off and Jeffrey on top. In the winter, we think we're being really racy if we even take our pyjamas off.'

Ben chuckled softly. 'I'm sorry, I shouldn't laugh.'

'He's so stuck in his ways that he still insists on wearing knickers rather than boxer shorts, preferably white ones. And wild horses couldn't persuade him into a pair of those little hip-hugging things. I think they look very sexy.' She flushed as her mind wandered to the type of underwear that Ben might be wearing. He was definitely a hip-hugger type. All week, his visible panty line had been noticeable by its absence. 'I shouldn't be telling you all this. I feel like I'm betraying him.'

'Do you still love Jeffrey?'

'I love him,' she said. 'I just don't know if I love him enough.' She pulled her dress down, smoothing it over her knees. 'I don't think my discontentment lies entirely with him, it's more to do with being discontented with myself.' She hugged her knees to her chest. 'I seem to be unable to move forward in my life. I feel as if my tank's been running on empty for years and now suddenly I've ground to an abrupt halt – miles from the nearest petrol station.'

'There might be one at the Tesco's down the road,' Ben suggested lightly.

Kate laughed, but shook her head. 'How did I expect T'ai Chi to open up the universe for me when I can't even get to grips with something as simple as the white crane animal play? Everyone else is swooping and soaring and I seem to be chained to the floor. I don't think I'll ever get airborne. It's mortifying the life out of me, Ben! That's what I feel like – I feel like a white crane who wants to spread her wings.'

229

'Don't worry. You'll get there.'

'That's what Sonia said. I'm not so sure.' Was that little ripple she had felt during the wood element exercises too minuscule to count? It was more likely to have been a muscle spasm than a connection with the universe. And if a tiny tremor in a broomstick was such cause for terror, how would she cope with encouraging her toes to leave terra firma?

'Do you know that white cranes mate for life?' Ben asked softly.

She turned and looked directly at him. 'At the moment that seems like a very depressing thought.'

He grinned and brought them back to earth. 'Does Madam think a chilled glass of champagne might help to lift her out of the doldrums?'

She gave him a grateful glance. 'That sounds like a truly wonderful idea!'

Kate watched Ben as he opened the champagne with a practised flourish. He handed her a frothing long-stemmed glass.

'What shall we toast?' she asked.

He held his glass out to hers. 'To white cranes spreading their wings.'

'White cranes,' she echoed and chinked her glass against his.

'And to us,' he said, his eyes searching hers.

'To us,' she answered unsteadily. They touched their glasses again, letting them linger together.

Ben got busy unpacking the picnic, while Kate spread the

gingham cloth over the grass. She helped him to open the little tubs of food. 'This looks lovely,' she said, nibbling at a prawn sandwich.

Ben lay propped up on the grass, stretching his long body parallel to the gingham cloth. They ate quietly, enjoying the food without the need to talk. Kate stared happily out over the fields. 'I collect fridge magnets, Ben,' she said dreamily. 'I have to buy one whenever we go on holiday. I've got castanets from Spain, a hamburger from America, a gondola from Venice and tulips from Amsterdam.'

'I think you need to get out more.'

She laughed. 'I do, don't I?'

'I'm sure that as your children get older you'll have time to turn your mind to loftier pursuits if you want to.'

'I can't blame the children, it's my own fault. Major world events barely touch me,' she said. 'There can be earthquakes in South America, floods in Bangladesh, bombs in Beirut and it all passes me by. But let there be snails on my busy Lizzies and my day is completely ruined. How pathetic can you get?'

'You're very hard on yourself.' He frowned at her. 'Working in an advertising agency as I do is hardly the stuff that world peace is made of, but we can all make our contribution. You just have to find the right niche.'

What was her niche? Reorganising the freezer so that she could fit in an emergency Sara Lee double chocolate gâteau? Kate Lewis's contribution to world harmony – never knowingly being caught without cake.

The sun was sinking steadily, giving a warning hint of the dusk to come, and there were a few clouds marshalling themselves on the horizon preparing to fling a bit of rain around. What did Sam say about yin and yang? After the sunshine there must always be rain? This was the natural order of things, the balance. She hoped the balance could wait until after their picnic.

Ben was sitting up now, watching the sun set. He rested his arms on his knees and looked straight ahead. 'Kate,' he said softly, 'have you ever felt totally connected to someone?'

She would have thought he was giving her a line, except he stumbled over the words. And she had felt it too.

'Deep inside, I mean. At a level I don't fully understand.'

'Not before,' she replied, and her own speech was stilted and uncoordinated – like Jeffrey trying to dance to a reggae beat – or any beat for that matter. 'I felt it during the Pushing Hands exercise today. Guy said we should discuss it.'

'For me that was just the confirmation of it. I've never felt like this about anyone else.'

'Don't say that,' she whispered.

'It's true.' He glanced over the gingham cloth at her. 'And I know you feel the same.'

'What can we do about it though? I'm married, Ben.'

'You're not happy with him.'

'I'm not happy with myself!'

They both stared at the horizon as if the answer might lie there.

'There must be hundreds of pretty single girls where you work. Ones with bigger chests and smaller bums and cute little turned-up noses.'

'There are a few,' Ben grinned.

'Why me?' Kate persisted. 'Why a married woman of thirty-five who still has a penchant for wearing blue eyeliner long after it could be considered fashionable?'

'There's no answer to that question,' he shrugged. 'And you know it. Why anything? Why does every workman who ever comes to your house take two sugars in his tea? Plumber, electrician, double-glazing fitter, British Telecom engineer . . . whatever. It's always tea and two sugars. Why?'

'I don't know why,' she answered in a tiny voice.

'And neither do I.' They looked at each other.

Ben selected the fattest, reddest strawberry from the punnet. 'Here.' He took it by the stalk and held it out to her. 'Peace offering?'

Kate leaned towards him, taking the strawberry in her mouth until Ben's fingers touched gently on her lips. She bit down and the sweet juice ran into her mouth. 'Mmmm.'

Smiling, he picked another one and slipped it into her mouth, staying close to her, watching her as she devoured the strawberry. He trailed the back of his hand over her cheek and stroked his fingers tenderly along the line of her jaw. 'You have a very strong jaw,' he said. 'Lots of tension.'

'I clench it in the night.' Kate swallowed hard. 'I'm grinding my back teeth away. My dentist always tells me off.'

He bent his head towards her, pausing with his mouth

close to hers, and she didn't move away. Ben flicked the tip of his tongue across her lips, slowly, teasingly. 'You taste wonderful.'

'Like a strawberry?' Kate's voice shuddered.

He tasted her again. 'Exactly like a strawberry,' he confirmed.

He tilted her head back, covering her mouth with his, breathing his heat into her. His hands were twisting into the hair at the nape of her neck. Energy spiralled within her, coming up through her body to focus on the sensual touch of Ben's lips. He made her feel transformed from a boring housewife and mother into a whirling twirling ballerina on top of a music box. She felt the breath catch in her throat as he ran his hand over her Laura Ashley sundress and grazed his thumb over the tender swelling of her nipples. She heard herself gasp. 'Ben . . .'

His mouth travelled down along her throat, easing inside the neckline of her dress, while his fingers continued their delicate assault. What was Sam saying about using martial arts techniques to neutralise and deflect an unwanted approach so that you don't get hurt? Except that this approach was very much wanted. Her hand stayed his fingers. 'Ben,' she said, 'this is wrong.'

He broke away from her with a heavy sigh. 'It feels very right.'

'I know.' Kate massaged her forehead with the palm of her hand. 'But it isn't.'

Moving away from her, he sat resting his thumbs against his lips. 'I want you,' he stated simply.

'I can't do this to Jeffrey. He doesn't deserve it.'

Ben stayed silent.

'You know nothing about me, Ben. You don't know that I failed my maths O-level, or that I can play the piano up to grade seven, but never practise now, or that I can't ride a bike to save my life, or that at my age I'm still frightened of the dark.' She pushed her fringe back from her face and stared at him. 'And I know nothing about you.'

'That doesn't mean there isn't anything between us.'

'It scares me,' she said.

'That's the last thing I want you to feel.' Ben slowly rubbed his hands over his face and then made to pack away the picnic. 'We'd better get back.'

'Not yet.' Kate put her hand on his arm. 'Just hold me.'

'If I hold you there's no guarantee my hands will behave,' he warned her.

'That's a risk I'm prepared to take.' She sat between his knees, her back against his chest. He wound his arms around her, drawing her to him and she could feel his heart beating against her ribs as he nestled his face in her hair.

The sun was setting in the sky, dusk bringing a chill to the air. The clouds had deepened to a rich indigo in a velvet blue sky, colour-washed with a pale swish of tangerine above the corn. For the moment, the rain had stayed away. But it was due, you could taste it on the breeze. They sat not speaking, Kate resting her head on Ben's shoulder listening to the steady rise and fall of his breath, feeling the heat of his body permeate through her. *I could stay like this for ever.*

'Can we be just friends?' she asked, snuggling against him.

'No,' he said sadly, tightening his hold on her. 'I don't think we can.'

Chapter Twenty-Six

'Oh, shit,' Jeffrey said quietly. He wasn't sure what was worse – the terrified screams or the livid orange paintwork. His eyes followed the twisting tubular track to the top. It looked an awfully long way up. But at least it meant that you couldn't see the fear on the victims' faces. He wiped his palms together. They were sweating. Profusely. *OBLIVION*, the sign said. *THE WORLD'S FIRST VERTICAL-DROP ROLLERCOASTER.*

Why was he allowing himself to be coerced into queuing up to go on this? he wondered. Last week he had baulked at climbing a gentle 170 steps to the pinnacle of the Bridgewater Monument – and now here he was, preparing to be hurtled at 4.5 Gs over a sheer drop into a yawning chasm of a hole strapped to nothing more substantial than a theatre seat. What's more, he had been queuing systematically since seven o'clock this Friday morning, when they had set out on this pursuit of folly. He had queued along the motorway, he had queued again to park, then to part with the best part of eighty quid for the four of them and now he was queuing up for a white-knuckle ride, just before he probably queued up to vomit.

The last time he had visited Alton Towers was as a boy on a school trip. There had been no lavish theme park then, just pleasant gardens, a rundown house and a half-hearted attempt at a cable car ride which went all of 200 yards. By the time you had queued it was quicker to walk. So some things never change. The only thrill he had got was from snogging Janet Eccleston (she of the hand-up-the-skirt incident) behind a beautiful purple rhododendron bush, which had fostered a lifelong aversion to kissing in public and a lifelong love of gardening.

Kerry and Joe were delirious. They had turned from wannabe pensioners into unruly adolescents overnight and he wondered what Kate would think of the sudden transformation. A bit of illicit bunking off had clearly unleashed their wild side. He didn't think the children had been taken out of school before in the pursuit of pure pleasure. Kate was very firm about that sort of thing. But then again, so was he. Usually. Natalie had once again phoned Hills & Hopeland to break the glad tiding that their most loyal employee was shunning his bought ledgers in favour of a little self-inflicted fear. He'd never bunked off work before this week, and this certainly couldn't be called the pursuit of pleasure for him. *What was it then? The pursuit of Natalie?*

He looked at the object of his desire and she gave his hand a quick squeeze, which made him sweat even more. Jeffrey surveyed the scene. The piercing screams at regular fifteen-second intervals (yes, he was counting) were jarring his nerves to well beyond previous levels of endurance. There was a minimum height requirement for *OBLIVION*, which meant that there were several very short and

238

disappointed children wailing at their distraught-looking parents. If only they knew how lucky they were! Couldn't these people put a maximum age limit or a blood-pressure monitor on this thing, to save *him* the embarrassment of bottling out? Jeffrey pushed his glasses onto his nose, a nervous tic he seemed to be developing nicely, and read the warning poster at the entrance to the ride:

Please be absolutely sure you wish to proceed. We do advise that you do not try to analyse what you are about to experience. As you will eventually come to realise, sometimes ignorance is preferable to absolute knowledge. What we do guarantee is that once you leave, you will never be quite the same again . . .

Jeffrey felt himself go pale. Very bloody encouraging.

There was a gaping concrete tunnel where the queue for *OBLIVION* snaked out. Kerry and Joe, bouncing excitedly, took him by the hands and dragged him to join the tail. Was it unseemly for a grown man to have a temper tantrum? He probably would have dug his heels in the ground if it hadn't been solid black tarmac. Natalie was bouncing excitedly too and it was a sight that was particularly disturbing to the equilibrium.

He distracted himself by staring fixedly at a bank of video screens flashing rapid disjointed images and playing the sort of loud repetitive music that could only be enjoyed if you were dropping Es – or so he imagined.

'What does oblivion mean?' Joe asked.

What indeed? Wasn't that what he was heading for – oblivion? A state of complete forgetfulness, tumbling down

239

a long dark tunnel somewhere between dream and reality, the end of existence as he knew it.

'It means you get totally wasted,' Natalie responded enthusiastically, when Jeffrey failed to speak.

Joe's eyes lit up. 'Great!'

Great.

A man with a dark collarless suit and a sombre expression popped up on the video screen. '*Welcome,*' he said. '*You have been designated for OBLIVION. The decision to come here was not your own.*'

Too right, mate, Jeffrey agreed. The decision to come here was taken by a very fanciable and fearless young Australian woman with the backing of two born-again delinquents. This was possibly the last place on earth he wanted to be – with the possible exception of Milton Keynes shopping centre on a Saturday afternoon.

'*This will be the ride of your life, during which you will free fall face-first into blackness.*'

Oh goody.

'*A free-falling object is something which falls under the sole influence of gravity.*'

He could feel Natalie close to him, the pressure of her arm lightly against his. That's what he was, a free-falling object, but under the sole influence of Natalie, who was a stronger force than anything as wimpish as gravity. Since he had first clapped eyes on her, something within him had felt seriously out of control, hurtling helplessly towards danger.

'*Unfortunately,*' the besuited man continued tonelessly,

'*in this instance, that object will be* YOU.' There was a malevolent smirk on his face and Jeffrey noticed that his mouth had gone dry.

The video showed a ticker-tape sequence of a bright red ball falling downwards. '*Free-falling objects accelerate as they plummet downwards,*' the man informed them. Elementary physics, Jeffrey reasoned with a spark of calm superiority. To illustrate the point the ball dropped faster and faster, until it hit the ground and cannoned off the screen. '*It is a pity,*' the unctuous smile was back, '*that, unlike the ball, people don't bounce back.*'

Jeffrey felt a cold trickle of sweat worm its way down his spine.

'*In fact, if Newton's Second Law of gravity is applied to your predicament, it could mean you are about to be trashed.*' A pleasant grin.

Very elementary physics. Could the same thing be said about his marriage? Was that about to be trashed too, if he continued this dangerous and risky free fall? He looked at Nat's beautiful face and her mane of messed-up blonde hair with an expression of extreme anxiety. There was a loud beeping noise and the word ANXIETY flashed in vibrant red letters on the screen. Jeffrey looked round him suspiciously. Natalie smiled encouragingly and they shuffled forward in the queue, edging towards the next bank of video screens and ten paces nearer to *OBLIVION*.

'You'll be right, Jeffers,' she winked.

The screams continued unabated.

The next video sequence spiralled onto the screens. '*In*

241

stressful situations like this, the body's fight or flight response system is activated. Muscles tense, heart rate speeds up and there is an increase in body temperature.'

There were all sorts of muscles tensing which shouldn't have been, and Jeffrey's heart rate was about to shoot off the Richter scale.

'For those about to descend into OBLIVION, extreme anxiety may even cause spontaneous combustion.' A whirling skull on the screen graphically burst into flames. *'Make sure you are wearing flameproof underwear,'* the man smirked.

Jeffrey was wearing the underwear that Natalie had bought him, complete with tortoise-shell buttons.

'Daddy.' Joe was kicking the barrier in a way that said his patience was wearing thin, the thought of experiencing extreme anxiety or being trashed simply sliding off his slender ten-year-old shoulders. 'I want to be on it now.'

'We're nearly there,' Jeffrey assured him. 'Just hang on for a bit longer.'

Why couldn't he take his own advice? All he had to do was hang on for a bit longer and Natalie would be gone from his life, back to Jessica's house and the goldfish and the gerbils. And Kate, his wife, his love, would be safely home from her T'ai Chi course and, like Dr Death in the video here, he would revert from a heaving mass of flame into a calm man in a sensible suit once again.

'Have you ever suffered from vertigo?' He was beginning to want to hit this bloke. *'Do you suffer from acrophobia, the fear of heights?'*

242

He had all sorts of fears these days. Some irrational, some less so. Fear of getting old, fear of losing his hair, fear of losing his job, fear of staying in the same job for ever, fear of never hearing the word promotion, fear of Kate finding out that Natalie had been buying him underwear.

'*Typical acrophobic symptoms are accelerated heartbeat, churning stomach, sweating palms and dizziness.*'

It sounded a lot like being besotted with an Australian au pair. '*After experiencing OBLIVION, some people may want to wipe the event from their memory. We should point out that you may have to relive it in your mind over and over and over and over . . .*'

The man on the video shrank to a little dot, to be replaced by whorling patterns that reminded Jeffrey of a Spirograph he had had when he was a boy. They had reached the top of the tunnel now and were almost at the start of the ride. The breeze was funnelling towards them, cooling his heated face, but the screams were significantly louder.

'Fuck,' Jeffrey sighed to himself.

DON'T LOOK DOWN! warned a big orange sign. He ignored it and looked down at Natalie. They had reached the edge of *OBLIVION*. Where did they go from here, apart from down?

Back on the video the spiralling images had been replaced, once again, by the same man, who looked distinctly more demonic this time. '*Everything has been designed for your comfort,*' his sugary voice was teasing. '*This ride is perfectly safe.*'

243

A little man in white popped up on his shoulder. The good side. The voice of reason. '*If it is safe, why is it called OBLIVION?*' he asked in fear.

It echoed Jeffrey's sentiments perfectly.

The alter ego continued, his voice rising to a shrill pitch: '*Have you ever seen anyone who's survived it and come out the other side?*'

Sneer. '*It is natural to have slight feelings of anxiety at this point. Just relax and prepare for a pleasurable experience. There is no cause for concern.*'

There *was* cause for concern. There was a wonderful wife to consider and two lovely children. Two children who were now hopping innocently from foot to foot in anticipation. Jeffrey smoothed his damp palms down the sides of his jeans.

'*Have you heard the screams?*' the voice of reason asked.

The beat of the music quickened and the queue jostled forward. Eager.

'*This ride is perfectly safe,*' the dark-suited man repeated smugly.

'*How do you know?*' There was panic in the other man's voice. How indeed? Jeffrey thought. It was a step once taken, that couldn't be undone. You had to live with the knowledge that you had fallen, face-first, for ever.

They were at the front of the queue now. Jeffrey turned round, the crowd behind him were pushing him forward. There was no way out. Natalie was grinning from ear to ear, displaying teeth galore, unaware that this ride meant so much more to him than she could imagine. The children

244

were ahead of him, their bright smiling faces now slightly tinged with fear.

'Ooo,' Kerry said worriedly and Joe looked suspiciously as if he wanted his teddy bear, Mr Growly, the one he pretended he didn't need any more.

Jeffrey was herded into his seat with a hefty push by a man in an orange jumpsuit. He could hear his breath labouring in his chest, like it did when he was climbing the long steep hill up the eighteenth hole at the golf course, heading back to the sanctuary of the clubhouse.

The smug man was speaking again. '*Just sit back and enjoy the experience*,' he smirked.

It was easy for him to say. Did he have family commitments? A bright orange harness was clamped unceremoniously over Jeffrey's head. His fingers trembled.

'*This is it!*' the panic-stricken man on the video yelled. '*You're nearly at the point of no return.*' He knew that. He had known it all the time, from the moment he had first met her. '*Are you sure you want to continue?*' What else could he do? He was being pushed inexorably towards the edge. His brain told him he shouldn't be doing this, but when he opened his mouth to say so, nothing came out.

'*Hasta la vista, baby! Goodnight, Vienna!*'

Clunk. They were all fastened in, sixteen people suddenly gone very quiet. '*Get out now while you still can!*'

There *was* no getting out. It was already too late. Far too late. Not seconds, not minutes, but six days too late.

'*Have a pleasant trip.*' The dark side had won. He was heading off on a course that he couldn't stop.

There was a churning of hidden machinery and, with a jolt that sent shock waves up his spine, the ride chugged out of its station, climbing steadily to the summit high above them and vertiginously high above the ground. Jeffrey's jowls juddered; he hadn't realised until now that he even had jowls.

By the time they reached the top, he was gasping for breath. Natalie's smile didn't waver and there was an expression of utter glee on her perfect features. Her hair floated magnificently on the wind. Only the excessive raising of her eyebrows showed any hint of fright. The two rows of theatre seats jerked to a sudden stop, perched on the very edge of nothingness. One minute he had been looking at a cloudless blue sky, now he was face down towards a gaping black hole and Jeffrey wondered briefly exactly what was, or wasn't, holding them up.

There was smoke billowing copiously from the hole in the ground. 'Oh my God,' he said in breathless awe, 'it's on fire.' His fingers gripped the safety bar. 'It's on fire and no one's noticed. They're going to drop us into it.'

'It's a special effect, Dad,' Joe assured him through chattering teeth. 'It's supposed to be there.' He clutched at his orange harness, his breath coming in shorter pants than the ones he wore to school. 'Just chill out, Dad.'

Chill out. He looked at his daughter. Kerry's face was white, her mouth opening and closing soundlessly like a goldfish. And what of him? The terror had numbed him. There was no feeling in his arms. His eyes were dry, his hands wet. His teeth were stuck to his lips.

Natalie placed her hand on his arm and looked him squarely in the eye. 'It'll be all right, Jeffers. You won't come to any harm. I promise you.'

At that moment, he would have believed anything she told him. He looked at his hands, rigid with tension, gripping the flimsy-looking bar that was the only thing protecting him from certain death as a squished mess on the ground. His knuckles, as promised, were white. There was a moment of intense peace and acceptance, before his stomach shot to his feet and his brain rattled violently in his skull. It was only a matter of time before the screaming started. This truly was the point of no return.

As they were launched over the edge into *OBLIVION*, Natalie turned to him and in a matter-of-fact way said, 'Just don't look down.'

Chapter Twenty-Seven

Kate was standing with her hands resting on her tummy, her eyes resting on Ben.

'Circle the hands slowly round the *Tan-Tien*, just below the navel,' Sam instructed. 'It should be a small physical movement, all the work is going on deep within your belly. Feel the growing warmth, hold it inside.'

She had been feeling warm all week without the need to circle her *Tan-Tien*. There was a burning at the back of her neck and a feverish flush to her cheeks.

'The fire element,' Sam said, 'is possibly the hardest to harness. It represents heat, desire, passion and joy. If we have an imbalance in this area it can become out of control, literally, spreading like wildfire inside us. The problem is that it then consumes us and leads to burnout.' He glanced at several of the men in the group, including Ben. 'All you high-flying executives have been warned!'

And what about us neglected housewives? Kate thought. What do we do if we've got a raging fire inside us that won't be harnessed? Fire might represent joy as well as passion, but how could she feel happy when today was the last day of the course – the last day she would spend with Ben? Sam had said that in the cycle of life, fire could

248

be overcome by the water element. Would returning to the shallow puddle of her life quell the flames that had been fanned within her?

'Are you feeling hot?' Sam asked them all.

Very hot, thank you, Sam. The rest of the class nodded dutifully.

'Let's finish there,' he said. 'Keep that joy inside of you for the rest of the afternoon and we can unleash it at the end-of-course party tonight! And now let's bow out to each other.' Right fist, left palm. *I mean you no harm.*

The group disbanded, wandering off to collect scattered belongings deposited under the shade of convenient trees. Ben fell in step beside her as Kate headed back towards the Priory.

'You look subdued,' he said.

'Yes – I'm sad that the course has ended so soon.'

'And you still haven't found the meaning of life?'

'No.' *But I've found someone who would give my life meaning. Does that count?*

'The party should be fun.' Ben looked as downhearted as she did, but at least he was putting a brave face on it.

'Yes,' she answered without enthusiasm.

'Someone's bought a cake.'

'Nice.'

'And sparklers.'

'Very nice.'

He tilted her chin with his finger. 'Don't be sad,' he said. 'Not on our last night together. I'll wait for you at the front of the Priory.' He looked to her for confirmation. 'About seven?'

'Seven,' she said automatically.

Back in her room, Kate flopped onto the bed and massaged her eyes with her fingertips. She wasn't going to the party. How could she, when all she really wanted to do was curl into a corner and weep? She couldn't face saying goodbye to Ben. What could they say to each other? *It was nice meeting you. So long and thanks for all the fish. We could have made each other deliriously happy if only I wasn't a wife and mother ...* How could she tell him what she really felt, when she wasn't even sure herself?

She would pack and go home now – sneak out like a thief in the night. No backward glances. No what ifs. Back to the safety of her des res in Acacia Close. Kate pulled herself off the bed, took her suitcase out of the cupboard. She dutifully began to pack.

Kate lifted the new nightdress she was clutching to her chest and regarded it critically. Marks & Spencer's finest. It was a married woman's nightie. Warm and functional with absolutely no attempt at glamour. As Sonia had pointed out, it was one small step up from pink rosebuds and this was her attempt at being a femme fatale. She rolled it into a tight little ball and threw it, with more venom than accuracy, at the wastepaper basket.

Placing the last few items in the case for their journey back up the A41, Kate clicked it shut. What now? There was nothing else to be done. It was time to leave. Jeffrey would be pleased that she was home early. It would be a nice surprise. Although he wasn't a man who was overly keen on surprises. Being on the receiving end of a kissogram was probably one of Jeffrey's worst nightmares. She ought to phone him at work and let him know her change in plans. She would hate to dash home and find that he'd taken the children to the cinema or Pizza Hut. Home alone with nothing but fridge magnets and floating candles for company. The thought made her shudder.

As she picked up the phone to dial Hills & Hopeland, there was a quiet knock on her door. She hurriedly replaced the receiver and smoothed down her hair. It must be Ben. He would see the case and would know she was planning to tiptoe quietly out of his life without the courtesy of telling him. The gentle knock came again.

Kate went to the door, and bravely opened it. Sam stood leaning on her doorframe.

'Can I come in?' he said.

'Yes. Of course.' She stood aside.

He threw a glance at the packed case. 'You're giving the party a miss?' His eyes were soft and sympathetic. 'Not in the mood for celebrating?'

'Not really.'

He took her hand and pulled her towards the bed, sitting her down next to him. 'I wanted a few words with you before you left, Kate.'

She shrugged, not understanding. 'Why?'

'You've been finding this week a bit of a struggle, haven't you?'

251

She nodded without speaking. *Don't be nice to me, Sam, you'll start me snivelling!*

'Persevere, Kate,' he advised. 'Sometimes, to learn to fly at all, we have to fly in the face of what's expected of us.' He squeezed her fingers, lightly as if he were scared of crushing them. 'Only then can we truly be the person we really are, rather than the person we've forced ourselves to be or let ourselves become. Do you understand what I'm trying to say?'

She nodded dumbly again, but it was such an infinitesimal and painful movement, she wasn't sure that it had registered.

'If you've been joined at the hip with someone for a long period of time, it can take a while to learn to stand on your own two feet, let alone to then take both of those feet off the ground so that you can begin to soar free.'

A tear escaped from Kate's eyes and she rubbed her hand over her face.

'Do you remember what I was saying earlier about the fire element, how it can cause burnout in high-flyers if it rages uncontrolled inside you? The same goes for lovers too.'

So, her Chi had been gyrating its hips at Ben more obviously than she thought.

'With the wild passion there may be sparks, fireworks, the crackle of electricity, but let it get out of control and it'll consume you from the inside out. Fire makes us act irrationally. For balance in a relationship there needs to be earthing too. Friendship, caring, stability.'

'But what if that's all there is, Sam?' Kate asked bleakly. 'What if there isn't any fire left in a relationship? None at all. What then?'

'Then you have an imbalance.'

Kate forced a tearful laugh. 'I have an imbalance.'

'A serious imbalance,' he confirmed. 'There is a negative side of being too earthed. It makes for a solid and totally dependable relationship, but there's no growth or development in the partnership. Nothing moves forward. You lose all the sparkle and stop reaching for the stars together.'

When had she and Jeffrey last stopped to look at the stars, let alone reach for them?

'The weight of being grounded by another person will begin to drag the free spirit down. Eventually, they'll want to break free. To fly.'

'Isn't there another way? Isn't it possible for things to change?'

'Nothing's impossible,' Sam shrugged. 'It depends how long you are prepared to wait. But some people can't ever grasp the fire element, Kate – it's literally too hot for them to handle. They're frightened of getting their fingers burnt. Someone who has their feet rooted deeply in the ground may take years to feel safe with even a flicker of flame.'

'What do I do then?' she whispered. 'Should I throw myself on the fire and see if there is any underlying earth to support it when it eventually burns out? Or do I go back to the solid mountain of earth and anchor myself to the hope that one day something will set it alight?'

'I'm not here to be judgemental, Kate,' he assured her. 'I want to help.'

'By pouring cold water on my flames?'

'I wanted to point out the drawbacks.'

Don't you think I know them already, Sam?

'But, at the end of the day,' he continued, 'only you know what you really need.'

'Fire or earth? What a choice.'

He regarded her packed suitcase waiting near the door. 'By the look of it, you've already made your decision.'

'By the look of it,' she agreed.

He stood up. 'I'll let you go then.'

'Thanks, Sam,' she said. 'You're very kind.'

He wrapped his arms round her and hugged her. 'You'll be missed at the party.'

'I know.'

'Perhaps you should stay,' he said, letting her go. 'See it through to the end. It may make things clearer.'

'Still the ripples in the pond?'

'Perhaps.' He shrugged. 'There's something that may help. It's a sound that you can make to heal the heart. You say it quietly, internally – *aaah*.' He breathed it out gently.

'Just *aaah*?'

Sam grinned. 'It's not as easy as it sounds.'

'Nothing ever is.'

Kate followed him to the door. He stood with his hand hovering over the handle, hesitating. 'Do you want me to give a message to Ben?'

254

She shook her head, mouth set in a determined line. What was there to say? 'Can you love two people at once, Sam?'

He smiled ruefully. 'Not unless you're a Conservative MP, Kate.'

'Hills and Hopeland,' the sing-song voice at the end of the phone trilled.

'It's Kate Lewis,' she said, as she gathered the final few bits and pieces of her belongings together. 'Can I speak to Jeffrey, please?'

'I'm sorry, Mrs Lewis, he isn't here.'

'I thought I might just catch him before he left,' she said. 'Never mind.'

'He hasn't been here all day.'

Kate stopped in her tracks. '*All day?*'

'Your au pair phoned in this morning. He's sick.'

'*Sick?*'

'I thought you knew.'

'I'm away. On a course,' she explained.

The receptionist tutted sympathetically. 'He's not been very well all week.'

'*All week?*' She was beginning to sound like a parrot.

'He had Wednesday off too and had to go home early every other day. We've been quite worried. It's not like him.'

You're telling me! It's not like him at all. If Jeffrey had a suspected brain tumour, he'd take two Hedex and carry on.

'Perhaps he's missing you,' the receptionist said coyly.

'Perhaps,' Kate said distractedly. *Or perhaps not.* 'Thank you. I'll try him at home.'

But the home phone rang and rang until the ansaphone cut in. '*Jeffrey and Kate are unavailable to take your call . . .*'

That was clear enough. But why was he unavailable if he was supposed to be at home dallying at death's door? What should she do – assume that he was too ill to get to the phone, jump in the car and zoom home to soothe his fevered brow? If he was so ill, where was Natalie? Who was looking after him? Who was looking after the children?

Kate tried his mobile. '*The Vodafone you have called may be switched off,*' a robotic voice informed her. '*Please try again later.*'

Kate narrowed her eyes, scowling at the receiver. Where the hell was he? She rifled through her handbag, fumbling around until she found her address book. Flicking through the pages, she found the number of their next-door neighbour, Mrs Barrett. Fortunately, she answered after three rings.

'Mrs Barrett,' Kate was feeling rather breathless now. 'It's Kate Lewis. How are you?'

'Oo, I'm fine, thank you, dear,' Mrs Barrett answered. 'My knees have been better, but I shouldn't grumble.'

She did. Constantly.

'Mrs Barrett,' Kate butted in, before she started to catalogue the rest of her ailments, 'have you seen Jeffrey today?'

'Now then,' she said. 'Let me see.' There was a pause, during which Mrs Barrett's brain seemed to be slowly clicking into gear. 'I saw them all getting into the car first thing this morning.'

Them all?

'Jeffrey and the children?'

'And that flighty-looking piece. Oo, I do beg your pardon, my dear.'

'Did Jeffrey look unwell?'

'Unwell? Why, no, dear,' she said. 'Not at all. He looked the picture of health. Laughing like a drain, he was, and the children.'

'And the flighty piece?'

'Her too. And the milkman hadn't yet been.'

'So, it was before seven?'

'They looked like they was off to the seaside for the day, way they were carrying on. Early start and all that horseplay.'

Horseplay? Kate didn't like the sound of that at all.

'Didn't the children have their school uniform on?'

'Not from where I was standing. Although I only caught a glimpse of them from behind the bedroom curtain,' she added. 'I'm not one for being nosey.'

Perish the thought! 'Is there anyone at home now?'

'I can't see the car from the window,' Mrs Barrett said in a muffled voice. Kate could imagine her craning her neck to get a better view round the Pyracantha Firethorn which they had planted especially to block it. 'Is everything all right, dear?'

'It's fine,' Kate assured her. 'It must have slipped Jeffrey's mind to tell me they were going out for the day.' *What else had conveniently slipped his mind?* 'I'm sure there's nothing to worry about.'

'Do you want me to go round there?'

Kate was beginning to regret phoning her. It would be all round the Close by tomorrow. She could imagine Mrs Barrett's arms folded over her cardiganed chest, recounting the tale to all who would listen, adding a few little embellishments along the way to make it a bit more juicy. 'No. Everything's fine. Really.'

'Well, you just let me know if there's anything I can do to help,' Mrs Barrett cooed sympathetically. 'It must feel very strange being all those miles away and not knowing quite what's going on.'

'I'll be back tomorrow,' Kate replied firmly.

'Right you are, then,' Mrs Barrett said. 'Bye bye for now.'

Kate put the phone down. So much for her plans to rush home to her husband and the bosom of her family. The white rose that Ben had picked for her still sat in her toothbrush mug on the dressing table. It was fully open now, its scent delicately fragrant against the slightly stale smell of a hotel bedroom, but the water in the mug was cloudy and needed changing, and one or two of the petals were starting to curl, turning brown at the edges.

What was Jeffrey up to? Why couldn't he have picked up the phone and called her? He seemed to be working on the same theory as her mother – that telephones were only made for receiving incoming calls and that the dial was largely ornamental. Here was she, trying to single-handedly circumnavigate the stormy seas of their marriage, while her husband was gallivanting around who knows where in the company of a dangerously beautiful blonde with legs like a particularly tall giraffe and teeth galore.

I'll be back tomorrow. That's what she'd said on the phone. Was she going to stay and see this through to the end then, after all? She looked at her case standing by the door, the phone sitting silently on the bedside table and the white rose blossoming forth in her toothbrush mug.

Chapter Twenty-Eight

Still bubbling in the afterglow of excitement, Jeffrey struggled to get the key in the front door. It didn't help that he was being harassed from behind.

'Come on, come on,' Kerry urged, sounding like Jeremy Paxman on *University Challenge*. 'I need to do a wee.'

'So do I,' Natalie agreed.

Joe hopped around silently, but with a purposeful sense of urgency.

Jeffrey was wearing a black and orange T-shirt which said I SURVIVED *OBLIVION*! on the front and a baseball cap in the same colour scheme with a catchy 'O' logo on the peak. Nat, Kerry and Joe were sporting matching outfits, except that Joe's baseball cap was worn back to front, which Jeffrey thought looked too ridiculous for words. He had splashed out on them in the souvenir shop in an impromptu moment of frenzied purchasing folly and had even bought the dreadful photograph of them all looking suitably frozen with terror from the booth at the end of the ride.

The front door swung open to sighs of relief as everyone raced for the bathrooms. Jeffrey smirked to himself. He was feeling vibrant, drunk with euphoria and a sense of achievement. He had felt the fear and done it anyway! The chorus of 'Wild Thing' strummed round inside his head.

Natalie appeared first. 'Great day, Jeffers,' she said, clapping him heartily on the back. 'I expect you'll need a nice cup of tea now?'

He nodded enthusiastically, before he realised she was mocking him. Then to his utmost surprise, she leaned over and kissed him, briefly, hotly, full on the mouth. He was still reeling as she wiggled away into the kitchen and put the kettle on.

The light on the ansaphone was winking at him.

'It's Kate.' His wife's voice filled the hall. 'I . . .' There was a strained pause. He hadn't spoken to Kate since Wednesday and then it had been a very half-hearted conversation. The sort of tense exchange you had with a double-glazing salesman you were trying to get off the phone as quickly as possible. Perhaps he should have called her last night, but with the barbecue and the plans to be made for Alton Towers ... Excuses. There was a tremor to Kate's tone. 'I'll catch up with you later. When you get back from wherever you are ...'

Jeffrey frowned.

The next message made him frown even more.

'Jeffrey,' cut-glass English tones rang out. 'Miles Hopeland here. Wanted a few words with you, old chap. It hasn't gone unnoticed that you've been missing from the office a fair bit this week and I'd like to discuss it with you. Please will you call me at home as a matter of urgency.'

Uh oh. *It hasn't gone unnoticed*. Pay-back time. Jeffrey glanced at his watch. It was getting late. Which music should he face first? The merry dance he seemed to be leading Kate, or the funeral march from Miles Hopeland? No doubt the firm had found out he wasn't sick or rather he *was* sick – but of his own volition and due to an excess of Gs and candy floss, rather than a deadly virus. Whichever way, he *would* be sick by the time Miles had finished with him.

He'd phone Kate first and put her mind at rest. It was the last day of her course and he didn't want to upset her by telling her that he had been discovered bunking off work and had been sacked. She would never find the meaning of life if she found out instead she had an unemployed husband, and he didn't want to feel responsible for her failure as well as his. Jeffrey put his head in his hands. He couldn't quite believe how calmly he was taking this. It was true that his life had flashed momentarily before him – graduation, marriage, birth of two children, first Mercedes, first set of golf clubs, pension rights. But there was a vague sense of detachment, a peaceful acceptance of the situation, a quietening inside of him. Perhaps this was the catalyst he had needed. He could set up his own firm, become a consultant – that was all the rage – or sell up and buy a smallholding in the Outer Hebrides and do bed and breakfast for people who couldn't afford to go to the Seychelles.

As it turned out he couldn't tell Kate anything. He phoned the Priory, but they couldn't find her anywhere. She wasn't in her room and she didn't answer their paged calls. Jeffrey replaced the receiver. It would have to wait until she got home.

He padded through to the kitchen, where Natalie handed

him a cup of tea. It was just as he liked it – steaming hot, not too much milk, too much sugar. He sat on a chair at the table and swallowed it gratefully.

'Who was on the ansaphone?' Nat asked.

'One call was from Kate,' he said, 'and the other one was the senior partner of my firm requesting the pleasure of a phone call. Urgently.' Jeffrey pursed his lips. 'It has come to the attention of the powers that be,' he informed Nat, 'that I have been forsaking my post and providing paltry excuses for doing so.'

She raised one eyebrow quizzically.

'I think Hills and Hopeland and I will shortly be parting company.'

'Real life, Jeffers! They can't sack you for blagging off for a few days.'

'I think you'll find they can,' he said.

Natalie crossed her long legs, a look of concern flitting across her face. 'You'll talk your way out of it,' she reassured him. 'You could charm a koala bear out of a eucalyptus tree.'

'Thank you for your faith in me,' he smiled, 'but Miles Hopeland is no koala – a dingo, perhaps. But no koala.' Jeffrey swigged some more tea. 'Anyway,' he said bullishly. 'I'm not sure that I want to. My career's been going nowhere fast for years. I'm in as much of a cul-de-sac as this house is.' He gestured around him. 'Perhaps the time has come for change.'

'Take some time to think about this before you phone him.' Nat sounded worried.

'No,' Jeffrey said, pushing away from the table. 'I think I'll phone him now, while I'm in the mood.'

'Please, don't do anything rash.'

'I have spent my life not doing anything rash,' Jeffrey replied rationally. 'Until this week.' He stood up, scraping his chair across the terracotta glazed tiles with a determined air.

'Sit down for a while,' Natalie cajoled. 'Finish your tea.'

'I have finished my tea, Nat.' He turned his cup upside down to prove it. 'And a splendid cup of tea it was, too. I shall miss your tea-making skills.' He looked at her and their eyes met.

'I'll miss you too, Jeffers,' she said softly.

A lump rocketed to his throat. The bravado he had been feeling evaporated instantly and an intense sadness flooded his heart.

They looked at each other for a few moments longer.

'I'd better make that call.' Jeffrey shrugged at her and turned away.

Five minutes later, he returned to the kitchen in a daze. He looked down at his hands and saw they were shaking. Natalie was biting her fingernails.

'Did you get through to him?' she asked nervously.

Jeffrey nodded speechlessly.

'Was it what you expected?'

'No.' It wasn't what he had expected at all.

'Was it bad?' she prompted.

'No,' he managed. 'No. It wasn't bad.'

264

'Did he want you to leave?'

'No,' he said. 'No. He didn't.'

'Did he give you a warning?'

'No. None at all.'

'Jeffers!' Natalie cried. 'I can't stand this. Dish it!'

He looked up at her, face blank with bewilderment. 'He promoted me.'

'He *what*?'

A slow grin spread over Jeffrey's face. 'He bloody well promoted me!'

'He didn't!'

'He did!'

She ran across the kitchen, grabbing him, squeezing him in a bear hug, dancing, whirling round the table, shrieking with glee. They stopped, breathless with exertion, laughing, both of them panting heavily.

'Ah, I bet this calls for another nice cup of tea?'

'I think it calls for something a bit stronger than that.' Jeffrey reluctantly let go of her and with a flourish produced a bottle of champagne from the fridge. As he wrestled with the cork, Natalie plucked two Wallace and Gromit tumblers from the cupboard above the kettle and Jeffrey let the champagne fizz over into them.

'What are we celebrating?' Kerry leaned in the doorway, looking as if she hadn't quite enough energy to stand upright.

'I've got a promotion.'

'Great.' She looked unimpressed. 'Joe and I are knackered.'

265

'Tired,' Jeffrey corrected.

'We're knackered and we're off to bed.' She gave him a wave. 'It's been cool, Dad.'

'Cool,' he agreed.

'And this is cool too,' Natalie said, clanking her tumbler against his. 'Who am I drinking to?'

'The new partner of the widely respected and reputable firm of Hills and Hopeland, accountants to the stars!'

'A partnership?'

'I can hardly believe it.' He sank onto a kitchen chair and gulped his champagne. 'They thought I was sneaking time off to go for interviews.' Jeffrey laughed. 'There was a rumour going round the office that I was being head-hunted for a top job with Price Waterhouse.' He looked at Natalie and she was grinning back. '*Me*? I've always wanted to be head-hunted,' he said. 'It sounds so glamorous.'

Natalie sat down next to him and tipped some more champagne into their tumblers. 'I'm so pleased for you,' she said, clutching his hand. 'But it's probably no more than you deserve.'

'After all these years.' Jeffrey shook his head in amazement. 'I thought I'd become like part of the furniture. A filing cabinet in the office of life. Useful to have around, but no one really looks at it or appreciates how much you'd miss it if it left.'

'We take a lot of things in life for granted . . .' Natalie agreed solemnly.

He glanced up at the sudden change in her tone.

'. . . People most of all.'

A few of the bubbles in his champagne burst. Natalie emptied the bottle and threw it in the bin. There was a slight weave to her step, as there had been when they had first stepped from OBLIVION. He felt a bit wobbly himself. His head was reeling and he could feel the flush of alcohol on his cheeks.

'Fucking hell,' he said with a nervous giggle which followed a rush of momentous realisation.

'I'm starving,' Natalie announced.

'Me too,' he agreed as his stomach gave a confirming rumble. The last meal they had eaten were four soggy quarter-pounders at a table cunningly disguised as a bubblegum pink cartoon car in the McDonald's at Alton Towers. Already it seemed like a million years ago. One way and another, it had been a week of new experiences.

'We could wait while I prepare one of Kate's health-conscious and well-balanced meals,' she slurred. 'Or we could improvise.'

'Improvise,' Jeffrey dictated, feeling reckless.

They had a bowl of Coco Pops floating in banana milkshake, followed by Häagen-Dazs Cappuccino Chocolate Chip ice cream straight from the carton with a shared spoon. There was something decidedly smutty and sexy about spooning ice cream into a stranger's mouth – if you could get over the fact that they might have germs. They lingered too long over the kitchen table until their bottoms started to go numb on the hard chairs. Jeffrey wandered off to rummage in the dining-room cupboard until he found another bottle of champagne and they drank it warm, knocking Wallace and Gromit's heads together with unrestrained hilarity.

'Let's take the rest of this through to the lounge,' Jeffrey muttered through lips that felt as thick as a pair of pork sausages.

They tumbled onto the sofa, Natalie curling her legs beneath her. Jeffrey drained the second bottle. 'It's been a great week,' he said woozily, forgetting in his haze of Moët & Chandon that Natalie had tattooed both of his children, permanently mutilated his daughter, caused great expenditure on reglazing, obliterated his bank account and most of his food, and had induced nausea several times in several different guises.

'It has,' she agreed, letting her head hang back over the cushions. 'A real bonza week.'

She returned herself to an upright position and stared at him, the slate-grey cat eyes snapping sharply into focus. 'I mean that,' she said.

'I don't want it to end,' Jeffrey answered softly.

'All good things do.'

It would be so easy to kiss her, just one small movement and he could do it and it would seem like the most natural thing in the world. Natalie moved towards him, closing the gap. She put her tumbler on the coffee table and took Jeffrey's from his clenched fist and placed it next to hers, so close that Wallace and Gromit's heads were virtually touching.

His heart was hammering in his ears and his palms had gone cold with fear. The clock on the mantelpiece was ticking loudly into the silence. It had been a wedding present from some long-forgotten friends and he had always loathed the noise it made. 'I think we'd better go to bed,' he said, suddenly sounding very sober.

'I could take that one of two ways, Jeffers.'

He sighed and it sounded like the longest, saddest sigh in the world. 'I'm a married man, Nat. However much I might want to, I can't do this.'

'If you're a married man, where's your wife?'

'As you well know, she's on a T'ai Chi course, finding herself.'

'She could, at this very moment, be doing exactly the same thing.'

He shook his head. 'Kate isn't like that.'

'How do you know?'

'She bakes cakes for the school fête,' Jeffrey said. 'That's not the stuff adultery is made of.'

Natalie put his fingers to her lips and licked them, slowly, lazily, as she'd licked the ice cream from his spoon, sending tremors of desire through his body. 'No one would know.'

'I would.' Jeffrey pulled his hands from her grasp. 'I'm not the type of person who can do casual sex, Natalie.'

She giggled seductively. 'We could get dressed up, if that would make you feel better.'

'I could sleep with you tonight, pretend that it meant nothing and watch you walk out of my life.' He looked at her. She was young, beautiful and very, very tempting. 'But I'd be lying,' he said. 'And the hardest person of all to lie to is yourself.'

Chapter Twenty-Nine

The trees surrounding the Priory terrace had been dressed with sugar strands of tiny white fairy-lights that twinkled like stars. Strains of mellow jazz drifted on the air, falling and rising with the fizz of conversation. The air was sultry, treacle-thick, and needed a thunderstorm to blow it apart. It was a magical setting for a party.

The rest of the students were already there, drinking tall glasses of Pimm's stacked high with ice and cucumber. Kate was observing it all going on around her, threading her way through the mass of bodies, watching out for toes and handbags and uneven paving stones, but she wasn't really there at all. It felt as if she was outside of her body, seeing it all happen to someone else. Smiling, nodding, saying hello, while her mind was occupied elsewhere. How could they have come to the end of the course so quickly? The week had gone by and yet she had only blinked her eyes. She had barely begun to know Ben and yet, so soon, she would be without him again. What would happen now it was all over? Ben squeezed her fingers, bringing her back to earth again, leading her through the crowd.

'Drink?' he asked.

She nodded and Ben went off to fetch her a glass of

white wine. She saw Sam edging his way through the throng and suddenly he was next to her.

'Fire?' was all he said.

'Water,' Kate smiled in return. 'I'm trying to go with the flow for once, rather than paddling upstream.'

Besides, Mr Earth had gone AWOL when I tried to phone him.

'I'm proud of you,' he said, and pecked her cheek.

Ben was back. He took her hand again, shrugging off the simpering attentions of the Fur Fabric Four (who were looking distinctly pie-eyed only halfway down their Pimm's), and led her to the edge of the gathering. They leaned against one of the low sweeping branches of the Cedar of Lebanon, secluded from the main hub of the party.

'I feel really awkward,' he confessed. 'It's as if I want to fit a lifetime's talking into one night, but I don't quite know where to start.'

'Don't say anything, Ben. It will only make things more difficult.'

'We've been together such a short time.' His eyes were racked with uncertainty. 'And now that I've found you, I don't want you to go.'

She put her finger to his lips, silencing him. 'There's no point in torturing ourselves with this. We can never be more than we are now. Tomorrow, I'll go back to my family, and life will continue as it always has.'

'Did you find what you were looking for from the course?'

Kate let the sturdy branch take her weight. 'In some ways I found *more* than I was looking for.' She gave him a sideways glance. 'And in other ways, I feel as if I'm still floundering around. I never did get to grips with being a white crane and now it's too late. Perhaps I'm not cut out for flying.'

'You are,' he said. 'And don't let anyone else convince you otherwise.' He took her glass, his eyes twinkled mischievously. 'I'm not sure if I'm cut out for dancing though.'

Kate grinned. 'I take it that's a hint,' she said. 'End of serious talking.'

'No,' he said. 'We can talk later. Now, I just want a reason to touch you.'

He took her hand and pulled her into the circle of dancers who were shuffling round the saxifrages on the terrace. As he held her to his chest, she could feel they were both trembling; the heat of the night rushed through her body and the spiralling energy twirled inside her until she felt totally merged with Ben. It was like one of those films in which the mirror-ball above the dance floor throws spangles of coloured light over the hero and heroine; everyone else blurs until they no longer exist and they're alone, whirling together, oblivious to everything but themselves. There was no one but Ben. The Fur Fabric Four could have done a moonlight streak with nothing but a cocktail umbrella between their teeth and Kate would never have noticed.

They swayed in time with the music, dance after dance, grateful of the excuse to hold each other tight.

'You dance wonderfully,' she murmured.

'You're very kind,' he answered with mock formality. His face was against her hair, his hands on her back – hot, disturbing. He lowered his voice. 'Stay with me tonight, Kate.'

She looked up and met his eyes. 'Yes,' she whispered.

He searched her face. 'Are you sure?'

'Yes.'

'Do you think they'd notice if we left now?'

'Yes,' she said.

'We'll miss the sparklers.'

'And the cake.'

Strains of 'Love is the Drug' drifted towards them on the heavy breeze. In a locked embrace they stumbled round.

'*I say go, she say yes*,' Bryan Ferry warbled.

'Go?' Ben said.

'Yes.'

And they threaded their way through the party animals who were intent on pouring Pimm's down their throats as if it was the last thing they would ever do. Sonia would have been in her element, Kate thought.

Ben curled his arm round her waist, guiding her back towards the Priory. He cleared his throat. 'Your room or mine?' he asked huskily.

She thought of the pots of assorted wrinkle creams, firming creams, softening creams all lined up on the dressing table, mentally berating her nightly beauty routine which ensured she went to bed greased up like a cross-Channel swimmer. The functional nightdress was still half in, half out of the wastepaper bin. 'Yours.'

They crossed the cobbled courtyard and wound their way up the staircase towards Ben's room with the stealthy movements of criminals. How could she be acting like this? Kate asked herself. She was the only girl in her class at school who wouldn't steal sweets from Woolworth's pick 'n' mix counter, even though her friends assured her it wasn't real theft because you could eat the evidence.

Ben smiled at her reassuringly. 'This bit's always the hardest.'

Is it? This was the first time she'd ever even contemplated anything like this and a niggle of doubt asked her how regular an occurrence this was for Ben. Was he used to leading compliant women to his room in the still of the night? What was she doing, agreeing to spend the night with a man she hadn't even kissed? He might be awful at it! The only other person she had kissed – *really* kissed – apart from Jeffrey was Paul Taylor when she was fifteen, a snatched moment of passion at a school disco. He had been all tongue and dribble and cold sores. It lasted about ten seconds and she was convinced she would get pregnant because she was two-timing her steady boyfriend. Kate glanced cautiously at Ben. He didn't look anything like Paul Taylor. In fact, her heart did barrel rolls just watching him. He was bound to be an awfully good kisser. As he fiddled with the key in the door, her insides juddered alarmingly.

His room overlooked the croquet lawn and the majestic Cedar of Lebanon. It was larger and more plush than hers, and it was with some relief that Kate saw there was a double bed dominating the room rather than her midget-sized single jammed up against the wall. The scent of him filled the room – fresh, clean, spicy, sexy, unmistakable. *Eau de hunk*. He was tidy. She liked that in a man. There were no clothes lying around, just some loose change, his wallet and a travel alarm on his bedside table. A bottle of cK One stood by the mirror on the dressing table.

She could see the terrace from the window; the party was carrying on unabated. The music was louder now, sexier, pulsating and people were dancing with the type of abandon that would once have been innocently labelled 'gay'.

Ben came up behind her and wrapped his arms round her. 'You're shivering,' he said. 'This is probably the hottest night of the year. You can't be cold?'

'Terrified,' she admitted.

'Why?' He gave a half-laugh. 'There's no need to be. Just relax.'

Kate pulled away from him and perched on the study desk that also came as an added feature in Ben's room. She looked at her feet. 'I'm scared in case you ask me to do something that I haven't done before.'

'You're a married woman,' he said, catching her hand. 'A mother of two.'

Kate grimaced. 'This isn't a good time to remind me of that.'

'What can I possibly ask you to do that you haven't done before?'

'I don't know. I'm not even sure I'm aware of all the

275

options.' She hugged her arms to her body. 'Jeffrey has been my only boyfriend. He was my first tentative kiss, my first fumbled petting, the first, and only, man to make love to me. If I haven't done it with Jeffrey, I haven't done it at all.'

Ben laughed softly.

'Don't laugh at me!'

'Just let it happen, Kate.' He came towards her and framed her face with his hands, feathering kisses on her mouth, moulding his body into hers. 'It would be nice to take you to places you've never been before.'

'There are lots of places I've never been to before,' Kate warned. 'I've never been to Bognor, for one, but I'm not sure I'm in a tearing hurry to go there.'

'You'd love it!' he teased.

'I'm frightened to do this, Ben.' She wriggled uncomfortably. 'I feel so inadequate,' she whispered. 'I'm a walking mass of stretch marks, gashes and childhood scars. You won't know whether to make love to me or play noughts and crosses.'

'You are so beautiful,' he said lovingly. 'The decision's already been made.' Ben buried his warm mouth into the soft skin of her neck and began to unbutton her blouse.

'Oh,' Kate replied weakly.

Chapter Thirty

Jeffrey lay on his bed, arms stretched out above his head. He and Natalie had shuffled drunkenly up the stairs together, and had shuffled a bit more on the landing outside his bedroom door, exchanging looks of longing and indecision – on his part. He had never been any good at this sort of thing. He put it down to lack of practice and a certain emotional naivety when it came to the opposite sex. Kate, he could just about cope with, but other women were a complete mystery. The moment went on too long. Then Natalie had spun on her heels and marched purposefully towards her own room. And the sinking of his heart was matched by the bubble of relief he felt in letting her do it.

He wondered what Kate was doing now. He hoped that the course had been all she had wanted, and that she would come home feeling refreshed and ready to face new challenges. And what would he feel when tomorrow came? He was looking forward to her coming back. *Wasn't he?*

There was a knock on the door and he flicked the duvet over him in case it was Kerry. Before he could speak, the handle twisted and it creaked open on its hinges.

Natalie stood in the door, framed by the light from the moon. She was wearing a wisp of silk that was probably

277

supposed to be a dressing gown and her normally tousled hair looked suspiciously as if it had been brushed.

'Hi,' she said.

Jeffrey sat up in alarm, clutching the duvet to his chest. 'Is there something wrong?'

'Yes.' Her lips were full and pouting. She came to the side of the bed. 'I'm in one room and you're in another.'

'Natalie . . .'

Untying the belt from her dressing gown, she let it fall to the ground in a careless heap. Her naked body was young and firm, her skin translucent in the darkness. The pierced belly button was very much in evidence. Somehow it didn't seem nearly as innocent on Nat as it did on Kerry. It was aggressive, sexual and very scary. The tattoo was yet to come. Never in his wildest dreams – and there had been some pretty wild ones lately – had he imagined he would get a private viewing of it. She sat on the bed, curling her legs beneath her.

Her smile was feline in the extreme and Jeffrey could feel his heart pounding nervously. 'Do you always wear your glasses, Jeffers?' she purred.

'Only when I need to see,' he answered with a voice that decided to change key every other word.

She reached out and took them from him, placing them on the bedside table.

'Do you prefer the light on or off?'

Jeffrey jerked his shoulders tightly in a movement that was supposed to resemble a casual shrug. 'I'm sort of an off man.'

Natalie clicked the light on, flooding the bedroom with a harsh light which reminded him of his neighbours' halogen security light which lit up like Blackpool Illuminations every time a hapless cat – usually Erstwhile – strolled by. Catching the wisp of silk, she threw it over the lampshade and the room was instantly suffused with a soft rosy glow. 'That's better,' she said with a half-smile. 'Now we can see what we're doing.'

He wasn't sure they should be doing what they were doing at all. In fact, he was convinced they shouldn't. Nor was he sure he wanted to see it bathed in a rosy glow. This was quite a departure for someone whose idea of debauchery was a nip of brandy in his bedtime Horlicks. 'Nat, this is making me feel horribly weak-willed.'

'You're a man,' she said. 'It gives you the perfect excuse.' Natalie began to gently prise his fingers off the duvet. 'There are more ways than one to enjoy a white-knuckle ride,' she informed him.

He was hanging onto the edge again, knowing that there was no escape from what was about to happen.

Natalie tossed the duvet to the floor. He was naked and ready. She slipped to the end of the bed and began licking, kissing and biting his toes, slowly, tantalisingly, exquisitely.

'This is sheer lunacy,' he gasped.

She said nothing, but continued her tender assault, working her way up his body – ankles, calves, knees, thighs ... Oh God! His hands clutched convulsively at her hair, her face, drawing her into him. Oh, good grief. *OBLIVION*. Jeffrey looked down and surrendered himself to the sensations.

Chapter Thirty-One

This was how it must feel to be Tangoed, Kate decided. Ben was taking her on a rollercoaster ride of passion and with each heart-racing dip and turn she was unfurling like a flower, becoming instead the Whore of Babylon.

His love-making was a total revelation to her. She didn't know whether she was up, down or inside out, whether she wanted to laugh or cry, but she knew that she felt more wanton and wanted than she ever had before – and was revelling in it! Ben's body was quite a surprise too. She'd only ever seen Jeffrey naked in the flesh. She always knew there'd be different sizes and shapes of erections, but she never knew they had different personalities. A bit like cats really – they might be all small and furry, but they had very different ways of getting what they wanted. Jeffrey's always looked polite and kind, very cheerful, good-mannered. But Ben had stood there every inch a man, looking, well . . . very *cocky*. There was a thrusting certainty about him that said 'You are in the hands of someone who knows exactly what they're doing.' And he did.

He was a skilled lover, there was no doubt about it. Tender, demanding, exciting. She surrendered herself to him and let him play her body like an instrument – *and he was hitting notes she never knew existed.* Ben was sliding down her body, flicking his tongue over her burning flesh, darting it in her belly button. Kate was surprised, she'd never thought of the belly button as an erogenous zone before. Previously, she'd always had a pathological fear of anyone touching it – a bit like the feel of theatre seats or chalk down a blackboard – yet this was giving her the same sensation as sticking your tongue inside a Walnut Whip.

She'd never had oral sex with Jeffrey. They'd talked about it enough, but had never actually done the dirty deed. You could say they'd only paid lip service to it. Was she the only person in the world who hadn't done it? According to *New Woman*, quite possibly. Everyone was at it. Give it six months and they'd probably be doing it on *Neighbours* too. Sweet thirty-five and never been licked.

His mouth moved lower, tasting her skin, lapping at her like a cat with milk. He was spreading her before him and feasting greedily on her. As his hands parted her thighs and his tongue tasted the parts that no one else had ever reached, Kate tried to remember to breathe, which was proving quite difficult given the relentless assault on her body and senses. Her head was swimming, a Catherine wheel was spinning in her stomach; showering her with tingling sparks from the inside out. She felt like Alice in Wonderland discovering unknown pleasures that begged her to Eat Me, Drink Me. Love Me. And she never wanted it to end.

*　*　*

When they were sated, for the third time, Kate lay on her stomach while Ben stroked her back with an intimacy that she and Jeffrey had never achieved even after fifteen years of what, essentially, had been a happy marriage. A shaft of rich pain cut across her pleasure, but the guilt that she expected to accompany it failed to materialise. What would he think if he could see her now?

Her arm rested above her head and she was watching Ben's eyes. 'I can't believe we've done this,' she said disbelievingly. 'This is the sort of thing other people do. Not me.' Her head flopped languidly on the pillow. 'What now, Ben?'

His fingers trailed over her skin in lazy twists and turns, writing I LOVE YOU along her spine. There was a sheen of perspiration on her skin that shimmered like phosphorescence in the light of the moon. 'You feel warm,' he murmured. 'Do you want to cool down?'

Kate's lips curved into a smile. 'What exactly did you have in mind?'

'Come on!' He leapt from the bed, tugging her hand.

'Where are we going?'

He was edging towards the window. 'You'll see,' he said, pulling gently at her again. 'Come on!'

Reluctantly, Kate got out of bed. 'I don't know where my clothes are.'

'You won't be needing them.' Ben lifted the tall sash window, which creaked in protest. The night air was still hot and heavy, covering the ground like a thick blanket. He was up on the windowsill before Kate knew it.

'Ben, you'll fall!'

'I won't. Here . . .' He helped her up next to him. 'There's a fire escape.'

She crouched naked on the sill next to him, trying unsuccessfully to cover herself with her arms.

'People will see us,' she hissed.

'Who?'

Kate surveyed the scene. Ben was quite right. There was no one around. The window overlooked the terrace where the party had long since died; its only traces were a few used paper plates discarded in the shrubbery and some brightly coloured strings of party-poppers wound round the odd unsuspecting saxifrage. There were no lights on in the Priory, nor the accommodation wing, but two spotlights shone out from the darkness picking out the ramparts against the night. The ornate wrought-iron fire escape wound straight down to a grassy mound which bordered the main house, which was then just a mere slither away from the croquet lawn.

'Let's go.' He stepped out onto the fire escape.

'Where to?'

'You'll see.' He grinned, his teeth looking whiter than white in the moonlight.

Kate put her foot gingerly over the sill. She was going outside, naked in the dark. She didn't think she'd ever been outside in her birthday suit before, not since she was about three years old on Bournemouth beach and then she'd had considerably fewer bits to be bashful about.

Ben smiled back at her encouragingly as he led the way,

pitter-pattering carefully down the fire escape in their bare feet. At the bottom, the grass was cold and damp between her toes.

'Let's keep to this side,' Ben said, putting his arm round her. 'Away from the lights.'

'Supposing there's a security camera,' Kate whispered anxiously.

'Then we'll be giving the guard something to talk about!'

They stuck close to the edge of the trees, crouching down as they ran, ducking under the Cedar of Lebanon, making themselves small, lightning quick. Entering the more dense area of the copse, the darkness enveloped them. It was black as pitch and cooler under the umbrella of trees. Ben held her still. 'If we stand here for a few moments, our eyes will get used to the dark,' he said.

It didn't help that she had the distraction of his hands roving her body while they were waiting, but sure enough, out of the blackness, the grey fuzziness of indistinct shapes started to form in front of them.

'Walk slowly,' Ben instructed. 'Don't look down. Your feet will get used to feeling their way round obstacles.'

They made their way up the path, past the place where they had eaten their picnic. Kate could feel the rough dampness of leaves, twigs and bracken beneath her soft feet. As they climbed higher into the woods, the path became steeper, the ground softer, more yielding under her step. She could hear Ben's breathing just behind at her shoulder, senses alert, conscious of their nakedness. The blood was zinging through her veins, she could feel every pulse, every beat of her heart and there was a lightness to her spirit that had been missing for years. At the very top they broke out into a clearing. They were on a high, exposed ridge which jutted out proudly, dominating the surrounding countryside.

The moon was full and high, blue-white in an ebony sky. Solid black clouds massed, stage right, thick, threatening, laden with the weight of gathered rain. They were backlit by the celestial torch, silver-edged with dramatic filigree. The stars were low, close, sheltering beneath the coming storm. In the distance, faraway lights of tiny towns gave off a subtle golden glow on the horizon, speckled with the amber pin-pricks of streetlights. A sharpness spiked the air, clear and refreshing, prickling the senses to life. The breeze had quickened.

Ben held her hand and they walked together to the edge of the ridge. There was a vertical drop in front of them – sheer until it reached the flatness of the plateau of fields spread out beneath like a safety net.

Kate turned to him, pressing her body against his, suddenly scared, desperate, vulnerable. 'Make love to me,' she begged. 'Now.'

'Not yet,' Ben said. 'I want you to fly with me, Kate.'

A trickle of terror rippled through her. 'I can't,' she gasped.

'What did Sam say? Sometimes you have to take a leap of faith.' He urged her towards the edge of the precipice. 'It's time.' He turned towards the drop. 'Take my hand.'

'I'm scared,' Kate murmured, clutching him.

'Don't be. I'll be with you.'

She followed him and stood right at the edge. Her toes curled over into nothingness and she felt a tremor of fear and exhilaration shudder through her. Ben spread his arms wide, exposing his body to the night. Hesitantly, Kate did the same. The breeze trailed its fingers through her hair, lifting it from her face and her neck, carrying it on the wind, soothing her. It licked over her breasts, hardening her nipples to aching points, before it breathed over her belly and between her legs, stirring exquisite sensations in her loins.

'Remember the white crane, Kate,' Ben said from the blackness. 'Spread your wings.'

The wind whirled round her, warm and chill eddies teasing and flirting with her body, sending out tendrils of air to stroke her skin, intimately caressing her. Leaning into it, she let the tangible nothingness support her, lift her, exalt her. She moved her arms tentatively, offering uncertain wings to the taunting moon.

'Reach for the stars, Kate,' Ben said. 'Look. They're so close, they're almost within your grasp.'

He was right, they were a hair's breadth away from her. All she had to do was stretch out.

She focused on her breathing, high and tight in her chest and she dragged it from her belly, swelling through her body, bursting against her lungs until it broke out of her mouth with an anguished cry. A surge of power filled her arms, lifting them as if driven by pistons, thrusting them through the air like an oar cutting through water. Lunging,

286

beating, sweeping. Her arms moved again, gathering the air to her, cradling it in the curve of her wings, before the powerful uplift raised them in supplication to the sky again.

And then her heels lifted, her legs melted away, the ground fell from beneath her, the strong hands of the wind supported her belly. She was rising. A lightness surrounded her, the strong movement in her arms propelling her upwards, breaking the gravitational pull of the earth.

'Oh God,' she breathed. Still higher and higher, she soared, head up towards the stars. Her whole body was pulsating to a steady primeval rhythm, like the ebb and flow of an ocean. As she looked down, the fields and the ridge were laid out beneath her, insignificant in their earthly solidity. She was weightless, unfettered, hovering above the ground. Free.

Hot tears splashed from her eyes, running cold down her cheeks, before the breeze brushed them tenderly away.

'I'm flying, Ben. *I'm flying!*'

Chapter Thirty-Two

The sun was bright and yellow in the sky like the sun in Teletubbyland. It flooded the bedroom with unnecessary brightness and Jeffrey rolled over, now modestly covered by the duvet again, blinking against it. Natalie was gone.

He sat bolt upright in bed and stared at the clock. Not that it did him much good. Fumbling around until he had found his glasses, he looked again. Eight o'clock. He strained his ears to catch tell-tale noises that said she was in the en suite bathroom or downstairs preparing breakfast. But there was nothing. Just a deathly silence. A silence that in crime novels always signalled that something was seriously amiss.

He threw back the tangled duvet and it was there staring at him. A psychedelic pink notelet, one of the ones Kate kept by the phone. There was a message scribbled on it.

Jeffers – it wasn't lunacy, it was beautiful, fun, sexy and fulfilling. Wild thing! Your wife's a very fortunate person. Nat x

Jeffrey looked bleakly at the wreckage of the sheets, the smears of lipstick and mascara from Natalie's face on the pillow slips, and thought that if Kate could see him now, the last thing she would consider herself was very fortunate.

His sleep had been fitful, without any of the usual

contented post-coital drowsiness. He had woken in the night, still haunted by a dark shadow of disbelief that he was actually in his bed – in his marital bed, in his marital home, his marital children just down the hall – with another woman. Natalie was curled against him and his arms were wrapped tightly around her. She was breathing deeply, like a slumbering child. Her cheeks were pink from exertion, a delicate flush from her orgasm still colouring her throat and her blonde hair tousled. This was the first time he had ever been in bed with a woman other than Kate, and to say it felt strange was an understatement. The contours of her body were different, but he and Natalie fitted together just as easily, curving together with the easy comfort of spoons.

He pushed the image out of his mind. His body felt as if it had been filled with heavy-duty porridge and he plodded to the bathroom trying not to encourage too much unnecessary movement in his cranium. The shower battered his body with sharp little needles and he regretted having to wash the imprint of Natalie's scent from his skin. Why had she gone from the bed so early? Had she stayed all night or had she slipped away as soon as he was sleeping soundly? Perhaps she had gone back to her own room or was sitting downstairs reading the paper, waiting for him to wake. He sniffed the air for the delicious aroma of freshly brewed coffee. Nothing. Not even the less delicious aroma of freshly spooned Nescafé.

He shaved with extreme care, feeling every scrape of the razor over the sensitive skin beneath his stubble. Things had changed. The face that stared back at him looked the same – but something was different inside. He couldn't put his finger on it, but he knew that deep down things could never be as they were before.

Jeffrey hopped round the bedroom trying to make his uncooperative legs thread into his uncooperative jeans. What would he say to Natalie? Was there a correct way to thank someone the morning after? Would there be a coolness to their demeanours after the passion of last night? Or would they fall into each other's arms and carry on where they had left off? Was Natalie having regrets? Was he?

He headed downstairs. She wasn't there. He checked in the lounge and, when it was clear she wasn't in the kitchen, the garden. But there was no sign of her. She must still be in bed. It was easy to forget that Natalie had also been over-zealous with the champagne.

Jeffrey made two cups of strong instant coffee, careful not to clang things together too loudly, and crept up the stairs with them. He paused at the children's doors. There was no sound from Kerry's room so she must be asleep, as she always played her CDs at full volume from the minute her eyelids let in light, and Joe was still snoring gently. Oblivion, it seemed, came in different forms for different people. Jeffrey tiptoed past their rooms and tapped gently on Natalie's door. There was no reply. He tapped a little louder and then waited a few moments, heart pounding unsteadily, before pushing the door open. The bed was made, the duvet smooth and untouched, the matching cushion at a pert little angle as always. Wherever Natalie was, it wasn't here.

Jeffrey headed back down to the kitchen and sat at the table drinking his coffee, which tasted bitter. Why had she sneaked out without saying goodbye? Had she been trying to avoid him, or did she simply have something pressing to attend to at the other house before Jessica's return? After a few minutes of fretting, he decided there was only one way to find out. He crossed to the kitchen phone and flicked through the pages of the address book for Jessica's number. As he dialled, he mentally rehearsed what he was going to say and the tone he was going to say it in. Bright and breezy? Worried and concerned? Sexy and sultry? *Can I do sexy and sultry?*

It rang unanswered. Jeffrey sat down with his cup of coffee, looking miserably at the one going cold next to it. The *Telegraph* shot through the letterbox, making him jump; he went to collect it and then sat at the table for the next twenty minutes pretending to read it, while his mind re-ran erotic images from last night. It was no good. He was going to have to go and find her. He scribbled a note for the kids using one of the psychedelic pink notelets. *Had to pop out. Get your own breakfast. (Not crisps!!) Back soon. Dad XX*

Grabbing the car keys from the hook, he sprinted out to the car and set off for Jessica's house.

There were no signs of life and it reminded him sharply of the rockery-stone-through-the-window debacle, so

Jeffrey contented himself with a sedate knock, followed by a slightly less sedate ring of the doorbell. Jessica's next-door neighbour put her head cautiously over the dividing fence. She too seemed to have her senses on red alert after the incident just a few short days ago.

'Can I ask what it is you want?' she said, looking suspiciously as though she wished she had a large Rottweiler with her. 'We've had a bit of trouble round here lately with hooligans.'

Hooligans? Jeffrey had the good grace to blush.

'I've come to see the au pair – Natalie,' he explained. 'She's been looking after my family while Jessica's been away.'

'Oh,' she said, looking semi-placated. 'I'm afraid you've just missed her.'

'*Missed her?*'

'She left in a taxi about ten minutes ago.'

'Left?' Jeffrey sounded desperate even to himself. 'Where did she go?'

'I don't know,' she said, in an I'm-not-bloody-Mystic-Meg tone. 'She was carrying a large backpack.'

Jeffrey was back in the Merc before the sentence was finished. The station, he thought. It was the only conceivable place she could be going.

Leighton Buzzard Station had been revamped a couple of years earlier. From the charming, crumbling Gothic building of yesteryear had emerged a red Lego-style construction, with absolutely nowhere to park outside without the risk of being crushed by the number 42 bus from Luton. Today, however, that risk was the last thing on Jeffrey's mind.

He had driven at breakneck speed down Soulbury Road, careless of the frequent speed traps, holding the steering wheel with a death grip. Bats recently departed from hell probably went slower. Now he slewed the Mercedes at a reckless angle to the road, eschewing the double yellow lines, the DO NOT PARK HERE, EXIT ALWAYS IN USE sign, the VeryNice vans for hire he had blocked in and the fact that two wheels were on the pavement.

Jeffrey ran across the road, dodging between taxis, and shouldered through the automatic doors which leapt apart at his approach. She wasn't in the ticket hall. Was that good or bad? He looked round him, eyes darting from side to side. Then: there she was on the platform, her backpack weighing her down.

Tearing up the stairs in the concourse, he burst through the doors and onto the platform like the men in Impulse adverts do. Except he'd forgotten to grab a bunch of flowers on the way. He stopped. What was he going to say to her? Natalie turned and looked at him.

'Where are you going?' he blurted out.

'What are you doing here?' Nat blurted back.

They stood looking at each other in silence.

'I asked first,' Jeffrey said, when it looked like nothing else more suitable was going to fill the gap.

Natalie hung her head. 'I'm going away.'

'Where to?'

'Does it matter?'

'It does to me.'

Natalie folded her arms. 'We shouldn't have done what we did, Jeffers. I betrayed Kate's trust. So did you.'

God, she looked dreadful. Her face was pale and blotchy, despite the tan, her eyes were bloodshot and there were tangles in her hair that needed a good comb taking to them. Jeffrey's heart twisted.

'I don't want you to leave,' he said brokenly.

'Why do you want me to stay?' she asked harshly. 'So that we can carry on with me as your bit on the side?'

'It's not like that,' Jeffrey cried. 'As well you know.'

'You love Kate,' she said.

'How can I truly say that I love Kate, when I can do what we did?' Jeffrey raked his hair. 'I have no regrets.'

'I do,' Natalie looked at him sadly. 'It was a mistake.'

'A mistake?' The blood drained from Jeffrey's face. 'You said – and I quote – "it was beautiful, fun, sexy and fulfilling".' He counted the words off on his fingers as accountants do.

'And a mistake,' she added flatly. 'It was a one-night stand, Jeffers. Nothing more. They happen.'

'Not to me they don't!'

'The train now arriving at platform four is the late-running 9.35 service to London Euston ...'

Jeffrey looked stricken at the tannoy which dangled above their heads. Then he stared down the railway track. The train was arriving.

'Don't go,' he begged. 'Wait for me. I'll get some things

and come with you. We can travel round Europe together.'

'And Kate?'

'She'll understand.'

Natalie didn't look convinced.

'No,' he said. 'She won't understand, will she?'

Natalie shook her head. 'This is a dream, Jeffers. You're a married man. Single income, wife, two children, oppressive mortgage. They depend on you. And you, in turn, are completely dependable. You could no more come with me than you could turn to drink and drugs and become a rock star.'

'I could try,' he said desperately.

'Besides,' the harshness returned, 'I don't want to be with someone who cheats on their wife.'

Jeffrey looked horrified. 'I have never cheated on my wife,' he protested. 'Until now.' He felt tied by his inability to express his feelings. Feelings were something to be developed over time, not blurted out into the ether before you'd had a chance to examine them from every angle. 'This is different for me, Nat.'

'I knew you'd take it too seriously, Jeffers,' she said. 'It meant nothing to me.'

'Nothing at all?'

'It was good,' she said. 'But don't let one minor aberration ruin your life.'

'It was *not* a minor aberration.' There were tears in his eyes.

The train pulled into the station.

'I am begging you, Natalie,' he implored. 'Please don't leave now. Let me have time to sort this out.'

'There's nothing to sort out.'

'I love you,' he said, before he realised he hadn't checked that anyone was listening.

'And I *like* you, Jeffers,' she said softly, smiling for the first time. 'You're a great bloke.'

'You *like* me?'

'I like you a lot.' Natalie leaned forward and kissed him on the mouth.

It was warm, tender, sweet and Jeffrey's insides screamed silently with the pain of it.

'I have to go.' She pressed the button and the doors of the train slid open. Hoisting her backpack onto her shoulder and without a backward glance, Natalie stepped inside.

Jeffrey abruptly turned away, his mind frozen. There was no way he could bear to watch her leave and there was nothing he could think of to do or say to make her stay. What could he offer her? She was young, single – a free spirit – and he was old, older than time itself, manacled by responsibility and Conservative with a big fat capital C. *Let her go, let her go, let her go.* He concentrated on his breathing which was slow and laboured, and the more he breathed, the more he was able to push down the waves of grief that were rushing up inside him like the torrents of a swollen river bursting through the solid restraints of its banks. Biting his lip and jabbing his car key as hard as he could into his palm, he walked slowly and deliberately out of the station. He heard the whistle blow and the clatter of the wheels as the train set off. He kept his eyes fixed straight ahead and made himself put one foot in front of the other, one foot in front of the other, one foot in front of the other, never turning round. So he didn't see Natalie's face pressed hard against the window. Or the fact that she was weeping.

Chapter Thirty-Three

They made love on the ridge, beneath the stars, before creeping slowly back to Ben's bedroom in the early hours of the morning on cold, clandestine feet. The Priory was still and peaceful, framed dramatically by the gathering clouds, its slumbering occupants unaware of the naked, shivering adventurers stealing back to the safety of its walls. Now a grey watery dawn was breaking and Kate was lying in Ben's arms as he stirred from his sleep and his hands started meandering deliciously over her body.

'Good morning.' He spoke it softly against her lips.

'Good morning.'

'How are you?'

'Desperate to go to the loo,' she breathed.

Ben opened one eye. 'How romantic.'

'I'll only be a minute.'

'I'm counting,' he said, kissing her again before snuggling down into the duvet.

She slipped out of bed and the room was chilly and strange and she opened the wardrobe door by mistake instead of the one to the bathroom. When she did find it, her feet went into shock as they hit the cold tiles and she hopped from foot to foot as she made her way across to the mirror.

The sight that greeted her was not pretty. Her hair was standing up on end and her lips were stuck to her gums and she wondered if Ben realised he had just made love to Ken Dodd. The mascara smears and the bags under her eyes combined to make her resemble an insomniac Basset Hound. Her tongue looked like it had seen a ghost.

Kate eyed Ben's toothbrush longingly. Oh, for the feel of bristle and the tang of spearmint. She hesitated, fingering the tube of toothpaste. Would he mind her using it, or should she just have a quick run round with a blob of Macleans on her finger? Wasn't it strange that she could share his body so easily and yet his toothbrush was a different matter entirely? It was a very intimate thing to share. The thought of getting back between the sheets with bed breath galvanised her into action and she scrubbed vigorously. After a cursory search for a comb, which Ben didn't appear to possess, she ran her fingers through her hair, tugging at the worst of the tangles, before she gave up and decided he would have to make do with her looking ravaged, rather than ravishing.

Kate then sat on the loo and tried to wee quietly; of course the sound seemed intent on reverberating round the bathroom. It was unheard of, taking all this trouble just to get back into bed in the morning; after fifteen years of marriage Jeffrey had seen it all. There was nothing about her appearance that could shock him. He had, after all, witnessed the birth of both of their children, so there were no secrets there. These days, she and Jeffrey seemed to conduct most of their conversations while she was sitting on the loo. It was the only place in the house that they could get any privacy with two wannabe teenage children. Was Ben the sort of man she would feel comfortable talking to while she was sitting on the toilet? She felt so comfortable with him and yet awkward at the same time. Perhaps it was just the newness of spending time with someone who was still really a stranger that made her feel so unsure. And maybe that's where she had gone wrong in her marriage. It was probably hard to keep that sparkle of romance alive when you had an intimate knowledge of each other's bodily functions.

By the time she returned to the bedroom, Ben was propped up on his elbow. He was almost wide awake and looking anxious.

'What's wrong?' she said, smoothing his hair as she slipped back into the crook of his toasty warm body.

He took her hand and drew a slow, deliberate circle on the centre of her palm as he looked at her. 'This is the Palace of Anxiety,' he said. 'The *laogong* point. It relates to the heart.' He held his palm to hers, which was slightly damp and decidedly anxious. 'Concentrating this spot helps us to open up emotionally.' He joined their *laogong* points together and a strong current of energy flowed between them, confident, sure. 'Kate,' he said, his voice serious. 'Come away with me.'

She giggled nervously. 'For a dirty weekend?'

'No.' His pale blue eyes were earnest, searching. 'Permanently.'

'Leave Jeffrey?' The thought took Kate's breath away.

300

'I love you.'

'I can't just leave,' she said. 'I have people who depend on me. I've got two children, a cat that no one else remembers to feed and an appointment at the hairdresser's on Monday at two o'clock. What would happen to Kerry and Joe if I left? I'm the sort of person that doesn't let other people down.'

He took her face in his hands, stroking his thumb over her cheek. 'But what do you want, Kate?'

'I want you to love me again.' Tears were starting to form an untidy queue behind her eyes. 'I don't want this to end.'

'It has to, Kate,' he said softly. 'There has to be a last time. And, unfortunately, it's fast approaching.' He smiled, but his eyes were as grey as the harsh dawn sky. 'Unless you say yes.'

'Can't we carry on? As friends?'

'*Could* we be just friends?' he asked soberly. 'I don't want this to turn into some seedy cloak-and-dagger affair.'

'I couldn't do that either,' she admitted. 'Even if the flesh was willing, how would I get away? I'm a housewife – we're not known for the exotic nature of our business trips. Even Jeffrey might notice if I said I was popping down to Tesco's and didn't come back for three days.' *Although sometimes I do wonder.*

He shrugged, but it wasn't an easy movement. 'So, it has to be all or nothing.'

Kate sat up and hugged her knees to her chest. 'We should never have started this.'

'But we did start it, Kate.'

'I should have listened to Sam and stayed in Standing Firmly posture,' she said reproachfully. 'All that flying business – I must have left my head up in the clouds. If I'd made sure my feet hadn't left the ground in the first place, I wouldn't be in this mess now.'

'You've started to break free, Kate, and sometimes it hurts to recognise that. It's part of moving on. Growing. And growing often involves pain.' He tenderly stroked her neck. 'Particularly when you begin to outgrow someone you love.'

'But what if standing still and moving forward both involve pain?'

'Then it's a very difficult decision to make.'

'Thanks!' Kate smiled ruefully.

'Where does your future happiness lie?'

'I don't know,' she said miserably. 'Sam's still, quiet pond is having a million rocks thrown into it all at once.'

He squeezed her hand hard. 'I want you to come with me.'

'I can't do that.' Kate huffed wearily. 'Despite this – us – I do still love Jeffrey, you know.'

'But how much of that love is now borne out of habit rather than passion?'

'Habits become habits because they're very comfortable props. They're also fiendishly difficult to give up. Old habits die very, very hard.'

'Do you want to live like that?'

'They need me,' she said flatly.

'And what do you need?'

'Me?' Kate said it like it was a new concept. She shook her head. 'I suppose that's what I came here to find out.' She gave him a sad, sweet grin. 'I just didn't expect it to be six foot tall and sporting a crew cut.'

'I think I know exactly what you need to make you happy, Kate.'

'Do you? Well, I wish you'd tell me because I haven't the foggiest idea any more.'

'You need someone to help you reach for the stars.'

'I take it that person would be you?' She risked an ironic smile.

'Will Jeffrey take you there?'

'Jeffrey isn't generally a flying sort of person. He is definitely a feet flat on the floor man. He gets airsick when the plane's still sitting on the runway.'

'Don't waste your life grounded by duty,' Ben said.

'I can wait until the children leave home to get my life back.' Kate flopped against the pillow with a miserable snort. 'It won't be that long.'

'How old's Joe?'

'Ten.' So he had spotted a fatal flaw in her argument.

'Eight years until he goes to university. Perhaps you might wait until they've finished studying, or they're married, or they have children.' Ben set his mouth sadly. 'The reason you came here is that you're unhappy *now*.'

Eight years was a long time to spend in limbo.

'Then it'll be just you and Jeffrey and you won't want to leave him then because he'll be lonely. Suddenly, fifteen years will have gone by – the best years of your life – and you will still be trapped by duty. You'll be fifty and no nearer to finding out who you really are.'

She opened her mouth to protest, but what could she say? So much of it was true. The future stretched grimly ahead of her. She clamped her mouth shut and stayed silent.

'What does your heart want to do?' Ben prompted.

What indeed? Controlling her heart was becoming like steering a particularly difficult Tesco's trolley. It was veering erratically all over the shop. She knew exactly which way she should want it to go, but was having a devil of a job making it obey her.

'Are you going to negate your own desires by doing what duty requires of you, or are you going to think of yourself for once? People sometimes have to move on, no matter how painful that decision is or how much hurt it causes.'

'At what cost?' Kate's eyes were troubled. 'I wish I could be like that. I wish I could just do what I wanted and walk away without looking back at the fallout. You can't just pick people up and put them down when you've finished with them, like smelly dishcloths.'

'People do it all the time.'

'Not if they have any integrity. I couldn't be like that. Sometimes, I wish I could.'

'And this is one of those times?'

Kate nodded without speaking. She looked at him. He was carefree, exciting, daring. Not to mention drop-dead gorgeous. Her life would be so different with Ben. With him she would be a person again rather than a wife and a mother. The brief time she had spent with Ben had been the happiest she could remember for a long time. There was a strong connection between them that was too deep-rooted to ignore. And on the other hand there was Jeffrey. Safe, dependable, reliable, solid. The Volvo of husbands. She had been with Jeffrey for ever. Could she simply turn her back on that and walk away? They had been through so much as a couple, there was a lifetime of history that would always bind them together. But, at the end of the day, was it enough to make her stay for another lifetime?

She was back to the conversation she'd had with Sam. What did she really want? The heat and passion of fire, or the sure slow security of earth? But knowing what she wanted and knowing what she felt compelled to choose were two entirely different matters.

'I can't desert them, Ben,' she said, sounding stronger and more convinced than she felt. 'It's too soon. I can't rush a decision like this. I hardly know you. Perhaps . . .'

'Ssh,' he said, putting his finger to her lips. 'Then this is the end.'

He drew her down to him, covering her mouth with his, tender, insistent and unbearably sad.

The end. Even the thought of it made her feel sick to her stomach.

Sam forgot to mention that after the soaring heights of ecstasy and pleasure would come deep, debilitating pain. Yin and yang. The natural balance.

Chapter Thirty-Four

Kevin was leaning on his car when Jeffrey stumbled out of the station. He was wearing red checked trousers, a bright yellow jumper with FORE! emblazoned on the front and a faintly sardonic smile.

'Fancy meeting you here,' he said flippantly.

Jeffrey stared blankly at him.

'I followed your car,' Kev explained. 'I thought it was Nigel Mansell at first, the speed you were doing. But then I thought, No, Nige doesn't drive that fast.'

'She's gone.' Jeffrey's voice was bleak with despair.

Kevin's mouth set in a line. 'I take it we're talking about the Aussie from heaven?'

'She's gone,' he repeated, dazed.

Kevin sighed. 'Come to the golf club,' he said. 'My four ball will have to do without me today. Besides, they only strip me of every cent I've got. Bloody bandits.' He put his arm round Jeffrey's shoulders and steered him towards the Merc. 'I'll buy you a nice cup of coffee and you can tell Uncle Kevin all your cares and woes.'

Jeffrey shook his head. 'She's gone.'

'Jeffrey, old bean.' Kevin clapped him on the back. 'The record's stuck. Now, you'd best move that car quickly, before you get a yellow boot. Okay?'

Jeffrey nodded obediently

Kevin looked at the Merc and tutted. 'Dear oh dear. The only person I know who can park worse than that is my dearly beloved wife.'

Jeffrey nodded so much Kev thought his head might drop off. He massaged his hands across his forehead in exasperation.

'FOLLOW ME!' Kevin said loudly in the voice he normally reserved for Sonia's deaf Aunty Lily. 'There's no chance you'll find the fucking golf club in this state,' he added under his breath.

'I love her,' Jeffrey said, staring at the tar-coloured coffee untouched in front of him. Was it true that too much caffeine gave you the tremors? If he'd drunk it, that would perhaps give him an excuse for the trembling he felt inside.

'You *lust* her,' Kevin corrected. 'That's a very different thing altogether.'

Jeffrey wrung his hands together. 'I don't know what to do.'

'There's nothing *to* do, mate,' Kevin said, tucking heartily into his second bacon bap. 'You've had a Gillette GII ...'

Jeffrey looked blank. 'A what?'

'A close shave.' He swiped the tomato sauce from the corner of his mouth. 'From this you must learn.'

The car park was packed, but the clubhouse was like a grave. Everyone sensible was out playing golf, the thing Saturday mornings were invented for, whipping the dew from the grass and performing some overt male bonding, before they had to rush home to the family and do chores and shopping at Tesco's and wash the car.

Kevin leaned back in his armchair, raising a knowing finger. 'The best things in life might appear to be free, but on closer examination you'll see they usually come with a hellish price tag.' When there was still no response from Jeffrey, he decided to resort to song: 'You need to pack up your troubles in your old golf bag and smile, smile, smile . . .'

'For God's sake, shut up!' Jeffrey snapped. 'My life has ended.'

'One tiny grain of sand on life's endless beach has been washed away . . .'

'Fuck off!'

'Mate,' Kevin sighed, regarding the crumbs on his plate, 'that type of woman eats pathetic little men like us for breakfast. We are bacon baps to them – tasty, but we only fill a hole for a few hours. They see us as a challenge. They think nothing of turning our lives upside down for one night's fun.'

'It wasn't fun,' Jeffrey objected. 'Well . . . it was. But it wasn't *just* fun. It was more than that. And I thought she felt it too.'

'How much fizz had you drunk?'

Jeffrey glared at him.

'I know,' Kevin said with resignation. '*Fuck off*.'

'Natalie's different. I know she is.'

'Well, perhaps she is,' Kevin allowed. 'But you can't risk

it. Look what you've got to lose. It's taken you years to build up your rather enviable lifestyle. Are you prepared to watch it all go into the back pocket of some jumped-up little lawyer with matching his and hers Porsches and a barn conversion in the country?'

Jeffrey said nothing.

'Frank reckons Kate's better-looking than Liz Hurley.'

'And what does Frank know about anything?'

'Naff all, mate,' Kevin said with a shrug. 'But then what do any of us know?'

'He can't even make a decent cup of coffee!' Jeffrey slammed his cup on the saucer until coffee slopped onto the table.

'That may well be the case.' Kevin tried to sound soothing. 'I'm simply trying to reintroduce some logic into this tawdry scenario.'

Jeffrey sat up. Is that what it looked like to the outside world? A tawdry scenario? It certainly didn't feel like that inside.

'You are letting passion take over from *ration*,' Kev quipped with a self-satisfied smile at his own wit.

It was easy to see that Kevin spent his working day running a marketing department, Jeffrey thought bitterly.

'You now need to concentrate on some damage limitation, my friend,' Kevin advised. 'You must make sure that Kate never, ever, *ever* finds out about this. Do *not* get the urge to confess your sins. Honesty, believe me, is never the best policy.'

'I've never lied to her before,' Jeffrey said. 'Not big lies.

I did once forget our wedding anniversary and had to rush into the garage on my way home from work to buy a tatty card and some wilting flowers. She guessed that it had slipped my mind, but instead of owning up, for some reason I chose to lie my way out of it. But that was the only time. It was stupid and awful. How can I keep a secret like this from her?'

'It might help clear your conscience, but bear in mind she'd be wearing your bollocks as earrings sooner than you could blink!'

Jeffrey did blink.

'Women don't forget these things,' Kevin continued. 'And, despite what they may say, they don't forgive either.' He gave him an Uncle-Kevin-knows-best look. 'Keep it in, batten it down and let it stay that way, otherwise it'll nibble away at your marriage like a slug at a bloody lettuce. First the edges will be chewed away, a bite at a time, slowly, slowly, until eventually it's so riddled with holes that it isn't worth hanging on to. It'll be fit for nothing but the compost heap.'

The average marriage lasted fourteen years these days, Jeffrey thought. He'd read it in the *Telegraph*. That probably meant if the seven-year itch didn't get you the first time, it hit you twice as hard when it next came round. Was it possible for people to make a lifelong commitment now, when that meant thirty, forty, fifty years – more? Even fourteen years sounded like a long time compared to most of their friends. If he and Kate lived to be seventy, they'd have been married for nearly fifty years.

How many people made their golden wedding anniversary? Was it even realistic to believe that you could love the same person for so long? Once he had thought so.

Kevin drained his coffee, shuddering theatrically as he swallowed. 'If you want my advice . . .'

Do I have a choice?

'Forget Natalie. Forget she ever existed. File her in that tidy little brain of yours in a compartment marked DO NOT OPEN and concentrate on papering over the cracks.'

How could he do that when there would be so much to remind him of her? Every time they went to Ashridge Forest, she'd be there. Every time he caught a glimpse of his child's belly-button ring. Every time he ate burnt food. How could he forget the feel of her skin, the taste of her mouth, her body wrapped so deliciously round him. She had opened his heart, when he never realised it had been closed.

'Do you want some more coffee? A cup of tea instead?'

Jeffrey shook his head. 'I'd better get back. I left the kids to their own devices.'

'At least you know the house will still be standing, mate. You have a lot to be thankful for.'

Jeffrey stood slowly from the table. 'I'll have to run the hoover round before Kate comes home. Tidy up a bit.'

'I take it that Natalie's skill with her hands didn't run to wielding a duster?'

Jeffrey glared blackly at him and then broke into a reluctant smile. 'No,' he said.

'That's better.' Kevin patted him on the back.

311

They walked out into the car park, greeting acquaintances in similarly garish clothing bearing golf bags. The sun was still shining and life was going on despite Jeffrey's domestic drama.

'Do you think you can manage to get home in one piece?'

Jeffrey nodded.

'Phone me if you need to, mate,' Kevin offered. 'Any time.'

'Thanks,' Jeffrey said quietly as he slid into the Merc.

'It'll get easier, you know,' Kevin assured him through the car window.

Jeffrey sighed and let his hands rest wearily on the steering wheel. 'Will it?'

'Yeah,' he said. 'Not overnight. But it will.'

Jeffrey started the car engine. 'Tell me,' he said, 'how come you know so much about all this stuff?'

Kevin pressed his lips together and a shadow crossed his eyes, but it could have been the sun passing behind a cloud. 'My seed has not always been confined to the garden of marriage,' he said enigmatically, before he turned and walked briskly away.

Chapter Thirty-Five

Ben and Kate sat together at breakfast, slightly apart from the rest of the group, on the edge of the jokes and banter of those in high spirits at the thought of going home. Neither of them had any appetite. Was it obvious to the others that they were lovers now, not just friends? Did their lingering glances give them away – their loving looks? The fact that they were the only two looking depressed at the imminence of their departure? Had no one noticed the fact that they had gone to an inordinate amount of trouble to arrive separately, and the quiet fuss they had made about being forced to take the only two remaining chairs, which happened to be together? With all this talk of Chi and energy flow and goodness knows what else, could they not see the vibes that were palpably throbbing between them?

Despite Kate's feelings that they might as well have had a neon sign above their heads declaring *We had it off last night!* their classmates did not look up from their eggs and bacon, which they all attacked with gusto despite the evidence of several hangovers from the party.

Only Sam, it seemed, had guessed their secret and he smiled sadly at them over his plateful of sausages. Her feet were entwined with Ben's under the table and in spite of her resolve to stay with Jeffrey and all other good and wifely intentions, she knew she wanted to be doing this furtive foot-fondling for the rest of her life. She wanted to touch Ben's leg under the table, to stroke his knee, to brush her fingers lightly along the length of his thigh. Their surreptitious glances grew steadily more desperate as the hands of the clock in the dining room contrived to whizz round as quickly as they could. Ben was the first to abandon his breakfast. Pushing his plate away, he said, 'I've got to go and make a phone call.' He lowered his voice. 'Come up to my room when you've finished.'

Kate watched him stride out of the dining room with a hideous sense of foreboding. She had finished, she thought, eyeing her congealed egg and a mess of fried tomatoes that looked like something's disgorged entrails. *I just want to know what it feels like to be without you.* Even for a few minutes it was very horrible. Empty. Desolate. Would this be a constant part of her make-up from now on or would it, at some given time in the future, just stop – like a rundown clock?

Everyone else was swapping light-hearted stories about the previous evening's celebration – who had said what to whom, who had spilled drinks down whose blouse, whose hands had wandered with overt bravado to places where they shouldn't. No one mentioned that she and Ben had slipped away too early to be considered polite, and they all laughed too loud at things that weren't really funny with a forced *joie de vivre* that somehow seemed put on for her benefit. Kate glanced at the clock again. She ought to be leaving soon or Jeffrey would start to worry. *Wouldn't he?*

Ben had his phone clamped to his ear. The line was terrible, snap, crackle and popping like a bowl of Rice Krispies. 'Fi?' he shouted, as he strode backwards and forwards across the room flinging clothes into his case.

'Is that you, Ben?'

'Have you remembered that you're supposed to be coming to collect me today?'

'Of course!' she replied indignantly through the interference. 'I'm on my way.'

'*Now?*' His heart plummeted.

'I'm halfway up the M40,' Fi informed him brightly.

He glanced at his watch. In his mind, he'd bargained for Fi forgetting and needing to be cajoled out of bed, thus giving him another couple of hours with Kate. He'd imagined a stroll in the sunlight, a secluded clearing – anything to stretch time and delay the minutes before they had to part. Trust this to be the one day in Fi's life when she decided to be punctual!

'I'll be there in the twinkle of an eye,' she promised. 'This baby moves a darn sight better than Old Faithful!'

He had yet to tell her that the garage had rung to say Old Faithful was unlikely to move ever again.

'Has the course been good?' she yelled.

'Yes.'

'You still sound bloody miserable.'

I am bloody miserable.

Fiona waited until the fresh spurt of crackling had subsided to a mere hiss. 'Does this mean the fair lady didn't succumb to your not insignificant charms?'

'I don't want to talk about it,' Ben said firmly.

'Is that I don't want to talk about it, *yes she did*? Or I don't want to talk about it, *no she didn't*?'

'It's none of your business.'

'Yes, it is,' she insisted. 'If it's yes she did, and you're sounding this suicidal, then it's very bad news indeed, Benjamin.'

'It is bad news,' he said with a heavy sigh.

'Oh fuck,' Fiona tutted. 'Don't do anything stupid!'

Stupid? What counted as stupid by Fiona's standards? Falling in love with a married woman? Losing your head as well as your heart? He had already leapt the bounds of his own stupidity. He could look back on this in time and say it was inevitable. He and Kate were meant for each other. *Why couldn't she see that?* It was bound to happen. The attraction was too strong. But, at any time, they could have stopped it. Either of them. A well-timed no instead of a passion-filled yes. If only life were so simple. It was very easy to be logical when Kate wasn't two feet away from him.

Fi's voice broke into his thoughts. 'I'll be there as soon as I can.'

Don't rush! Dawdle. 'Drive safely,' Ben warned.

'I always do!'

'You don't,' he corrected. 'You've had five smash-ups in the last two years.'

'Yeah, but the others always came off worse,' Fiona protested.

And who was going to walk away the least hurt out of this tangled wreckage? Would it be him or Kate?

'Stick to the speed limit,' he said.

'See you soon!' she breezed and the line went dead.

Ben looked forlornly round the room; he pictured Kate curled naked on the bed next to him – one of the many cherished images he would carry away with him. The scent of her was still in the air, on the tips of his fingers, on his lips. He pressed his hands to his temples and tried to stop his brain working. Soon it would be gone.

Kate's lips had gone dry and she licked them nervously, before knocking timidly at Ben's door. It didn't look like the same doorway in the daylight as it had in the dark; she must have been concentrating on things other than the decor the last time she approached it, she thought with a wry smile. She was about to knock again when Ben opened the door.

'Hi,' he said.

'This is terrible,' she said, wandering into the room and sinking onto the bed. 'I hadn't wanted to face saying goodbye last night. Now it's even harder.'

Ben sat down beside her and wound his arms round her. 'There's never an easy way to do this.'

'We might never see each other again,' Kate choked.

'It's the only way.' Ben kissed the top of her head.

'There must be something else we can do!'

'Like what?' he said. 'You've made your choice, Kate. You have to stick to that.' Ben smiled wickedly. 'Unless you want to change your mind?'

How could she tell him that it was changing every five seconds? And when it wasn't changing, it was having doubts.

Kate put her head in her hands. 'I want you both.'

Ben laughed. 'That's generally known as being greedy.'

'This is the hardest thing I've ever had to do. Even giving birth was like shelling peas in comparison.' Sorrow was breaking her heart.

'I'll always love you, Kate. If you ever need me, I'll always be there for you. Waiting.'

'But how will I know where you are?'

'You'll find me. Trust your instincts.'

'I'm going against all that my instincts are telling me now,' she said wretchedly.

'I don't know what to say, Kate, to make it any easier. This has to be your decision.'

'I bet you're sorry that the wine tasting was cancelled,' she joked tearfully.

'But then I would never have tasted the bouquets of your flesh.' He pressed his mouth to hers and they clung to each other, kissing silently, sadly, fiercely as only people who know they are about to part kiss.

'How do we end this?' Kate started to cry, single tears rolling over her lashes. 'I can't be the first one to walk away.'

'I'll come down and take your bags to the car for you.'

'I couldn't bear to watch you walk away from me either.'

'Then this is going to be very tricky,' he said too lightly.

There was a brusque knock on the door, before it was flung open. A burly woman bearing a pile of sheets barged through it. 'I need the room vacated,' she barked. 'The next course is coming in.' And she dumped the fresh linen next to them on the bed and stood there looking bad-tempered.

'We need a few more minutes,' Ben said politely.

'I'll give you five,' she snapped and stomped out again.

'Not the most romantic of endings,' Ben commented. 'I bet Robert Redford never had to put up with this.'

Kate laughed through her tears. 'No.'

He took her hand and kissed the back of it. 'We can't delay it any longer, my Katie.'

'You go first,' she said, standing up and smoothing her skirt. 'And I'll stay here. No ... I'll leave. No ... you leave. No ...'

She burst into tears. Ben stood up and held her against him.

'Turn round, walk out and don't look back,' he instructed. 'Go to your room, collect your case and drive straight off. Short, sharp, swift.'

'I can't.'

'You have to.'

'As easy as that?'

'What else can we do?' Ben pleaded. 'You're a wife. A mother. You have people who depend on you.'

'You forgot the cat,' she sniffled wetly.

319

Ben smiled. 'The cat would be bereft,' he conceded.

'I need you,' Kate sobbed. 'How will I fly to the stars without you?'

'If it's destiny, Kate, we'll be together,' he said seriously. 'Somehow, some way. Things will work out. Maybe the timing just isn't right. Like Sam said, if we put our trust in the universe it will give us what we need.

'Now go,' Ben said, holding her tight. 'Just keep walking. Don't turn round.'

She kissed him for the last time. Then she turned and went. Out of the door, out of the corridor, out of his life – and she didn't look back, not once. Not even when she heard him shout, 'I love you!'

Chapter Thirty-Six

In the leafy driveway of number 20, Acacia Close, Joe was kicking a football against the garage doors. The sky had turned a pasty grey and a spiteful breeze was making the summer trees shiver with cold. No doubt the teeth of the Teletubby sun were chattering somewhere as it hid behind the clouds.

Having parked the car in a more traditionally sedate arrangement than earlier, it had taken considerable effort for Jeffrey to relax his death grip on the steering wheel and coordinate his body through the motions of getting out of the driver's seat. Even now, his fists were bunched so tight, the muscles in his shoulders felt like steel girders. Jeffrey stumbled from the car, still feeling dazed and disorientated.

Joe was wearing his *I SURVIVED OBLIVION!* T-shirt and probably would do until it walked to the washing machine itself. He watched his son and wondered would he ever feel so carefree again? Would there be a time when his biggest worry would be keeping greenfly off his sweet peas, whitefly off his busy Lizzies and blackfly off his nasturtiums? When would he be able to think of Natalie and not get a sharp pain in his chest that threatened to stab the life out of him? Joe scored an imaginary goal and cheered himself. Why couldn't he be that age again, but with the added benefit of wisdom that hindsight had supplied? Jeffrey closed his eyes and let the pain wash over him. *Would I do things differently?*

'Where's Natty?' Joe asked as Jeffrey walked on jelly legs across the gravel.

'Gone,' Jeffrey said.

Joe stopped kicking the ball and stared at him. 'Where?'

'You know she wanted to go to Europe?'

Joe nodded.

'Well,' he said hesitantly, 'she decided to go a bit earlier than she'd planned.'

'Why?'

Jeffrey crouched down and picked up the ball, twirling it in his hands. Anything, rather than look at his son's bleached face.

'Sometimes grown-ups change their minds.'

'Didn't she like us?' His lower lip started to tremble.

'Of course she did.' Jeffrey put his arm round Joe's shoulder. 'I think she liked us a lot.'

'Then why didn't she say goodbye?' he burst out.

'Saying goodbye to people you like is very hard.' There was a constriction the size of Joe's football lodged in Jeffrey's throat.

'We could have made her stay.'

Jeffrey hugged his son tightly. 'I don't think so,' he said. 'Let's go inside. I've got to tidy up before your mother comes home and sees the state of the place.'

'I don't want Mummy to come home,' Joe said bleakly.

'She's boring.' He looked up at his father. His eyes were round and trusting. Kate's eyes. 'Natalie was fun. I wanted her to stay for ever.'

Jeffrey swallowed uncertainly. 'So did I, son. So did I.'

The radio in the kitchen was blaring out unheeded, the television was offering lively competition from the lounge and sounds of Kerry practising her keyboard jerked inconsistently from the dining room. Jeffrey went into the kitchen and snapped the radio off. He supported himself on the work surface and breathed deeply before turning to the task in hand. *Tidy up*, his brain said, and he searched for the plastic carrier that held all the necessary requisites for the job. Clutching a duster and Mr Sheen, he decided he would start with the bedroom. Do the worst first. Polish and spray Natalie out of his life.

He launched himself up the stairs, taking them two at a time, collecting clean sheets from the airing cupboard on the way. He stopped abruptly at the bedroom door, unable to move. The scent in the room caught at his nostrils, heavy, musky, sexy. *Natalie*. The evidence was all still there. Untouched. Like a murder scene. The tangle of sheets. The smears of make-up. The psychedelic pink note, complete with Natalie's endearments on Kate's bedside table next to frilly Jilly Cooper. All that was missing was the blood. *That's because the bleeding's going on inside, where no one can see it*.

He ripped the sheets from the bed, screwing them into tight little balls and forcing them into the bursting laundry basket. The washing machine would need to go on too. *Do I know how to work it?*

Jeffrey was smoothing down the fresh, unsullied sheets when Kerry appeared in the doorway. 'Joe says Nat's gone.'

He grabbed the psychedelic pink note and pushed it under Kate's pillow out of harm's way, before turning to face his daughter.

'It didn't look like she'd slept in her bed,' Kerry said. And his daughter was suddenly thirty-two not twelve.

'Perhaps she was just very tidy,' he said weakly and Kerry eyed the duster and Mr Sheen doubtfully.

'I heard some funny noises.' Kerry kicked her toe against the carpet. 'Was she sick?' His daughter's gaze burned into him. 'Like Clarissa's daddy's girlfriend?'

'No.' Jeffrey cleared his throat guiltily. 'That was me. I had too much champagne.'

'Adults!' Kerry tutted. 'Why don't they ever grow up?'

Jeffrey looked more sheepish than Shaun the sheep. 'I'm sorry I disturbed you,' he said wanly.

'Mummy will wonder why she's gone.'

Kerry, I'm still wondering too! 'I know.'

'Do you want me to help you?' she asked. 'You look a bit weird.'

'No.' Jeffrey shook his head. 'I can manage. You carry on with your keyboard practice. We've still to face your mother with the pierced belly-button confession, so you'd better do something to get in her good books.'

'I could put the sheets in the washing machine.' She cast a look at the laundry basket. A look that was just too knowing for a twelve-year-old. *Why, if adults never grow up, do children grow up so fast?*

'Do you know how it works?'

'Daddy! Of course I do! I'm a girl!'

She strode into the room and purposefully picked up the wicker basket. 'I'll leave you to get on with this,' she said. 'You've got to squirt the polish on the duster first and not straight onto the wood.'

'Why?'

'Mummy said so.' She headed towards the door.

'Kerry.' Jeffrey picked up the duster. 'What did you have for breakfast?'

'Jammy Dodgers.'

'Kerry!'

'You said not to have crisps. You didn't say we couldn't have biscuits.'

'Don't tell your mother,' Jeffrey warned her.

'I won't even tell her that you weren't here,' she said tightly as she left the room.

Jeffrey squirted the Mr Sheen carelessly and the cloying smell of it made him nauseous. Where was Natalie now? Was she risking the delights of the Eurotunnel, heading for the art galleries of Paris, the crumbling beauty of Venice, the romance of Prague? Or would she have got as far as Euston Station and be regretting shunning the cultural wasteland of Leighton Buzzard and the more obvious charms of its occupants? Would she, in fact, even now be rushing homewards through Hemel Hempstead and back to him? Jeffrey rubbed the duster half-heartedly over the dressing table. He doubted it.

Perhaps it was for the best. What sort of life would they have had together? Who would have sorted out the year-end accounts for his clients at Hills & Hopeland if he had just upped and left them in the lurch? And what about Kate and the children?

There was a picture of his wife in a silver frame. On the night of their engagement? Possibly. The occasion had been lost over time, due to the alarmingly steady depletion of his brain cells. She was as beautiful now as she had been then. Jeffrey ran the duster lovingly over her face, tracing the smooth skin that was now more wrinkled, tenderly polishing her nose. He had come so close to losing Kate. Marriage, these days, was like a sandcastle on the beach. No matter how well it was constructed or how big or fancy a moat you dug round it, the advancing tide would inevitably try to wash it away. What could he do to hold it together against the constant battering? Should he just rejoice in the fact that they had come this far, so much further than most, give up the fight and let nature do her worst? Or should he keep on trying to shore it up, piling on sand when the cracks started to show and the walls started to crumble? And what if you smashed one sandcastle to the ground and started all over again with a new one? Wouldn't the same thing happen eventually?

Looking round the bedroom, he saw that no trace of Natalie remained. She was gone. Out of his life. But what of his heart? Would a simple rub round with Mr Sheen do the same trick? He felt more tired than he had ever felt in his life. Kate would be home soon, expecting life to go on as normal. He would have to pull himself together. He would heave himself up by his boot straps, gird his loins – whatever that meant – and do all those singularly British things that added up to soldiering on. From now on, he would put everything into his marriage to make it work. He would never take Kate for granted again and he would never, ever, *ever* so much as look at another woman as long as he lived.

Jeffrey looked in the mirror and didn't recognise the careworn man who looked back. His face was as haggard as Mick Jagger's and suddenly his eyes welled with tears for the loss of simplicity in his life. Clutching the duster to his heart, Jeffrey Lewis – staid, sensible, Conservative-voting accountant – crumpled to the floor and wept like a child.

Chapter Thirty-Seven

It was pissing down. The blistering hot summer week had turned as cold and cheerless as November. After the sun, now comes the rain. Balance. Just as Sam had forecast. Kate's feet echoed emptily on the glistening wet cobbles of the courtyard as she made her way back to her room. The Priory looked grey and gloomy, the trees had closed in and all the flowers in the manicured beds were weighed down, bent heads dripping with water.

The only good thing about the rain was that no one could tell she was crying. Her heart screamed at her to turn round and run after Ben, but her body plodded stoically on. In her mind she knew this was exactly the right thing to be doing for everyone.

She reached the accommodation wing and then stopped in her tracks. What if she was shutting the door on the one thing that could make her happy? What if she was letting Ben walk out of her life when he was the one person who could lift her from the ordinary and the mundane?

This was insane. She had to find him and stop him. Great splats of rain splashed onto her head from the overhead guttering like a Chinese water torture.

No – wait – hang on. She was married, with children. Could she selfishly walk away from all that to pursue her own happiness? What would she do with the children? Where would they live? If she took them to live with Ben, it would disrupt their schooling – they'd have to leave all their friends. But they could stay with Jeffrey and she could see them at weekends . . . Would they turn to drink, drugs and prostitution because they came from a broken home? Wasn't that what *World in Action* was about every week? Good Lord, what was she thinking of?

Turning on her heels, she dashed inside the building, setting off towards her room with a determined stride. After three paces, she ground to a Tom and Jerry-style halt again. There were ways of making this work. Perhaps Ben could buy a cottage in one of the villages and commute into London, so that she could see them during the week. What would he think about that? Did he want children? Did he want her children? Someone else's children? Perhaps Natalie was so enchanted by their perfect behaviour that she would dump Jessica's marauding tribe at the drop of a cork-brimmed hat and move in to Acacia Close permanently, thus solving all childcare arrangements in one fell swoop. She wondered how well the week with Natalie had gone. It had been so difficult to tell with their guarded phone conversations. Jeffrey had said so little.

Where was the balance in this? The scales swung heavily from one side to the other. It wasn't possible. *Was it?* Kate chewed her nails. People did it all the time. What were the statistics now? One in two marriages consigned to the scrap heap. Was Ben worth all this? In a moment of stillness, the pond became calm and clear. Yes.

Now all she had to do was tell him.

Kate ran back across the slippery cobbles of the courtyard. She raced up the stairs and along the corridor to Ben's room, pushing past the trolleys stacked with mops, buckets, towels and tea bags. His door was open and she skidded inside. The cleaner was busy making the bed with clean sheets and Ben's bag had gone.

She sped back down the stairs, across the cobbles again and slid into the reception area. A queue of people were waiting to pay their bills and Kate hopped and hovered and barely hung onto her patience until she was at the head of it.

'Can you tell me if Mr Mahler's checked out, please?' She leaned over the desk and tried to read the list upside down. 'Ben Mahler.'

The receptionist trailed her finger slowly down her computer screen. 'Yes,' she said finally. 'He's already left.'

'Is it possible for you to give me a contact telephone number for him?'

The smile took on a brittle edge. 'I'm afraid I can't divulge confidential information about other residents.' *It's more than my job's worth.*

'This isn't confidential,' Kate said in a lowered voice, aware that the queue behind her was building up to lunchtime-in-a-post-office proportions. 'We promised we'd keep in touch. It's just that with all the rush to pack up and vacate the rooms . . .' Her voice tailed away.

'I'm sorry,' the receptionist said.

Kate's Chi sank to her sandals.

'But you've only just this second missed him. If you rush, you might catch up with him in the car park.'

It flew back up to her throat.

'His wife came to collect him a few minutes ago.'

There was a loud ringing in her ears. 'His wife?' Kate stammered. Now her Chi didn't know where the hell to go. 'Mr Mahler isn't married.'

'Isn't he?' She didn't look convinced. 'I assumed it was his wife. A very pretty blonde.' She lowered her voice and leaned towards Kate like a co-conspirator. 'She certainly wasn't old enough to be his mother – though she could have passed for his daughter.' The receptionist turned back to her computer screen, chuckling at her own joke.

A very pretty blonde. Not just a plain ordinary pretty blonde. But a *very* pretty one.

'You'll need to hurry,' the woman prompted. 'Or you'll miss him.'

I'll miss him. Kate knew that already.

'Next, please!' the receptionist said and the queue shuffled forward.

Kate's feet had rooted to the ground. Never had the Standing Firmly posture been executed so perfectly. Nothing would move. Her entire body was immobilised with shock. *Ben's wife?* She had to be wrong.

331

Chapter Thirty-Eight

'Where have you been?' Fiona complained. 'I've been waiting for ages!'

Ben lugged his case to the car, trying not to inspect it too obviously for newly acquired dents and trying not to trawl the car park to see if Kate's car was still there. He looked back at the Priory. It was a harsh building in the wrong light. There were damp patches on the walls where the gutters leaked and the glorious stained-glass windows looked drab now in the rain.

He could see his bedroom window from here and the fire escape, and his eyes wandered the track they had taken across the grass and up into the woods. A vision of Kate naked, offering herself to the sky, burned from the back of his eyes. This week would stay with him as long as he lived.

'I asked at Reception, but they hadn't a clue where you were. I was about to send out a search-party . . .' Fi halted mid-flow. 'You look terrible,' she said. 'Truly terrible.'

'I feel terrible,' Ben answered.

Her face creased with concern. 'Put that down,' she instructed, wrenching his case from him, 'and come here!' She flung her arms round his neck and hugged her to him. He slid his hands round her tiny waist.

'You've lost weight,' she said.

'I haven't, Fi,' he insisted. 'You're being melodramatic.'

'I thought this course was supposed to relax and regenerate you?'

'The exercise has done wonders for me,' Ben said. 'It's the workout of the heart that's causing me grief.'

Fi gave an exasperated huff. 'What am I going to do with you, Ben?'

'Treat me gently,' he suggested.

'I phoned Chris in the office and I have some particularly awful jokes to tell you to make you laugh,' she said.

He grinned in spite of himself.

'By the time we're halfway to Hampstead, you'll have split both of your sides open and will have forgotten all about little Miss Perfect. Mrs Perfect,' she corrected.

Ben's face fell.

'Sorry,' Fi said apologetically.

He tried to give a light-hearted shrug, but couldn't make his shoulders move at all.

'What can I say to make it right?' she asked.

'Nothing.'

'Shall I tell you a bad joke instead?'

Ben laughed. 'Go on.'

'Get in the car then, while I try to remember the punch line.'

He put his arm round her shoulders and hugged her to him. 'What would I do without you, Fi?'

'That is a question I often ask myself, Benjamin,' she said, breaking away from him and heading towards the car.

'I take it you're driving?' Ben asked, leaning on the roof.

'Well, I'm not in a rush to swap this for Old Faithful.'

'Ah!' Ben slid into the passenger seat. 'There's something I've been meaning to tell you . . .'

It may not be his wife, Kate thought, but whoever it is, he's certainly very fond of her. She stood at the entrance to the Priory, next to the revolving door half-hidden by a tumbling Clematis Nelly Moser. It was all woody and bare at the bottom and would need a good pruning when it had finished with its candy-stripe burst of colour. You had to be very careful with clematis, they were touchy about being chopped at the wrong time and would drop dead as soon as look at you. Jeffrey would know exactly when to nip it in the bud.

The receptionist was right. She *was* a very pretty blonde. And tiny. And young. And Kate was watching Ben laughing, joking and cuddling her.

Could Ben have been married and not told her? Kate heard about people like that all the time – men who went to conferences, removed their wedding rings and all memory of the wife and children they had waiting at home. Was Ben really like that? How could he have been holding her and swearing undying love for her only minutes ago and now be draped – yes, draped was a good word – round this rather nubile girl. Wouldn't she have been able to tell? Even if he wasn't married, they were clearly what the *Daily Mail* would call 'an item'.

Emotionally, she felt very naive in the ways of the world.

Having spent half of your life with the same person didn't equip you very well for the slings and arrows of the modern mating game. He was probably having a good old laugh at her – the dowdy bird with the blue eyeliner who was good for a summer-school shag, but nothing more. Kate closed her eyes.

When she opened them, she saw that Ben had got into the car with the blonde at the wheel, and they were driving away.

Kate trudged back to her tiny bedroom where, for a while, she sat staring blankly at the wall. The beautiful white rose that Ben had so gallantly given her, had finally died. Its velvety bruised petals were scattered on the dressing table. It had bloomed so briefly and now it was dead. Perhaps everything was like that – only perfect, as fresh as a daisy, for a very short time. What was the old game? He loves me, he loves me not? Did it work with roses as well as daisies? She held a petal to her lips and gulped back her tears. There were only twenty-four petals. *He loves me not.* She counted them a second time and then checked behind the dressing table to see if any had fallen down. Twenty-four. Ben had said that every rose had twenty-five petals. She had trusted him and he had lied to her after all. What else had he lied about?

Chapter Thirty-Nine

'Fi, can you stop the car?' Ben said. They were at the end of the drive, waiting to join the stream of traffic on the main road. 'I need to make a call.'

'I've got a mobile. The wonder of modern technology means that while I drive, you can talk.'

'Just pull in over here,' he begged. 'Only for a minute. It's personal and I need some fresh air.'

Fiona viewed him suspiciously. 'You cannot fail to have noticed that it's raining small domestic animals.'

'I won't be long,' he said and, grabbing her phone, jumped out of the car. He leaned on the back of the boot and put the phone to his ear, hitching the collar of his jacket up against the pelting rain. Pretending to talk animatedly, he smiled broadly at Fi, who was watching him through the rearview mirror, a disdainful expression on her face.

After a few moments, Kate's BMW appeared in the driveway. She was inching along in a queue of other cars. Ben held his head down and, thanking God for the congestion on rural backwaters, watched her furtively. She had been crying again.

There was a noise beside him. The clearing of a throat. And, as he tore his eyes away from Kate, Fiona nudged his arm, making him drop the phone. He scrabbled on the ground to pick it up out of a puddle.

'I suppose you realise you were making that call with my sunglasses case?' she said sardonically.

Ben stood up and examined the metal case. 'Oh.'

Fiona took it from him and wiped it dry on the side of her jeans. Then she slid her Ray Bans out, putting them on even though it was still raining. 'Here's the phone,' she said, offering it to him. 'At least, you haven't ruined it.'

Ben patted his pocket sheepishly. 'My own's in here.'

'Get a life, Ben,' Fi suggested. Her eyes followed Ben's gaze to the blue BMW. She pulled her sunglasses down to the tip of her nose and stared at Kate, who was stuck behind a Range Rover. 'That's her, is it? In the Bavarian bollard bruiser?'

Ben nodded miserably.

'She looks sweet,' Fi said in surprise.

'She is.'

Fiona leaned against the boot of the car next to him. 'Does she know how you feel?'

'Yes.' Ben swallowed hard. 'I love her.'

They watched Kate in silence.

'So what are you going to do about it?'

'I don't know.'

'If you love her you should let her go,' she advised.

His jaw set tightly and he kept his eyes fixed ahead. 'That's why I'm standing here like a complete prat watching her drive away.'

Fiona put her hand on his arm.

'You'll survive. After a fashion. We all do. Physically, you'll be unscathed, but emotionally you'll be permanently crippled.'

Ben sleeved the raindrops from his nose. 'Thanks.'

'If it's any consolation, she doesn't know what she's missing.'

A gap in the traffic appeared, which coincided with a gap in Ben's breathing. It was time for her to go. Hope seeped out of him into the puddle at his feet. *Don't go!* his brain screamed. *Look round! See me! Love me! Change your mind! I have no weapons to fight this!* And then Kate pulled out into the road, swung the car away from them and was gone.

'Let's get back in the car,' Ben said shakily. 'We're getting wet through.'

Fiona didn't move. 'This is probably totally the wrong time to say it,' she gulped, 'but I still love you, Ben.'

The rain was running down her cheeks and he brushed it away with his thumb. 'I know.'

'Life isn't fair, is it?' she asked quietly.

He looked down the road, but Kate's car had disappeared. 'Never,' he said, and held on to Fi as if his life depended on it.

Chapter Forty

Kate lasted as far as the dual carriageway before she had to find a lay-by. Swinging in by the bright blue P sign, she stopped next to the concrete bin overflowing with takeaway cartons and dented lager cans, and cried for a solid five minutes. In an attempt to make it more constructive, she tried to turn it into the aaah sound to heal her broken heart, but it came out like aaargh and just made her feel stupid. Afterwards, she dried her tears, tidying the smears of mascara with a damp tissue in the rearview mirror. The pain was like cutting yourself, she thought. You had to put a bit of plaster on it and carry on regardless. The scar would always be there to remind you, but soon you'd forget just how much it had hurt when it happened. Eventually, it would fade to a mere hint of a blemish that you only noticed from time to time.

It was time to be getting back. Back to life. Back to reality. She cast one last look at her blotchy face and decided that no one at home would take a blind bit of notice anyway. Perhaps this had all been a dream. A fantasy romance created by a bored brain that was tired of busying itself baking bread and battling with bed linen as if it really mattered. Now, more than ever, she needed something else to think about other than the daily domestic round that had dragged her down to this level of discontentment in the first place. She was disappointed that there had been no blinding flashes of inspiration on the job front, no sudden urge to rush into the Bradford & Bingley and start that dizzying climb to become Building Society Cashier of the Year, no brain-tingling certainty that opening a tearoom would make her feel a vital part of the human race or no yearning to turn her dining room into a home factory and churn out mohair teddy bears for dreary Sunday craft fairs. But then she hadn't really given it due consideration; instead she had given in to a dangerous distraction, when she was a woman not known for her flights of fancy.

Kate slid the BMW into gear and accelerated away from the squalor of the lay-by. She forced herself to smile, snuffling away the last of the tears as she did so. It *had* been fun meeting Ben. She would have treasured memories of him – the white rose that started it all, the picnic, the night on the ridge, the way he had laughed, the way he looked at her, the way he had loved her. *Had* he loved her? For a short while she had believed it.

Would Jeffrey be able to tell that she'd had an affair, just by looking at her? The way you were supposed to be able to tell if someone likes butter by holding a buttercup under their chin? Was there a special glow that would give her away the minute she walked through the door?

Number 20, Acacia Close hadn't changed at all. Though why she had expected it to in the mere space of a week, she wasn't sure. Was it because she had changed? Kate was a different person from the woman she had been seven days ago. A stranger in her own body, a stranger in her own home. She was a woman with a secret. Someone who had strayed from her given path and had found the excitement of the woods both thrilling and scary at the same time. Now she knew for certain that once you had ventured into the unknown, you could never feel quite the same. You might have the security, the knowledge that the route you were treading would hold no surprises, but the sense of adventure would always be missing.

The rain had all but stopped and the sun was nudging the clouds out of the way. The gravel drive squelched rather than crunched to herald her arrival. Bright pink Chinese peonies peeped out from the herbaceous border, stems stooped with the effort of keeping their heavy heads upright. They were interspersed with the bright yellow punk-spiked heads of dandelions and she knew that, if the rain held off, she should spend the afternoon gardening. A light bulb pinged on in her brain – perhaps that was where her vocation lay! What if she took a course in horticulture and trained to be a landscape gardener? She could tell a daisy from a dianthus at fifty paces. And she certainly had enough experience of the dirty end of a spade. Wouldn't it be rather nice to be paid for wrestling with someone else's weeds for a change, rather than continually losing the fight with her own? It was a thought.

The front door swung open and her husband appeared. He was rubbing his hands together and twitching from foot to foot, like he did when he was nervous, or when they were going on holiday, or doing anything that couldn't quite be classified as 'routine'. And there was something different about his appearance. She couldn't believe how much Jeffrey's hairline had receded in one week for a start and his face looked tired, older. Perhaps it was the strain of coping with the female version of Skippy the bush kangaroo. Kate grinned wickedly to herself. Maybe Natalie wasn't the angel that Jessica had made her out to be. Jeffrey was smiling too, but it wasn't his usual easy grin. This was the insincere rictus of a game-show host, painted on with Panstick. She almost waited for him to shout, 'Kate Lewis, come on down!'

Instead, he sauntered over to the car and said, 'Hi.'

'Good grief,' Kate replied as she got out. She stared at him open-mouthed. His hair hadn't receded at all, it had been shaved within an inch of its life. 'It's . . .'

'Radical?' Jeffrey supplied.

'For you. Yes.'

Jeffrey did a twirl. Which was a particularly strange thing for Jeffrey to do. 'Do you like it?'

'I love it,' she said. 'I'm just a bit stunned. What on earth possessed you?'

'I thought it was time for a change.' She saw a hint of a blush in Jeffrey's fair cheeks. 'A new me.'

'Well, it's certainly that.'

'Come on,' he said. 'Let's get your bags inside. The kettle's only just boiled.'

They went round to the back of the car and she opened the boot.

'Kate,' Jeffrey said hesitantly. His eyes searched her face. Could he see her betrayal writ large? Was the evidence there in her expression? He took her hand and squeezed it gently. 'I have missed you.'

'Have you?'

'Yes.' He slipped his arms round her waist and kissed her full on the mouth. His kiss was warm, comforting, familiar and yet, not Jeffrey at all. This kiss was bordering on the realms of licentious behaviour. Whenever they started doing this sort of thing on the television – which they did frequently – Jeffrey sprang into action, hurdling the coffee table in one fearless leap and switching it off before it corrupted the children. Kate resisted the urge to look round and see if the neighbours were watching. It couldn't be classed as usual behaviour for her to be snogging in the street, let alone Acacia Close. But then she'd done quite a few things in the last week that weren't like her at all. What had come over Jeffrey, though? Had Natalie been giving him too much red meat? He broke away from her, smiling his sweet, guileless smile.

He heaved her bags out of the boot and steered her towards the house.

'The rain's been awful, hasn't it?' he said. 'Still, the garden needed it.'

Only Jeffrey could come up with a statement like that.

The lounge was in darkness. Joe and Kerry were watching *Star Trek: Deep Space Nine* on the video. And they were squabbling about whether it was better than *Star Trek:*

The Next Generation or ancient *Star Trek* with the fat bloke who wore a wig and the boring one with pointy ears. Her son was wearing a baseball cap the wrong way round and his feet were on the coffee table. Kerry's hair sported a single multi-coloured cotton-bound braid which she was sucking along with her thumb. A sort of unfinished Bo Derek effect. There were two orange stripes on her cheeks that looked like slivers of smoked salmon. Dark rings circled her eyes and a garish red slash adorned the space where her pretty pink mouth used to be.

Kate wanted to rush out and check that she had come to the right house. It had said number 20 on the gate, she was sure. But somehow, she had left Enid Blyton and returned to *The Simpsons*.

'Mummy's home,' she said, uncertainly.

They both looked at her and waved. 'Hi,' they managed before turning back to the television.

'Who did your braid?' she asked Kerry.

'Natalie,' her daughter said, still transfixed by Worf doing battle with the Klingons.

'It's pretty,' she said.

'Thanks.' Kerry sucked it some more.

'And the make-up?'

'Natalie. The lipstick's Tart Red.'

There was no disputing that.

'You can borrow some of mine if you like.'

'Yours are a bit too pale for me,' Kerry said, still watching the intergalactic battle. 'But thanks.'

Kate stood there for a few minutes while they ignored

her and then let her feet plod her through to the kitchen, where – it was comforting to see – the designer-scuffed cupboards still looked like they needed a fresh coat of paint. Jeffrey was concentrating on the serious business of making tea. Hadn't her husband noticed that their children had turned from Rosie and Jim into perfectly normally surly, rebellious pre-teenagers while she had been away?

'What's happened to the kids?'

'What do you mean?'

'Kerry seems to be wearing the entire contents of a Max Factor factory.'

'Natalie's been encouraging her to experiment.'

'She looks like the Bride of Dracula.'

'It does take a bit of getting used to,' Jeffrey admitted, tapping the teaspoon against the cups in an agitated manner.

'Doesn't she know that a hutchful of innocent rabbits have had their eyelashes glued together so that she can wear that lot without her skin dropping off?'

'I think she's put being an environmental activist on hold for the moment.'

'I've been gone for seven days, and in that time they've gone to pot.'

Jeffrey glanced up at her. 'I thought that's what you wanted?'

'It's a bit sudden, isn't it?'

'They've started to come out of themselves,' he said. 'Aren't you pleased?'

'Pleased?' *Well, yes. But perplexed, too.*

'Besides it's not pot they've gone to, it's Alton Towers.'

So that's where you were! 'I tried to phone you yesterday.' Kate struggled to keep an accusatory note out of her voice. 'At the office. They said you were sick, but you weren't at home.'

'I *was* sick,' Jeffrey said bravely. 'Sick of work. Sick of routine. Sick of Hills and bloody Hopeland.' He mashed the tea bags fiercely. 'So we all went out for the day. It was Nat's idea. A fitting end to her time with us.'

'You took the children out of school?'

'It won't hurt just once.'

'And a day at Alton Towers has brought about this rather rapid personality change?'

'Natalie's helped too. She's been a big influence on them.'

'In a week?'

'She has a very forthright style.'

'Where is she now?'

'Gone.' Jeffrey's voice sounded curiously tight.

'Gone?'

'Yes.'

'When?'

'This morning.'

'And when is she coming back?'

'I don't think she is.'

'But I haven't paid her,' Kate said.

'Haven't you?' Jeffrey looked surprised. 'Neither have I.'

'Has she left an address?'

Jeffrey hung his head. 'No.'

'A phone number?'

'Nothing.'

'I can't believe she's just upped and left without payment or leaving a forwarding address.' Kate raked her hair. 'Jessica said she was very reliable.'

'Perhaps she was having an off day.' Jeffrey looked evasive.

'How am I going to explain this when they get back from Florida and are Natalie-less? They adored her. They thought she was Mary Poppins and Mrs Doubtfire rolled into one, with a sprinkling of Eva Herzigova added in for good measure.'

Her husband looked shame-faced. Kate put her hands on her hips and tried to look threatening. 'You didn't upset her, did you, Jeffrey? You did get on all right?'

'We got on fine.'

'Are you sure?' There was definitely something he wasn't telling her.

'Can you get the milk?' Jeffrey said brightly.

Kate wandered to the fridge. Her fingers ran over the surface of a cutesy china house they had bought in Prague. It was supposed to be reminiscent of the splendid thirteenth-century architecture there, but bore no relation to it. That was to have been a romantic weekend for her and Jeffrey, but she had developed food poisoning from the meal on the plane, Jeffrey's wallet had been pick-pocketed on the metro and, when they got back to Heathrow, the car had been vandalised and the stereo stolen. She hadn't bought a fridge magnet from Northwood Priory, but perhaps it was too upmarket for that sort of tat anyway. The one holiday that had left a deeper imprint on her than any other, and she had nothing tangible to remind her of it. But then, it wouldn't do to be reminded of Ben every morning when she started to make the packed lunches. It wouldn't be a great way to begin the day. She pulled the fridge door open and stopped dead. There, between the Heinz tomato ketchup and a packet of Wall's pork sausages, propped against the Utterly Butterly was a psychedelic pink note in Jeffrey's fine, copperplate writing. *Don't ever leave us again!* it said.

'Oh, Jeffrey.' Kate crossed the kitchen to wind herself round him. 'That's very sweet.'

'I mean it, Kate,' he said. 'Things haven't been the same without you.'

A blind man on a galloping horse could see that!

Kerry came into the kitchen, sat down and slumped over the table in a perfect parody of pubescent ennui.

'*Star Trek* finished?'

She grunted.

'Did the Klingons win?'

'Oh, please,' Kerry said. 'Do they ever?'

Not in thirty years. Some things *definitely* never change.

'Anyway,' Jeffrey said lightly. 'Tell us all about your course. We're dying to hear, aren't we, Kerry?'

Kerry looked a long way away from dying.

'Well,' Kate took her tea and sat at the table with her daughter. 'It's been enlightening.'

'What were the other students like? Were they all older?'

'No,' Kate said. 'There were a few crumblies around, but it was a surprisingly young crowd. In fact,' she giggled, 'there were an awful lot of women with pierced navels and tattoos about.'

Jeffrey and Kerry stiffened visibly.

'What have I said?' Kate asked, looking from one to the other.

Kerry glanced nervously at Jeffrey. 'Now?'

He shrugged, even though there was a worried slant to his eyebrows. 'It's as good a time as any.'

Without preamble, Kerry lifted up her jumper and the belly-button ring glinted in the sunshine.

'Oh, my God,' Kate said. She'd come over all hot and unnecessary. Her baby was a woman! Her baby was a woman! Panic attack! Panic attack! *Sink your Chi, Kate. Sink your Chi, otherwise it's going to shoot out of the top of your head and make a mess all over the kitchen.*

'I've got a tattoo as well,' her daughter said flatly. 'On my bum.' She stood up, pulled down her leggings and swivelled round to show one cheek of her bottom.

Kate was feeling faint. 'Who's Ronan Keating?'

'Boyzone,' Jeffrey said.

'It's only fake.' Kerry tried to view her own backside. 'Natalie said real tattoos drove mothers wild.'

'I like it,' Kate said stoically.

'Do you?' Kerry eyed her suspiciously.

'It's very trendy.' *No wonder Natalie had legged it before she got back!* 'I was thinking of getting one done myself.'

Jeffrey spluttered into his tea.

'Cool, Mum,' Kerry said, hitching her knickers as she walked out of the kitchen.

Kate held her hand to her forehead, lest she swoon. 'Did you agree to that?' She pointed to where the belly-button and the bottom had been.

'Only after the event,' he admitted. 'It's grown on me though.'

'Is there anything else you want to tell me while it's confession time?'

Jeffrey flushed from the neck of his polo shirt to the tip of his ears.

'Joe hasn't been expelled for drug dealing? The cat hasn't pooed on Mrs Barrett's front doorstep again? You haven't resigned from Hills and Hopeland?'

'I've been promoted,' Jeffrey said. 'A partnership.'

'Why didn't you tell me sooner?' She put her arm round him, squeezing him and kissing him on the cheek. 'Jeffrey, that's fantastic!'

'Is it?' he said miserably. 'A golden handcuff to chain me to my desk for the next twenty years.'

Kate let go of him and sank back, staring in amazement. 'I thought it was what you'd always wanted?'

'So did I.' Jeffrey snorted unhappily, making ripples on the surface of his Darjeeling. He looked at her, eyes imploring. 'There must be more to life than this?'

Kate's mouth went slack and she wondered how much damage her falling chin would do to the designer glazed terracotta tiled floor when it hit it.

350

Chapter Forty-One

Kate stared at herself in the mirror, lining up the cleanser, toner and moisturiser ready for her nightly fight against ageing. She pulled some pretty cotton wool balls from the glass jar in front of her and paused with them in her hand. Hidden between the layers was another pink note. I love you. She smiled to herself. Jeffrey was such a sweet and gentle man, how could she have overlooked those qualities? Probably because most of the time, it was demonstrated through quiet, background gestures, rather than a showy in-your-face display. He wasn't a roses and champagne man; Jeffrey was a cup of tea and shall I rub your shoulders? material. With a little thrill of pleasure, Kate folded the note and slipped it into her dressing-gown pocket.

On the surface it felt like nothing much had changed, but the energy within Kate was fizzing up like a glass of Perrier water, gentle little bubbles bursting pleasantly as they came to the top, releasing her worries into the air. Refreshing. Perhaps things wouldn't be so bad, after all.

It hadn't occurred to her that Jeffrey was capable of being unhappy too. Strangely, it was comforting to know that he was struggling inside as much as she was. Perhaps they were both going through a midlife crisis, one last fling at rebellion before they settled down for their dotage. She sincerely hoped not. What about those people who went across the Sahara on a camel in their seventies or appeared on *Mastermind* in their eighties? Surely they hadn't sat comfortably, never venturing off their Dralon three-piece suite since their mid-thirties? Like T'ai Chi, it was all a matter of mind intent.

It was nice to be home. The house had taken a lot of blood, sweat and years to make it so comfortable, but now it was indelibly stamped with their style. There wasn't enough lime green or evidence of earth colours for it to be deemed fashionable, but it suited them both. She ran her finger over the dressing table, not ostensibly checking for dust, but pleased nevertheless that there wasn't any. The children had been dispatched for the night to her mother's house. Jeffrey had organised it, along with a Chinese takeaway – to keep her in the Oriental mood, he said – and a decent bottle of white wine. That, combined with a long soak in a bubble bath, had gone some way to soothing her jarred and shell-shocked body. Soon Ben Mahler would be a thing of the past. She flinched at the mere thought of his name. How soon? A week, a month, a year – sometime maybe never? Kate popped the cotton wool back in the jar. Routine could go to hell for once. She would do a Joan Collins and flounce into bed naked and in full make-up – see how the new Jeffrey would cope with that!

Padding to the bathroom, Kate collected her dirty laundry from her case. She lifted the basket lid and peered inside. Another note. *I love you lots!!!!* Kate chuckled and gave the note a kiss before consigning it to the growing collection in her pocket. She tipped the T-shirts and the leggings inside, hesitating only to look at the pair of knickers she had worn last night. Like the discarded nightie, they were pretty, pink, functional and marginally bigger than could be considered sexy – married women's underwear. She would always think of Ben when she was wearing them and she'd always wish that she'd worn something sexier. Hugging them to her in a pathetic little gesture, she felt the tears well up inside. She had got nothing of Ben to take away with her. Not even a photograph. Only her memories. How soon would she forget the sound of his voice, the mischievous spark in his eyes, the softness of his skin? She wanted to hold him in her brain for ever, never letting him go. But perhaps that wasn't the wisest thing to do.

She could hear Jeffrey whistling good-naturedly in the kitchen, clashing the crockery together as he unloaded the dishwasher, chatting to Erstwhile about the joys of Kit-E-Kat, locking the back door. Would she ever make love to him again and not see Ben's face? Every time Jeffrey touched her, would she wish it was someone else? She dropped the panties on top of the pile of clothes, closed the basket and returned to the bedroom. Folding back the duvet, she plumped up her pillows, trying to smile through her sadness.

She heard her husband say goodnight to the cat and start to climb the stairs. He was singing 'I'm in the Mood for Love', making up the words that he didn't know, and Kate couldn't help giggling.

Jeffrey crashed through the bedroom door with a flourish. 'Da, da!' he said, and held out the horrendously ornate silver tray that they only used at Christmas when they were serving mulled wine and mince pies to their boring neighbours in an attempt to be festively sociable. On it sat a bottle of champagne, two glasses – and a long-stemmed pure white rose. Kate's heart lurched when she saw it.

He produced a box of matches from the pocket of his dressing gown like a magician producing a white handkerchief, and samba-ed round the room lighting strategically placed candles that he had obviously concealed earlier.

'Aromatherapy,' he said, blowing out the match. 'Exotic Garden. Sensual, seductive.'

He pounced on the bed and to Kate's nervous delight, growled like a tiger. 'Let me pour you a glass of champagne,' he said wickedly.

This was like going to bed with a stranger, Kate thought to herself. Something she knew all about now. Oh God, could she carry the weight of a guilty conscience round with her for the rest of her life? She peered at her husband, still singing cheerfully. Did Jeffrey suspect anything? She didn't think so.

He handed her a fizzing glass and offered a toast. 'To us,' he said.

'To us,' Kate echoed guiltily.

'So,' he took her hand, 'do you think the week away was worthwhile?'

'I think I've learned a lot.'

'Do you feel more settled?' He traced his finger over her palm.

'I'm not sure,' she said, avoiding his eyes. 'I still don't know what I want from life. Not exactly. I thought I might look into doing a course in garden design or something like that. Set up a little business. Something that I could work round the school holidays for a few more years.'

'I can't believe it,' he said delightedly. 'I've been thinking exactly the same thing!' Jeffrey slugged back his champagne. 'I realised when my promotion came through, it isn't what I want long-term. Accountancy isn't for me.'

'*It isn't?*' She was astonished.

'No. Balance sheets bore me to death. They're squeezing the life out of me, Kate. I don't want to be stuck behind a desk for the rest of my life.'

'*You don't?*'

'I want to get my hands dirty! Run barefoot in the grass!'

'*You do?*'

Jeffrey was getting very animated. 'Kate, you could train first. Start the business while I carried on supporting us. Then after a couple of years, when you were established, I could give up my job and join you. I could take a course in my spare time . . .'

'You don't have any spare time.'

'I'll make some.' Jeffrey squeezed her fingers. 'This is important, Kate. I need a dream. I don't want to be deskbound,' he said passionately. 'I want to reach for the stars!'

Kate's universe was shifting and she wasn't sure if she was ready for it.

'I've got something else to show you too!'

Jeffrey was in full flow. The steady stream had burst its banks and was determined to wash everything familiar on the landscape away in its path. He reached under the bed and after a few moments of grappling, pulled out a very large box which he plonked on the bed.

'Go on – open it!' His eyes were bright.

Kate fumbled with the hastily wrapped package, pulling out reams and reams of tissue paper until she reached the treasure. 'Rollerblades,' she breathed.

'You said you wanted to try it.'

'So I did.' She looked nervously at Jeffrey. 'But I've got no sense of balance.'

'I thought you might have learned something from T'ai Chi.'

She had, but nothing that would help with rollerblading. 'It still isn't the meaning of life.'

'But it's a start,' he said comfortably. 'I've bought them for us all. I thought we could do it as a family.'

'Even you?'

'Even me.'

The sight of Jeffrey on rollerblades would definitely be one worth seeing.

He looked at her endearingly. 'From little acorns and all that . . .'

Acorns. Wood. Growth, blossoming, reaching up. A fresh start.

'I suppose we could give it a go,' she said, a huge smile breaking out on her face.

'However,' he said with a twinkle in his eye, 'I don't think you'll be needing them *just* yet.' Jeffrey dumped the box on the floor. 'And I don't think you'll be needing this either.' Tenderly, he slipped her dressing gown from her shoulders, caressing her skin, making her shudder with expectation.

'Jeffrey . . .'

'Kate,' he said with a sigh, stilling the movement of his hands. 'There's something I've been meaning to ask you.'

She was aware that she was shivering inside. 'What?'

'I hate being called Jeffrey. All my life I've been called Jeffrey and I've always loathed it.'

'You've never said.' Here was another big surprise.

'Well, I'm saying it now. Do you think you could start calling me Jeff? Or Jeffers?'

'Like Natalie did?'

'Did she?' He frowned. 'I hadn't noticed.'

She looked at her husband's guileless, honest face. Was that the face of a man capable of betraying her? He couldn't possibly have done. Not Jeffrey. Jeffers. *Could he?*

'Anything else?' she asked.

He grinned. 'I think that's enough to be going on with.'

'Thank goodness for that.' Kate exhaled the breath she

357

had been holding for the last few minutes. Straightening up, she saw the corner of another pink love note peeping out from under her pillow.

'Why, Jeffers,' she fluttered her eyelashes, waving it in front of him, 'is this for me?'

The grin froze on her husband's face. His handsome features blanched and there was a fleeting look in his eyes that she couldn't fathom. Fear? Regret? Remorse? For some unknown reason, Kate felt an icy chill round her heart.

Jeffrey gently took the pink sheet from her hand and crushed it with his fist. 'It's just words, Kate,' he said in a voice that didn't sound entirely steady. Her husband tossed the crumpled pink paper to the floor. 'I want to do everything in my power to show you how much I love you, how much I need you.'

He threw the duvet on the floor, letting the cool night air caress their bodies. 'Have I told you, Kate Lewis, that you are the most beautiful woman on earth?'

'Not recently, Jeff Lewis,' she said and the words caught in her throat. In a moment of still, calm clarity, Kate suddenly realised that in the search to find herself how close she had come to losing Jeffrey. To losing everything.

He slid down the bed, feathering her body with kisses, teasing her, planting kisses on her toes, her feet, her thighs, hot tongues of flame licking her body. Fire. Passion. Kate held her breath, shuddering, delighting in the sensations. As she turned her head, she caught sight of the perfect white rose in the moonlight. Ben's image drifted before her eyes, laughing with her, holding her, loving her. She could fly now. He had taught her that she could do anything. All she had to do was try. All she had to do was believe in herself. She could soar across the sky and find him, whenever she wanted to, wherever he was...

Kate squeezed her eyes shut, whispered, 'Goodbye,' once more to Ben. Wrapping her arms around her good, kind husband she held on to him as tightly as she could so he wouldn't see that she was crying. Kate Lewis had finally found herself.

If you enjoyed *More to Life Than This*, you don't have to
wait for more!

Carole Matthews' new novel,

A Cottage by the Sea

is out now.

Read on for the first two chapters, and join
Grace, Ella and Flick by the sea, for a week that will
change all of their lives.

Be ready for love, laughter, tears and friendship . . .

Chapter One

'*Destination*,' the dulcet tones of the sat nav announces. '*Destination*.'

Harry stamps on the brakes and stops dead in the middle of the road. There is nothing as far as the eye can see. 'Where, you bloody stupid woman?' he asks it, holding his hands aloft in supplication. 'Where?'

'*Destination*.' She is insistent. '*Destination*.'

The sat nav has the disdainful, upper-class tone of my old English teacher. She always hated me too. Normally, we call the sat nav Auntie Flossie. Today, neither of us is really speaking to her.

'Can you see anything, Grace?' he asks.

I gaze out of the car window. It's beautiful here. The road stretches ahead of us, unbroken, and there's not another car in any direction. The verdant green fields lie unspoiled beneath the unbroken acres of sky. There isn't a single man-made building in sight to mar the view. It's untamed, remote. And I guess that's the crux of our problem.

'Not really,' I admit. But it's fantastic and I hear myself sigh happily.

'Well, she says we're here.' It's clear that Harry is rapidly losing the will to live. 'Can you just look at the map, please?'

I scrabble at the road atlas on my knee. It's a tattered wreck and what remains of the front cover tells me that we bought it from a supermarket in 1992. Helpfully, inside it has a little red circle where all of their branches are – but none of the major roads built since that year, of course. Somewhat worryingly, there are no helpful red 'supermarket' circles anywhere in the area. According to this map, we are in total supermarket wilderness.

In fact, there's not very much near here at all. Currently, the only thing I can see are the miles and miles of rolling fields, hedgerows thick with flowers and sheep. Plenty of sheep.

'Fucking place,' Harry complains.

He is not a happy man. His hands are gripping the wheel again and his knuckles are white. His handsome face, however, is scarlet, becoming borderline puce. My husband, I know, would rather be in Tuscany or Thailand or even Timbuktu. Anywhere, in fact, rather than on our way to a cottage in Wales for a week.

'We can't be far away,' I offer, keeping my tone placating.

The polar opposite to Harry, I'm just thrilled to be here. My dearest friend, Ella Hawley, has invited us to stay with her and her long-term partner, Art. Ella's spending the rest of the summer in Wales and I just can't wait to see her. She's only recently inherited this cottage, but I've heard so much about it over the years that wild horses, never mind a grumpy husband, wouldn't have kept me away. Ella's also invited our friend Flick, but whether or not Flick will turn up is an entirely different matter. You can never quite pin Flick down. I hope she makes it as I haven't seen her in ages and it will be so lovely to catch up.

Outside the chilled atmosphere in the Bentley – only some of it due to the effect of the über-efficient air-conditioning – the sky is a blue more usually seen in the Mediterranean and beneath it, on the very edge of the horizon, a silver ribbon of sea shimmers invitingly. We can't be far away because Ella's cottage is by the sea and, if we drive too much further, we'll be actually in it.

'*Destination*,' the sat nav repeats.

She now sounds slightly weary with life. As am I.

'Get a grip, woman. We're not at the destination,' I tell her firmly. 'Even I've worked that out.'

'Grace,' Harry says, teeth gritted, 'do you mind? We can't stay here in the middle of the road all day.'

To be honest, Harry and I haven't really been speaking since we stopped at Magor Services just before the Severn Crossing. The service station was like a glimpse of hell with queues a mile long for everything and the place stuffed with families screaming at each other. Harry couldn't get anything to eat but a plastic ham sandwich on white bread and he's very much a smoked salmon on wholemeal man. His temper, already frayed by the amount of holiday traffic on the road, shredded to breaking point.

It hasn't helped that we've been on the road since silly o'clock and that there was a ferocious tailback to get over the bridge and into South Wales. On top of that, it cost us nearly a fortune to cross. Cue much muttering under Harry's breath that people should be paying to get out of Wales, not into it.

'We could have been halfway to the sodding Seychelles by now,' he mutters darkly.

In theory, I suppose we could be, but there's so much

else to consider when flying somewhere. It starts with all the vaccinations – nearly the cost of the holiday in itself. Invariably we require malaria tablets too, which make me feel dreadful. The whole experience is just so stressful. All the glamour of flying has long gone. I always feel as if I need another holiday when I've flown for thirteen or more hours just to get back from somewhere. Your memories of the island paradise fade very quickly when faced with a four-hour-long queue for passport control at Gatwick or Heathrow followed by a week of hideous jet lag.

'I hate long-haul flights nowadays, Harry. You know that. For once, isn't it nice to throw the cases in the back of the car and just drive?'

I get a grunt in response.

Despite my husband's reticence, I'm so looking forward to this holiday and am so desperate for it. Work has been nothing but stress this year – the financial climate forcing everyone to tighten their belts, and where I work is no exception. I'm an accountant, the staff partner in a small but successful firm based in north London. We have only ten staff but, believe me, they're a full-time job to manage. I've just had a small mutiny on my hands after we told them that there will be no company Christmas trip this year. Normally, we take the staff and their

other halves on a long weekend jaunt during the approach to the festive season. In the past we've been to Paris, Rome, Bruges. All very lovely. All on expenses. But this year we're going to have to do without. Every single one of our clients is watching the pennies and I think it looks right that we should do so too.

I feel the same about our own holidays abroad. More

often than not, Harry and I go away at least twice every year. How can that be acceptable when so many people are struggling simply to pay their mortgages? I'm more than happy to have a summer staying at home, although I don't think Harry much likes the sound of it. So, when Ella asked us to come down and spend some time with her at the cottage, it seemed like the perfect solution. To me, anyway.

Harry wasn't keen, of course. Even as we set off he was bemoaning the fact that it would be more 'basic' than he prefers. My other half likes to lie on a sunlounger for two weeks and be waited on hand and foot. He doesn't care if there's culture or scenery. He just wants heat, a swimming pool and alcohol on tap. He likes a turndown service, a chocolate and perhaps an exotic bloom on his pillow every night. Those things don't really interest me. Don't get me wrong, I've enjoyed my fair share of luxury holidays too. But sometimes it can be just a tiny bit *boring*. Does that sound ungrateful? If you're typically British and fair-skinned, there's only so much sunbathing you can do if you don't want the boiled-lobster look. So this year I'm really looking forward to having a holiday in my own country for the first time in many years. I'll get to catch up with my dearest friends. Harry and I will get to spend some quality time together without having to go halfway round the world. It'll be fun. I'm sure. Just the tonic we need.

'Shall we aim to get there before nightfall, Grace?' Harry says tightly.

So I pull my attention back to the map and try to work out exactly where we are.

Chapter Two

The fact that I get to hook up with my lovely friends is the icing on the cake for me. Again, I'm not sure that Harry feels the same way. My husband isn't overly fond of my friends. He says that I change when I'm with them. I think, half of the time, he doesn't like it when he's not the centre of attention and you know what it's like when old friends get together.

Ella, Flick and I all went to university together in Liverpool over ten years ago and, as such, go way back. We're more like sisters than friends and are inseparable. I feel as if we grew up together. Those formative years shaped us into the women we are today. Ella Hawley, Felicity Edwards and Grace Taylor. I smile to myself. We were quite the girls back then. A force to be reckoned with. Mainly due to Flick, I have to say. She was the one who dragged us kicking and screaming into the thick of student life. I'm sure Ella and I would have stayed at home in our skanky rooms every night, studying, if it hadn't been for Flick. Ella's the arty, thoughtful one. Flick is the fabulously pretty, fickle one. I, for my sins, am the steady and sensible one. Though we're ten years older now and, supposedly, wiser, our roles haven't changed that much.

We all took different courses at university, but found ourselves in the same halls. We hooked up at one of the events in Freshers' Week – I can't even remember what now – and have been together through thick and thin ever since.

After that first rollercoaster year when we struggled to get our studying to keep pace with our partying, we escaped halls and moved as a team into a totally hideous flat at the top of a draughty Victorian house in one of Liverpool's less salubrious areas. I only have to think for a minute how awful it was and it makes me shudder. The carpet had that terrible stickiness of a back-street pub and, as we were on the top floor, the windows had never been cleaned. They still hadn't when we left two years later. Learning how to exterminate cockroaches, mice and silverfish together is always going to be a lifelong bonding experience. Though it always seemed to be me, with rubber gloves and dustpan, who had the job of clearing up the resulting corpses.

Not only did we share the same hideous flat, but we also worked in the same hideous bar. Honkers. I don't have to say any more, do I? There's a fantastic, sophisticated nightclub scene in Liverpool. Honkers wasn't part of it. We used to run a sweepstake between the three of us – five pounds at the end of the night to the person who got the most gropes. One point for a bottom grope, two points for a boob grope. Flick had the dubious honour of winning most nights.

We put up with the groping, largely without complaint, simply to earn some extra cash to supplement our drinking – sorry, our studies. If someone got a feel of your tits they tended to give bigger tips. Oh, happy days. Our shared horror only helped to make our little team stronger than ever. Even though we had no money and lived in a fleapit, they were good times. We had fun together. Mostly. But there were heartaches too and we vowed then that nothing would ever come between us. Not men, not fame, not fortune. It's fair to say that it's just the men that have troubled us thus far.

Harry doesn't like it when we spend hours reminiscing about a life and a time that he wasn't involved with. I'll admit that when we get started on the 'good old days' we do get a bit carried away with ourselves. Once we get going, we can talk for hours. You can't help but do that with good friends, can you? It's not as if we have huge reunions every five minutes. We all have busy lives and often only manage to get together every couple of months for a catch-up. We normally go out for a glass of wine and a pizza, nothing more exciting than that. We haven't had a girls' holiday together since we all went to Prague on my hen weekend over seven years ago now. So, as reluctant as he is, I'm sure that Harry can't begrudge me a week with my friends.

'I'm dying of thirst,' Harry says sullenly.

My heart sinks. What he means is he needs alcohol. I think this interminable car journey is the longest I've seen him go without a drink lately. I don't quite know what's going on, but recently there have been far too many late nights at work, too much restorative red wine. When he does eventually come home, I can't prise him away from his iPad or his mobile phone. It seems as if he'd rather spend time doing who knows what on Twitter than be with me. It pains me to say that I can't remember the last time we had a conversation that wasn't in raised voices. We've been married for seven years, but I can't see us making another seven at this rate. It's not so much the seven-year itch as the seven-year slump. The last few months in particular have been just awful and, as a couple, we're as far apart as we've ever been. We get up at different times, go to work, eat dinner separately. Sex is a distant memory as I'm usually in bed and long asleep by the time Harry climbs the stairs. The weekends are no better. Harry's taken to shutting himself in his office and I mooch round the house by myself until I too give up trying to have fun and resort to the distraction of paperwork. It's no way to live. It's barely half a life. We are living to work, not working to live.

If I'm honest, there are times when I've felt like walking out. The only thing keeping me from doing that is the fact that I remember the Harry who I married – just about. The man who was charming, sophisticated and great company. It's simply a phase, I keep telling myself. It can't be roses round the door all the time. But sometimes it's hard when I look at the stranger sitting next to me.

We're both desperate for this break and I'm so hoping that we can spend some time together, relaxing, having fun and getting back to how we once were. That's all we need, I'm sure. Time. Time to sort things out. Time to have a laugh. Time to work out where it's all gone wrong.

I glance across at him. He's still a good-looking man. Tall, once quite muscular, but now that he's drinking more there's a hint of a paunch as he's never been one to embrace the idea of vigorous exercise. We used to like walking, but now it's all I can do to get him out of the flat at the weekend to go for a stroll down the road. The distance between our front door and the pub is the only walking he likes to do these days. His blue chambray shirt is straining slightly at the seams. I daren't suggest a diet as that would only be another reason to argue, but I'm gently trying to introduce healthier options into our evening meals. Harry's older than me. At forty-four, he's twelve years my senior. Not a lot these days, I guess, but I wonder if it will become more of an issue as the years pass. Still, we have to patch up where we are now before I can worry about the future. I want to run my hand through his hair. It's cropped short, greying slightly at the temples. He hates it when I touch it.

This person was once the life and soul of the party. Harry only had to walk into a room to make it light up and I was in awe of him. He was always so confident, so assured, that it spilled over on to me and I blossomed in his love. We were great as a couple. We might never have had a wild passion as such, but we were solid. Or so I thought. We fell into step nicely. As a couple the whole was better than the sum of two parts. I sigh to myself. Now look at us. Two people circling each other, never quite in time. This holiday will do us good. It will bring us back together, I'm sure. Because, more than anything, I want my husband to fall in love with me all over again.

Harry's voice breaks into my thoughts. 'Found out where we are yet?'

'Yes,' I tell him. Though, if I'm honest, I'm not *exactly* sure.

Anxiously, I twiddle one of my curls as I try to figure

out where we are on the lines and squiggles of the map. I wasn't blessed with the map-reading gene, hence our heavy reliance on the sat nav. 'It's just over this hill. I think.'

With a tut, he stomps on the accelerator and we set off again. A few minutes later, over the brow of the hill as I'd predicted, I'm mightily relieved to see a sign for Cwtch Cottage – pronounced Cutch, so Ella tells me.

'This is it,' I assure Harry and we turn into a narrow track.

We slow to walking pace as the lane is bordered by high hedgerows on each side, with a tall line of grass right down the middle of it, like a secret passage. We squeeze our way towards the cottage. Already I feel as if I'm entering a different world.

'I hope this doesn't scratch the paintwork,' Harry grumbles.

I feel stupid in this car. A Bentley doesn't fit with the scenery. Frankly, it doesn't fit with me at all, but it's Harry's new toy. His pride and joy. He treated himself to it a month or so ago when he had his annual bonus from work. Though I've no idea why anyone would feel the need to spend so much on a car. It's an insane amount of money to blow. To top it off, he bought a personal number plate too. He loves its gleaming black showiness. I just wish that we had something a little more anonymous. Something in beige, so that the local vandals won't feel the need to run a key down the side of it. This car is criminal damage waiting to happen. To me a man with a flash car is like him walking around, waving his willy. Though as I hardly ever drive now – who needs to in

London? – I don't feel that I can really impose a low-key choice of car on my other half. If this is what Harry wants, then who am I to argue?

A profusion of wild flowers blooms in the hedgerow, glorious shades of pink, yellow and white. I open the window to let their colourful heads trail over my hand. The scent is heady.

'You'll get seeds and all sorts in the car,' Harry says. 'Next summer there'll be dandelions growing in the carpet and we'll wonder why. Shut the window.'

Reluctantly, I do.

Thankfully, a short and bumpy ride later, Ella's cottage comes into view. 'We're here!'

The sight of it takes my breath away. Cwtch Cottage stands in splendid isolation on a rocky promontory at the entrance to a small, secluded bay overlooking the sea. It's a simple structure, long and low, painted white, and I don't think I've ever seen anywhere quite so beautiful.

'Oh, look at it, Harry,' I say. 'Wasn't this worth that awful journey? It's stunning.'

Ella had shown me photographs of the cottage, but they just hadn't conveyed how spectacular the setting was. There's an unbroken view right to the horizon where the sea meets the sky.

Harry brings the Bentley to a standstill at the end of the bay and stares out of the window, open-mouthed. 'Christ, there's nothing here.'

'It's wonderful.'

The tight band that seems to be melded to my heart these days eases slightly. I think I can actually hear it sigh with relief. Tears prickle behind my eyes. You can keep your Seychelles and your Maldives, this is paradise to me. How I wish we were staying here for two weeks or even longer. A week seems barely adequate.

My husband is less moved by the surroundings. The expression on his face is bleak. 'Where's the nearest pub?'

'I don't know. Ella said that it was quite remote.'

'You're not bloody kidding.'

'Oh, Harry.' I kiss his cheek. 'It will be lovely, you'll see.'

'I haven't seen anything for miles.' He punches his digit at his mobile phone. 'No signal either.'

Smiling, I offer up a silent prayer of thanks. A whole seven days without having to compete with Twitter!

I put my hand on his arm. 'I'm really looking forward to this. We can have some time just to be together, to chill out, to put things right.'

'There's nothing wrong with us,' Harry says crisply.

But there is, I think. We both know that there is.